Danny King was born in Slo... Hampshire. He has held a num... stacker, postman and magazin... dozen muddy building sites ar... England between 1985 and 199... all published by Serpent's Tail, and the BBC sitcom *Thieves Like Us,* and widely regarded as Britain's third-best hod-carrier-turned-writer. He lives in Islington with his wife, Jeannie, and son, Charlie, and has his own tools.

dannykingbooks.com

Praise for Danny King

School for Scumbags

'Wayne Banstead is an engaging character; the set pieces…are first class; and the action sequences are fast, exciting and funny. Amoral, anarchic and un-PC, *School for Scumbags* is a lot of fun' *Guardian*

'Intelligent, witty and an eloquent comic creation' *Big Issue*

'A corker of a novel…great, swindling fun' *Time Out*

'Witty, pacey and definitely not for kids' *Heat*

'The perfect antidote to Hogwarts fever' *Daily Sport*

'Great fun' *Daily Telegraph*

'*Just William* for adults and all those sick of Potter' *Daily Mirror*

'A rite of passage of a bunch of Bugsy Malones learning the hard way that there is honour among thieves. A sweet book, basically, though I'm sure Danny King would hate me for saying so' *Sunday Express*

The Burglar Diaries

'An absolutely hilarious, laugh-out-loud book by someone who has been there' Bruce Reynolds, mastermind of The Great Train Robbery

'Occasionally hilarious, if morally dubious, *The Burglar Diaries* is well worth buying – and definitely worth half-inching' *GQ*

'This is the sweet-as-a-nut, hilariously un-PC account of the jobs [Bex] has known and loved – the line-ups, the lock-ups and the cock-ups. If ever there was an antidote to *Bridget Jones's Diary* this is it. *The Burglar Diaries* is the first in a series. Long may it run' *Mirror*

The Bank Robber Diaries

'*The Bank Robber Diaries* is the best (and funniest) British Crime novel since *The Burglar Diaries*, also written by Danny King' *Ice*

'Once again the comic genius and hilarious one-liners have you warming to the anti-social protagonists of Chris, Sid and Vince; more cock-ups than hold ups ... a thoroughly un-pc but rewarding novel' *BBM*

'A second tale of wickedly un-PC caper crime' *Publishing News*

'Extremely funny' *FHM*

The Hitman Diaries

'One of the few writers to make me laugh out loud. Danny King's brilliant at making you love characters who essentially are quite bad people' David Baddiel

'It's blokeish humour ahoy in this thoroughly enjoyable tale…King's writing is sharp, and he has a real penchant for dialogue as spoken by criminals' *Maxim*

Blue Collar

Danny King

First published in 2009 by Serpent's Tail,
an imprint of Profile Books Ltd
3A Exmouth House
Pine Street
London EC1R 0JH
website: www.serpentstail.com

ISBN 978 1 84668 701 3

Designed and typeset by folio Neuadd Bwll, Llanwrtyd Wells

Printed in the UK by CPI Bookmarque, Croydon, CR0 4TD

10 9 8 7 6 5 4 3 2 1

For our adorable son
Charlie Stewart Milo King
with all our love **X**

Acknowledgements

First and foremost, I have to thank my esteemed editor, John Williams, for getting behind this book and for helping me shape it into the story you're about to read. It's no exaggeration to say that if it wasn't for John, I wouldn't be the writer I am today and Oddbins in Cardiff would've closed down by now. Extra-special thanks must also go to the good people at Serpent's Tail, particularly Pete Ayrton, Rebecca Gray, Niamh Murray and Ruthie Petrie, for continuing to show a level of faith in me that's rarely seen outside ufologist chat-rooms. Thanks also to Mark Philpott of Waterstone's for press-ganging the readers of Eastleigh into buying my books. To Simon Key and the fine folks at the Big Green Bookshop in Wood Green for keeping literature alive in N22 and for their generous hospitality. For Araceli and Gemma for coming along to say hello and hear me read when some five thousand pubs must've been open across London that same evening. For Jeannie for bringing me a cup of tea just now. For Andy Rivers at bykerbooks.com for publishing my short 'Burglar Diaries' story and for wearing a shirt during our interview despite coming from Newcastle. For Danny Marsh at the Norwich School of Art & Design for publishing my story, 'The Echo', in his college's 2008 anthology. And for Dan Chant, Robert Splaine, RJ in Australia, Steve Pickwell, Elizabeth Earle, Dave Cobb and Maggie Kaye for all their support over the last year. It's very much appreciated. Finally, an enormous debt of thanks must go to Helen & John, Dot & Mike, Robin & Denise,

Ralph, Claire & Thomas, Andrew, Petra, Filip & Kajá, Cliff, Amanda & Abigail, Clive & Jo, the ladies at Jeannie's book club and everyone else who's contributed so generously to Charlie's wardrobe and nursery. Thanks to you, all the royalties from this book can now be spent on beer and puzzle magazines. Thank you, one and all.

1 Polite awakenings

I don't know if you've ever done this, but waking up somewhere unfamiliar after an almighty night on the sherbet is an incredibly confusing experience.

At first, you just lie there with your eyes open, unable to focus or hone in on anything, and frankly, reluctant even to try. It's all just lights and shapes, a bit like when you were a baby, but that's fine with you. Just as long as you're nice and comfy, as long as your nappy's empty and your feet aren't two dirty great blocks of ice, then why bother even trying? Your bed's all lovely and warm and you haven't got work today…

Hang on! A quick jolt of panic as you race an even quicker finger across the old brain calendar and double-check the day, before you're able to relax again, sink back into your stupor and drift off, safe in the knowledge that this is a genuine Saturday morning. And not just a practice one like last Thursday.

No, that's that; everything's hunky-dory and you're all done for the week. You're able to take it easy and write off a small chunk of your life until lunchtime when you'll give Jason a bell to see if he's up for a couple of pints and a bucket of balls down the golf range before you give any thought to tonight.

There's only one thing.

When, and more importantly why, did you decide to hang a load of bits of bamboo from your bedroom ceiling just over your bed?

OK, maybe this has got a little bit specific but this was what

I found myself wondering after one phenomenally successful Friday night down the dogs.

I'd been Michael Winner all night long and won nine out of thirteen races. Straight up, absolutely incredible. All right, I'd only put a couple of quid on each time and I'd never got anything more than twenty or twenty-five quid back on any single race, but I still walked away with a couple of hundred quid in my back pocket. I was absolutely made up. Fantastic. I didn't have a clue what I was doing either. Well, I'm no expert. All I did was have a quick look at the form guide, ask luckless Jason which one he was going to stick his money on then go for one of the other ones, usually the one in the stripy waistcoat running in the middle of the track, and hey presto; four-to-one plus my stake back? Stick another fifteen quid in that pocket of yours, young man and see who's up for a high-five. No? No one? OK, never mind, what's next?

Of course, there was always the slight niggling regret afterwards that I didn't cash in my mortgage and/or my gold teeth and stick the lot on any of my winners but to be honest I'm not brave enough to bet big. It's only a bit of fun for me. A night out, a few beers and a bit of a laugh. I work too hard for my money to go chucking it away on dogs, horses or scratch cards.

No, it's just a bit of fun. And what fun it had been too.

Of course, it narked Jason off something rotten, particularly when the only time I didn't win anything was when he stuck his two quid on the same dog as me. What a Jonah! Still, somebody's got to cough up if I'm going to be kept in scampi and chips for the rest of my life.

And champagne?

Oh God, yeah, that was right, I'd been drinking champagne last night too. Jesus, I must've been in a good mood.

It was at this moment that the bed gently rocked and a lovely warm pair of buttocks pressed back against my thigh. I almost smashed my head into the bamboo mobile in surprise and pulled back the covers to see who I was in the bed next to.

It wasn't Jason. Thank fuck for that.

But who was it?

And hang on a minute, where was I?

And how did I get here?

And *Christ almighty*, how much did I have to drink last night? My poor old aching head.

I quickly ran through the evening's events in my mind but there was a total blank where the post-dogs memories should've been. Like someone had nicked the tape or recorded *Dad's Army* over it by mistake. What did we do last night?

I've never been one for blanking out before, and indeed, reckon it's all a load of old codswallop when people tell you they can't remember what they did the previous evening.

'Here, Tel, you remember dancing on the table in the pub, flashing your arse at everyone and chinning old Stan?'

'Er... no.'

But this was different. This was a genuine, bona fide, couldn't see the woods for the trees, missing-in-action memory blank.

I couldn't remember a thing.

Not a thing.

And this seemed like a shame because I appeared to have pulled an absolutely corking bird at some point in the evening.

'Blimey, how did I do that?' I either said or thought, as I cradled my thumping skull between ten nicotine-stained fingers.

The lady in question was still sleeping, so I let her sleep for the time being and tried to get my bearings. What had I done last night? And who was she?

After a few seconds, she slowly turned beneath the sheets so that she was now towards me and I was able to see her face.

I still didn't recognise her, not at all, and I hate to admit this but I had a terrible attack of the scumbags and wondered if I'd splurged my winnings on a prostitute. If I had it would've been the first time in my life, so I couldn't really see that. Besides, this didn't look like a prostitute's bedroom. Nice lilac sheets, an enormously thick and fuzzy duvet, half a dozen fluffy pillows and stuffed toys all over the shop. Actually, the place was a bit of a mess what with the piles of clothes, shoes, books, ornaments and bric-a-brac cluttering up just about every available surface. No, if this girl was a prostitute then she was in desperate need of one of NatWest's small-business advisers to come in and sort out her place of work, because she was scoring low on a few basics.

Also, I still had my pants on, and what sort of prostitute leaves a bloke in his trolleys all night?

No, this girl was no prostitute, and certainly no prostitute I could afford, though I still had one last lingering doubt knocking around with my headache that made me wonder if I shouldn't just tap her on the shoulder and ask her if I owed her anything at all.

Perhaps not.

So, who was she?

I didn't know, but whoever she was, she was absolutely gorgeous. Shoulder-length blonde hair, a spotless complexion and a face as cute as a vicar's daughter's. She was still sleeping for the moment and looked peaceful to the point of angelic. She had a few traces of make-up around the eyes and lips, though she didn't look like she really needed it. She had a tiny upturned mouth, half a button where her nose should've been and lashes that looked like they could've picked up Radio 1 – even on the motorway.

She was, for want of a better word, *luvvlie*.

I laid my head on the pillow next to hers and stared at her delicate features for about five minutes until all at once she screwed her brow into a tangle of pain and coughed the word 'fuck' into my face.

'Oh fuck, oh fuck, my head, my head. I'm in so much pain,' she sobbed, curling up into a ball and pulling at her hair and eyes.

She eventually opened them and I saw that they were like little emerald islands, floating in two bloodshot pools of regret.

'Please, get me a tablet. Please please please,' she pleaded, giving me directions to the kitchen and begging me to hurry.

I found the kitchen roughly where she'd described it and nosed through half a dozen cupboards before locating a big box full of tablets and plasters. I selected some suitably dynamic painkillers and knocked back a couple myself, then returned to the bedroom and asked the patient if she wanted one or two.

I was close, and watched her shotgun three in quick succession and drink a big glass of water before sinking back beneath the covers. I climbed in after her and tentatively tried a bit of snuggling. To my continuing surprise she seemed all for it so we settled down and nestled in each other's arms, groaning, moaning and wondering who the fuck the other was.

To older generations, this probably seems like absolutely outrageous behaviour, especially on the part of the girl – or 'slag', as I believe they were sometimes tarred back then.

'I didn't share your grandad's bed until after we were married and I didn't see him after that first night for another eighteen months because he was away fighting the Germans,' my grandmother once told me, which I took to mean he'd either been in the trenches in the First World War or turning over BMWs with the Official England Supporters' Club.

Well, you know, that was fair enough for back then but times change. Not always for the better, I grant you, but they change all the same, and like it or lump it you have to change with them or else get left behind.

I'll give you an example of what I mean. OK, here it is; now, I like to think of myself as an old-fashioned kind of romantic. I'm not really interested in bed-hopping my way through life and chalking up another carcass for the lads. Some blokes are like that, but not me.

Don't get me wrong, I'm not interested in kids or donkeys either and honestly enjoy/suffer from the same urges as everyone else. I seriously do and can't think of many things better than lying in the arms of a beautiful woman – albeit in my pants. But I'd take a beautiful woman I knew and had a relationship with any day of the week over some saucy anonymous barmaid with enormous knockers and three days to live. That's just what I'm like. I like the women in my life to be in my life for a bit longer than that bloke who came around a few years back to tune all our videos to get Channel 5.

Actually, I think I'd probably just like to find a wife, though I'll keep that under my hat for the moment as that's the sort of comment that usually goes down even worse with women you've only just met than 'How much?'

So, with that all said and done, here's the example. A few years ago – and I'm talking twelve or thirteen here – I was on holiday in Gran Canaria with a couple of my mates when I met a really nice girl. I can't remember her name, I'm afraid, but she ticked my romantic job sheet down to the last box and had my insides doing loop-the-loops just smiling at me.

I met her on one of those stupid jeep safaris that drives you up into the mountains and takes you on a tour of the island's accident black spots. She'd sat next to me in the back of the last jeep and we'd got on really well. Everything I'd said came out as funny and fascinating, at least to her it did, if not to the other passengers, who had to endure seven hours of merciless giggling and flirting – the poor bastards.

Anyway, after our day in the mountains, me, my mates and the new love of my life's mates all met up for dinner and a night on the slates. We had some lovely food, a few gallons of Harvey Wallbangers and danced into the wee small hours, jumping up and down and making up our own lyrics to 'Come On Eileen' when we gave up trying to work out what Kevin Rowland was singing. It was a really great night. Really really really. Then, at about four, the club closed and it was time to say goodnight. By this point, me and my sweetheart were all but inseparable. I know it sounds stupid but I'd grown genuinely close to her over the course of the evening. To me, this wasn't just some silly holiday romance or a one-off knee-trembler, this was the start of something real. Something life-changing. Long after this holiday was over, I was going to see this girl again. And again. And again. And as luck would have it, she only lived in Hertfordshire, so this was more than just a pipe dream. That day, on that mountain, in that jeep, and under that sun, I'd met the girl I was going to spend the rest of my life with.

So when my mates, her mates and her discussed the idea of going on to this little twenty-four-hour bar down by the beach to get in a few last drinks, I told them I was going home. Seriously, I said this.

'It's been a fantastic night but I'm dead on my feet and I'm going home. Have a couple for me and I'll see you tomorrow,' I promised my confused future wife, giving her the gentlest of little kisses before strolling off into the night like Sir Galahad with a particularly bad case of concussion.

What an idiot!

What a dick!

So why had I done this? Simple – because I desperately wanted to see her again and I didn't want to go ruining everything by getting really drunk and cheapening our love by trying to hang out the back of her on our first night together. I was more than happy to wait and utterly convinced that I was doing the right thing by her and that she would recognise my honourable intentions. Coming from a typically proud working-class family, I'd been brought up to believe this sort of nonsense.

I reiterate, what a dick!

Almost inevitably, both my mates banged her in the bog while I was tucked up in bed back at the hotel thinking noble thoughts and I never saw her again.

Both of them? I mean, I could've just about understood one of them, but both of them? And in the bog?

'She was well up for it,' Paul and Andy had explained the next day. 'I think you loosened her up a bit, know what I mean.'

'How could you do that? You know I liked her.'

'Well, you went home. She didn't know why you did that and was all confused.'

'What, so you both gave her one to clarify my position?'

'You should've come along, then, mate, if you liked her an' everything. You were well in there, you were.'

'Oh, what, you think all three of us could've banged her, then, do you?'

This was a real wake-up call for me, and from that day on I dropped my naively chivalrous gentlemanly tactics in favour of striking while the iron was hot. It's unfortunate, but that's just the way it is these days. Because if you're not willing to take a girl to a twenty-four-hour bar when she wants to be taken to a twenty-four-hour bar, there's no shortage of blokes who will.

And so this was probably the reason I found myself waking up in the bed of a knee-knockingly attractive girl, whose name I didn't know and whose life was a complete mystery to me, a dozen or so years later.

All I knew about her in fact was that she slept in lilac sheets and didn't have anything near my grandmother's patience.

2 What's in a name?

We both drifted off to sleep again after our headache tablets got to work. Even me, in spite of all the questions and excitement that naturally come from finding a beautiful blonde in bed with you on a Saturday morning instead of your work boots and half a kebab.

I finally came around again at about ten, when I sensed someone moving about at the foot of the bed, and found I was no longer cheek-to-cheek with a mysterious blonde.

She'd already made it into some grungy jogging bottoms, vest and T-shirt before I knew what was going on and looked apologetic about getting dressed.

'Just my running gear,' she explained sheepishly. I waited for her to demonstrate by running straight out of the house, but instead she asked me if I wanted a cup of coffee.

'Do you have tea?' I asked, not being one for coffee.

'Er, yeah. Darjeeling? Earl Grey? English Breakfast?'

'Have you got any Tetley's?'

The girl thought for a moment and told me the nearest thing she had was English breakfast tea.

'Will that do?' she asked.

Failing a trip to the shops it was going to have to, so I told her to go easy on the milk and heavy on the sugar, but she disappeared off to the kitchen before I could tell her how many chocolate biscuits I wanted on the saucer.

Sensing a little awkwardness on her part, I took the

opportunity to search for my clothes and pulled on everything I could find, though my socks had a five-hour headstart on me and were nowhere to be seen.

The girl returned with two cups and caught me pulling on my shoes.

'Oh, er, here, I… did you still want your tea before you go or do you have to go now?' she asked, stumping me with that one. I hated difficult questions.

Now obviously – obviously – I wanted to stay, discover her name, get to know her, take her for dinner, dance with her through the night and spend the rest of my days doing everything I could to make her happy, but that wasn't really the question, was it? The real question was, did I want tea before I went?

I tried reading between the lines and working out what she meant but I'm hopeless at this sort of thing. I always have been. What did she mean? Did she mean, 'Here, you can drink this tea if you like but then you have to go'? Or was she trying to say, 'I've made you some tea as agreed, but to be honest I'd prefer it if you just went now to save us any further embarrassment'?

I slowed my shoelace-tying down to a snail's pace to buy myself precious seconds to pick apart each word and ended up having to flip a coin in my head. It came down tails, but that didn't matter as I'd forgotten to pick a side and ended up reaching for a cup.

'Thanks,' I said, then took one look at the lukewarm milky piss she'd brought me and kicked myself for not legging it when I had the chance.

We sat next to each other on the bed and sipped our drinks against a backtrack of hanging silence. There were so many questions I wanted to ask, such as her name, who she was, what she did, how we'd met, how we'd ended up back here, what had happened once we'd got back and had she seen my socks, but ironically, she was the last person on earth I could ask these things. I mean, can you imagine it? All night long we'd been making sweet tender love and promising our hearts to one another then, mission accomplished, a few hours of kip and I was drinking her tea and asking her, 'Er, sorry, who are you again?' No, not tempting.

I plumped for keeping my mouth shut, scouring the room for anything that would spark a memory and crawling along carefully with both feelers stretched way out in front of me.

'So, how do you feel?' I asked after a while. 'A bit better?'

'No, not really. I feel just awful,' she replied.

'Hangover or self-loathing?' would've been the obvious follow-up question had we been either aliens, Americans or drugged up to the eyeballs on truth serum.

'Yeah, I'm not feeling too clever myself,' I settled for volunteering. 'What happened to the others?' I eventually asked, figuring I was on safeish territory with that one as I'd been out with Jason and girls generally didn't go out on a Friday night on their own unless they were lonely beyond desperation or undercover WPCs trying to catch serial killers.

'Don't you remember?' came the question I'd been dreading, a lot earlier than expected.

'Er, yeah, no, it's fine. No, no, of course I remember,' I babbled, before asking. 'Why, what happened?'

The girl let that one go and filled in a few of the blanks for me. Me and Jason had apparently drunk ourselves into newborn wobbly antelopes off the back of my winnings (though she omitted to say where we'd been drinking or who we'd been drinking with) and a cab had come along and taken Jason away without me even noticing.

'Don't you remember, you kept buying him drinks and asking me where he was for ages after he'd gone?'

I played that one out in my head but none of it looked like anything I'd seen before.

'Oh yeah, that's right,' I replied so unconvincingly that I

could've probably got a job on *EastEnders* had the casting director been sat on the bed with us.

'You also kept on calling me Jo all night. Do you remember that?' she then said.

'Oh... bollocks. Sorry about that.' I frowned, Jo being the name of my last girlfriend. How embarrassing, though it did narrow the field down slightly as far as my new blonde friend's name went.

'That's all right. I was probably just as plastered as you by the end of the night,' she said with a slight shrug. 'I always get smashed on champagne,' she confessed.

I rarely did myself and remembered why the moment I stuck a hand into my pocket and pulled out nothing but the cotton lining and my bus fare home.

'Oh, are you going, then?' she asked when she saw me examining a handful of coins and fluff. I hadn't intended to, but I could almost see the bottom of my cup and all of a sudden the girl seemed even more distant than ever.

Only a few minutes earlier we'd been cuddled up in bed all nice and snug but suddenly there were clothes and clear daylight between us and we could barely look each other in the eye. This wasn't what was supposed to happen. This wasn't what was supposed to happen at all. When I'd first woken up next to her it was like all my birthdays had come at once, or at least that the tooth fairy had finally delivered, but before I'd had a chance to spark up a big fat self-congratulatory cigar, the opportunity was suddenly sliding away from me and I didn't have a clue how to slow it down.

One thing was alarmingly clear, however. I was thirty seconds away from finding myself out on the street and once I was out there, I was out there for keeps. This girl, her bedroom and my socks would be gone for ever.

But then, wasn't that going to happen anyway? I mean, just

look at her. Oh, you can't, can you, it's a book? Well, then allow me; she was as pretty a girl as any I'd ever known and she had a lovely quiet sort of way about her that made me want to bundle her up in cotton wool and reassure her that everything was going to be all right, although her demeanour could just as well have been down to the fact that there was some strange bloke in her bed who'd seen her arse and her bamboo mobile. She was athletic, well spoken and obviously a bit trendy. She knew what to wear, if not how to hang it up, and she lived in a spacious, pricey-looking flat that was decked out in ethnic chic-a-brac. And most unusually of all, she looked around about my age (early thirties) yet had no wedding ring or confused little kid peering out at me from the bedroom doorway to show for it.

She was, in short, absolutely fantastic – which naturally meant she was way out of my league.

If I'd seen her in the pub, I'm sure I would've glanced over at her from time to time and thought wishful thoughts, but I would never have gone up to her and introduced myself. There would've been no point. I would've stood no chance. Don't get me wrong, I ain't got four heads or an ant's nest for a face or nothing but still, you have to have some sort of idea about the weight division you're punching in otherwise you just end up picking yourself up off the canvas every Saturday night. And this girl was a first-round knockout if ever I saw one.

Which made our imminent parting all the more inevitable, no matter how gut-wrenching.

'I'd probably better shoot off,' I finally replied, reluctantly setting my cup down on the chest of drawers next to the bed.

The girl agreed and said that it was probably for the best, considering the catastrophic state we were both in, and I noticed her face softened a little as I rose to leave. Probably gratitude, which was something at least. Well, I had no desire to run her through the wringer squeezing excuses out of her, so I decided to let her off the hook and hoped that she would think better of me for it after I'd left. Not that that would do me any good, but then again you can't spend your whole life dropping to your knees in tears that every day's not Christmas, can you? No, you just have to get on with it and be a man. Take it on the chin. Turn the other cheek. One set all, God save the Queen and... oh, bollocks to this, let's just get out of here, shall we?

'Right, well, that's me, I guess. Thanks very much for the tea. English breakfast, you say? I'll have to look out for it. Right, have I got everything? Keys? Wallet? Mobile?' I frowned, filling my pockets and suddenly looking forward to that lunchtime pint even more than ever.

'I'll see you to the door,' she said, bolting out of the bedroom and skipping down the hallway towards the front door.

I passed her at the front door and wondered if I should try to give her a kiss or not. I wanted to, of course. Who wouldn't? She was beautiful and I was never going to see her again. Perhaps I could even nick a quick squeeze of her knockers while I was at it, or would that be pushing it? Probably, so I simply stopped just in front of her, held her gaze for the briefest of seconds then pressed my lips to hers.

Remarkably, she didn't stumble back or slog me around the chops with one of her wooden elephants or nothing, but instead responded to my kiss and slipped her arms around my waist. I couldn't believe it. I was kissing her. I was kissing this beautiful girl. And she was kissing me back?

I'll tell you what else I couldn't believe; I couldn't believe I'd waited until we were both dressed and stood next to an open front door to try this, considering where I'd been only twenty minutes earlier. What a mug. I weighed up the situation and wondered if there was a realistic chance of getting her back inside and out of her jogging bottoms, but kicked myself when I realised I'd missed the boat again. Being one of life's big cowards, I'd waited until the moment of 'now or never', like my mate Doug, who finally worked up the courage to ask out the girl he'd fancied for years the day before she moved up to Dundee, or my Uncle Brendan, who sent the old girl in the fish and chip shop dirty texts from his deathbed, and like the pair of them found there was no time to do anything about it when we came up trumps.

'Thanks for putting me up for the night,' I said, deciding against asking if there was anything else I needed to thank her for.

'You're welcome, it was fun,' she told me, the guilty glint in her eye giving my guts one last punching, then all too soon I was outside.

My inner voice screamed at me to ask her for her phone number. Ask her for her name. Ask to see her again. Ask her anything, anything at all, just don't let her shut that door…

…but in the end I did none of these things.

I simply smiled manfully at her one last time, told her I'd see her around some time and sighed as the door closed between us.

What a loser.

I waited for a couple of seconds to see if it was going to reopen but it didn't. It stayed right where it was and pursed its letterbox into a frown at my complete lack of resolve.

I half thought about knocking again, but my odds were lengthening with every hesitation, taking me from an even-money favourite when I'd woken up next to her this morning to a fifty-to-one outsider. What exactly I'd been waiting for was suddenly beyond me. I'd had nothing to lose by going for it – and I'm not talking about sex here, just human connection – but I'd decided not to risk it anyway. And now I was stood out here like a big chump with no chance of seeing her again, no different to if I'd made a ring out of an old discarded condom wrapper and asked her to marry me with it.

Seriously, what a big fucking loser.

I made a note of the number of her house, just on the off-chance

I found my bottle several years from now and decided to pop round and ask her out for a drink, then turned and started making tracks.

Talk about getting out of bed on the wrong side. This was going to annoy me all day, if not for the rest of my life.

I'd reached the end of the road and was picking up the pace in an attempt to get to the pub (any pub) before my disappointment doubled me over into a crumpled heap, when all of a sudden my mobile rang. It had a different ring tone from the one I normally had it set to but I just figured I must've switched it to something different the previous evening – dicking around with phones being the nation's favourite drunken pastime.

No name came up to show who was calling, just a number. I checked the number to see if I recognised it and rather confusingly I did.

It was mine.

How the hell was I calling myself when I had my phone in my hand? It could've only been my own self-confidence phoning up to explain where he'd been this morning.

As it turned out, it was a girl.

'Hello. Hello, Terry, is that you?'

'Yes. Hello, who's this?' I asked.

'It's Charley,' she told me.

'Charley?' I thought for a moment. 'I'm sorry, who?'

'Charley. You know, Charlotte?'

Charlotte? Charley? I didn't know anyone by either name, especially anyone who could phone me up on my own phone while I was still holding it.

I wondered if I'd flipped my lid and turned into a schizophrenic. It happened all the time in America, alter egos phoning themselves up to introduce themselves and suggest a killing spree. It's a lot more common than you'd think.

As it turned out, it was actually the girl I'd left just three minutes earlier, though I only finally twigged this when she relented and explained, 'You know, the one you left just a moment ago. The one you kept calling Jo all last night?'

'Oh, yeah, Jo... sorry, I mean Charley. Oh yeah, hi, hello, how are you?' I asked, my brain still in first gear.

'Still hung over,' Charley said.

'Sorry to hear that,' I told her, though I didn't look all that sorry standing in the middle of the street, suddenly grinning from ear to ear like a nutjob with a whole bowl of blancmange to himself.

She had my number? This was great. This was fantastic even. This was... still a bit weird with what was going on with my phone but I'd figure that one out later on, piece of crap. In the meantime, I had more important things to jump up and down on the spot about.

Like *Charley*.

She'd phoned me up. I hadn't even realised she'd had my number but that didn't matter now. All that mattered was that she'd phoned me up and, more importantly, that she'd phoned me up pretty much the second I'd left. Some people say that you're meant to leave it a couple of days and play it cool but Charley obviously didn't buy into this theory and had decided to strike while the iron was hot herself. Had she, like me, been biting her tongue all morning long, only to finally come to her senses and realise that life was too short to mess around? That if she had a shot at happiness, then she should go for it before it got away and sod the consequences?

Maybe. But if she had, that wasn't what she was phoning about. No, what she actually wanted was her phone back.

'You've taken mine by mistake. It's the same model as yours, remember?'

I didn't, but it did explain a thing or two. It also presented me with one last chance to make an utter dick of myself and see this unbelievably cute, beautiful, graceful, knockout stunner laugh in my face before she slipped from my life for good.

And this time, I was going to take it.

3   Jason and the Lagernauts

'Jesus, my head. I ain't drinking champagne again for a while,' Jason swore, a couple of hours later when I met him in my local, the Catford Lamb.

'What was it, wedding last night, or you two finally get a room together?' Tony the landlord chuckled, before shouting over to old Stan in the corner, 'Couple of pooftas we got in today,' in case old Stan didn't get it. Old Stan lifted his half a stout our way and agreed enthusiastically.

'What'll it be, then, girls, couple of pink gins?' Tony then asked.

Sensing this one was set to run and run I decided to take the wind out of the boring bastard's sails and told him I'd love a pink gin, but only if he was out of Campari. Tony gabbled excitedly and ran through a list of girlie drinks – sherries, shandies, Bacardis and Cokes, Tia Marias, white-wine spritzers and Martinis before eventually blowing himself out trying to recapture the moment. Me and Jason drummed our fingers on the bar as we waited for him to finish and old Stan went back to staring into his past.

'Port and lemon?' was his last throw of the dice, but that was basically it, Tony was a spent force, and me and Jason eventually got a couple of pints and a breather from the cabaret.

'Sandra gave me a right earful this morning,' Jason told me

when he resurfaced from his lager. 'I just blamed everything on you, though, and she was all right after that.'

I shrugged to show him that this was fine and asked him what he remembered about the previous night.

'Not much. Bits and pieces. Here, how d'you get on with that old posh bird?'

'Funny you should ask.' I smiled, all full of myself. 'I ended up back at her place, didn't I?'

'Did ya?' Jason gasped. 'You jammy bastard. How d'you get on?'

'I haven't got a clue,' I admitted.

I told Jason about the big pothole in my Friday night and he filled in a few missing shovelfuls where he could. Apparently, we were already pretty legless by the time the last race came around and that's when we met…

'What was her name? George or Bob or something? Some bloke's name,' Jason trawled, scratching his chin.

'Charley?'

'That was it. Her and…'

This time he didn't even have a lead on whoever Charley was with, so she got tagged with a simple shrug of the shoulders.

Anyway, Charley and her mate had been at the dogs as well the previous evening, which was a bit weird because the dogs didn't seem like the sort of place they'd hang out at, but apparently they were being ironic. In the past few weeks they'd been to the dogs, the bingo, a banger race, an amusement arcade and a darts tournament, all in the name of irony, which presumably only left a boxing match, a pie fight and a chimps' tea party before they could sign off on this whole working-class experience.

'So if we went and had our lunch in the Ritz in our work togs, that would be ironic too, would it?' Jason wanted to know.

'Yeah, I'm sure they'd love it,' I replied, my head full of images of posh waiters clapping their hands with delight as the pair of us trod cucumber sarnies and Hula Hoops into their carpet.

'And that's when we met them,' I think was where we'd got to.

I cast my mind back and vaguely remembered talking to a few people at the racetrack but none of them seemed to fit either Charley or her 'posh mate's' description.

'I'm not surprised, the amount you were knocking back mate. You remember when you got that double come up and you started knocking back double everythings to celebrate?'

I didn't.

Anyway, apparently at the end of the evening we'd somehow hooked up with Charley and her mate and I was all Billy Big Time with a couple of hundred quid burning a hole in my back pocket so Charley had said she knew a little boozer near by that was open late. Jason, apparently, hadn't wanted to go, but reluctantly tagged along to make sure these two sorts didn't rip me off for my winnings and only felt it was safe to leave me once I'd done the lot. What a mate.

'By the time the other one had disappeared you and that Charley were thick as custard, knocking back the champagne and wowed out to fuck that you both had the same phone,' Jason explained. 'You really don't remember any of this?'

I pulled the same face old Stan pulled when anyone asked him where he lived but none of the previous evening came tumbling back. Scary when you think about it. To get yourself into such a state that you could've done just about anything without even realising it. There must be blokes out there in this big wide world who started out on a Friday night with the intention of a few drinks and a bit of a laugh and ended up in prison, or worse still, in the ground, with no idea of how they got there. Silly really, the things we do to ourselves. Jason summed it up nicely one time when he said, 'Imagine if we ever managed to explore space and found another planet with life on it and there were these little green blokes who were perfectly sensible and hard working for most of the time, then once a week they all went down to a quarry and licked a big green glowing rock, then started smashing dustbin lids over each other's heads and puking up on the night rocket home. We'd think they were fucking bananas, wouldn't we?'

We probably would, but I bet we'd have a go on the rock ourselves when they weren't looking.

Anyway, I'm straying off the point. Nothing bad had happened to me the previous night and I was alive and in once piece and grateful for it. And that wasn't all I had to be grateful for.

'You mean you can't even remember if you gave her one or not?'

'I can't even remember if I gave *you* one or not.'

'Well, do you... you know... feel like you've had it?' he then asked, gesturing downwards with a drop of the eyes.

'No, I feel like I've been beaten up by a couple of tramps and dragged through several brewery hedges backwards but I don't feel like I've done anything that'll have the CSA cancelling my Sky subscription any time soon.'

'Not even in the morning?'

'No.'

'What did you do then?'

'Just had a cup of tea and went. Have you heard of English breakfast?'

'What, d'you mean like eggs and bacon?'

'No, like English breakfast tea?'

'No. What is it?'

'Well, it ain't Tetley's, I can tell you that.'

'Anyway, never mind all that. What about this bird?'

What about her indeed? I'd taken her phone back and almost choked it again, but at the last moment finally redeemed myself Robert Vaughn-style and asked her if she wanted to... was free to... didn't mind... had nothing better to do... was bored... stuck... etc... for a drink one night?

'Um...' she'd ummed, looking none too sold on the idea, so I'd braced myself for the inevitable 'see the thing is...' schtick and even started nodding magnanimously like I was well aware of what 'the thing' was. But then Charley pulled the rug from beneath my feet and said,

'Yes, OK, then. That would be nice.'

Yes?

OK, then?

That would be nice?

Did I hear her right? Well, yes, I'd heard the words but I was worldly enough to know that while 'no' always meant 'no' from a girl, 'yes' didn't necessarily come with the same twenty-eight-day money-back guarantees. I'd learned this from bitter experience when I'd asked this girl out a few times a couple of years back. I was working on this site down in Sutton – starter homes mostly, one- and two-bedroom maisonettes and flats – when this girl moved into one of the first places to be completed. She was as pretty as a pay packet and used to cause quite a stir when she stepped out for work in her clean and crisp business suit in the mornings. Don't get me wrong, none of us were ever rude to her or nothing. We just knew her to say good morning to and speculate about behind her back.

Anyway, after a few months me and Jason were sent off from the main gang around the back of her block to build a little retaining wall for the top soil. Miss Business Suit must've had that same week off because she was around most days. I guess it was a little less intimidating there being only the two of us in her back garden because she used to come out, chat to us and bring us cups of tea from time to time. And I must say she was even lovelier up close than she looked from thirty feet away in the gables. Nice girl too. Very friendly, bright and smart. A real distraction. That wall took longer to build than Hadrian's.

Anyway, to cut a long story ever so slightly shorter, eventually (when Jason had sloped off to the sweet shop) I managed to get around to asking her out. She'd said,

'Yeah, definitely, we must some time,' and nodded enthusiastically.

Now I'm no language expert but that sounded like a 'yes' to me so I allowed myself to feel all chipper and smug and even told Jason about it when he got back with the choc ices. Jason asked me when my date was but we hadn't quite agreed that much yet so I had to go back and ask her out again, this time with a few of the specifics nailed down.

Unfortunately, I didn't see again her for the next few days so I was forced to take the bull by the horns and knock on her door. Miss Business Suit answered with her usual smile, so I asked her if she was free at all this week.

As it turned out, she wasn't and blow me if she wasn't busy at the weekend too.

'Oh well, perhaps some time next week, then?' I relented.

'Yes, definitely,' she'd replied, so I'd gone back and told Jason that we were going out the following week.

'When?' the annoying bastard had asked me again.

Anyway, the following week came and went without so much as a sighting, so I was forced to stow my hopes away for another long weekend and even found myself looking forward to getting back to work the following Monday so that I could see Miss Business Suit again and get our date sorted.

Unfortunately, I still kept on missing her so eventually I went around and knocked on her door again. I knocked on three separate occasions but she was never in. I even considered hanging around for her after work, but I ruled that one out because I didn't want to look like a stalking fruity sex-case and I also wanted to get home for my dinner.

Eventually, I saw her a few days later when I was working in a footing with the rest of the gang, but I didn't say anything then because I didn't want to embarrass her in front of the lads, so I went round to her place after last knockings and just managed to catch her on her way out – the back door.

Once again she said that she was sorry but she was busy all week long but maybe we could go out some time the following week. Or the week after that. She'd let me know.

By this time all the lads had caught wind of it and thought we were going out. And I couldn't really blame them either, I mean, *I* thought we were going out, but I was wrong. And finally I had this confirmed to me one frosty morning when I saw Miss Business Suit leaving her flat with some pencil-dick who wasn't me. Actually, that's not fair on him, I don't know if he was a pencil-dick or not. All I know is that he actually got to go on dates with Miss Business Suit while I only got to ask for them.

Seven weeks, that went on. Seven weeks and I think I must've asked her out a total of five times before the penny finally dropped. Each time was a nerve-shredding heart-in-the-mouth stutter-fest and each time she'd said 'yes', but her 'yes' hadn't meant 'yes', not even her 'yes definitely'. It had actually meant, 'No, but I'm too embarrassed to say no. Read between the lines, Bungle'.

Oh, I'm not bitter, because it can't be easy being put on the spot by some knuckle-headed doughnut who can't take a hint, but then all it takes is a moment of courage and everyone knows where they are. A bit like asking in the first place – which is an awful, excruciating, miserable, tongue-twisting experience and one I've always hated.

Eye-openingly enough, that pencil-dick who wasn't me

became quite a fixture around Miss Business Suit's flat and they occasionally passed us by when we were working on or near the estate access road. One morning they both even smiled up and said good morning to us when Robbie called down a '*mawnin'*' of his own and she didn't even blink when she saw me up there next to him. It was like nothing had ever passed between us and there was an unspoken agreement that even if something had, neither of us should ever bring it up again.

I wondered if this was how I'd looked to Charley this morning.

I also wondered if Miss Business Suit's pencil-dick ever knew about it when she finally broke up with him or whether he just went around there one day and found the locks had been changed and some other geezer wearing his slippers.

'So you are going out with her, then?' Jason asked me, meaning with Charley. Forget about Miss Business Suit. That was just me reminiscing. I'm over her.

'I think so. I mean, she said yes and everything and I've got her number in my phone now, so I said I'd give her a call next week,' I explained, showing him her number as proof of my recent success.

'Nice one. You'll do all right there, my son,' he offered, clicking his tongue against his teeth and rubbing his hands together like Jiminy Cricket on a promise.

'Really? You think she likes me, then?'

'Oh yeah, posh birds love a bit of rough,' he winked, all congratulatory. 'Everyone knows that, don't they?'

Old Stan over in the corner rolled his eyes.

'Yeah, but do you think she actually likes me? You know, actually likes me for me?'

Jason stopped rubbing his hands mid-rub and looked at me as if I'd just taken the lid off a pot of snakes.

'Er, well, you know, sure, depends on what you're talking about,' he speculated. 'What are you talking about?'

'Well, is she only after me for a quick shag or do you think she actually likes me for who I really am?' I asked.

'Are you sure you don't want a pink gin?' Jason asked, by way of a reply.

'Oh, don't give me that old flannel, you've been happily married to Sandra ever since you met her in the sandpit, so don't come the old *Confessions of a Bricky* bollocks with me. You know what I've always wanted.'

'Well, yeah, Tel, but all I'm saying is you shouldn't size up every bird you meet as potential life partner material. You're setting yourself up for a fall every time. And with this Charley bird especially. I can tell you that for nothing,' Jason told me, as good as his word, for nothing. 'Just enjoy it for what it is and don't go twisting your knickers into knots over what it isn't because at the end of the day you're only going to shoot yourself in the foot before you've filled your boots.'

I think I got what Jason meant, although he could've just been trying to sell me his spare Toe Tecs again.

'So you reckon she's not properly interested, then? She's just after a bit of something else?'

'Oh no, I'm sure birds like that always go searching for future husbands down the dogs, Tel. When they want to get their hands on a real good one like,' he smirked.

At that moment Tony the barman came over and asked if we were ready for another drink. I was disheartened enough to go for several more barrels so I pointed to the Stella and stuck a hand in my pocket.

'What d'you think of posh birds, Ton'? Old Prince Philip over here reeled in a bit of a plum-sucker last night and is wondering what his chances of long-term happiness are like,' Jason asked the Lamb's resident expert on everything.

'Has she got money? I'd love to meet a bird with money. Get me out of this shithole,' he said without even having to think about it.

'I couldn't tell you,' I replied. 'Maybe.'

'Yep, posh old rich bird wants you to go and live in her mansion rent free you jump at the chance,' was his advice.

I promised Tony I would, then told him to send over a half of stout for old Stan in the corner before pocketing my change.

'Look, I don't know what this bird of yours is like but if you ask me she's probably just up for a spot of Lady Chatterley's with old ditch-digger McArse-Crack, so try not to go building her up in your mind because it probably ain't going to happen,' Jason laid out. 'Never the twain shall meet, as my old man used to say.'

As depressing as this all sounded, I'd come to much the same conclusion on the train ride home this morning. We might meet up again. We might get on like a mansion on fire. We might even go to bed and make sweet squeaks together but when all was said and done, we weren't going to be picking out baby bonnets in John Lewis any day in the future.

Perhaps Jason was right. Perhaps I shouldn't handicap every date with these sorts of lofty expectations, but it's hard not to get carried away when you meet someone you like after a year and a half of eating fish and chips off your lap in front of *Deal Or No Deal*.

Like I said, I'm not really the bed-hopping Jack the lad in tight trousers that some of my mates like to think they are. I'm just a normal bloke with normal aspirations and normal desires. I'd sown a few wild oats back in my twenties and as much fun as that was back then, it's not the sort of thing that would have me dodging the altar for the rest of my life to go on chasing it around discos into my sixties. I'd see old Stan in the Lamb every time I came in for a pint, and it terrified me, the thought that I might turn out like him; no wife, no kids, no family. No nothing. Just a half of stout and a seat in the corner.

'That's old Terry's stool that is,' I can hear them saying in thirty years' time. 'You can't sit there, he'll be in soon, the poor mad lonely old bastard.'

No, I'd like to get married and settle down and have a family. Sorry if that lets the side down, lads, but that's just the way I was built. So if I met a girl these days and I liked the look of her, I'd ask her out because I wanted to see her again. If I didn't, then I wouldn't, even if a few carefully spun compliments could've probably won us both a roll around in the nude, because there's no point. All that ever got you was a reputation as a wanker and a mobile you could never switch on.

So, I liked Charley. At least, I liked the look and the sound of what I'd seen of her so far, which, arse and bamboo mobile asides, wasn't that much, to be fair. But I liked her all the same. I liked her and I wanted to see her again. And not just to find out what expression a posh girl pulled when she was *really* enjoying herself (although there was that too) but because she seemed like someone I'd probably want to share a third date with. And then a fourth date after that. And then a fifth. And then a sixth and... and...

...and Jason was right. What odds would you give on a girl like Charley wanting to share a dozen dates with a bloke like me?

I had to face the facts, I was just a bit of rough.

Another box to tick on her ironic tour card.

4   Rainy Mondays

*A*fter a thoroughly miserable weekend spent staring at the clothes hanging up in my wardrobe and the cheerlessly unappealing bloke who brushed his teeth whenever I did, Monday morning turned up punctual as ever.

My alarm is set for half six, but I tapped the snooze a couple of times this particular morning so that I'd have to make my sandwiches and flask to the accompaniment of Jason leaning on his horn outside.

'You have a beer last night or something?' he asked when I climbed into the van.

'No, I just overslept,' I lied.

The sky was still tinged with darkness and we talked a little about how the nights and mornings were spreading themselves a little wider these days, but for most of the journey we simply stared out of the windows.

I like how everything looks first thing cock-a-doodle-doo in the morning. I'd prefer it if I didn't have a day full of gables ahead of me, but by and large I'm a morning person. Early mornings are a real no-nonsense time of the day. The only people who are up and about are people who have to be up and about. Nobody gets out of bed and goes for a walk or a drive at six in the morning if they don't have to, so for a couple of short hours the world's a neatly ordered and professional place to be. It's basically a world for grown-ups. There are no little ASBO ratboys kicking bins all over the pavements or molly-coddling mums gridlocking the streets driving their lazy fat bundles of preciousness half a mile up the road to school or smelly old pisshead work-dodgers venting their spleen at not being given the moon on a stick. Yep, this time of the morning was all right with me.

Oh, and in case you're wondering, yes, Jason's van is white.

We picked up Robbie as usual at the Thornton Heath roundabout and carried on to the site in Wimbledon. Only Dennis, one of the other hoddies, was here from our gang already, sat in his car with his eyes closed and his head against the glass, so Robbie jumped out, gave him a shout and the pair of them went off to start knocking up muck – which is what us chaps in the trade call cement when it's mixed up.

'Oi, don't knock up too much,' Jason shouted after them. 'Looks like we could have a drop of rain today.'

The skies had stayed dark despite the big hand making it around to a quarter past and I reckoned Jason might be right. There was a bit of wind in the air and a big flat shadow across the land which told me we could be home again by lunchtime.

That's the thing about working outside. After a few years you get to be able to read the skies like newspapers and these particular ones looked like they were ready to piss down on our heads all morning long.

'Two quid says it starts raining the moment we get up the ladder,' Jason offered, keen to recoup some of his dogs losses, but I'd done with gambling for the week. We watched the windscreen and the puddle across the road for the first couple of drops all the same, but none made themselves known.

Big Mick, the groundworkers' gaffer, slapped the front of the van as he mooched past and told us not to bother going anywhere with our tools. 'Gonna rain today, lads,' he said, but the rest of the gang was already arriving, so we figured we might as well make a show of it.

'They reckon it's going to chuck it down today,' was Stuart's

assessment when we met him at the bottom of the ladder. Nobby
agreed and said his missus had phoned up from Slough to tell
him it was already bucketing down there.

'What do we want to do?' Nobby asked, as Big John, Tommy
and little Mick all came over to join us. It was pretty obvious
what little Mick wanted to do from the way he'd left his hod
in the car but Gordon had the final say. He was the subby (the
subcontractor ergo the boss), it was his shout.

'Well, it ain't raining now, is it, so get up that ladder and lay
some fucking bricks, you lazy bastards. Mick, go and get a roll of
plastic from the compound and we'll get everything covered up
in case it starts coming down.'

The great rain debate went on for another half an hour, each
of us stopping every few bricks or so to feel the wind, until eight
o'clock brought a skyful of cats and dogs with it.

'Told ya,' Jason pointed out helpfully.

We covered up what we'd done and retreated to the van to
read the *Sun* and watch the rain teem down the windscreen in
rivers before Jason came to the conclusion that this was it for the
day and started on his sandwiches.

'Cheese and chutney again. I thought we'd seen the last of that
jar,' Jason frowned at his *Sandriches*, so named after their creator,
Sandra. 'What have you got? Wanna swap?' he asked, without
waiting to hear what I'd got. We thrashed out a deal that saw one
round of cheese and chutney and a Scotch egg coming my way in
exchange for my fish paste doorstep and a Club biscuit, then we
read our *Sun*s from cover to cover until we both needed a stretch.

The rest of the lads were holed up in a newly tiled house and
were debating how long to give it before they chucked in the towel
and called it a day.

'Any inside work going?' Big John asked Gordon. He had a
few windowsills and a couple of houses that needed scraping out
but nothing that was going to keep the nine of us in Caribbean

holidays so he told Robbie to go and wash the mixer out and the rest of us to point up the few courses we'd laid and go home.

'How depressing,' was the general consensus.

I checked my watch. What was that, half an hour's worth of work? Gordon would probably give us the hour but that wouldn't add up to more than ten quid once we'd covered the cost of our petrol and cheese and chutney.

'Still, worth it, though, weren't it?' Robbie reckoned when we dropped him off at Thornton Heath roundabout and told him we'd see him tomorrow.

'What are you going to do today?' Jason asked, when he pulled up outside my place.

'I don't know. You up for a quick half at lunchtime?' I tried.

'No, can't, I'm afraid. Sandra'll have me working on the kitchen, so no booze for Jason today,' Jason said, talking about himself in that weird other-person way he sometimes did whenever Sandra was calling the shots. I sympathised with the both of them then climbed out of the van and into the rain. 'Meant to piss down again tomorrow,' he called up the path after me, then pulled away and went home to give himself a hand with the kitchen.

I had a shower, a cup of tea and a couple of digestive biscuits, in that very order, then stood at the kitchen window and looked out at the rain for a bit. It was really coming down.

There's something about watching rain that's spellbinding. I particularly love it when the wind gets hold of it and really whips it against the window, though this can lose a lot of its allure when you're cupping your hands against the outside of the double glazing and looking at a set of keys, an umbrella and your mobile phone on the draining board. I was an angry man that day, I can tell you.

Still, that was then and this was now. And for the moment I was inside, clean, dry, fed and suddenly very, very bored.

I hated being rained off when I had nothing else to do. Losing the money's always bad enough in itself, but spending the day rattling around inside your flat while the rest of the world's at work can leave you depressed to the point of tears by the time CBeebies comes on. It's OK if you've got jobs that need doing or there's some snooker on the box that needs watching but I had neither today so by one o'clock I had the fridge out of its hole and a bottle of Ajax in my hand just to give myself something to do.

Of course, the other reason I was so restless was because Charley's number kept taunting me from my mobile.

I picked it up every now and then just to check that I still had it and even wrote it down on a piece of paper in case my SIM card decided to commit suicide just for a laugh. Her 0s and 7s and 5s and 6s looked so inviting from where I was standing that I keyed them in just to hear the sounds they made, then tried the same thing on my landline to see if they made the same sort of beeps. Naturally, I hung up before I got to the last digit, as it was only Monday and you didn't phone a girl up on Monday if you'd only met her on Friday. Not unless there was a war on. Even I knew that. So I weighted down her number with a cup so that it wouldn't get blown through the gap under the door and down a drain when my phone exploded and wandered back into the kitchen to look for something else to do.

As luck would have it, my kettle needed descaling and I remembered seeing a descaling block in the box of cleaning products when I dug out the Ajax, so I killed another half an hour defurring its element before finally losing the will to live.

This was ridiculous. Why couldn't I phone a girl on the Monday if I'd only just met her on the Friday? Who had made up that stupid rule? All weekend long Jason, Tony and old Stan had been telling me I had to wait until at least Wednesday before calling Charley and I'd nodded like a pigeon and promised them that I wouldn't even think about it. But seriously, why couldn't I? And why the fuck was I listening to old Stan?

I marched back into the living room and picked up her number like I meant it. It was now almost twenty past two and if I had to twiddle my thumbs for another forty-eight hours before I could even phone her and listen to her racking her brain for excuses, I was going to go off my chump.

I recalled her number and pressed the green button and instantly felt like runner-up in a cream-cracker-eating competition.

It started to ring at the other end, so I took a quick belt of water before she answered and brought it all up through my nose when it went down the wrong way.

'Fuckig… urgh… ug… guurr,' I told Charley when she said hello.

I coughed out the worst of it as urgently as I could and half thought about asking if it was OK if I rang back on Wednesday, but the ball was now rolling so I had to go for broke. 'Sorry about that, fucking swallowed some water down the wrong way just as you answered,' I explained. Hang on, did I just say 'fucking' or was that in my imagination? 'Er, anyway, I just wanted to give you a quick ring and see how you were. How are you?' I asked.

'I'm fine, thanks,' Charley replied, dropping her voice a little. 'Much better than Saturday anyway. I stayed in bed the whole day.'

'Oh, really?' I pondered, then wondered if that sounded pervy, like I had my hands down my pants as I was talking to her or something.

'So, how are you?' Charley then asked.

'I'm good. Rained off today,' I explained.

'What?'

'It's raining today. Can't work when it's raining.'

'Why? Are you made of sugar or something?' She chuckled.

I quickly double-checked to make sure I hadn't rung Gordon by mistake then explained that it wasn't me who didn't like it, it was the people who bought our houses. They were the ones that weren't so keen on paying good money for walls with no muck between the bricks.

'So what are you up to? Having a day in front of the TV, are you?' she asked.

'God, no, I'm just...' I thought about telling her about the kettle and the back of the fridge, then thought better of it. '... reading, you know.'

'What are you reading?'

'The telly guide, and there's nothing on.'

Charley's snigger of polite laughter quickly tailed off into a sigh and I heard the word 'anyway' without her actually having to say it.

'Where are you?' it was my turn to ask.

'Work. The office. So I can't really talk... that much,' she explained in hushed tones, then explained to one of her colleagues her end that she was talking to 'no one'. I decided to press ahead and keep this as brief as possible before she really was and asked her if she was free at all this week.

'Sure. What day?'

Any day was good with me. In fact, right now would've been just about perfect, but I figured one of us ought to stay at work and earn some money if we were going to buy that house together one day in the future, so I went ahead and suggested Wednesday, figuring old Stan would go along with that.

'Wednesday's good for me. Where do you want to go?'

Hmm, good question, and one to which I hadn't given even a jot of thought. Normally, when I went out, I just went up the Lamb. Occasionally, I went to the bookie's. Even more infrequently, I went to the dogs. I wondered which of these Charley would fancy.

I quickly nipped to the front door, opened it and rang my bell.

'Oh, hang on a minute. I think someone's at the door. Can I call you back in a second?' I asked.

'Sure, give us a call,' Charley permitted.

I hung up and took a few minutes to run around inside my own head in a sweat. Where did I take her? What did we do? This was a first date, so I had to bowl her over with something special.

Bowling?

Some good irony points there but I wasn't sure it said what I wanted it to say about me. Also, I didn't really want to spend our entire relationship going to funfairs, snooker halls and donkey rides just to prove to her how earthy I was. No, I had to show her my classy side, so that she saw me as someone to look up to, or at least someone she didn't have to look all that far down at, which called for dinner.

Just one thing, what did posh girls eat for dinner? I didn't know. But then, that was because I hadn't been to a posh restaurant in... well, ever really. I'd been to Indians and Chinese before but usually only after the pub closed when I had double vision and double everything with poppadoms and prawn crackers please.

Still, everyone liked a Chinkie's, so why didn't I take her to the best Chinkie's in the West End and Chinky Town itself. Or perhaps that should be Chinatown from here on in.

Yeah, that was a smashing idea. Really show her that I knew my way around the best places in London and that I wasn't just some Catford kebab head.

Naturally we'd have to meet for a couple of cheeky cocktails first and it would have to be somewhere central, a short walk from Chinatown that was easy enough for her to find. Leicester Square was the obvious solution. It was central, flash and just the sort of place a bloke in the know would sweep a young lady off to.

I dug out the Yellow Pages to look for bars but mine stopped just north of New Cross, so I gave Jason a quick bell and asked him if he knew any pubs in Leicester Square. He didn't but Sandra had been to a place called All Bar One right in the Square itself with a couple of the girls one night and she sold it to me completely when she told me that this place belonged to a chain of boozers that were specifically designed for women. No grungy little fleapits with frosted windows, tattered carpets and blokes swapping guns under the table, these were big, airy places with a fine selection of wines and more handbag handles than you could catch your coat pockets on.

It sounded like just the ticket.

I phoned up Charley all excitedly and gave her the itinerary.

She paused for a moment, then chuckled and asked me if I was serious.

I had been up until she'd chuckled and asked me if I was serious, but now I was just plain confused. What was wrong with that? It had all the basic components that any date should have: booze, food, bright lights and handbag handles.

Charley stopped chuckling when I didn't start and told me she didn't mean to mock.

'Oh, well, no, it sounds lovely, and Leicester Square's great and all, but I was thinking of somewhere a little less touristy,' she said, making me wish I'd suggested the Lamb and the fucking bookie's after all. 'I'll tell you what, do you know the Workers' Social?' she asked.

'Which one?' I asked.

'No, silly, it's a bar. In Noho.'

Noho? Where the hell was Noho? And what did she want to go to a Workers' Social for? I figured Charley was probably still on her ironic kick but I suddenly didn't mind. I'd take a date of darts and dominoes and having a sing-song round the piano in the corner over a night of spilling egg fried rice all down my front any day of the week given the choice. With this in mind, I told her I knew it well and that I'd see her there at eight sharp and hung up the phone sporting the first smile my face had seen since I'd left her place two days earlier.

5 The workers ain't that social

It took me ages to find out where Noho was in the *A–Z*, my search being slightly hampered by the fact that there isn't actually anywhere called Noho. It's just what trendy people call the streets north of Soho. Robbie put us straight the next day and said he even knew the Workers' Social because a mate of his brother's worked there in the evenings, and he scribbled down the name of the street for me.

'Shit place it is. What you want to go there for?' he asked.

'Yeah, what's wrong with the British Legion in Wowo?' Jason smiled, all pleased with himself for about five minutes until it started pissing down again. 'Oh, what is this?'

Wednesday proved a bit more productive and we actually got eight hours under our belts, much to everyone's relief. I beamed with excitement and whistled 'Zip-a-dee-doo-dah' all day long until a vote was taken and the lads packed me off to the other end of the site to fill in joists. I couldn't wait to see Charley again and as much as the clock tried to drag its heels, it couldn't hold our date off for ever and the wait was finally over.

Well, almost. I arrived in Noho half an hour early and found the Worker's Social right where Robbie's brother had left it.

It wasn't exactly what I'd been expecting. From the outside it was all neon signs, blacked-out windows and miked-up bouncers, a light year away from the working men's clubs I remembered going to with my old man when I first left school. But that was like nothing compared to what I saw when I actually walked through the door. The place wasn't even half finished. It was all breeze-block walls, exposed lintels and concrete floors. Cables and pipes ran between exposed wooden joists in the ceiling and even the bar was just a slapdash, badly pointed bare brick wall topped off with an old scuffed-oak surface. Most astonishing of all, though, were the seats in this place. They'd all been cast out of concrete. Even the tables. I could see the impressions where the wooden frames had been dismantled after they'd set.

Forget about a piano in the corner, this place needed a muck mixer.

Still, I'm not such a big lug that I can't appreciate a bit of variety and I recognised this place for the cutting-edge trendy theme bar it was. Did seem a bit odd calling it the Workers' Social, though. Wasn't exactly the sort of place I could see my dad heading down after a hard day on the sites. It also wasn't subsidised.

'How much?' I almost choked.

'Three seventy-five,' the expressionless barman repeated.

'Three seventy-five for half a lager?'

That's right, half a lager. The builders hadn't got around to putting any pumps in yet either so the only beers they sold came in bottles, which meant the price of a pint worked out at about £7.50. Oh yeah, my old man would've fucking loved this place, all right.

I found a vacant Flintstones table with a clear line of sight to the entrance and sat myself down.

It was now a quarter to eight, which meant Charley would be here in fifteen minutes and this realisation released a thousand butterflies to buffet me from the insides. I don't think I'm naturally a cowardly sort of bloke and will happily scale the tallest scaffolding, stand up to the biggest bully and tackle the meatiest spiders, but women were another matter altogether and about the only thing on this planet that could reduce me to a tear-streaked gibbering wreck. My nerves soon started showing on the surface and I fidgeted and palpitated, shivered and wheezed as my limited-edition collector's beer sprinted through my body at breakneck speed.

Fortunately it was so dark and noisy with a constant thump thump thump of monotonous DJ funk that no one around me even afforded me a glance, and when my watch finally struck eight, I lifted my eyes to the entrance and kept them there for a full ten minutes.

No one even resembling Charley came in during that time and when my watch just kept on ticking away regardless, my anticipation finally cracked and my hopes began to crumble.

She wasn't coming, was she? Charley wasn't coming.

We got to quarter past and I couldn't hold on any longer. I bought the second instalment of my pint and retook my seat to wait some more.

Twenty past.

I'd put so much stock in seeing Charley on the stroke of eight that for her not to be here and sitting across from me twenty minutes later was almost too much to bear. Worse-case scenarios started filling my head and images of Charley suddenly sitting bolt upright in the middle of *EastEnders*, shrugging, then sinking back into the sofa to watch the end (and then possibly *What Not to Wear*) filled my head. I even began to picture her having a right good laugh at my expense when all of a sudden my phone beeped inside my jacket and I received a text message.

I ripped it out of my pocket and pressed half a dozen wrong buttons before I realised the keypad was still locked. I took a deep breath, carefully typed in the correct code to unlock the keypad, then read my message.

Fucking Car Phone Warehouse.

Apparently I was entitled to two free ring tones if I upgraded my handset with them in the next month. All I had to do was pop into my nearest store for details and give them a share of my wages for the next year.

'You big cunts!' I shouted into my phone, then looked up to see Charley standing in front of me and smiling.

'Good news?' she enquired.

'Oh, shit, sorry, I didn't see you there,' I explained, as mortification and relief swept over me all at once. 'Shit, do you want a drink?' (*Stop swearing!!!*)

'Yeah, please. A glass of dry white wine would be nice.'

I rushed to the bar and almost strangled some bloke next to me when he cut in front of me, ordered half a dozen different cocktails, a cup of espresso, asked what crisps they did, asked the barman if he knew a guy called Curtis – played the bongos apparently – paid by credit card, then got so sidetracked comparing record bags with some other sandal-wearing dipstick that he didn't notice the barman waiting patiently for him to tap in his PIN number to the little handheld verification machine. In fact, we would've probably both still been there today had one of us not pointed out to the other that all his records and/or teeth were likely to get smashed in if he didn't sort himself out and fucking hurry up.

That shifted things along nicely.

'Sorry about that,' I told Charley when I finally retook the seat opposite her. 'A right palaver that was.'

Charley said it was no problem and thanked me for the wine, then smooched momentarily with the rim of her glass and smacked her ruby red lips with satisfaction.

'Lovely,' she sighed.

And I had to agree, she certainly was.

In fact, she was more lovely than I remembered. Tall, crisp, sparkling and sharp. Charley scrubbed up great and looked more like the sort of girl you'd see in a catalogue than anyone you'd normally find opposite me. She blazed with femininity and wore herself better than any woman I think I've ever been on a date with before. OK, let's not get carried away here, I was only five minutes into our date and I admit that I still knew very little about her, but judging by her cover, she looked like a fantastic read.

'Who were you talking to up at the bar?' she asked while I was still collecting my thoughts.

'Oh, no one, just having a bit of a laugh with old matey, that's all,' I explained. 'Anyway, cheers. You finally made it.'

'What? Oh, yeah, sorry, I'm late. Were you waiting long?'

She'd turned up at twenty-eight minutes past eight. The maths were pretty simple.

'No, I just got here myself,' I decided to tell her.

Charley said that was good, because she was a bit of a klutz with time. All her friends were always saying that she was always late but that wasn't fair because she really tried. I lied and told her that I completely understood, then asked her if she'd had a good week so far.

'It's been such hard work,' she told me. 'I've been in meetings with the client all this week about the upcoming campaign and even though they green-lit the overall strategy months ago, we can't get them to agree on the key targets. How can you push a campaign forward if you can't even agree on the basics?'

I was fucked if I knew, so I told her she just had to try and make the best of it, then asked her what she did and what she was talking about?

'I'm an advertising account manager. Don't you remember?'

'Let's just pretend, for the purposes of this conversation, that I don't,' I said, then came clean when she asked me what that meant.

'Well, anyway, I handle a particular advertising account and liaise between the client and our team who plan and run the campaign.'

I nodded anyway.

'And it's just been a bit of a nightmare getting the client to agree to our proposals. There's always something they don't like and they're forever insisting on last-minute changes.'

'I see,' I saw. 'Er... so who's your client? Would I have heard of them?' I asked.

'Naldesco. They make food products, cooking sauces, tinned meals, condiments, that sort of thing,' she said. 'They're very big.'

'Well, you're doing a bang-up job because I eat nothing but Naldesco tinned pies,' I reassured her.

'Christ, I hope not, for your sake. Anyway, there's no such thing as a Naldesco tinned pie. They make tinned pies but they're marketed under the brand name of Auntie Kate.'

'Urgh, hang on a minute, I've had one of those, they're horrible,' I blurted out, before I could get the cat back in the basket.

Luckily Charley agreed.

'Yes, they are, but I don't work on that account. Naldesco's got a lot of brand names and subsidiaries: Auntie Kate's pies, Cotswold Country Sauces, Highland Heaven Puddings, Tonbridge Traditional Treacle...'

'All knocked up in a big decommissioned missile silo next to Sellafield, I expect,' I joked, but Charley just nodded and said pretty much. 'So which account do you work on?' I asked.

'I'm handling a new account for a new range of table sauces. Rocket Man Sauces.' She smiled apologetically, then added, when she saw I was slightly confused, 'You put them on your chips and suchlike. The bottles are shaped like rockets and we're considering releasing a range of action figures to be sold alongside them so that children can wash out the bottles when they're done and use them as toys.'

'Well, you can't argue with that,' I said.

'It's an age-old trick, give away a free toy and kids will pester their mums to buy them it regardless of whether they like the product or not.'

'Yeah, I used to get my mum to buy Weetabix when I was a kid because it had *Doctor Who* scenes on the box and little cardboard figures inside,' I shared with her for some reason. 'I was always chuffed to bits when I got a Dalek, but no matter how many boxes we got through we never found a sea monster. I mean, there were three of us, me, my brother and my sister, all eating Weetabix around the clock. You'd think that, in all that time, we'd have found at least one sea monster, wouldn't you?'

Charley sympathised and agreed it had been a bad time for everyone.

'Do you think they deliberately held some figures back so that people kept buying and buying and buying Weetabix to complete the set?'

'Now there's a thought.' She smiled knowingly. Bastards, I knew it.

'So, it's not going well, then? With your client?'

'They want to go saturation right away, but we're concerned about a negative backlash and want to build up, targeting individual towns and cities first of all to give the main campaign a launching pad, so to speak.'

'That's right,' I agreed. I tried to think of a follow-up question to ask, about saturating launching pads and stuff like that, but I didn't really understand what she was talking about and I was worried if I pressed her further on the subject she might twig this, so I settled on a more obvious line of questioning. 'So what flavours do you do, then?'

'It's not me,' she assured me, but told me that for the moment Rocket Man Sauces came in spicy tomato, barbecue, curry and sweet & sour flavours, otherwise known as lunar, solar, cosmic and galactic space fuels.

'And are they nice?'

'No.'

'Oh,' I said, somewhat surprised. 'I bet that makes your job a bit harder, then, doesn't it?'

'Not really. Not from a marketing point of view anyway. It's not the taste angle of this product we're pushing,' she explained, confusing me even more.

'But hang on, the moment someone buys this stuff and ruins their dinner with it, it's game over, isn't it? No matter how many laser guns you've got on the bottle,' I pointed out.

'There are no laser guns on the bottle, the designers have gone more retro space exploration rather than sci-fi with the look of the packaging.'

'But how does that matter when the stuff inside taste like something out of *Ghostbusters*?'

Charley didn't think it was all that important, though. It wasn't in her brief so it wasn't her concern.

'Besides, we can't do anything about that aspect of the product, so why worry about it? We have to focus the campaign on the positives and let Naldesco concern themselves with that side of things.'

It was a fair point, I guess. Me and Jason simply laid the bricks we were told to by our governors. It wasn't down to us what shape the houses were, how many bedrooms they had or even what bond we laid. That had all been decided years before between the architects, the building firm and the local authority. We were the monkeys. They were the organ grinders. Charley didn't quite see herself as a monkey but didn't get a chance to expand on her point of view because at that moment some shaven-headed bouncer came over and told me I had to hop it.

'What?'

'Come on, let's go. No arguments,' he said, giving me directions over his shoulder with one of his stumpy thumbs.

'Hold your horses, what's this even about?' I protested, standing up to face him. It was then that I saw my little mate with the record bag and never-ending bar round standing just behind him with a surly puss and some bloke who looked like record bag matey's psychological back-up.

Oh dear.

'Outside,' the bouncer repeated, making to grab one of my arms.

I pulled it away and gave him some free advice about keeping his hands to himself, which he told me he'd take into consideration, and I got myself all set to stick one on him the next time he laid a finger on me, when I suddenly remembered Charley.

I looked down at her and saw her emerald eyes full of fear and confusion and I knew it would be all over between us the moment I chinned one of my new mates standing in front of me. That's when I decided to holster my fists and resort to my brains.

'Keith, can you come down here a moment?' the bouncer asked his microphone and I had an emergency flash of inspiration.

'Here, do you know Alan?' I asked the bouncer.

'Alan who?'

'Alan Law. Robbie's brother.'

But the bouncer didn't know him.

'Terry, what's going on?' Charley finally asked. I acted all baffled and told her it was probably just some silly misunderstanding, but I knew she wasn't going to buy that for very long, especially once me and Kojak started demolishing the place with each other. Our date would be well and truly over.

'Are we going to have trouble with you?' the bouncer enquired, so I tried to appeal to his better side.

'Look, mate, I don't know what the problem is, but I'm on a

first date here,' I explained, playing my joker. 'Can't we sort this out like grown-ups?'

But a stomp stomp stomp stomp stomp stomp on the stairs brought another grown-up into the proceedings and it was obvious that this grown-up had grown up eating his greens.

'Wass up, Kev?' the man mountain asked, his eyes firmly fixed on my lapels.

'This one here won't leave,' Kev told him.

'Is that right?' he asked.

Well, it had been up until about two seconds ago but now I wouldn't have put my house on it.

I noticed Charley was still sat in her chair, albeit uneasily, and I couldn't blame her really. Was she really going to stand by some trouble maker you couldn't take anywhere and follow him out into the street after he'd been kicked out of her swanky local in less time than it took to warm up her seat? No, of course not. What sort of a sophisticated girl about town needed aggro like that when there were no end of apes hanging in Noho's trees and she had all the bananas?

'You can go out on your feet or on your head, it's entirely up to you,' all seven foot of Keith said, listing my options in no particular order. I didn't hold out much hope but I thought I'd try one last throw of the dice before I was dragged upstairs by the jacket anyway.

'*You* don't know Alan, do you? Alan. Alan Law, Robbie's brother,' I pleaded, holding out my hands to stop the big man's advance.

This momentarily checked him in his tracks and he took a moment to look me up and down as the question melted over his face.

'Yeah, I know Alan. And Robbie as it happens. Who are you, then?' he asked suspiciously.

'I'm Terry, I work with Robbie down in Wimbledon,' I told

him, hoping this would count for something and that he wouldn't simply tell me to say 'hallo' to Robbie next time I saw him as he slung me head first into the bins.

'You on the hod with Robbie, then?' he asked.

'No, the trowel. He runs our bricks,' I explained, noticing that I was actually being given a chance to explain something rather than just being threatened with the door, and I glimpsed a chink of light.

'Yeah, I know Alan really well,' he happily admitted. 'Top bloke, he is. I used to do a bit with him down Docklands when it was all going up.'

I didn't have a clue what Alan and this enormous bloke used to do a bit of 'down Docklands when it was all going up', it could've been tarmacking, chippying, drug smuggling or beating up taxi drivers for all I knew, but I nodded and looked as chuffed about it as I could before hitting him with the first favour of our new-found friendship.

'Look, Keith, mate, I don't know what's going on here, I seriously don't. What's this all about?'

Keith didn't know so he turned to his mate Kev for answers. Kev told him that I'd threatened to beat up the bloke behind and Keith took a look over his shoulder and cocked his head sympathetically.

'Who said that? I never said any such thing,' I lied as fast as I could. 'I just asked the bloke if he could see his way clear to getting a move on because he was taking all night pissing about with his little mates while I was stood behind him waiting to get served. OK, I admit it, I swore and told him to get "a fucking move on", but I certainly didn't threaten him,' I insisted. 'What am I, a hooligan or something?'

'That's rubbish, he said he was going to break all of my records and teeth if I didn't get out of his way,' matey with the record bag and bruised ego finally piped up.

I tried to look as wronged as I humanly could and my acting got an unwelcome boost of authenticity when his mate bullshitted that he'd heard me say as much, which was as big a lie as my own as he hadn't been anywhere near either of us when I'd offered to do a Norris McWhirter on the little fucker's record bag.

I clocked the changing expressions on Keith and Kev's faces as the bag ladies launched into their own little tirade and I got the distinct impression that the cavalry were starting to side with Big Chief Whispers with Menace after a while. Bag matey and his little yapping poodle might've had the facts in their corner but they'd underestimated the importance of presentation and the more they banged on about me and what I'd said, the more it sounded like they were telling the doormen their job. Not a fantastically smart thing to do, so I figured now was the time to trip them both us with my peace pipe.

'Look, I'm sorry if you thought I was out of order for asking you to hurry up, but you have to admit you were mucking around ordering teas and coffees on your credit card, then jabbering on to your mates while the barman was waiting for you to type in your PIN number,' I pointed out, for the benefit of our bouncers, then stuck my hand in bag matey's direction and offered, 'No hard feelings?'

Naturally, bag matey snorted with derision and folded his arms in defiance to show me that he didn't do deals with thugs. That was when Kev apologised to Charley and me and even told me I was 'all right'.

'What? But he threatened to beat me up,' bag matey protested with outrage.

'Just get over there and let's have no more of this, OK. The man's just trying to have a drink with his girlfriend,' Kev told him. Charley shifted in her seat to show me what she thought about that particular can of worms and Keith gave me the thumbs-up and asked me if I ever got down the White Horse.

'Occasionally,' I once again lied for seasoning.

'But he should be thrown out of here,' bag matey continued, then added for some reason that he knew the DJ.

'Then do us a favour and go and lend him some of your records, he seems to have been playing the same one for the last half an hour,' I suggested, making both Keith and Kev nod in agreement.

'Fucking dreadful, inne?' Kev confirmed.

Bag matey couldn't let it go, though, and insisted on seeing the manager. Keith told him he'd be seeing the double yellows out front if they had any more trouble out of him, before wishing me all the best and shooing the pair of them away with a few well-chosen words, sixteen of which were ironically:

'*I'll* smash all your fucking records in if you don't pack it in, now behave yourself.'

I retook my seat opposite my dumbfounded date and promised her that I didn't know what the hell had just happened there. And you know what, I really didn't.

OK, so I'd bared my knuckles a bit with old bag matey but it was only an expression. You know, a sort of 'hurry up or I'll smash your face in' born of frustration. If he'd taken it seriously there was nothing to stop him barking back instead of running off and crying his eyes out to the bouncers. I mean, he was the one with all the mates in here, not me.

And besides, over and above everything else, couldn't he see how out of order he was for doing what he'd done? I mean, he was the one that had quickly cut in front of me. He was the one that had ordered half a dozen complicated cocktails and a cup of espresso and monopolised the barman so that no one else could get a drink for over fifteen minutes. Not me. He was the one that had been laughing and joking around once he safely had a drink in his hand without sparing a thought to concluding his business so that other people could get served. Was bag matey such a complete me-first merchant that he couldn't see how inconsiderate this was and understand how much it might wind up the blokes spitting feathers behind him? It didn't help that this place thought they only needed one barman, but that was beside the point. His actions had been keeping me from my beer for a full quarter of an hour while my date sat waiting in the corner. You'd have thought if he had any sort of shame he would've actually felt embarrassed and apologised for his behaviour, wouldn't you?

I would've, had the record bag been on the other shoulder.

'Oh shit, sorry, mate. Here you go,' I would've said.

At which I would've got a somewhat frosty:

'No problem, ta,' for my troubles and that would've been that.

After all, pubs are places for grown-ups, ain't they, not spoilt little brats who couldn't see that there was anything wrong with hogging all the swings for the whole of playtime just because they got to 'em first.

I decided not to go sharing any of these thoughts with Charley as I figured this would just put a dent in my cool handling of the situation, but it did twist one thing into sharp focus that I hadn't really given much thought to up until this moment.

And that was, we weren't in Catford no more.

6 Money can't buy you love

I didn't go home with Charley at the end of our date. Not because of my near-punch-up, but because it was a work night and I had to be back in south London to press my snooze button the next morning. Not that there was any sort of invitation, you understand. We'd just had a couple more drinks, tried to pick up the conversation where we'd left it and chucked in the towel at around half past ten.

I thought I'd blown it. Or rather, I thought matey had blown it for me because the shadow of my barney hung in the air like a bad smell for the rest of the evening. In fact, I'd already written off the whole date as just one more thing to get annoyed about come Judgement Day when Charley texted me as I was on my way home.

'I had a great night. I can't believe those fucking prats. Are you free on Saturday?'

Actually, that's not strictly true. What her text had really said was this:

hd gr8 nite :-) cant blv wot hpnd wth thos gIs :-@ u3 sat :-D :-(?

At first I thought something had gone wrong with my phone again and it wasn't until the next morning when Jason turned my phone on its side that I realised that the :-)s were actually little faces and not just really shit punctuation.

'Sandra sends me them all the time. I thought she was texting me while wearing her oven gloves the first time round but no, they're little faces. See, happy and frowny? For yes and no.'

'I see.'

Truly bizarre. And I don't mean Charley's text shorthand. I mean the fact that she wanted to see me again. It's funny how two people can come away from the same date with completely different ideas about how the evening has gone, isn't it? It had happened to me a few times in the past but this was the first time I was the one who hadn't thought the evening had been a blistering success.

What was it that Charley had liked about the evening? We'd chatted and joked and a couple of times I'd even managed to make her laugh, but it had been a long way from great. I don't mean from my own point of view. No, I'd loved the evening because Charley had been there. So as far as I was concerned the evening had been great. I just couldn't figure out why Charley had thought it had been great too.

'Will you stop annoying me and talk about something else, for crying out loud?' Jason pleaded from the other end of the scaffolding. 'Christ, it's like someone reading out Marjorie's problem page all morning long.'

'You know what your problem is, Tel?' Big John said, addressing me with the tip of his trowel. 'You've stuck this bird up on a pedestal from day one without even getting to know her. Perhaps she did have a great night. Perhaps she's all as chuffed and as giggly and girlie as you this morning. I don't see how she could be, but you never know.'

'Yeah, she's probably on the other side of London, slapping down some bricks and having exactly the same conversation,' Jason pointed out, as he cut and buttered a brick.

'You don't know what sort of blokes she'd been out with in the past,' Big John then said. 'She might've been out with all sorts: boozers, wife-beaters, two-timers, cokeheads. They're a right load of bad boys those rich Flash Harry City types, you know?'

'That's true,' Jason confirmed, which instantly underpinned

Big John's statement as a fact. Two brickies' opinions carried that sort of weight, you know.

'She could've had the lot, you know. Compared to them, you could be Sir Galahad and Sir Lancelot all rolled into one,' Big John said, twirling his trowel around in his hand. 'You're a nice bloke, you are. What's up with you? Why wouldn't she like you? Sort yourself out.'

'Nah, I go wit' Jays,' Nobby perked up from the other end of the flank. 'She's probably just after a bit o' rough. Ah put money on it that she was aching to see you smack tha' fella in the gob las' night. I bet she would'a wet her knickers and sucked you off all the way ta hospital if ya had.'

'Yeah. Or there is always that,' Big John admitted, rolling muck on his muck board to get a nice big trowelful before spreading it along the wall.

My love life focus group continued with such advice up until tea break when the conversation landed on football island and got shipwrecked there for the rest of the week.

I'm not much of a football fan, to be honest. I'll watch the odd England match and get as excited about it as the next guy come World Cup time. I'll even occasionally ask Robbie how Crystal Palace are doing, them being my nearest local league team, but by and large the government could outlaw the game and I don't think it would make a jot of difference to my life. Not like Robbie. It would be an utter disaster for him. And not only because he wouldn't have anywhere to go at the weekends – and anything to talk and think about at all other times – but because he'd suddenly find himself up against an enormous pool of unskilled and unemployed labour and I bet Wayne Rooney could shift a few bricks if he put his back into it.

'He'd have to for two hundred grand a week,' said Robbie, prompting one of those 'if I had a million pounds' conversations which ended in a shouting match when Stuart insisted on risking his in stocks and shares rather than sticking it in the bank and living off the interest like the rest of us planned to do.

'Jesus, isn't it five o'clock yet?' grumbled Jason.

I didn't do much on Friday night. I had a couple of pints in the Lamb but went home early so that I'd be fresh as a daisy for Charley the next day.

I texted her when I got in but no reply came back, which meant she was either playing it cool, was too drunk to notice or had taken her own life because I'd not texted her for the whole of the evening.

Or she was too busy getting banged in the bog by those two blokes I went on holiday with twelve years ago, of course, which was equally possible.

When her reply did finally arrive, Saturday morning, it was heavily encoded.

wnt2 cum ∧ 2 cnbry + mt 4 drx 2nite :-)

'What the fuck...?' I muttered, trying to decipher it, before giving up and simply phoning her.

'What do you think? Are you up for it?' Charley asked, after the initial 'oh hi, how are you?'s.

'OK, let's do it, I've got the microfilm. Let's telex HQ and get out of here.'

It turned out what Charley's text had actually said was this:

'Do you want to come north to Canonbury (∧ being north London, you see) and meet for drinks? Such a thing would make me smile.'

I played it cool and told her I might wander by if I had nothing better to do, then put down the phone and rushed into the shower, shaved, trimmed my nails and flossed, and spent the next seven hours throwing shirts about the bedroom and shaking the clock.

Nine hours later I pulled up at a nice little pub in a Canonbury back street, got myself a pint and pulled a newspaper out of my back pocket. If nothing else, I'd at least learned from our earlier date.

Charley arrived a respectable fourteen pages later and shed her grin for a couple of seconds to plant a breathless and excited kiss on my lips before shaking herself out of her coat.

'I'm not late, am I? I couldn't find my keys anywhere,' she explained, pulling the arms inside out and dumping the whole lot over the back of her chair.

'Not a bit of it. White wine?' I offered.

'Actually, can I have a beer? The same as whatever you're having.'

'Half?' I double-checked. Charley laughed like that had been a joke so I pretended it had and got her a pint.

'How have you been? Tell me about your week,' she said, when I sat back down.

My week had been much like the previous five hundred. Jason had called around in the van, picked me up, driven us both over to some half-built housing estate and together with a load of other blokes, we'd finished a little bit more of it. The only things that ever changed about my job were the blokes around me and the weather above me. It had rained at the start of the week, dried up towards the end and we'd finished half a dozen gables, a couple of footings and four murder lifts, which are what us brickies call the brickwork around the upper storey of a house for reasons no one's ever been able to explain to me. All in all, it had been a spectacularly ordinary week, though I did put something of a gloss on it and scared her to her toes with a story about how Robbie had overloaded the boards again and how the scaffolding had plunged right beneath my feet, though in truth it had only plunged by about two inches. And it had happened to Big John, not me.

Still, Charley looked suitably blown away at my action-packed week full of danger and dare-doing and made me promise to be careful in future. I half thought about telling her that danger went with the territory, darling, then realised that if I did, everyone in the pub would be quite within their rights to throw their drinks over me, so I simply assured her that, the odd overloaded scaffolding board aside, most sites were pretty safe places these days.

'And how about you? How's the campaign going?' I asked in return.

Some progress had been made. Naldesco had agreed to sit down and listen to what the agency had to say about the benefits of a regional strategy, so Charley was pulling stats and data from similar past campaigns to smack 'em over the head with and make a bit of a fist of it.

It's bonkers when you think about it really, isn't it? All this fuss, money and talking over something you're going to empty over your chips – and just once in all likelihood. You'd think it would be simple, wouldn't you? Stick an ad on the box along the lines of: 'Buy Rocket Man Sauce. It's fantastic', run it six or seven million times until we're all ready to kick the telly in every time it comes on, then repackage the product and repeat the process a year later when Naldesco finally gets the message that we don't want any. That's what everyone else seemed to do. Just because it was Rocket Man Sauce, it don't mean it was rocket man science, did it?

'Remind me what you do for a living again?' Charley asked in her defence.

I gave her that one but still, it was stupid. You'd think intelligent, well-educated people would have better things to be doing than wasting their time on this load of old rubbish, wouldn't you? No wonder we hadn't found a cure for cancer yet.

I thought better of sharing this last observation with Charley and we got on to the subject of our families. Both sets of parents were still alive and while Charley was an only child, I had the full set, an older brother and a younger sister.

'How do you get on with them?' Charley asked.

'Fine,' I replied. 'I go round there for tea once in a while, borrow a couple of tools off my old man every now and again and call in on my sister when I need a few shirt buttons sewing on, that sort of thing,' I explained.

Charley wiped a mock tear from her eye and asked me if I ever saw them when H&S Hire and Sketchleys weren't closed. She didn't quite phrase it like that, but that was the general gist.

'But do you get on with them? Do you love them?' she asked. 'Do you tell them that you love them?'

'Well, yeah, you know, I don't know, I mean, we don't go around bawling our eyes out in front of each other and plastering the old man with kisses whenever he's off the bog, but we do all right. Same as everyone else, I suppose,' I babbled, a touch off balance in the face of such questions. 'Well, what about you? What are you like with your old folks, then?' I countered, figuring attack was the best form of defence.

'My mum's cool. I speak to her most days and tell her about my life.'

'Have you told her about me?' I asked.

'No,' she said, saying all there was to say on that particular subject. 'And my dad's lovely, though he worries about me constantly. I guess being his only daughter and all that. I'm Daddy's little girl and always will be to him. He's very protective of me.'

'Is he here now?'

Charley laughed and told me he was waiting outside in the car with a cricket bat.

'What does he do for a living?'

'He's an investment banker.'

I didn't really know what an investment banker did but it sounded like one of those bowler-hatted sorts of jobs that got you enough money to buy a house in Berkshire, cover it with ivy and park a Mercedes outside it.

'Do all his pens come with little those chains on the end to keep 'em attached to the desk?' was about the only thing I could think to ask about investment banking.

'Yes. It stops representatives from the CBI sticking them in their pockets when he's not looking,' Charley confirmed.

'Smart.'

We talked for a few more pints, interspersing fact with nonsense as we got to know each other inch by inch and I learned a couple of things about Charley that both surprised me and watered down my optimism all in one.

For a start, she was minted. Not super-rich, shopping at Harrods and a big plate of caviar and chips at the Ritz every night, but she still had a few quid in the bank all the same. See, while it turned out that thinking up ways to sell Rocket Man Sauce paid twice as much as it did to build houses, she also didn't have half the outgoings I did as her flat was completely paid off – though not by her.

'My dad bought it for me when I moved to London. Like I said, he worries about me and didn't want me having to live in a dodgy area just because I couldn't afford to buy a place somewhere nice.'

All the same, that called for a 'Jesus!' if only because I wasn't even a fifth of the way into my twenty-five-year mortgage to buy my ex-council flat in Catford, which probably qualified as Dodge City in Charley's old man's books.

'It's a bit embarrassing really,' she sheepishly admitted.

I thought about this before concluding that it shouldn't be.

'We'd all have one if we could,' I said. 'If he's got the money and doesn't mind parting with it, then why not? Better than chucking it at the bank if you don't have to. Oh, I forgot, he works for the bank, doesn't he? Well then, even better.'

And I meant it too. We pay out so much money that we don't have to when we're skint. Take my place, for example; I bought it for just over ninety thousand pounds with a ninety-five per cent mortgage five years ago and if I stay alive, healthy and in work, by the time I finish paying it off in the year 2027, I will have paid back something in the region of a hundred and eighty grand for it. That's over twice what the flat cost. I've checked the mortgage paperwork and it's all there in black and white. Unbelievable, isn't it? The thieving bastards. Your house is the most expensive thing you'll ever have to buy and you have to pay double for it if you don't have the wherewithal to buy it outright the first time around.

Naturally, Charley's old man, being a thieving bastard himself, probably worked all this out with one of his chain-linked pens and saw that plundering his ISAs for his daughter was actually the best way of keeping money in the family anyway. OK, so Charley now had his... whatever her flat cost – a quarter-of-a-million, I wouldn't be surprised – but wasn't she always going to get it anyway? The moment he popped his clogs the lot would've been turned over to her anyway. Charley was his only daughter, so what difference did it make if she got an advance on her inheritance and put it to good use while he was still around to enjoy seeing her put it to good use? And actually that's not true either, come to think of it, Charley wouldn't have got the lot because the taxman, an even bigger thieving bastard than Charley's dad, would've had half of it away in death duties before she could've even stuck a black dress on, so if you think about it, it actually made a lot of financial sense just to give it to her now. If her flat had cost a quarter of a million pounds and if she had done the normal thing and got a mortgage and then waited for her dad to fall off his perch in order to get her hands on his money, she would've had to have paid out something like three hundred and seventy five grand to the bank and the taxman alternately to be no better off than she was as things stood right now.

Put like that, who could blame her for letting her dad buy her a flat?

Still, spoilt cow.

'So your wages, what do you do with them, then? Just chuck 'em in the bank and dip into them when you want a new pair of socks, or do you blow the lot on taxis and holidays?' I pried, quite improperly, but the question was crying out to be asked.

'No, I have bills to pay, just like everybody else,' she assured me, though she must've had radiators in the front garden and an extension lead running up to Blackpool's Golden Mile to have made a dent in her fifty-grand-a-year salary, as far as I could make out. 'And I have a few investments and a pension to manage,' she added, and I was almost tempted to ask if she wanted me to have a whip-round, but I wasn't sure she'd see the funny side of that if she was already embarrassed about having been given a flat – in pricey Canonbury.

The second thing I learned about Charley that put a crimp in my expectations was that she'd had surprisingly few long-term relationships. She'd had the odd month-long fling here and there, of course, and a boyfriend while she'd been at university, but for most of the last couple of years she'd used a basket when she'd gone to the supermarket instead of a trolley and spent her Saturday mornings reading her *Guardian* rather than lying in his arms. She was, for want of a better expression, on the shelf, which was a lovely old expression that my dad used to use about my sister before she met Cliff whenever he wanted to hear her scream. The question was, though, why was Charley on the shelf?

Did she choose to go it alone or were her expectations so

phenomenally high that Romeo himself would've had a job getting her to come along on his plus-one invitations?

In which case, what the hell was I doing shopping on these shelves? I couldn't afford any of this stuff. Of course I couldn't. And sooner or later the store detective was going to rumble me for the undesirable I was.

'Penny for them,' she said, when she saw me all pensive. I should've held out for more as I knew she could afford it but I went ahead and took her money anyway.

'Just wondering what a nice girl like you...' I started, before she comically interrupted.

'...is doing in a place like this?' she suggested, though she would've been closer to the mark if she'd tacked on the words 'with a bozo like you'.

'No, I mean, why you're not seeing anyone? Why you haven't got anyone? I mean, you're great. You're pretty, funny, clever, nice company. I can't figure it out.' (I could've also added 'and fucking loaded' but didn't.)

'I don't know,' Charley mused. 'Maybe it's because I'm a lesbian.'

'See, you've even got that going for you too,' I said, ticking the last box on my own particular card and calling bingo.

'I could ask you the same,' Charley pointed out.

'Well, I ain't gay, if that's what you're getting at.'

'What happened to Jo? Your last girlfriend. Why did you split up with her?'

That caught me a little offguard. I'd forgotten Charley knew about Jo and I didn't feel particularly comfortable talking about old girlfriends with her. Still, the question had been asked so I told her the truth.

'She did something that I didn't like. Something I could never forgive her for.'

'What?' Charley asked, suddenly all ears.

'She moved all of her stuff out of my place and married the manager of my local Safeways,' I told her. 'Of course, it's Morrisons these days, they took it over, but that doesn't really have anything to do with the story.'

Charley gasped. 'Is that true?'

'Yeah, they've changed the signs and everything.'

'No, I mean about Jo? She left you and married someone else?'

'Yeah,' I admitted and shrugged. Well, what else was there to do?

'I'm sorry, Terry,' Charley frowned. 'Were you very upset?'

'Not really. It had been on the cards for some time in all honesty. We weren't really getting on and sometimes you can just tell when a relationship's run its course.' I sighed.

Charley reached across the table and laid her hand on mine.

'One thing did annoy me, though,' I then confessed.

'What was that?'

'I can't go to bloody Morrisons any more. I've got to drive another mile up the road to Sainsbury's and they don't do the same spicy poppadoms I like.'

'I feel your pain,' Charley sympathised, and for one brief moment I almost forgot that I didn't have a hope in hell of hanging on to the girl who was smiling warmly at me from across the table.

Almost.

7   Idol hands

At eleven o'clock Charley started looking at her watch and fidgeting.

I sensed our evening was coming to an end and wondered what happened now. Should I try my luck and suggest a nightcap back at hers or should I do my usual stupid gentlemanly bit, kiss her hand, take a manly bow and get a large doner kebab for the train ride home?

'Well, I've had a really lovely evening,' Charley said, giving me a look that filled my mouth with the taste of onions and chilli sauce. 'But I guess we should be going. We don't want to end up like last week.'

What, in bed together? I wondered.

'You're right,' I said, looking about for puddles to lay my coat across. 'Well, I've had a really nice night too. Perhaps we could go out again another night, maybe in the week again?'

'Yeah. Or maybe we could go back to my place now,' she suggested.

'Yeah, or maybe we could do that,' I agreed, and followed her out of the pub in a semi-daze.

'I don't want you to get the wrong idea about me,' she said, when we got outside. 'I'm really not in the habit of doing this sort of thing.'

Funnily enough, neither was I, which was why it was so fantastic that it was happening now. As for getting the wrong idea about Charley, I wasn't sure I'd had a right one yet, so I was more than happy to give my brain the rest of the night off and let my heart take things from here – with back-up provided by the lads downstairs.

'That's OK, I don't think anything of you, I promise,' I duly promised, wondering if that had come out right.

'You're a fast worker. Most guys save that line for the next morning,' Charley pointed out.

'Er, no, that's not what I mean,' I fumbled, but Charley assured me it was OK, she knew what I meant.

'So you'll respect me in the morning, huh?' she asked.

'I'll worship you in the morning,' I replied, causing my brain to leap out of bed and come charging downstairs in his slippers to see just who the fuck was letting my feet have a go on my mouth.

'From thinking nothing of me to worshipping me? You really are a fast worker.' Charley smiled, holding my gaze for a moment before slipping an arm around my waist and giving me a kiss.

Charley had a nice kiss. Her lips touched mine. They parted a little and we tasted each other's mouths with tenderness and restraint. Not like some of the birds I've known. After a few glasses of wine Jo used to kiss like that thing John Hurt got stuck to his face in *Alien*, while Helen before her used to attack my mouth like her tongue was trying to defect from her own head and make it over to mine to start a new life. Still, neither of them were as bad as Jill the Goth. I only ever went home with Jill once. Once was enough. She'd been OK in the pub and in the cab home, but then when we'd got back to her place she sank her teeth into my tongue during our first smooch and held me fast, as I hollered, howled and tried to gouge her eyes out.

I honestly thought she was going to bite my tongue off and scrambled across the room and away from her when she finally let me go, checking my mouth for blood and the windows for bars.

'Pain is good,' she simply smirked.

My lips, mouth and tongue didn't go anywhere near any part of Jill again and after a quick glass of water I made my excuses (namely, 'You're fucking bananas and I'm out of here') and ran off into the night. I couldn't even get anything to eat on the way home as my tongue hurt so much and it spent the rest of the weekend bathing itself in ice creams and quivering behind my teeth whenever strange women looked my way.

'You've got a nice kiss,' I told Charley when we pulled back from each other.

'Thanks. I should have, I've been practising on my hand all afternoon.'

Which again made two of us.

Charley twisted the keys in the lock and I followed her inside. Her place looked a little different from how I'd remembered it. I think I'd over-romanticized it in my head, like I have a tendency to do with all things, adding a couple of storeys here and dimmer switches there. It was still nice, certainly a lot nicer than my place, but it could've been nicer still. It had a lot of potential; a bit of decent skirting board, get rid of that cracked architrave, new tiles in the kitchen, lino in the bathroom, brass fixtures (which were my own personal favourites) instead of the basic plastic ones the builders had put in and new paint, carpet and doors throughout and Charley could've stuck ten grand on the price just like that.

'It's like having my very own Laurence Llewelyn-Bowen,' Charley said, handing me a glass of brandy. 'You know, the guy off *Changing Rooms*?'

I remembered the show if not the guy's name who'd presented it, but disagreed with Charley's assessment. I wasn't so much Llewelyn-Bowen, more one of those blokes in the background with no lines who did all work when the cameras were off and who silently longed to knock a bucket of bricks on to Laurence's foppy head whenever he walked past.

'Still, it could use a builder's touch,' Charley said, then took a sip of her drink and added: 'I think we both could.'

I realised she was right and put away my measuring tape and embraced her passionately.

'Please be gentle with me,' I said, sweeping her up in my arms, then putting her straight back down again when she turned out to be heavier than she looked. Size ten, my arse!

We entwined right there on the sofa and started pinging buttons and pulling zips until we were in such a tangle that we had to momentarily disengage to shake our trousers off. When we did, I found that Charley had on matching lacy purple underwear that looked more expensive than my car and I realised it'd probably had more say in me being here than I had.

'Let's do it right here on the sofa,' Charley whispered.

'For starters,' I replied, wrestling with her bra strap until admitting defeat and asking for a favour. Charley's fingers tweaked her strap and her bra fell away to reveal a beautiful pair of Charleys. 'Very nice,' I either thought or said, I can't remember which, and a moment later her knickers joined her bra and some more of my socks on the floor.

Being the self-styled gentleman I am, I'll leave the descriptions at the bedroom door, if you don't mind too much, even though I was doing her in the living room. I've probably said a bit too much already in all honesty, telling you what colour her pants were and how many tits she had, so I won't go on any further. All I'll say is that she was soft, lithe, delicious and she didn't try and bite my fucking tongue off.

And you can't ask for much more than that.

We lay curled up on the sofa afterwards, kissing gently and

tracing our fingers across each other's bodies as we stared deeply into each other's eyes. Mine suddenly felt as heavy as concrete blocks but I pulled out all the stops to keep them open for as long as possible in an effort to soak up every square mile of this pink and perfect vision of loveliness while it lasted.

'How long has it been for you?' Charley asked.

'What?'

'Since you last did that,' she said, clearing up the mystery of whether we'd done it the previous week once and for all. Well, that or the reason she hadn't replied to the previous evening's text.

'A little while,' I told her, reluctant to go into specifics.

'How long's a little while?' she pried.

'A little while's a little while,' I sidestepped.

'More than two weeks?' she asked, almost making me laugh in her face.

More than two weeks? Of course it was more than two weeks. Christ, I was going to be telling my mates I'd *just* done it with a stunningly beautiful bird four months from now so a fortnight of abstinence didn't actually qualify as abstinence. It qualified as 'I'm sorry, I can't come to the phone as I'm doing it right this very minute'.

'More than a few weeks,' I finally replied, though I could've elaborated and told her she could've bundled those weeks up into months if she liked and there'd still be quite a few of them too.

'How many's a few?' Charley pressed.

'A few's a few,' I explained, before trying to baffle her with some nonsense. 'When Winston Churchill said we owed "so much to so few", he was talking about five or six hundred RAF pilots, but when my granny told me that she still had "a few good years" left in her yet, she was talking about anything between six months to three years, so it depends on the context.'

'I see. And is your granny still alive today?' Charley fished, sensing a clue in my shpiel.

'No, unfortunately,' I said sadly. 'No, she was shot down on a routine reconnaissance mission over Biggin Hill.'

Charley blinked a couple of times but resisted the temptation to ask me if I was serious.

'Anyway, what about you?' I countered. 'When was the last time you... er...'

'Got banged?' Charley finished for me.

'I wouldn't have put it quite like that.'

'Oh yeah, so how would you have put it?' she asked.

I thought for a moment.

'Got done,' was the term I finally plumped for.

'Nice,' she said.

'Yeah, anyway, how long is it since you last got done?'

Charley gave that one some thought, then said that perhaps it was best if we didn't play this game after all, presumably because she somehow knew that this was the answer that would rob me of the most nights' sleep in the weeks to come.

That put a nice little awkward crimp in the conversation and neither of us knew what to say next for a few moments, so instead we just lay there, gently stroking each other's skin with our fingers and sinking into the lilac pillows.

After a while, Charley turned one of my hands over in hers and examined it.

'You have very big hands,' she said, squeezing my fat fingers and prodding my calluses.

This had been pointed out to me by girls before, usually in a 'urgh, aren't your hands rough and horrible' kind of way, so it was something I was a tad self-conscious about.

'Sorry,' I automatically apologised, worried that she was angry with me for sandpapering her tits for the last twenty minutes.

'No, don't apologise, I like them. They're men's hands.' She then went on to tell me about some solicitor bloke she once went out with who used to have hands spindlier than hers and who used to moisturise three times a day with hand cream.

'It actually got a bit creepy him touching me. My friends all said he had a handshake like a wet fish.'

I didn't even know wet fish shook hands, but I liked that Charley liked my hands, though in all honesty they were just the product of fifteen years of handling bricks. I wasn't genetically any more manly than her solicitor mate, if that's what Charley was getting at, and I'm sure if he ever got a job with us he'd soon sling his hand cream in the bin when he saw the benefits of having hands your could put your fags out on.

I told Charley about when I'd first started on the sites as a teenager. Back then I'd had kid's hands, as kids tend to have, and for the first couple of weeks I went through agonies I can't even begin to describe as my fingers found themselves a long way from the classroom. Those first couple of weeks, everything I touched hurt, especially in the evenings after work. I couldn't even pick up a cup of tea without shrieking in pain and my old man used to love the nightly spectacle of watching me trying to eat my dinner without using a knife and fork. Then the next morning it would start all over again. Bricks, blocks, scaffolding poles and planks, each one feeling like someone had wrapped it in barbed wire overnight.

'You should've just worn gloves,' Charley said, like this had never occurred to me.

'You can't, even a good pair of gloves falls to bits after a week or so, and even when they're new, grit always finds a way inside the fingers, especially in the winter when everything's wet, you can't avoid it. You might as well go through the agonies and let them toughen up.'

I wondered why I was telling her this. Was I trying to impress her with more tales of dare-doing, like the scaffolding collapse adventure from earlier on, or was I simply colouring in a little more of my background for her? Probably a bit of both, if the truth were to be told, though it's always nice when people show an interest in your life and the things you've done, even if these things are pretty ordinary.

'Well, I like your hands,' Charley said, giving my fat sausage fingers a little kiss. 'I like them a lot.'

'That's good, because my hands like you,' I replied, returning her kiss.

Before setting my hands to work again.

8   The greaseless spoon

I've never really liked Sundays. I think it has something to do with all the Sundays we had to endure as kids. When there was nothing to do because nothing was open and no one was ever around, primarily because Sunday dinner time is bang smack in the middle of the afternoon, where no meal has any right to be, let alone an enormous great one like Sunday's, with peas, carrots, cauliflower and cabbage piled sky high, all boiled and about as appetising as my bedroom a couple of hours later.

And there was never anything but a load of old depressing dregs on the telly: *Songs of Praise*, *The Antiques Roadshow*, *Last of the Summer Wine* and *All Creatures Great and Small*, all topped off with *That's Life!* It certainly was and a miserable one at that for most of us until the nineties came along and someone had the stunning idea of actually opening a few places on our national day off so that we didn't have to sit around staring at the wall and sobbing quietly about the prospect of work or school the next day. We could go to the pub, go to a restaurant, go to the pictures, watch the football or even do a bit of shopping if we were so inclined. Suddenly we had a choice. Naturally there were a few miserable old gits who thought it was their divine right to tell the rest of us what to do and lobbied to 'keep Sundays special', but they were massively outnumbered by the dancing majority who were just thankful to finally have something to do to take our minds off our fucking Mondays.

Still, I think all this came just a little too late for me to ever be able to fully appreciate them. The rotten, miserable, dreary Sundays of my youth were just too deeply ingrained on my psyche so that it didn't matter how many bowling alleys opened up near my house, I could never fully shake off that overwhelming sense of wall-climbing lethargy that hung around my neck all day long and went off the dial if I turned on the box and found *Ski Sunday* on.

That said, this particular Sunday certainly went a long way to redress a lot of that wrong when I opened my eyes and found Charley purring gently beside me. She looked even lovelier than she had done that first morning I'd woken up next to her, though maybe that had something to do with the fact that I knew she wasn't a prostitute and stinging me five hundred quid for the privilege.

A slow stirring soon turned into a stretch then Charley sent her limbs to the four corners of the bed and let out a yawn that sounded like Bambi desperately screaming for help as she was strangled in an icy stream. Don't ask me how I know that, by the way.

'Morning,' she said, when she opened her eyes and noticed me staring down at her.

'Morning,' I replied, as I watched her rein in her arms and drag my neck with them. I was just starting to wonder what a bloke had to do to get a cup of tea around here when Charley let me in on the secret.

'Put the kettle on, will you?'

Of course, it was suddenly so obvious.

I got out of bed, pitter-pattered barefoot to the kitchen and looked through a few cupboards. I had no problem finding Charley's English breakfast tea, but then that was only because there was hardly anything for it to hide behind. She had a jar of coffee in there next to the tea, a few tins of tuna, a bag of pasta and six – yes, count them – six half-finished boxes of Weetabix.

In the fridge, a splash of milk, a dollop of butter, a few jars of pesto, sun-dried tomatoes and an assortment of condiments, but there was nothing you'd really call food in there. There was certainly nothing I'd call food in there.

She didn't live on this stuff, did she?

I wasn't sure. I also wasn't sure I fancied my chances of getting any breakfast this morning.

'Tea up,' I said, returning to the bedroom and handing Charley a steaming hot cup of English breakfast.

'Oh, it's a bit strong, isn't it? Can I have a drop more milk in mine, please?'

'You can if you want to go out and buy some. That's all the milk gone,' I told her.

'Oh yeah, I think I need to do a shop,' she remembered.

'No, I think you needed to do a shop six weeks ago,' I corrected her. 'This goes beyond needing a shop. What the hell do you eat in the evenings?'

'I don't know; pasta, Weetabix, that sort of thing,' she told me. 'I usually eat with friends quite a lot too,' she then said, filling my head with visions of skinny posh girls sitting around on crates eating handfuls of dried cereal straight from the box.

'I'll tell you what, I'll treat you to a slap-up café breakfast a little later if you like,' I told her. 'Before that, though, why don't you put your tea down?' I suggested, then slid back into bed beside her.

Charley took me up on both offers and forty minutes later... sorry, I mean an hour and a half later, we were walking down Upper Street keeping our eyes peeled for eggs and bacon.

We passed a perfectly decent-looking café along the way but Charley dragged me straight on past it and reassured me that she knew a much better place a little farther down the road.

That was fine with me. I had my own particular favourite

café in Catford that wasn't the closest one to where I lived but it was worth the extra two minutes in the car for the grub they slopped out.

That said, the Funky Zebra looked a different kettle of sausages altogether.

'Is this a café?' I asked in confusion when Charley pushed the door to go inside. 'It looks more like a cake shop.'

'Come on,' she simply told me.

Inside, the place looked even less like a café than it had done outside. The walls were lined with books, there were enormous great overgrown plants in every corner and a coffee machine the size of the Tardis off up near a big bright deli counter. What was most weird, though, was the fact that there was hardly anywhere to sit. Don't get me wrong, it was a roomy enough place in itself, but all it had were six little silver tables, each surrounded on all sides by big leather armchairs that seemed to fill the room, occupied by roll-neck-wearers who looked in no particular hurry to say goodbye to their empty plates. There was also a queue. Five other couples waited patiently to be seated while the tossers at the tables folded and unfolded dirty great broadsheets and drank little thimbles of jet-black coffee.

How I didn't start tipping people out of their seats and slapping glasses off faces after five minutes of clock-pointing is beyond me.

'This place is really popular,' Charley told me.

'Yeah, I can see why. It's great, isn't it?' I replied after another five minutes of holding my empty guts.

We finally got seated a full fifteen minutes after arriving. Some gormless Janet- and John-a-likes finally folded their papers away and started putting their coats on. I charged straight over before any of the smart bastards behind us decided they'd quite like to start their Sunday with a smack in the gob, but unbelievably the moment I appeared, Janet and John suddenly went into first gear,

John tying and untying his scarf half a dozen times in an effort to get it just right, while Janet sat back down and made a phone call on her mobile.

'Are you two going or what?' I finally had to ask.

I couldn't understand how they hadn't noticed the half-dozen people patiently waiting to be seated when neither of the inconsiderate fuckers had been distracted by cutlery for the last twenty minutes.

'In our own time,' John haughtily replied. He should've got one straight in the chops just for that, but he was lucky, Charley was standing just behind me, and I didn't want her thinking I couldn't go anywhere without threatening to punch somebody's lights out, so I simply hovered over the pair of them, folded my arms and started whistling.

And I ain't very good at whistling.

I didn't get more than a verse into 'Hit The Road, Jack', before Janet and John decided to do just that before any more spit landed down the backs of their necks and finally we had a table. Charley cast me a disapproving look as we sat down, but really she should've been casting it Janet and John's way. Surely they were the ones in the wrong, not me.

For a moment I wondered if chronic inconsideration was some sort of class thing. I mean, first that dickhead in the Workers' Social and now this. Perhaps these spoilt little posho brats were so used to getting their own way all the time that they'd never had to learn basic consideration for others and the higher they climbed up the social ladder, the more they used their elbows on everyone else.

It was a possibility, but I wasn't really buying it. Charley wasn't like that, just as I'm sure a lot of middle-class poshos weren't.

If anything, I reckon it was more to do with the fact that most people in these places were probably just a bit too polite for their own good to say anything, so all the me-first merchants knew they could get away with it. Neither this place nor the Workers' Social looked like the sort of place you'd worry about getting your eyes blacked in so what was there to stop a selfish git from doing a bit of queue-jumping or table-hogging if they were so inclined? Not a lot that I could see, but sooner or later they'd do it to the wrong person. It always happens. I've seen it dozens of times before and no doubt I'll see it dozens of times again. You simply can't get away with being a wanker for ever. It's a basic rule of life. So why not show everyone else a bit of common consideration and save the already overburdened NHS the trouble of having to put your face back together when some mental Jock on his football travels blunders into the Funky Zebra looking for a deep-fried Mars bar?

'Sorry, but I thought he was off and he only sat back down when he saw me coming over as a sort of fingers-up at me,' I explained.

'Well, people feel intimidated when they're being rushed,' Charley replied, and I wanted to ask her if they also felt intimidated when they were being launched head first through plate-glass windows, but I already knew the answer to that one. 'Anyway, what shall we have?'

I looked at the menu and found a full English at the top of the page.

'Do you like eggs Benedict?' Charley asked.

'Yeah, which one was he again? Face in *The A-Team*, wasn't he?' I replied, made up by the fact that someone had finally asked me this question a mere twenty years after I'd first thought up the accompanying gag.

Charley had never seen *The A-Team* and didn't know what I was talking about so she pointed it out on the menu and asked me again if I liked them.

'No,' I told her, then added, 'Don't know. Never had it.'

'Well, how do you know you don't like it if you've never had it?' she asked.

'I've never been run over by a dumper truck either but I know I probably wouldn't like that,' I reasoned.

'What sort of answer's that?' Charley asked.

'My final one,' I informed her.

'Well, it's your loss, because it's delicious,' she pointed out, presumably to try and break my spirits. 'Go on, why don't you have it?' she then went on, tapping my menu with hers.

As much as I liked Charley, I didn't want to get browbeaten into having something horrible to eat that I didn't want to eat when I'd already lined up my taste buds for a full English. At the same time, though, I didn't want Charley to go off thinking I was just some big dummy who hadn't made it past Farley's rusks yet either, so I quickly weighed up my options, tutted a few times, wobbled my big fat lip, then told her, 'OK, I'll have the eggs Benedict with you, then.'

'I'm not having the eggs Benedict,' she told me.

'You're not? I thought you were.'

'No, I'm having the haddock and eggs Florentine,' she said, almost knocking me off my chair in disgust.

'Urgh, what the hell's that?' I heaved, my eyes scampering back down the menu in horror. Charley reached over and pointed it out to prove that she hadn't just made up some disgusting concoction to laugh at my reaction.

'There.'

'You're joking, aren't you?' I double-checked.

'Of course I'm not,' she assured me, and I almost honked up all over the table when I saw that it had cream and spinach in it as well as haddock. No, surely that wasn't right? People really ate that?

'What's it like?' I asked warily.

'I don't know,' Charley replied.

'What? You mean you haven't even had it before?' I gasped in astonishment, my revulsion skyrocketing by the second.

'No, but it sounds lovely.'

'No it doesn't,' I had to point out. 'Don't have it. It'll be horrible.'

'Don't you like smoked haddock?' Charley asked.

'God, no,' I replied.

Charley thought for a moment then asked me if I'd ever actually had it. What a question! Of course I hadn't.

'Then once again, how do you know you don't like it if you've never had it?' she asked, and for a moment I shat myself thinking she was going to make me have a plate-load of that filth just to teach me a lesson.

'Look, I know what I like and I know what I don't like. And I just like bacon and eggs,' I explained in my defence.

'Well, it's got eggs in it.'

'Yeah, and fish and spinach. You drop either of them on my dinner and see how fast you get it back. And these are in my breakfast!'

Charley almost laughed. Almost, but I'm not sure she entirely knew what she was laughing at.

'You don't like spinach?'

'Urgh, no, I don't,' I told her.

'And have you ever actually had it?' she asked, sensing a pattern.

'Yes, actually, I have,' I replied, shooting the pants out of that particular theory.

'When?'

'When? I don't know. When I was a kid. At school. It was horrible,' I told her triumphantly, resting my case.

'And you haven't had it since?'

'Of course I ain't. Why would I? Not if it's horrible.'

Charley wasn't sure where to start, so we both put down our menus and waited for a few seconds while she ordered her thoughts. Not that I could see how she was going to talk her way round me on this one. I mean seriously, if something's horrible, it's horrible. Full stop. End of story. Get it away from me and bring me some chips. Falling into a ditch full of stinging nettles hurts like fuck no matter how many times you do it. This was an open-and-shut drawbridge.

'Have you ever drunk beer?' Charley finally asked.

'Well, it's a bit early for me, to be honest, love,' I said, checking my watch. 'I'll stick with the bacon and eggs for now if you don't mind, but we can go for a cheeky one around lunchtime if you want.'

'When you first tried beer, and I mean your very first sip, what did you think of it?' Charley asked. I cast my taste buds back to my twelfth birthday and sucked my mouth.

'I don't know,' I reflected. 'I didn't really like it, to tell the truth, but that's got nothing to do with this,' I cut in, before she could pop the cork and celebrate her monumental cleverness.

'It has everything to do with this. Your taste buds change, they refine as you get older. Just because you didn't like spinach as much as you liked Wotsits when you were a child, it doesn't mean you're not going to like it now, does it? It's very good for you,' she underlined.

'So's jogging. At least, that's what they say, but you won't catch me running around the park like a berk on Saturday mornings when I could be in the café having bacon and eggs,' I said, expecting full agreement on all the points I'd just made. But Charley just dropped her eyes and let me in on something that should've probably occurred to me already.

'I sometimes go jogging on Saturday mornings.'

'Oh,' I ohhed, then started backtracking so frantically that Charley almost caught a couple of shoes in the face. 'No, I didn't mean it like that. There's nothing wrong with jogging. I think jogging's great and I really admire...'

'Let's just drop it,' Charley cut me off, using the worst four words a girl can use on an early date short of saying, 'I'm telling my dad' or 'I'm really a geezer'.

'I just… I… sorry. Really, I'm sorry.'

'Shall we order, then?'

'Good idea,' I readily agreed, then spent the next three minutes working myself into yet another one as I waved my menu about in an effort to attract the attention of the Zebra's ovulating waitress and drag her away from the long-haired herbert with half a ton of scrap metal in his face and the scuffed guitar case he'd decided to come to breakfast with.

'Oi, for fuck's sake!' I finally had to yell across the café, winning me dirty looks all round and a roll of the eyes from Charley. 'Sorry, I was just trying to get the waitress,' I explained, and the sullen young cow duly waddled over with a scowl slapped all over her puss. I looked down at her feet to see why she was walking the way she was and saw that her full-length skirt was actually just a big long tube which never gave an inch and which made her look like one of those ex-fatty weight-watchers you see in the papers who pose for the cameras standing in one leg of their old trousers. As hip and trendy as her skirt undoubtedly was, I couldn't help but wonder if she'd chosen the wrong outfit for a job in the catering industry and was sorely tempted to suggest she saved it for school sports days or rolling down hills in.

'Yeah?' she yeahed, doing her best to swivel about on one leg inside her confines to show me how little she cared about me, my breakfast or this stupid crappy waitressing job.

Call me Sherlock Holmes if you like, but to me she smacked of someone trying a little too hard to give off an aura of total disinterest. Why? I couldn't tell you. Maybe she was just working here for a bit of cash until her real career took off and that really she was a poet or an artist or a musician or a designer or something. Something cool. Something creative. Something amazing. I hoped so for her sake as one thing was clear, she sure weren't no fucking waitress.

'What d'you want?' she asked, finding a pencil behind her ear and giving one end a chew.

'Can I have the haddock and eggs Florentine, please?' Charley asked, prompting our one-legged waitress to scribble *H e F* down on her pad then stare at me.

'And I'll have the... er, the...' I read the expression on Charley's face and finally gave in. Oh, bollocks, go on then. '...the eggs Benedict, please.'

'You want Tabasco on that?' Zebedee asked me.

'What? Urgh, no! Jesus, people put Tabasco on it?' I gasped. What sort of a breakfast was this anyway?

'Actually, scratch that last order,' Charley suddenly cut in. 'He'll have the full English.'

Our waitress started scribbling it down before getting confirmation off me and I had to kick up a stink to get my eggs Benedict reinstated.

'No no no, don't listen to her. I'll have eggs Benedict.'

'Look, Terry, just have your full English, it's what you want to have anyway,' Charley said, but I couldn't, not now, things had gone too far.

'No, I want the eggs Benedict. I want to see what it's like,' I insisted.

'No you don't, you want the full English.'

'No, I want the eggs Benedict.'

'You don't.'

'I do.'

'You don't.'

'I do.'

'Can you make up your minds, please, as we've got other customers waiting?' our waitress pointed out, though this hadn't seemed to be a factor when she'd been sniffing around Frankenstein over yonder.

'Terry, honestly, I don't care what you have, so just have whatever you want,' Charley pressed home.

'Good, then I'll have the eggs Benedict,' I told the waitress, handing her my menu to signal that my breakfast think tank had turned in its results.

Charley just frowned and shook her head, but if you think about it I'd been backed into such a corner that there really wasn't anything else I could do. Fucking eggs Benedict! I didn't want it, Charley was now dead set against it and our waitress probably wouldn't get two yards from the kitchen without tripping face first into it, but suddenly I had to have it. And what's more, I had to like it.

'Drinks?'

I looked to Charley and simply asked for 'the same' when she chose a suitably stupid coffee.

'OK, that'll be with you in a minute,' our waitress lied, before hopping away.

'Seriously, Terry, you should've just had what you wanted to have,' Charley continued, and I could see that this one was likely to rumble on all day so I did what I could to take the wind out of Charley's sails by telling her that I could have a full English any day of the week and that it was good to try something new for a change and a load of other old codswallop that I thought she wanted to hear until our breakfasts arrived a mere half-hour later.

Jesus, I decided simply to think this time around. *So that's what eggs Benedict looks like, is it?*

I don't know if you've ever had eggs Benedict but here's the deal. It looks just like half a Bacon & Egg McMuffin with custard and dead insects dumped all over it. And what the hell were they?

'Asparagus,' Charley informed me, when she saw my confusion. 'Have you never had asparagus before either? Try it, it's lovely.'

So I did and found it tasted exactly how it looked, only it was cold and therefore even more revolting.

I poked my McMuffin about with my knife and fork, trying to scrape all the dead insects (or chives) off the top in order to get a clean bite of it, and finally looked up to see Charley watching me like I was doing card tricks.

'Nice this, isn't it?' I reassured her, and you know what, I genuinely meant that, albeit only in the face of what she'd got for breakfast. Oh yes, I'd got off lightly all right and no mistake.

I tucked into my breakfast using the old one-mouthful-of-food-quickly-followed-by-a-gulp-of-coffee-to-wash-away-the-taste technique and managed to get halfway through it before I'd done all my coffee.

'Shame we haven't got any Rocket Man Sauce. I could do with a squirt of it around about now,' I told Charley. 'What's yours like?'

'It's lovely. Here, try a little,' she said, loading up her fork like she meant it.

'Er, no, I won't actually,' I panicked, making my chair squeak as I backed away from a load of oncoming haddock. 'I'm pretty stuffed already and I won't be able to get through mine if I've got to have some of yours too.' Especially not without something to wash it down with, I didn't add.

Charley withdrew her fork from my face and I breathed a sigh of relief as she defused it herself. That said, I was still all dried up on the drinks front so I called Zebedee over again and asked her for two teas and a can of Fanta if she found a moment before she clocked off tonight.

'What, are you getting a fizzy drink?' Charley asked, and my shoulders sagged when I realised I'd done something else wrong.

'I'm just thirsty,' I tried. 'I always have a can of drink when I'm at the café. It's just a bit salty if I don't.'

The bacon or ham or whatever it was they'd hidden under my

custard and eggs was that really smoky type of bacon that Jason liked and it was making me the thirstiest man in the world. A can of Fanta was just what the doctor would've ordered, had he been here and as thirsty as me.

'I don't drink sugary drinks, just water. Sugary drinks just make you more thirsty and are loaded with calories.'

I looked on the side of my can when it arrived and saw that she was right, at least about the calories. It didn't seem to say anything about making me more thirsty, though. I suddenly felt all self-conscious and childlike about my Fanta and didn't drink more than three sips, just enough to finish my eggs Benedict and show Charley an empty plate.

'Is that what you drink on the building site, then, fizzy drinks?'

'No, I just have a flask of tea or drink from the standpipe, which is just screwed into the mains,' I said. 'Mind you, I've seen some of the hoddies drink from the water butts before, and Robbie even drinks from them after he's added the Feb mix.'

'What's Feb mix?'

'It's chemical. A plasticising agent that makes the muck more manageable on the trowel. The hoddies add it to the water butts when they're knocking up. It smells a bit like diet cola when it's mixed with water which is presumably why Robbie likes to drink it, though he reckons it don't half give him gut rot.'

Charley gave this some thought.

'I think Robbie's going to die at an early age.'

'Well, we all know that. Even Robbie. But like he's always saying, he'd rather live in his twenties than his sixties, live fast, die young and leave a good-looking corpse, the silly bastard.'

'And what about you? Do you want to be like Robbie too? Live fast, die young…' Charley asked.

'… and drink Feb mix from water butts,' I finished for her. 'No thanks. I'd probably like to live a bit faster than our waitress here but I'm too old to be thinking about dying young these days. I'll just have to make the best of it and see if I can't leave a nice-looking old man for my widow to cry over.'

'So you're planning on getting married, then, are you?' Charley teased, making me go red. Boy, these were rocky waters I was navigating.

'Maybe,' I finally replied. 'One day. If I find the right lady.'

I figured this was a nice safe stock answer and Charley nodded like she understood perfectly. This wasn't really a conversation to be exploring on our second date (or was this our third?). No good could come of me declaring that Charley was that selfsame right lady and if she just bided her time a few more dates and stopped trying to make me eat haddock Florentine then nothing would give me greater pleasure than to get down on one knee, take her hand in mine and ask her if she'd mind awfully spending the rest of her life with me. Does that sound a bit impulsive? Apologies if it does but what can I say? I liked her.

Big John once told me that he knew he was going to marry his Glenda the moment he met her. Knew it in his bones, he did, and sure enough, twenty-five years and four kids later they finally tied the knot last year. And a lovely do it was too.

And that was how I felt about Charley. I liked her from the very first moment we met (or woke up together) and I felt it in my bones. She was the one for me.

'Shall we get the bill, then?' I suggested.

'Halves?' Charley offered.

'Not a bit of it, my treat,' I insisted, though I kind of wished I hadn't when I saw how much it all came too. And that was for half a custard-covered Egg McMuffin?

Probably a good job I didn't get the full English after all.

9 The waiting game

The thing that surprises most people when they see bricklayers work is just how fast a house goes up. You look at your average house, look at all the bricks and blocks it takes to build one, and then at the team of handsome devils whose job it is to put it all together, and I couldn't blame you for thinking it might take anything up to a month to finish the job. But it doesn't. In actual fact, with a gang the size of ours, seven brickies (when Gordon's out of the pub) and three hoddies, it actually only takes a bit under a week to build a house. And that's from the first blocks laid in the footings to the muck smoothed over around the chimney pot. Not that it stays smooth for long, mind, because in practice the bricky who smooths it over almost always writes his name in the soft muck for posterity. It doesn't really do any harm. Not if it's small. I mean, who's going to see it up there facing the sky as it is, other than birds and eagle-eyed 747 pilots? Brickies have been signing off their work as far back as the pyramids and I'll stick my neck out here and bet that if you were to take your house apart, brick by brick, somewhere in there you'd find a man's signature and a date. Something like, 'Albert Cooper, Aug 4th, 1923', which is nice if you think about it, though before you start getting too dewy eyed about this fine old bygone craftsman, just bear in mind that besides building your house, old Albert and all his mates also probably pissed in every room as they were slapping it together. Another fine tradition that I think you'll find dates back to the pyramids.

Well, it is a long old walk to the Portaloo and we have got work to do, you know.

Naturally, you don't build each individual house in one go, as other trades have to have their say as it's going up. The groundworkers have to backfill and concrete the footings, the chippies have to add the joists, and then the roofing trusses, and the scaffolders have to come along and raise the scaffolding as we complete each section, so in reality, we're actually probably working on a dozen different houses at different stages of development at any one time.

OK, there are six basic bricklaying stages to building a house. The first are the *footings*, the parts of your house that are underground and laid on the solid concrete foundations, which stop your house from sinking into the mud and getting subsidence, that's assuming the Paddies have dug down far enough, and that largely depends how close in the calendar we are to the Derby. When these are done, the lot is backfilled and concreted over to form a solid base. This is the ground floor of your house and it's called an *oversite*. We build up as far as we can reach, almost to the tops of the doors and windows, and then do all the internal downstairs walls as well, and then the scaffolders come along and lift the scaffolding. This next stage is called a *joist lift*, and we continue on up for just a few courses of bricks and put in lintels and RSJs where they're needed, then the chippies come along and lay the joists for the first floor. The whole thing then becomes known as a *band lift*, because it's usually a solid band of brickwork with no windows from here on up until we reach the bottom of the first-floor windows, at which point our good friends and esteemed colleagues, the scaffolders, once again come to our assistance. The next stage is called the *murder lift*, and we build up around the first-floor windows and again add lintels and RSJs where we feel they're warranted, then the scaffolders lift the whole thing up to roof level and all of a sudden the chippies get interested again. 'Blimey,' they think. 'We've got some roofing trusses that would look great up there,' and up they scamper to make a lot of noise with their hammers and saws until the house has the skeleton of a roof in place. Our role is almost at an end at this point. We brick up the *gable* ends, then seal the cavities with slates and flat tiles, then the scaffolding gets raised one final time and some lucky young fella gets to finish off the chimney, smooth over the muck around the pot, which is called the *flaunching*, and sign off the entire job with the tip of his trowel.

In this particular case, the lucky young fella in question was me, and I wrote in the soft green muck '*Terry ♡ Charley, 2008*', then looked out across the horizon when I was finished. It was a perfect autumn day. Fluffy white clouds hung in the sky and drifted slowly by, pushed on by a gentle breeze to pass shadows across the hustle and bustle below. It was actually a very beautiful sight. The skies often can be, particularly if you're able to admire them from a position of elevation, but they were wasted on me this particular day. I might've been up on the roof but my spirits were way down in the footings with the rest of the gang. And you know why?

Because Charley hadn't phoned.

It was Thursday afternoon, four whole days since I'd last seen her. We'd parted amorously enough, with hugs and kisses and promises to speak to each other as soon as, but then Charley hadn't lived up to her end. I know it was only a day afterwards, but I texted her on the Monday evening anyway just to see how she was, and then again on the Tuesday when I didn't get any sort of response, but still Charley hadn't replied. It was then that the paranoia started creeping in and by a quarter past four on this particularly fine Thursday afternoon it had swallowed me whole. Something was up. I didn't know what but something was definitely up.

Why hadn't I heard from her? Why hadn't she responded

to either of my texts? Why didn't she want to talk to me? And why was I the one moping over a silent phone? I was the bloke, for fuck's sake. Surely I was the one who was meant to dick her around.

I resisted the urge to text her for the third time or leave a frantic voicemail message on her mobile or landline. At least I had that much going for me, but not much else, to be perfectly frank.

See, when I'd said goodbye to her on Sunday after our horrible breakfast, I'd genuinely thought I'd cracked it with Charley. I'd seen her a few times, we'd spent the night together and we'd never even run out of things to tell each other. She'd updated me on all the latest Rocket Sauce news and I'd educated her all about band lifts and oversites, so why had she suddenly gone quiet on me? Some might argue that it was *because* I'd educated her about band lifts and oversites, but I couldn't see that. OK, so it might not have had goose bumps popping out all over her body, but by that same token she'd shown a genuine interest in what it took to build a house. I mean, it's an interesting subject, isn't it? We all have houses. At least, most of us do, and it's good to know how the everyday things around us are made, I reckon. I'd been interested in what it took to push Rocket Man Sauce on the rest of us. I hadn't necessarily understood half of it or why the hell anyone would want to bother, but I'd still found it interesting all the same. Hadn't she felt likewise?

Had I bored her?

I hoped not. I'm admittedly not the cleverest bloke in the world and I'm sure I'd have trouble keeping up with her if she suddenly put her grey matter into fifth gear and started talking about something clever like... like...

See, I don't even know what. That's how dumb I am.

Politics? No, I read the papers. I could talk about them lot of crooks if I wanted to.

Economics? I had a mortgage. I had savings. I even had a pension. And the housing market is a barometer for the UK's economy, everyone knows that, so blokes like me and Jason felt the peaks and troughs of the nation's fortunes long before the Hooray Henrys in braces up in the City did, so I could probably stand my own on that subject too.

No, the more I thought about it, the more I realised it all boiled down to eggs Benedict. I should've just had it, liked it and shut the fuck up. I should've even suffered a mouthful of hers if I'd thought about it. But I hadn't. I'd argued with her. Over eggs Benedict? What an idiot. What a tosser. I'd lost the woman of my dreams over a disagreement about eggs Benedict and in the process found out what it would feel like to swallow a real-life cannonball.

What an arsehole.

I don't think it helped either, that crack about me hoping to get married one day when I met the right lady, because I had met the right lady. Only I'd been such a plank that I'd gone and talked her right out of my life.

And all of a sudden, everything was too late. I'd gone from taking the first few tentative steps on the road to a lifetime of love and happiness with the best girl in the world, only to turn back for Alphabetti Spaghetti the moment the grub got a bit grown up. Not that I had much of an appetite at the moment, you understand. What a fuckwit!

You can probably now see why it wasn't within my powers to appreciate the beauty of these late afternoon skies. You can also probably now see why Gordon had stuck me up here on my own, away from the rest of the lads. Well, fair enough, I suppose. I was starting to bore even myself going on about it these last three days. They needed a break from me. It was just a shame I couldn't get a break from myself.

'Tel? Tel? Terry? You all done?' Robbie shouted up from the deck, a fresh hod of muck on his shoulder.

I gave him the thumbs-up to show him that I was, so Robbie had a quick check about to make sure Ebenezer, our site manager, wasn't anywhere around, then slung his muck into the nearest hole to save himself having to carry it all the way back to the mixer.

'She rung you yet?' he then shouted up. I shook my head. 'Well, yo' can' spen… ne resta… lif' 'orryin' 'bout wheth… ' … sin' 'e … … ife … 'ork or … ot, … … an' …stal …'an … 'ou. Ah mea… …se's t… …ay… ' …'s …m … … …'matoes?' he elaborated, apparently forgetting that I was on the roof and he was on the ground.

'What's he saying?' Dan, the chippy, looked up at me from the fascia board around the gable.

'I don't know,' I replied. 'But I'm sure it's probably good advice.'

Thursday came and went without a phone call too and I cut and buttered my way through most of Friday in a miserable trough of despair before my phone finally beeped and wobbled excitedly in my pocket to let me know that I had a new text.

I'd already made up my mind to climb into the mixer if this turned out to be fucking Car Phone Warehouse again, but my heart did a backflip when I pressed the green button and saw Charley's name.

soz 4nt gtg bck 2u – wks bn crzy :-(. im out 2nite but cll u tmw :-)

Which I translated to mean, 'Sorry for not getting back to you, but work (or the week) has been crazy (either really busy or amazingly fun). Here's a frowny face to show you either just how sorry I am or alternatively what an arse-ache the last few days have been. I'm off out tonight, but I'll call you tomorrow for reasons unspecified. Here's a smiley face which you can take to mean I'm either happy to do this, or I hope this makes you happy, or hooray it's the weekend or any number of other things, including I couldn't think of how else to end this text.'

I read the short message a dozen times and tried to read between the lines. It hadn't been exactly the most heartfelt message in the world but at least she'd finally texted, which was a definite improvement on five days of lip-wobbling silence.

'Happy now?' Jason asked, brushing the murder lift flank we'd just pointed up.

'Yeah, I suppose,' I replied, but I wasn't really. I'd waited all week long to hear from her and had finally been rewarded for my patience with a one-line text to let me know that she was off out with someone else tonight. Pardon me if I didn't giggle with boyish excitement and run around handing out cigars.

'Oh, for the love of fuck, give your brain the rest of the week off,' Jason pleaded with me. 'You're miserable when she doesn't text you, miserable when she does. I don't know what's the matter with you, mate, but I'll tell you this much, if you don't sort yourself out you're just going to make yourself unhappy moping over this bird and she ain't going to thank you for that.'

Of course, I knew he was right. I'm not that much of an idiot that I couldn't see that I was behaving like a right plate of eggs Benedict and that if Charley could see me like this she'd probably run a mile and have every right to do so. It's just hard sometimes, when you've convinced yourself that you've finally found the thing you've been looking for all your adult life, only to feel it slipping away from you for reasons you can't quite put your finger on. You try telling jokes and visiting water-slide parks under such circumstances, motherfucker.

'It's OK, I'm fine,' I told Jason, then started texting Charley back.

'Oi, what d'you think you're doing?' Jason suddenly said.

'What? I'm just texting her to let her know that that's all cool and that I'll speak to her tomorrow,' I explained.

'She hasn't replied to you all week and only finally gets back to you on Friday afternoon and you're straight on the buttons back to her without so much as a breather? What's wrong with you?' Jason said, snatching my phone away from me.

'Oi, give me that back.'

'No, you can have it back in the Lamb tonight and not before,' he told me in no uncertain terms, warning me off with his brick brush, before retreating to the other end of the scaffolding with my phone, muttering to himself, 'Texting her straight back like a great big plank after only five seconds. Unbelievable. *Un-fucking-believable!*'

10 Secrets and thighs

Jason eventually gave me back my phone at eight o'clock in the Lamb that night and I skipped and danced through big gay sun-drenched meadows when I saw that I had yet another text from Charley. That said, I almost went head over heels in a big pile of shit when a moment of paranoia flashed across my brain in the shape of Charley telling me she never wanted to see me again because I hadn't got back to her straight away.

'I can't deal with this game-playing shit,' being the phrase I feared the most.

Fortunately for Jason and my liver, no such text came up when I pressed the appropriate buttons and instead, an invitation appeared on-screen.

my frns bday tmw nite. wnt 2 cm ^ + hv drx in isl @ 7? :-)

A bit more backward and forward texting revealed that it was one of her friend's birthdays the following evening and that she wanted me to come along. Or more accurately, was giving me the option of coming along if I wanted. Which are two subtly different positions but let's not stare at our navel too much here.

Now, I have to say right off the bat that I wasn't exactly kicking the stable door to meet a load of posho strangers I probably wouldn't have a thing in common with and who would probably view me with scorn and amusement because I'd never had eggs Benedict up until quite recently, but I was desperate...

'Steady on,' warned Jason.

...sorry, eager to see Charley again, so I texted her back

and made out like I thought the whole evening sounded like a Saturday night knocked together in heaven and agreed to see her in some boozer called Signed For! in Islington at seven.

'What? Signed For!? What is that? Is that a pub or something or are you going for a drink in a sorting office?' Jason wanted to know.

'I don't know. You don't think I'll have to sign for everything, do you? Like my drinks and all that?' I was more worried about.

'Nah, probably just the name of the place. They come up with all sorts of weird names these days. It's almost like it's become a point of principle, you know, to come up with the most un-pub name possible for your new pub,' he speculated, prompting ten minutes of laughs as we competed to think up the most unlikely pub name imaginable, which Jason won hands down when he decided to call his future bar, nightclub and restaurant complex Fuck Off.

'Still, good sign that is, her wanting you to meet her mates,' Jason said.

'You reckon?'

'Oh yeah, shows that she's not ashamed to be seen out with you, which is definitely a step in the right direction.'

'Oh, cheers, that's nice, innit. Don't go giving me too much of a big head, now, will you?'

'Hey, don't knock it, mate. It's better than going out with a bird who doesn't want anyone to know you're knocking her off,' Jason said. 'I had a couple of them before I met Sandra, you know, and fun and games they are too.'

He then went on to tell me about this overly secretive secretary who used to work in the site office of one of the first sites he'd worked on when he first left school. I hadn't worked on that particular job myself so I had to take Jason's word for it that she was 'all right' rather than up to usual building site secretary specifications.

Anyway, what had happened was a couple of months of teenage flirting had resulted in a night of 'unstoppable banging' (Jason's words, not mine) when they'd accidentally bumped into each other in a pub one evening.

'It had been a real steam valve turner,' Jason gor-blimeyed, before filling me in on all the unnecessary details, such as what she'd looked like upside down and the exact colour of her pubes. 'Anyway, I go into the office to say hello to her the next morning, which is what I was led to believe was proper etiquette for a gentleman after he'd spent the previous evening rearranging her internal organs, and she just completely blanks me, like I'm not even there. I can't think what I've done wrong, but I beat a hasty retreat anyway and put it down to honest-to-goodness embarrassment. And I can't blame her, the things we'd done, like when she...'

'Just get on with the story,' I tell him.

'Right, anyway, a few days goes past and I bump into her in the compound again, though this time when we're both alone and suddenly she's right up for it again. We arrange to meet that evening after work and bingo, my numbers come up again. Full house. And then some.'

'OK, I get it, she didn't want the blokes at work knowing,' I reasoned, and I couldn't blame her for that. A building site full of giggling hairy-arsed halfwits hanging off the scaffolding and whistling at her knowingly every time she left the office for a drink from the Feb mix barrels.

'That's what I thought but she didn't draw the line at just them. My mates, her mates, our families, strangers in the street, in the pub, she didn't want anyone knowing about us. She comes back to my bedsit a couple of times a week or we occasionally go to some little out-of-the way boozer, but that's basically it for about four months. It's not like either of us were seeing anyone else at the time either. She just didn't want anyone knowing that we had something going on. How d'you like that for a long hard look in the mirror?'

'What happened to her?' I asked.

'I don't know. The job finished, she moved on and I never saw her again. As far as I'm aware I think I'm still technically going out with her because we never actually ended it or nothing. And I couldn't ring her to chase her down because she lived with her mum and dad and didn't want them picking up the phone on me, so she never gave me her number or told me where she lived. I liked her an' all.'

'Did she only ever let you do her up the arse as well, and always cup her hand over her fanny in a way that suggested she might have a cock and balls down there?'

'See, this is what always happens when blokes open up to each other. I'm baring my innermost here,' Jason said, before pointing out what a phenomenal gay I'd been about the whole Charley deal up until now.

'Sorry, mush. It was just too difficult not to say it,' I apologised.

'Oh yeah, I know. And it was a good one too,' Jason conceded.

'No, anyway, this little bird of yours was probably just a bit young and shy,' I said. 'I mean, how old was she? Seventeen? Eighteen?'

'Well, probably. I don't know. Anyway, the point stands that it's better to have a bird who's willing to show you off to all her mates than to have one who's too scared to stand next to you on your wedding day in case everyone starts thinking that she likes you. It just bodes a bit better for your relationship. No, I think it's a good sign.'

All at once Tony, our eavesdropping landlord, leaned across the bar at us and picked up the baton.

'I shagged this bird once,' he told us. 'Had the biggest arse in the world, she did. Seriously, I couldn't believe it. It was enormous. Like that, it was,' he demonstrated, using his hands and a fair stretch of his arms.

Jason looked at me and nodded.

'Are you writing all this down?' he asked.

11 Friends

I arrived on the dot of seven the next night, with more of Jason's advice ringing in my ears (most of which involved not getting drunk and chinning any of her mates) and poked my head around the door. Charley didn't look like she was here yet, but the rest of Islington did. I squeezed inside and sidestepped my way through the throng in an effort to find the bar.

The reason for the crowd was immediately obvious. A big screen at the far end was showing some football match and the whole place was jumping up and down and yelling at the projected images of the players as if they could actually hear them. One particularly noisy brain donor was repeatedly asking the referee 'what the fuck' was the matter with him, and I took a moment to wonder if he was the sort of person who spent his days looking around the backs of mirrors when he wasn't shouting at walls.

Fortunately, the clock in the corner of the screen showed that they'd already played eighty-four minutes so I fought my way through the crowd, satisfied that I wasn't going to have to put up with an entire night of 'Football's Coming Home'.

There were at least five barmen and maids behind the bar, all of whom resembled fantastically trendy versions of the customers themselves, and despite the fact that hardly anyone else was waiting for a drink, what with the match reaching its nail-biting conclusion and all, it still took me a full ten minutes to get served.

Don't get me wrong, I'm not some sort of impatient juvenile

who eats his packed lunch on the bus on the way to school or nothing, I just couldn't work out how it took me ten minutes to get served when the bar staff seemed to outnumber waiting customers two to one. One long-haired herbert was brushing ashtrays, another one was charging about in circles announcing to the world that he was changing a barrel. One was stood around carefully inching a pint of Guinness closer to the top of a glass, while another looked like he was trying to reprogram the till in accordance with the instructions on the back of a packet of kettle chips, which left a single spiky-haired pixie to dance between the taps and take the odd order when she felt like doing someone a favour. It was maddening.

Yeah yeah yeah, here I go on about Catford again, but seriously, in my local there was only Tony, and he seemed to cope just fine without too many problems, even when the football was on. Tony was like an octopus behind the bar, pouring half a dozen drinks at a time and storing half a dozen more in his head so that no one went thirsty or wasted too much of their precious Saturday nights banging empty pint pots on the bar, so how the fuck did these feet-dragging beer-tap-dodgers get away with it?

'In your own time, please, love,' I eventually shouted over, only to be told she was already serving someone. That particular person had only been waiting half the time that I had, but he shrugged apologetically in my direction, which saved me from having to ask the bouncers later on if they knew any of my mates.

I finally got my pint, or at least about eight-tenths of a pint, precision pouring in this place being ranked about as highly as speed and geniality, and found somewhere at the end of the bar to perch until the final whistle blew.

Within five minutes of the match ending the pub emptied out, freeing up a stool for me, though Charley was still missing from the picture. I tried not to read too much into this, figuring she was just useless with timekeeping full stop, even when the place we were meeting in was in her own backyard, and sure enough a quarter of an hour later she arrived in full fluster with herself.

She didn't clock me straight away, but instead made a beeline for this big group of boisterous wankers who were sprawled across two enormous leather sofas who I'd been rolling my eyes at for the last fifteen minutes. I felt my shoulders sag as I watched her greet and kiss the entire party as she took off her hat, scarf and coat before finally looking around and noticing me in the corner.

She quickly scuttled over and gave me a kiss, then apologised for being late and asked if I wanted to come over and meet everyone.

'Not even slightly,' was the obvious answer, but I remembered what Jason had told me about Charley's approval and her mates' approval being index linked and realised one sure way of giving myself the elbow was to spend the night over here by myself, getting steaming and sporadically flicking my fingers up at everyone else on the other side of the pub.

'I'd love to. Lead on,' I told her, rising to my feet and then dawdling in her wake as slowly as possible to shave precious seconds off the inevitable.

'Everyone. Everyone. This is Terry. Terry, this is everyone,' Charley told the gang, winning me a few nonchalant nods and one outright frosty glare. Charley then turned and told me, 'I'm really glad you could make it. Oh, you've almost finished your pint. Let me get you another.'

'No, please, I'll get it. You stay here and I'll get you one as well. What do you want?' I insisted, my cup suddenly running over towards the tortoises behind the bar. 'Glass of wine?'

I retreated with our orders and managed to avoid all ten of the bar staff's eyes for a good fifteen minutes before the least lazy pump monkey finally recognised me as a man waiting for a drink and served me despite my best efforts.

'How much? Fuck me!'

Two minutes later I handed Charley a big glass of wine and clinked it against mine. 'It's good to see you again,' I told her.

'You too,' she agreed. 'Shall we sit down?'

I looked around for a couple of chairs to grab but rather ominously her friends were already shuffling up on one of the sofas to make room for either a couple of fag papers or the two of us.

'Come on,' Charley said, sinking into the space and dragging me down with her.

The sofas were pretty low so that I was now at cock and fanny level with at least half a dozen or so of Charley's mates who hadn't been lucky enough to find a spare square inch of leather to squeeze themselves into.

'Comfy,' I pointed out, tucking my elbows in and stretching my pint out two feet in front of me in an effort not to tip half of it all over myself every time somebody got up, sat down or smiled without warning.

'Terry, this is CT,' Charley said, introducing the bloke on the other side of me whose thigh was pressed hard into mine.

I resisted the obvious joke about him missing a couple of letters and simply shook his hand and smiled.

'How are you?' I figured I should ask.

'Good,' CT replied, regarding me carefully. 'So you're a bricklayer, are you?'

Charley had either mentioned me before or CT was fucking great at guessing people's jobs.

'Yes,' I confirmed, then debated whether or not have a stab at guessing his. I decided against it, not least of all as I really didn't want to get sucked into a 'so, what do you do?' conversation with some bloke I cared so little about that I couldn't even be arsed to ask him what his initials stood for. Don't get me wrong, I'm not a rude, antisocial bastard, even though that's the way it sounds.

I just wanted to be with Charley. I hadn't seen or even spoken to her all week long, and now that I finally had her in the same room as me, I just wanted to give her my full, undivided attention and fill in a few blanks from the past week.

Not that there was much danger of that. Not now that Charley was in full jabber with some posh bloke with trendy glasses on the other side of her and CT had begun mulling over what bricklaying meant to him.

'Very skilled work, bricklaying. People think you just slap them down but there's a real art to it,' CT informed me. 'Churchill used to lay bricks for relaxation, you know.'

'Yeah, well there was no shortage of work back then, I suppose,' I replied, crossing my legs to try and get them away from CT's.

'Good money in it too, I hear,' he then told me.

'That's odd, I keep hearing that an' all,' I said, wondering just how much Churchill was on. More than me I wouldn't be surprised.

CT nodded at nothing in particular and took a big sip of his wine. Wine? I responded by nodding away myself, just to show him that I was still tuned in, even though I was biting to get back to the safety of Charley before CT could turn the conversation on to football. But Charley was doing fantastically well without me and there was suddenly the danger of me looking like some big, dumb, ignorant, millstone date who couldn't fend for himself in company without throwing a big sulk or playing Beach Rally II on his phone, so I took the decision to let Charley enjoy all of her evening, and not just the part that featured me, and asked CT the inevitable.

'So, *CT*,' I remembered, trying my best to look interested. 'What d'you do?'

'I'm a producer,' he told me, turning slightly to fill in the gap my leg-crossing had just left.

'Like a greengrocer?' I double-checked.

'No, nothing so fancy, I'm a producer for the BBC,' he replied, catching me off guard and actually impressing me.

'Really? Which one? BBC1 or BBC2?' I asked.

'I don't work on any one single channel. I produce programmes across the board for all of them,' he explained, so I snapped my fingers and demanded examples. 'At the moment I'm working on a show called *Lost Touch with Reality* on BBC3. Have you seen it?'

I hadn't. Had anyone?

'It's basically a fly-on-the-wall-style thirty-minute show that catches up with and follows the fortunes of former reality stars. Remember Colin from *Car Pool*?'

I didn't even remember *Car Pool*, let alone Colin.

'We're working with him next week. Following him around for a week, at home, at work and, of course, in his car, to see how his fifteen minutes of fame has changed his life. It's that sort of thing,' CT explained.

'And how has it changed his life?'

'I don't know, we haven't filmed the programme yet, but if the others are anything to go by, he's probably lost all his friends, had an affair and turned into an unbearable, nasty twat.'

That was pretty good. I liked that one and warmed to CT a touch, though not so much that I was suddenly glad it was him I was snuggling with on the sofa and not Charley.

'Are they all a big load of cunts, then?' I asked, shifting my leg again to try to get the circulation going.

'Mostly. You get the odd occasional one who's nice but most of them do love to let their little bit of fame go straight to their heads. Well, it's inevitable really, if you think about it. I mean, who else is going to appear on reality shows other than people who think they've got something to offer already? Even rubbish collectors, believe it or not. Remember *Dustman's Holiday*?'

Of course not. I didn't pay my licence fee to watch dustmen going on holiday.

'No, I must've missed that one,' I simplified. 'So, who's the worst one? Who's the biggest wanker you've ever met?'

'Ah, now that would be telling,' he teased, passing up a perfect opportunity to tell me it was me.

'Oh, go on, don't be a cunt, just tell us. I ain't going to say nothing, am I. Go on, just tell us,' I prodded.

CT finally buckled and asked me if I remembered the first series of *Supermarket*.

'You're making all this up, aren't you?' I finally twigged.

'No, of course not. Didn't you ever see it?' CT insisted.

I was half tempted to tell him it was on at the same time as *Paint Dry Challenge*, but Jason's advice was still bumping around inside my head, so I plumped for acting all gutted that I'd been out every time it had been on and let him tell me about some prima-donna checkout girl who used to bollock the cameraman every time he missed her doing something interesting – which was all the time, according to her, and not once during the whole series, according to the cameraman.

'She'd then act it out for us all over again and get anyone else who'd been part of the lost scene to do the same and repeat what they'd said. Real fly-on-the-wall stuff it was,' CT said.

'No, sorry, I never saw it,' I apologised again.

'Don't worry, no one did. At least not any of her footage. That all ended up on the cutting-room floor.'

I wondered if they really did just drop everything on the floor of the cutting room? If it wouldn't be easier to maybe get a bin in there or something? I even thought about suggesting this to CT, but decided against it as I figured someone must've addressed this problem in the hundred or so years since they'd invented film-making and it was just an expression these days. I mean, I couldn't really have been the first bloke this had occurred to, could I? Surely the cleaners would've said something by now? Anyway, I had more important things to point out to CT, not least of all:

'You must be gutted, mustn't you? Working on telly and having to hang around with a load of nobodies all day long,' I chuckled.

'What do you mean?'

'Well, I would be. If I worked on telly I'd want to get to work with famous people, not a load of fucking binmen and checkout girls. Don't you ever get to work with anyone famous? Aside from Colin off *Car Park*, that is?'

'I've worked with a few in my time,' CT explained. 'I started on *Noel's House Party* when I first joined the Beeb, so I met my fair share of celebrities back then, but they're nothing special.'

'Who was the most famous?' I pressed.

CT thought about this for a moment or two then told me Mr T.

'Nice fella too. Then I went to work on *The Brain Game* with Ted Allen for a couple of series, but then Ted did his little disappearing act...'

'Oh yeah, I remember that. That was in all the papers, that was, wasn't it? What happened to him?'

'God, I wish I had a pound for every time somebody asked me that,' CT sighed theatrically.

'Get it a lot, do you?'

'Just once or twice a conversation,' he reckoned.

'So what did happen to him?' I asked again, not one to be deterred by a well-trodden line of enquiry.

'I don't know,' he shrugged. 'Most people think he owed a lot of money in gambling debts and took off rather than pay it back. I'm sure he's probably living in Venezuela or Vietnam or somewhere tropical these days, drinking himself to death and buggering the houseboy every Friday.'

'Well, it is the start of the weekend,' I pointed out. 'So do you know any famous people these days? Actors and that?'

'Lis is an actress,' CT told me, directing me towards a pretty little brunette on the sofa opposite.

'What's that?' Lis asked, turning around and catching me in mid-gawp.

'This is Terry,' CT told her, before making me freeze when he described me as 'Charley's boyfriend'.

I hadn't thought of myself as Charley's 'boyfriend' before and I certainly hadn't ever described myself as such, particularly in front of Charley, so it was a bit of a shock to the system hearing these words for the first time.

I had a quick feel next door to see if Charley had likewise turned to stone and found that she was still pleasantly soft and babbling away ten to the dozen to her trendy mate with the glasses, two arses along, so I unclenched my jaw and confirmed I was indeed 'Terry'. Though I left it at that.

'Hi,' Lis said, giving me a nod, then the rim of her glass a quick suck.

'I was just telling Terry that you were an actress,' CT explained a little further.

Lis baulked, like CT had just told me she got all her pants from Oxfam, but she got over it pretty quickly and told me she was, but that it was very, *very* boring.

'Fair enough,' I said, not wishing to press her for details. Not if it was boring.

We stared at each other in silence for a bit before I finally realised I should probably tell her something about my line of work if she didn't like talking about her own.

'I'm a bricky,' I told her, and backed up this revelation with the news that most blokes down the pub called me Tel the trowel. Lis looked around Signed For! accordingly. 'No, no, God, no, not this pub. No, my local, down in Catford. The Catford Lamb. Do you know Catford at all?'

Lis didn't.

'Oh well, you should check it out some time. It's a nice place. Honest.'

This seemed to confuse Lis even further and she looked to CT for the subtitles. CT just bypassed my babble, though, and asked Lis if she was working at the moment. Lis immediately perked up.

'Yes. Yes, I am. I'm working on a one-woman show with Carl that we're planning on taking to Edinburgh. It's called *The Lady of the Lamp*,' she told us enthusiastically.

'Florence Nightingale, huh?' CT ventured.

'Yes,' Lis confirmed.

'Who do you play?' I asked.

Lis asked me who I thought she'd play in a one-woman play about Florence Nightingale. Her fucking lamp?

'Well, I don't know, do I?' I said in my defence.

'I finally saw that advert you were in the other day,' CT then mentioned.

'Really? You were in an advert?' I asked, my interest stoked by the mention of proper acting. 'What was it for?'

'Oh, it's embarrassing,' Lis cringed, hanging her head to demonstrate.

'Fair enough,' I said, once again reluctant to press her for details. Not if it was embarrassing for her.

This time around, though, Lis didn't wait to be prompted by CT, eager no doubt to head off more stories about Catford, and told me how she'd been the young mum pushing the trolley with the little kid in it in the recent Morrisons advert. I couldn't quite place that one. Mind you, that was no surprise as I never really paid attention to adverts at the best of times, and I had a particular mental block where Morrisons were concerned after one of their managers had run off with my girlfriend.

'I'll look out for it, though,' I promised her, then decided to test the water and see if she was finally in the mood to talk about her job by asking her what else she'd been in.

'I was in a run of *Twelfth Night*, at the Salisbury Theatre, up until last month. And before that I played the part of older Belle in *Little Me* at the National,' she said.

'OK,' I nodded anyway.

'And I had two stints with the Reduced Dickens Company and a summer season at the Swan in Stratford-upon-Avon,' she added.

'Yes, I remember your notices,' CT applauded.

'What, from your landlord?' I suggested. 'No, seriously, though, what about telly?'

Lis finally saw what I wanted to hear and told me she'd been in the last Poliakoff drama, a BBC adaptation of *Vanity Fair*, a late-night political sketch show called *Eve & Stephen*, a dramatisation of the Blue Arrow trial and a dozen and one other programmes she could've easily been making up on the spot just to steal some of Colin from *Car Pool*'s glory.

'Right,' I nodded carefully, trying not to give away the fact that I hadn't seen or heard of any of the above, and even if I had, I probably still wouldn't have sat down and watched them even if I'*d* been in them myself. 'Great.'

'And of course you've done *Casualty* and *The Bill*,' CT nudged her.

'You were in *The Bill*?' I suddenly switched on. 'Fucking hell, smart. I love *The Bill*. Who were you?'

'I played a prostitute who'd been beaten up by her pimp,' she told me.

That didn't exactly narrow things down as far as plots on *The Bill* went, so she agreed to give me a quick blast in order to jog my memory. Lis dropped her head for a second, and I thought she was going to start crying that her career had come to this, soap opera charades for brickies in pubs, but instead she looked up and came straight at me in full character.

'You wanna sleep with me, Sergeant Carter? You wanna take me upstairs and have your way with me? Well, why not, everyone else does. But it's gonna cost you, darling, just like it costs everyone else. Forty quid and you can have whatever you like. Seventy and I'll even have my friend join us.'

I still couldn't remember the episode, but it sounded like a good 'un. I was just about to ask Lis how Sergeant Carter got on when I noticed the rest of the sofa had gone quiet and were now watching Lis grinding her tits at me. Including Charley. I figured an explanation was called for.

'She's just doing *The Bill* for me,' I told her.

'Well, make sure you get a receipt because seventy quid sounds a bit steep to me, fella,' Charley's mate with the glasses guffawed.

Charley laughed at that, as did half the people crowded around the two sofas, but I wasn't one of them. It seemed a bit too piss-takey for my liking, and as I didn't know anyone else here, I felt a little bit singled out. Actually, that's not true. I knew Charley among this lot but she was already back gassing with old cunty Four Eyes while I was sat here in the middle of a load of posho strangers suddenly feeling stupid.

And I don't know why I should've felt stupid either, because it wasn't really a dig aimed at me. Or was it? I wasn't sure. All I knew was that someone had scored a big clever laugh off the back of something I'd said and then left me to stew on it while he had his back slapped by all his cock-smoker mates.

I looked across at Lis to see how she'd taken it, but all she'd taken was the opportunity to slip away from the new bloke and she was now deep in conversation with some rugby shirt who was perched on the back of the sofa just behind us.

Only CT remained. Sipping his wine and nodding along slowly to the beat of the pub rhubarb.

I contemplated using up a little more of the evening by asking him if he'd ever thought about doing a reality show on bricklayers, but I wasn't sure just how much I wanted to sell him on the idea. I mean, yeah, it was probably a laugh for about half a day or so, having some documentary crew hanging around and filming your arse-crack, but months on end of the bastards getting under your feet while you were trying to work and pointing the cameras at you whenever you opened your gob to share your thoughts on old fatty jobsworth in the office or vanish a cheese sandwich? It had to get a bit much after a while. And what about the people who eventually bought our houses? I wasn't sure how much they'd appreciate stumping up their licence fees to watch a succession of tea-bloated brickies filling the very corners of their living rooms in which their tellies now stood with steam and gasps of relief. No, perhaps that reality would be a little too real for most folks to stomach of an evening.

Still, that said, it would probably be worth it if there were a few quid in it. Even if it was just cutting the odd ribbon at supermarket openings every now and again whenever the mayor couldn't make it. I'm sure there had to be a few grand in that sort of thing for Z-list celebs like myself and Colin. Definitely something to consider.

Whatever else I eventually decided to do, I'd almost finished my pint and didn't really fancy pitching CT my show with an empty glass in my hand, so I asked him if he was ready for another, then touched Charley's leg a few times to get her attention.

'Drink?'

'Oh, no, wait, surely it's my round, isn't it? Take my purse and get them out of that,' Charley said, trying to force her purse into my hand, but I resisted at all costs.

'No, it's OK, I'll get them,' I insisted, adamant that I wasn't going to be remembered as Charley's rough-and-ready date who couldn't keep his hands out of her purse all night long.

I made my way up to the bar and waited my turn again. After a few minutes Lis appeared next to me, so I asked her if she fancied a drink.

'No, it's OK, I'm getting a bottle of wine for the table, but thanks all the same,' she told me.

When I looked back at where we'd been sitting I noticed that most people were in fact drinking wine. As it happened, neither Charley nor CT had needed a drink as they were quite happily tucking into the bottles of red and white in front of them, so I wondered if I should buy one too. Not that I was going to drink any myself, you understand. I just thought I'd better make a show of a contribution. But then it occurred to me, if everyone was just buying a bottle and plonking them on the table, who was ever going to get me a pint back? I figured I had to keep either buying my own all night long or try and gatecrash a round.

About the only bloke drinking beer who'd I'd even come close to talking to was Charley's four-eyed mate with the big gob. I decided to swallow my pride and ask him if he wanted a pint anyway, figuring even if he didn't, it might get me into their conversation so that I could steal Charley back for myself the next time he took more than two seconds to ponder absolutely anything.

'Here, what's old matey's name? The bloke with the glasses? The one talking to Charley?' I asked Lis.

'Huh? Oh, that's Hugo.'

'Hugo? Really? People are really called Hugo? Get away.'

I called across to him anyway, feeling weirdly embarrassed to be shouting the name 'Hugo' out loud across a pub, and Hugo looked up after a while when he heard me, with no outward signs of shame.

'Do you want a pint, Hugo?' I shouted at him.

'Yeah, top man. Geezer. Geezer,' he replied, giving me the thumbs-up and shedding light on why he hadn't looked too upset about having his name shouted out loud in public.

'Who is he?' I asked Lis, when I'd gotten over his *Lock Stock* impression.

'We all went to uni together,' she explained.

'Oh,' I replied, and I should've probably left it at that, but at the last moment I stupidly noted, 'They seem to get on well together, don't they? Old Charley and Hugo?'

Lis nodded then replied all matter of fact:

'Well, it's not surprising really. They did go out with each other for almost two years.'

12 Specs

You know what, even if I had all the money in the world, or at least as much as Charley had, there's no way I'd buy a brand-new house. I've seen what goes into them and it doesn't exactly inspire me with confidence. Don't get me wrong, they ain't death traps or nothing. They ain't going to fall down around your ears or sink into your front lawn come the first drop of rain. But then, by that same token, I wouldn't count on them still being where they are in a hundred years' time like all the old Victorian and Edwardian jobs probably will be. They just ain't hard wearing enough.

It's all chipboard and dry-lining, plasterboard partitioning and plastic pipes. Even half the bricks we use today smash like china tea pots if you drop them from any sort of height. Not like the old Victorian bricks. Oh no, they knew how to build houses in those days.

Then again, I guess, back in Victorian times it was really only your rich Victorians who could afford to buy anywhere for themselves. Everyone else had to make do with two rooms and a bucket and a twenty per cent stakeholding in a big old brass bed ('Oi, you in the middle, after you with the bucket. And let's try and be a bit careful with it tonight for once, shall we? It's full to the fucking brim again'). Which is probably the chief reason why it's all the old well-to-do houses that are still standing these days rather than the slums, now that I come to think of it. That extra half-yard of quality that was meant to ensure these big old houses survived to be passed on from one generation to the next actually ensured they survived the old social order altogether, to a time when the descendants of the very people who used to serve upstairs and downstairs in them would come to actually own them. At least, they'd come to own a single laminated floor of them.

These days, however, the vast majority of new houses built are purpose built for normal working folk – and we all know what suckers they are. So building firms fit out the houses with the cheapest possible materials and pass on the savings to their pockets.

Like I said, there's nothing fundamentally wrong with the houses we build today and all of the materials come up to spec. But spec means minimum requirement. 'No shonkier than that, please. You can scrimp and scrape all you like but this is the very least we expect to see in there.'

And most building firms are only too happy to oblige to the letter.

Which is fair enough, I guess. They are in it to make money, but then are you really sure you'd feel the same way about that brand spanking new house you'd just hocked yourself up to the eyeballs for if you were to discover that all the materials used inside were the cheapest the builder thought he could get away with? I don't know about you, but I'm not sure I'd ever be able to look at the place in the same light again.

And this was suddenly how I felt about my relationship with Charley.

Meeting Hugo was like drilling into the wall and finding newspaper and spit where solid brickwork should've been. He was a real eye-opener.

'How's that, my old sunbeam? My old china. Sorted, geezer! Geezer!'

Well, first and foremost because Hugo had spent his formative years in a private school in Surrey, and not dipping pockets in Petticoat Lane, so I had to assume that the lingo and incessant finger-snapping were learned some time after he'd jumped naked off a stone bridge holding cocks with two other boys in silly fucking boaters. Which meant his whole demeanour was something of a put-on. But it was clearly the sort of put-on that Charley enjoyed. They looked right at home with each other, nattering, giggling and gossiping like the best of friends rather than the worst of scenarios, which is what I would've called Jo and that fucking arsehole from Morrisons had they walked into the pub and sat down next to me while I was trying to have a quiet drink with my new bird.

But Charley didn't show any signs of feeling uncomfortable about having Hugo around. Or, more to the point, about having me around. And she even made a point of pairing us off together a little later in the evening so that we could get to know each other. Just what I came out for!

Predictably, the first thing Hugo wanted to know was what team I supported. I tried to explain that I wasn't all that fussed about football but I'm not sure Hugo heard me over his own thoughts and observations about Arsenal and their domination over all forms of life on earth.

'...'cos those fucking Spurs cunts are getting far too lippy. I mean, where were they when we were playing in the Champions League year after year?' Hugo wanted to know. I couldn't tell him where Spurs were but personally speaking I was down Blockbusters most evenings because there was nothing but fucking football on telly. 'So, get down to Palace much, then, do you, geezer? I've got a season ticket, I have.'

It was that sort of conversation.

Whatever else you could say about Hugo, he was a friendly enough bloke. So friendly in fact that he offered me a 'line of chop' when I bumped into him in the bog a few pints later. I declined on the grounds that I wasn't really one of life's choppers. Something Hugo clearly was.

I don't know, though, he was a bit odd in all departments, and I got the distinct impression that he was either trying to impress or compete with me as the night wore on. And this behaviour increasingly pointed my thoughts back to Charley.

If she liked Hugo, liked his Mockney mannerisms and his Jack the Twat act, was that what she liked about me? Not that I was a twat (discuss), but my working-class credentials? I mean, we were clearly fascinating creatures, weren't we? CT had built a career out of filming us, Hugo couldn't stop climbing all over the furniture mimicking us and Charley liked to bring us down the pub for everyone to sniff at, so there was clearly something to us.

I don't know, perhaps it was just the beer doing my thinking for me, but that's how things started to shape up in my head. And I had met Charley down at the dogs, when she'd been on her little ironic tour, after all, so there was yet more grist to my mill, whatever that meant.

No, the more I thought about it the more I came to wonder if I wasn't just some sort of rough-trade trophy bloke she could hawk around in front of her over-educated mates for kicks and kudos, as that's what some posh birds did.

At least, that's what Jason reckoned.

That said, I had to take my hat off to Charley if that was the case because she was playing it all the way.

'Morning,' she sighed, looping an arm across my chest and curling up to me for a sleepy Sunday snog.

'Morning,' I replied, a little less sleepily, though that was hardly surprising seeing as I'd been wide awake for the last three hours.

'Did you have fun last night?' Charley asked.

'Yes, it was… very nice.'

'My friends are fun, aren't they? Did you like them?' she prompted, rubbing her leg against mine and kissing my neck.

'Yes, they were all… very nice,' I assured her, wondering if I should ask her about Hugo. Charley had never mentioned him to me before. Not even during our 'so when and who was your last?' conversation on our second date. What exactly I could take from that to beat myself over the head with all week long, I wasn't sure. I didn't sweat on it, though, as I was confident I'd be able to find something.

'CT said he liked you,' Charley said.

'Did he?' I mulled.

'What were you talking to him about?'

'Oh, I don't know. This and that,' I elaborated. 'Anyway, what about you?'

I rolled over on to my side, rolling Charley on to her back at the same time so that I was looking down at her.

'What about me?' She grinned cheekily, her green eyes focused on mine.

I paused to regroup, suddenly unsure if now was the right time to have this conversation. Or indeed, if there was ever a right time. *What's the deal with Hugo? You used to bang him, didn't you? Didn't you????* Oh, and I'll have three slices of toast this morning while you're at it, not just the usual two.

'Hey? What about me?' Charley pressed, bringing all four of her limbs into play to try and squeeze a few answers out of me.

'Yes,' I finally agreed. 'What about you?'

I quickly gave her a kiss before she was able to point out that she'd just said that and ordered my brain to take the rest of the morning off. It wasn't going to be needed for the next few hours and, besides, it deserved it.

Particularly in light of all the overtime it had been doing just lately.

13 Muckraking

The lads were chuffed to bits that I'd met a famous actress on Saturday night and one or two of them had even seen Lis in her Morrisons advert, though nobody remembered her from *Brideshead Revisited* or that poltergeist drama, I think she said.

'I can't even think which one you mean,' Big John said, scratching his head. 'Was it that one where the bird fell out of the window and she got stuck on the railings?'

'Er, yeah, I suppose. Must've been,' I agreed, figuring it didn't really make any difference to the story so why not?

'Oh, it was good, that one was,' he nodded, all impressed.

'Wha' wuz she like? Al'right, wuz she?' Nobby asked from the other side of Monday morning's joist lift.

'Yeah, she was nice enough, I guess,' I told him.

'Course, all thos lassies on th' telly haf'ta suck evr'one off ta git their jobs, ya ken tha', don't ya?' he then informed us.

'Do they?' Robbie asked, dropping a hod of muck down on Nobby's board.

'Oh aye, tha's well known, that is,' he confirmed, looking up from the soldier course he was laying across the patio lintel to fix Robbie in the eyes.

Robbie thought about this for a second then speculated that the bloke in charge of *Last of the Summer Wine* must be fucking devastated about his job then.

'I guess they let 'em off the hook when they get to a certain age. The actresses, like,' Jason speculated. 'Here's a lifetime achievement award and a part in *Miss Marple*, dearie. No, no, that's not necessary this morning, get up and put your teeth back in. No more auditions for you, darling.'

'Sounds a bit like the time I hired you,' Gordon sniggered at Jason from the chimney flank.

'Christ, I'll say,' Jason agreed. 'I didn't think you was ever going to stop sucking me off.'

We all had a good laugh at that. Even Gordon, who had a tendency to giggle like a schoolgirl when something tickled him, despite looking like a grizzly bear in a plastic hard hat.

Funnily enough, the lads were less than chuffed when it came to tales of Hugo. Jason asked if he wasn't actually just trying to rip the piss out of me, while Tommy thought it was par for the course with ex-public-school types these days.

'Not cool to talk like you've got a plum in your gob any more. No street cred in it. Much better to act like you were dragged up on some slum council estate, running guns for your crack-whore old lady and knife-fighting down the local snooker whenever you got five minutes. That's what'll get you a job in a bank these days, not a posh accent and a loada fucking O-levels.'

'What about real council estate crack-heads then? Wouldn't they get all the bank jobs going, then?'

'Don't work like that. They only take on council estate crack-heads who've been to Oxford or Cambridge. Is that what old matey did, then? Worked in a bank?' Tommy asked.

'No, he reckons he did something in marketing.'

'There you go, then. All about image, that game.'

As much of life was these days. The house we were working on being an excellent case in point. Nice place it was. Four bedrooms, detached, with a mock-Tudor finish. Mock-Tudor means that the front of your house (usually just the upper storey) gets a white rendering and then has fake wooden beams screwed to it, so that it looks like an old Tudor mortar-and-beam mansion. Of course, it doesn't really, but some people think it does.

Oddly similar are the sales staff from head office who come down to show potential buyers around. Like us, if they want to walk around on this site, they have to put a plastic hard hat on. Unlike us, though, if we ever see them in the pub up the road at lunchtime or after work, they'll still be wearing theirs, because wearing a hat makes you look like Bob the Builder. Of course, it doesn't really, but some people think it does.

'Maybe she's going out with you to get back at him,' Jason suggested. 'Have you thought about that?'

Curiously enough, I hadn't. At least, I hadn't up until Jason mentioned it.

'What d'you mean?' I asked, stopping in mid-cut-and-butter.

'Well, if this Hugo likes to play at being Johnny Clicky Fingers, everyone's favourite geezer from the streets, maybe Charley thought she'd bring down the real McCoy to rub his nose in it. Or even make him jealous. Win him back. A sort of 'you never appreciated me but this doughnut does, how d'you like those vinegar strokes, college boy?' That type of thing.'

Some of what Jason said tallied a little with some of my own thinking, but with a slightly different slant. For a start, I wasn't a geezer. I was a working man. In point of fact, I fucking hated 'geezers'. Geezers were the worst blokes down the pub. Forever on the ponce, or trying to flog you something you didn't want or bullshitting everyone's pants off about some incredible deal we could be a part of if only we didn't mind waving goodbye to three weeks' wages and never seeing it again when some other 'geezer's' van broke down and the cops... etc. I hated them. And so did Jason. Which was why we drank in the Lamb, a distinctly un-geezerly pub that was mostly frequented by working men, of both the suit- and overall-wearing varieties.

Geezers were just dickheads.

'Yeah, well, maybe she thinks you're one,' Jason said.

'What, a geezer or a dickhead?'

'Hey, it's your paranoia, you can be whatever you want, mate,' Jason shrugged, slotting the last brick into the course and giving it a tap with the handle of his trowel.

That was true. Not about the paranoia... well, that too. But more to the point that Charley thought I was some sort of geezer.

Hmm?

Oh, I didn't know.

It kind of reminded me of this story, though. Not exactly the same but similar. There's this bloke (I think I'll jettison the word 'geezer' from the rest of this anecdote) who drinks in the Lamb who lost a leg in the first Gulf War. Second battalion, Royal Fusiliers, reporting for duty, *sir*, he was. Had a couple of medals he used to wear around Poppy Day and cried whenever the Queen came on the box, that sort of thing. Anyway, he was forever bleating his guts out to anyone who'd listen about how he fought and died for his country and how the Fusiliers had deserted him in his hour of need with no pension and no parade, boo-hoo-hoo, 'give us a top-up there, Ton'. On the house, you say? Thanks mate, very generous of you, chief. You'd be a good man to be in a hole with, etc.'

Well, everyone felt terribly bad about poor old Paul, not least of all his girlfriend, Peggy. So one day Peggy wrote a letter to the Fusiliers branch of the Old Soldiers' Society, or whatever it was, pleading Paul's case.

A few days later two Fusiliers in full uniform walked into our pub and dragged Paul up to the bar by the scruff of the neck. They twisted his ears until he bought everyone in the pub a drink, then put the rest of his money into an old soldiers' charity box they'd brought along with them.

'Well,' I said to myself, 'those Fusiliers certainly know how to look after their own.'

Of course, Paul had never been in the Fusiliers. In fact, I don't think he'd even seen a real Fusilier before, so the only way they could possibly have been held responsible for the loss of his leg was if one of them had stopped mid-battle to phone back home and ask for a pizza to be delivered to his mum's house in Sydenham. As that turned out to be the road on which he'd lost his leg. Not the one to Basra.

I know this because the Fusiliers made him come clean in front of the whole pub.

Paul dropped his act shortly afterwards and spent the next six months feeling even worse about himself. Well, fair enough, I guess. I mean, he had still lost his leg. His new mates hadn't reattached that when they'd dropped by, had they? Only now, all of the sympathy had dried up and he had no one to blame but himself.

The free drinks had also dried up right along with the sympathy and Paul eventually took on a little light casual work to supplement his invalidity benefits.

Now it's incredible what a little bit of honest labour can do for a fella's self-respect and pretty soon the casual work led to a full-time job and as a result Paul lost a lot of the bitterness and resentment and eventually learned to stand on his own two feet. Er, well, you know what I mean. He also became the most generous bloke in the pub almost overnight.

'Sure you don't want one, Tel? My shout. Jason? Ton'? Stan? Go on, put your money away.'

I really like him these days. Paul the ironmonger is a much nicer bloke to know than Paul the war hero. Much more sorted. He still doesn't really like Iraqis, though he doesn't hate them anywhere near as much as he does Domino's Pizzas or the Royal Fusiliers.

Now, you may be wondering what all this has to do with Charley. Well, I got speaking to Peggy on her own one time and I told her I reckoned it all worked out for the best, her inadvertently grassing Paul up to the army, and you know what she said?

'What makes you think that was inadvertent?'

She didn't say too much else on the subject but reading between the lines I'd say she knew all along, or at least suspected, he weren't really in the war and this was just her way of shaming him out of his playacting.

Which led me to wonder if Charley was trying to do the same for Hugo.

You're not an East End wide boy and here's someone who'll see right through you in a heartbeat, so why don't you just cut the crap, be yourself and I'll go out with you again?

That was Jason's theory. Or was it mine? Can't remember who came up with it first.

Tommy was more inclined to believe that she just thought it was cool stepping out with a big dumb ape like myself in order to impress all her posho mates and show them just how 'real' she was, which made me this season's 'must have' accessory.

While Robbie maintained she was just enjoying having a dirty fling with a bit of rough.

'That's what these posh birds are into,' he reckoned. 'My mate reckons you can't walk into a greasy spoon on the A1 without tripping over some posh housewife on the pull while her old man's away on business. Laura Ashley knickers all over the car park, there is.'

They all seemed like plausible theories (except that one about Laura Ashley knickers. Pants that expensive don't get left behind) but it was Big John who really pissed on my apple cart when he suggested the most improbable theory of the lot.

'Christ on a donkey, Tel, has it ever occurred to you that she might just like you?'

14 Dinner dinner dinner dinner, dinner dinner dinner dinner, Batman!

That's what Batman's mum shouts out of the window when his dinner's on the table, according to Jason. Charley chose to text.

ct inv us2 dnr fri nite. u3? :-)

It took me half an hour trying to work out what the 'ct' part of the message meant and I went through any number of possibilities (Court? Can't? Cocktails? Coffee-time? Can Terry? Coded text?) before realising 'ct' meant CT. Her mate, CT. He was inviting us to dinner.

What, at his house?

Bit weird.

I'd never been to someone's house for dinner before, my mum and dad and my sister's being the exceptions, so I was dubious from the off. I mean, what if they made me something I didn't like? What if I didn't know which fork to use? What if I had to have a poo?

When you go for a bite in the pub, you can happily leave half your peas if they give you too many and disappear off to the bog with the paper for half an hour afterwards. It's not a problem. But around someone's house? They'd think I was some sort of rude bastard.

But then, wouldn't they think I was being an even ruder

bastard if I turned down their cordial invitation in the first place?

'We'd love to have you over for dinner on Friday night, Terry.'

'No, you're all right, mate. Fuck that.'

Between a rock and a hard place, I was. A rock and a hard place. What was wrong with the pub? That was all right, wasn't it? Even that terrible Signed For! Why couldn't we just go there if we wanted a drink and a bit of grub? Neutral territory for everyone, it was. No need to worry about accidentally spilling dinner all over the place or nursing an empty glass for half the night. You could just get up and help yourself in the pub. Do whatever you liked. But around someone else's house you were at their mercy.

Want a drink? I think you've had enough already.

Want to sit down? No, not there, here's your chair. It's the wobbly one.

Like spinach? That's a pity because that's what we're having.

Want some pudding? OK, but only once you've finished your spinach, mate.

Need to puke up? Not in my house, if you don't mind.

Like Robbie Williams? I can't stop playing his new album, I can't.

No, a Friday night around some posh bloke's house pushing peas around my plate and spitting feathers wasn't exactly my idea of the perfect way to unwind after a hard week on the sites.

'So are you free on Friday? Would you like to?' my mobile asked my ear.

'Erm... yeah, sure. That'd be great. Unless you'd rather do something else that evening, that is?' I offered in hope.

'No, no, I'm happy to go to CT's. He's a really good cook. He serves up some really interesting dishes.'

Oh, bollocks.

'That's that settled, then. CT's it is,' I heard some brain donor agree. I knew I couldn't very well leave it at that, though, otherwise I'd be walking in there blind with my guts going round like a tumble-dryer before I'd even caught a whiff of what horrors awaited, so I quickly double-checked something with Charley: 'Just one thing, when you say interesting dishes, what exactly do you mean?'

'Oh, relax, CT's dinners are gorgeous, just you wait and see,' Charley reassured me, though I distinctly remembered her saying the same thing about eggs Benedict. 'But, just to be on the safe side, is there anything you really don't like?' she eventually conceded.

I wasn't sure I wanted to run up my phone bill that much so I plumped for naming and shaming only my very worst food nightmares.

'Spinach, fish, tinned peas and Microchips,' I told her. 'Probably in that order too.'

'What are Microchips?' Charley asked.

'You know, those chips you get in a box that you do in the microwave. The adverts say they taste like the chips you get in the chippy but they don't.'

There was a conspicuously long silence on the other end of the phone before Charley promised me she'd have a word with CT.

'I'll tell him no Microchips for you, then.'

Friday afternoon once again came around as Friday afternoons reluctantly have a wont to do and me and the lads knocked off for the week and headed our own separate ways.

My own particular way once again took me north to Canonbury and it didn't escape my notice that I was the one who was again being asked to leave his patch, rather than the other way around. You would've thought that Charley might've volunteered to come south and see me in Catford just once by now, but no, yet again it was my turn to head north.

I blamed myself for this situation but in the early days I'd been so cock-a-hoop about seeing Charley that I would've happily crawled up to her place on my hands and knees with Hugo riding my back and *yee-harr*ing every step of the way. That's how spectacularly grateful I'd been.

Unfortunately, those early days had set a precedent for the rest of our relationship along the lines of, 'Want to see me this weekend? You know where I'll be', which left me in little doubt as to what the alternatives were. So I had a choice. I could either go north and see Charley again. Or I could stay in Catford and take all the plaudits my empty flat could throw at me.

The question was, which gave me a greater shot at happiness?

'I'm so glad you could both make it,' CT said, holding open his door and welcoming us with a smile. 'Please, come in. Come in.'

I shook CT's hand on the way past and followed Charley through to the kitchen. Candles flickered on a big old table in the middle of the room, illuminating three beaming faces that were already around it.

'Hello!' they called as one, craning their necks and offering their lips for kissing like a nestful of hungry chicks. Charley did a quick circuit of the table, planting smackers on the lot of them while I stood my ground and jangled my keys from a safe distance.

'Drink, folks?' CT offered, coming in at me from the side to take my coat.

'That would be lovely,' Charley replied. 'Here, we brought this.'

Charley handed him a bottle of red wine we'd bought in the offie on the way round.

'And these,' I added, opening up my carrier bag to show him the sixteen cans of Stella I'd picked up from the same shop.

'Like beer, huh?' CT deduced.

Now, I'll be the first to hold up my hands and accept that sixteen cans probably went a bit above and beyond for a sophisticated dinner party with candles and conversation (to be honest, it probably went a bit above and beyond for a punch-up at a bus stop) but the offie had had one of those offers on where you could buy so many and get so many more for free and that's just the way it had worked out. I could've either bought just four cans and left it at that or dipped a bit deeper into my pocket and taken advantage of their offer. There really hadn't been any middle ground. Of course, for just another couple of quid I could've got a whole crate, but I wasn't sure I wanted to turn up to my first dinner party with that many Stellas under my arm. No matter how good the deal had been.

I spent the next five minutes reorganising CT's fridge to accommodate all my beers before finally sitting down and popping open the first of the evening.

'Well, here's to me,' I said for a joke, but rather embarrassingly everyone lifted their glasses and joined in with the toast, which never happened down the pub when Jason did it. 'Er, yes, well, thank you very much.'

'Terry, this is Simone and Clive,' Charley said, introducing me to the couple opposite us.

'Hello,' I said, giving Simone a wave and braving the candles to shake the dead fish Clive had sticking out of his shirtsleeve.

'And this is Russell,' Charley then said, completing the introductions by grassing up the bloke at the end of the table.

'All right, how are you?' I offered.

'Absolutely wonderful, thank you. And it's so nice to finally meet Charley's new beau. I've heard so much about you,' Russell grinned, squeezing my hand and shooting Charley a knowing smirk.

'Oi, you, behave,' Charley objected, giving Russell a playful dig and distracting him long enough for me to get my hand back.

Hello, I speculated. *What's his game?*

'So, you're the builder,' Clive said at me from across the table.

'I've been looking for a good builder for the last six months. They're so hard to find, you know.'

'Well, don't come looking on my site, mate, we're a right bunch of cowboys, we are,' I assured him in an effort to head off this particular conversation before I found myself doing up his house on my days off for peanuts.

'Do you not take on private work, then?' Clive pressed, not taking the hint.

'More trouble than it's worth, captain. You can't make any money out of private jobs, not these days, not now London's flooded with Poles.'

'You don't like Poles?' Simone jumped in, taking issue with this last statement.

'No, I think they're great, I just couldn't afford to undercut them and carry on putting food on the table,' I replied, examining CT's crisp white tablecloth and worrying over just how much food I was going to be putting on his table before the evening was out.

The thing about the Poles was true, though. I mean, what Brit could afford to undercut them? Don't get me wrong, in their boots I'd do exactly the same. Come over here, live in a shoebox for a couple of years and earn enough money so that I could buy a nice place back home. Good on them. I don't blame them in the slightest for it. I simply couldn't do it myself because I was born and bred in London. My shoebox in Catford was all I could afford and it was mine for keeps.

'Well, I think the Poles do a fabulous job,' Simone declared. 'They're ultra-reliable and they're so much cheaper than British builders.'

'That's not very nice, is it, Sim?' Charley objected on my behalf. 'Terry is a guest, after all, remember.'

'I'm just being honest here. I'd want people to be honest with me. And it's true, British builders are extortionately expensive,' she explained as a matter of fact, then looked to me for a response.

I thought better about sharing my own particular thoughts on the subject, at least until I'd had the rest of my Stellas, and decided instead to simply ask CT what was for dinner.

'For starters, grilled goat's cheese with sun-blushed toms, toasted pines nuts and rocket...'

'Rocket? What, like Rocket Sauce?' I asked, wondering if Charley had put us together as some sort of focus group for her ketchup company – a telly producer, an advertising exec, three unspecified poshos and Britain's richest brickie. But CT just wagged his finger and he and Charley chuckled like I'd been joking or something.

'And for mains we're having baked salmon wrapped in Parma ham, crème fraiche and puy lentils, lovingly made by Russell here,' he warned us. 'With crème brûlée for dessert if you've got the room.'

I wasn't sure I would – my jacket only had three pockets.

Charley asked me if I was OK with that, so I put on my bravest face and promised her it all sounded lovely. Then, without warning, she did something she'd never done before and it momentarily struck me dumb (dumb as in unable to speak. Not dumb as in had never heard of rocket before); she took my hand in hers and held it beneath the table.

I don't know why she did this; whether it was to reassure me that dinner really wasn't as bad as it sounded or out of gratitude for not chinning her *Let them eat cake* mate across the table, or perhaps she just wanted to hold my hand underneath the table. I couldn't tell you. All I know is that I liked it more than I care to say and it made me forget my woes.

At least, until the starters started rolling out.

'Oh, this looks gorgeous,' Simone said, smacking her lips and leaning into her plate in a way that made me wonder if she wasn't going to bother with cutlery for this round.

Here, you can have mine as well, then, was the favour I desperately wanted to do her, but there was no getting out of it. I was nine years old all over again and I wasn't going anywhere until I'd eaten all my greens. How had that happened? I thought when I got this big, got a job and got my own place, I wouldn't ever have to eat something I didn't want to ever again.

'Here you, eat these turnips.'

'Oh yeah, try and fucking make me, mate.'

But dinner parties? I'd never bargained on dinner parties.

Now obviously, I'd never had goat's cheese before, but cheese was cheese, wasn't it? The same went for sun-blushed tomatoes, I presumed. They were just tomatoes, only *sun-blushed*? I was just having a cheese and tomato... what the fuck was that? Salad. Yeah, a cheese and tomato salad. With little sort of peanuts in it? What? Oh, fuck it, through the lips and over the gums, look out, T-shirt, here it comes.

Back when I was a kid, I developed a number of different strategies for coping with horrible food and one of them was to wolf it down as fast as humanly possible. No dawdling or chewing to taste, just hold your nose and chuck it back until it's all gone. It's a similar strategy to running through a tunnel of punches, which had been a particularly popular game in our playground.

Anyway, it seemed to do the trick because I did the lot in a bit under thirty seconds and was rinsing out with half a can of lager before the others were even on their second bite, though that wasn't surprising considering how much time they were spending gassing instead of eating. Their own particular strategy, no doubt.

'There is some more if you're hungry,' CT told me, consternation and confusion splashed all over his face.

'Gawd, *no thanks*! I mean, no thanks, that was just right for me. Very nice,' I replied.

It was a bonkers situation when you think about it, wasn't it?
I mean, we were all grown-ups, we were all expected to stand
on our own two feet, so why couldn't I just come out with it and
say, 'Actually, I don't really fancy any of the stuff you're dishing
up tonight. Nothing personal, I'm sure it's delicious, I just don't
fancy any of it myself. Still, you crack on and don't worry about
me. I'm perfectly happy to just sit here and get absolutely trolleyed
until the pudding comes out. Actually, thinking about it, is there
a chippy near by? I'm starving. Ain't had no dinner tonight.'

No, it didn't matter that that was what we were all thinking
– or at least I was. I wasn't allowed to say as much because
offending someone's feelings is deemed a worse taboo than
offending someone's taste buds. I tell you, this country.

Or at least, this particular colony of it. Try palming this stuff
off on my old man and you'd get it straight back across the table
at you.

After a while, CT turned to Charley and asked her if she'd
noticed it yet.

'Noticed what?' Charley replied, and for a moment I thought
CT was going to point out our complete unsuitability and the
goat's cheese down my front.

'My new piece,' he said instead, indicating over his shoulder
with a flick of the eyebrows.

Me and Charley looked towards the wall behind him and
furrowed our brows. Charley must've had better eyesight than
me because she cooed in wonder and commented that something
was wonderful.

I sharpened my eyes a few more twists and scrutinised the
back wall even harder but all I could make out was a pinboard
with a load of shopping lists and bus tickets stuck all over it.

'I'm sorry, what are we looking at?' I finally had to ask.

'CT has a new piece of art,' Charley announced in a smiley
way that told me there was an in-joke at work here. And by the

way, Simone, Clive and Russell smiled too, I could tell everyone was in on it but me.

I looked again, but still I couldn't see anything at all. I wondered if it was completely white, like the walls. You know, a 'look how avant-garde I am, I've got a white picture on a white wall' sort of nonsense, but seriously there wasn't anything there.

Except the pinboard.

No!!!

'The pinboard?' I cautiously asked, fully expecting them to tell me not to be so ludicrous and please could I take CT's new invisible white picture seriously, but astonishingly, I'd hit his battleship. It was the pinboard.

'Simone did it,' Charley told me, making Simone blush, and I could see why.

She'd got a normal, bog-standard pinboard and stuck on it bus tickets, train tickets, theatre tickets, receipts, flyers, including a couple of those dirty cards prostitutes plaster up in phone boxes, shopping lists and abstract doodles and enclosed the whole lot in a clear perspex frame.

Why she'd done this was anyone's guess. All I know is that she looked suitably embarrassed about it, sort of how I'd look if I got up and pushed over the fridge for no reason, and that everyone else was enjoying the moment.

'Is it one of the new ones?' Charley asked excitedly.

'Only twelve in existence,' Simone confirmed freely.

'What, there are more of them?' I couldn't help blurting out.

'It's Simone's new line,' CT then told me, leading me to wonder what her old line was, making wigs out of old banana skins?

'Hang on, I'm sorry, but am I being thick or something? What's all this about?' they forced me to ask.

'It's Simone's work,' Charley explained.

'What, laminating pinboards? Is there much of a market for that, then?'

'Don't, Terry, don't be rude,' Charley warned me, waking me up to the fact that I was on thin ice with this one. I looked across at Simone and Clive and caught the full force of two frosty glares.

'Sorry. No, it's very nice,' I reassured them, then thought better of adding that I had one just like it in my kitchen at home. Only mine was a work in progress.

Which just went to show the double standards some people had. Only ten minutes earlier Simone had defended herself for laying into my mercenary mates on the grounds that honesty was the best policy. Yet all of a sudden I was the rude one for raising an eyebrow when I found out that she went around doing stuff that would've seen my Great-Auntie Doris put in a home and never talked about again.

'So are you just borrowing it or have you actually bought it?' Charley asked CT.

'Oh no, I've bought it. It's all mine,' he boasted proudly.

Charley dealt a few congratulations around the table and the five of them talked of their excitement about Simone's upcoming exhibition, but no one even got near to asking the only thing I wanted to know. Namely, how much?

'Er… without seeming rude, can I ask you how much you bought it for, CT?' I finally cracked.

Everyone around the table clammed up when old money-grabbing Tel inevitably lowered the tone.

'Oh no, don't get me wrong. Seriously, I don't mean any disrespect, I'm just curious, that's all,' I explained.

'Well, I'm sorry, but I'd really rather not say,' CT apologised. 'It's not really my place.'

'Ah, no, that's fine, don't worry about it,' I climbed down, all embarrassed and in urgent need of booze. I filled the rest of my glass with my latest can and took a big reassuring swig. I wasn't sure how I was doing it, but somehow I was upsetting everyone around this table and I was starting to get to the point where I was almost afraid to open my mouth.

'I've got no problem with Terry knowing if you don't,' Simone then stepped in.

'No, oh, all right,' CT shrugged, then told me he'd paid sixteen hundred for it.

An enormous cloud of Stella sprayed across the table in Simone and Clive's direction as I choked on this figure, sending chairs flying in all directions as my fellow dinner guests leapt to escape my beer.

'Oh shit, sorry!' I gasped, my face all purple and sweaty as I coughed and honked on a lungful of lager. 'Went down the wrong way,' I croaked.

'Well, yes, quite,' CT agreed, taking stock and relighting the candles. 'Don't worry about it, it happens to the best of us, you know. Right then, tea towels?'

Charley patted me on the back and gave me a napkin to wipe the tears from my eyes.

'Sorry,' I rasped, incredibly embarrassed and apologetic.

Russell began wiping down the table while CT took away everyone's half-eaten starters and scraped them into the bin, now that everyone was suddenly finished.

'Are you all right?' was all Charley asked.

'Yes, thank you,' I replied, coughing out the last of my beer and standing my chair on end again. 'Oohh.'

'Good job Simone didn't tell you how much she normally sells them for, then, wasn't it?' Charley whispered, her lips curled into a barely concealed smile. 'Well, CT is one of her oldest friends, you can't expect her to charge him the full amount, now, can you?'

'I guess not,' I choked in response.

Now, I'm not going to get into this whole modern art debate because we all know it's simply a case of the emperor's new clothes here. Seriously, anyone with half a brain in their head can see that a load of bricks painted blue, or a video of a man hopping on one leg, or six buckets of paint upturned on a canvas or, in this case, a pinboard full of bus tickets, isn't art. And all the clever eggheads in the world insisting that it is and that I'm a thicky philistine ain't going to convince me otherwise. And I'll tell you the simple reason why – because I could do any of these things. I mean, blimey, who couldn't? Only if me or old Joe Knucklehead from down the road did do it, it wouldn't be considered art because we weren't coming from an artistic background. So I could paint a load of red arrows on a canvas and then cover it in crisps and it wouldn't be considered art. But if someone from the most exclusive, swankiest, wankiest art college in London were to do exactly the same thing it would be. That's just how it works.

Anything can be art apparently, but not everyone can do it. So there you have it in its clearest light – the emperor's new clothes.

Of course, every now and again someone shows these con men up for what they are by exhibiting the work of a new up-and-coming genius and roping in a load of nobby art critics to wax lyrical about it, before wheeling out some chimp in a beret and big floppy shirt who's drinking from a bucket of emulsion. And that's always great when that happens. I love it when they do that and I read all about it with a big grin on my face. But even this isn't enough to faze these boys because, you see, at the end of the day, it always comes back to us. We're simply philistines and we're not clever enough to understand it.

Perhaps not, but I understand this much; I might be a philistine, but I ain't no mug.

Sixteen hundred quid for a pinboard in a frame? I'm sure if I shopped around a bit I could find a Pole who knocked 'em out cheaper. Fabulous artists, the Poles. And so much cheaper than those unreliable British artists who, frankly, in my opinion, are more extortionately expensive than British builders.

'Here we are. Is everyone hungry?' Russell asked, a tablecloth change later.

He put my dinner down in front of me and I saw that it consisted of an extra-thin bit of bacon wrapped around a bit of salmon, sat on top of a load of really burnt peas (which I later found out were lentils. I'd heard of these before, but had never actually ever seen them) and all covered in cream.

OK, I'll admit it, I'm not the most sophisticated bloke in the world – no, seriously, I'm not – so I hadn't done that much posh grub in my time, but really, please, tell me, how was this nicer than a chicken dinner? Or a chicken curry? Or chicken and chips? Or chicken casserole? Or chicken nuggets? I mean, if I was having people around for dinner and I wanted to impress them (and the butcher's had run out of chicken) I'd get a steak in for everyone. A big dirty great slab of sirloin with onions, mushrooms, grilled tomatoes, a baked potato, a bit of salad and a scattering of mustard and pepper. I'd expect a good write-up if I served up six plate-loads of that to everyone, so what was the deal with the cat food challenge in front of us this evening?

Fish, as well? I'd specifically told Charley that I didn't like fish, and here in front of me was a fish, though she'd been as good as her word as far as the Microchips were concerned.

'Has it got bones in it?' I asked, digging open my fish with the funny-looking knife and fork I found by the side of my plate.

'No, it shouldn't have, I boned the fish myself this afternoon,' Russell told me, almost making me choke on my Stella again. Childish, I know, but he said it, not me.

Unfortunately 'shouldn't have' didn't carry the sorts of cast-iron guarantees I needed to commence Operation Wolf It Down again, so I had to rethink my options and selected a different strategy to beat this particular dish.

The 'eat a bit, drink a bit' option wasn't really a goer either, as I wasn't sure I'd be shown the same sympathy and understanding if I hurled a second mouthful across the table if it all got a bit too much for me, so this called for Strategy C.

'Here, CT, have you got any brown sauce?'

'Erm… er, yes… I think. I'm sure we must have,' he replied, looking at Russell in pity.

Russell himself chose not to say anything, he just stared at the dinner in front of me with a mixture of sadness and resignation in his eyes.

'You can't beat a bit of brown sauce,' I reassured everyone, and you certainly couldn't. Nothing completely annihilated something else's original taste quite like brown sauce. It was the napalm of all condiments.

'Here you go,' CT said, reluctantly handing me a plastic squeezy bottle as if it were a gun and I was his son. He looked like he desperately wanted to urge caution but wasn't quite sure how to go about it, so I quickly popped the lid and put him out of his pickle with a sweeping flourish all over my dinner.

'That got it,' I told him, and CT just agreed. It certainly had.

I mashed it all up together and stirred in half the lentils while I was at it, then helped myself to an enormous forkful before anyone could ask me if I wanted a bib, and I must say, it wasn't very nice. Even with half a bottle of brown sauce all over it.

'A sauce-on-everything man, huh?' Clive commented. I was going to tell him 'yeah, everything except pudding' but decided to hold fire until I saw what crème brûlée was.

I struggled on with my lot, determined that I should finish every morsel for fear of looking like a big ignorant rude dummy, and within four minutes it was mission accomplished. Bring on the pudding and then we're out of here. What time is it?

'Attend a lot of dinner parties, do you?' Russell asked.

'This is my first one,' I corrected him.

'Really?' he mulled.

After a while, CT turned to me and caught me by surprise when he confessed that he had an ulterior motive for inviting me along this evening.

'Dishwasher on the blink, is it?' I asked.

'Ha! No, but I'll bear you in mind the next time it is,' he chuckled. 'No, actually, it was something we talked about the other evening, in the pub. About making a fly-on-the-wall show set on a building site. Do you remember?'

I did, but I had only been joking at the time. It had just been a pub conversation. I mean, blimey, If I was taken seriously every time I opened my mouth in the pub I'd be doing a dozen consecutive life sentences by now and we'd all be at war with Wales.

'I actually think it's a really good idea and I'd like to pitch it to my commissioner in the next scheduling round if that's all right with you? What do you think?' CT asked.

'What, my building site?' I asked back.

'Ideally, yes, if we can get the agreement of everyone involved and the insurance to cover the crew,' he confirmed.

I turned to Charley and asked her if this was a wind-up.

'It's just an idea at the moment,' Charley downplayed. 'But I agree with CT that it could be really good. He's talked about nothing else all week.'

'What, me on the telly?' I triple-checked.

'Only if you agree. Like I say, ideally we'd like to come down and scout your building site, but if it's not suitable for whatever reason and your guys don't feel happy about it then obviously we'd look for another location, but it's the idea I'm really excited about. I think it's a wonderfully workable idea,' CT enthused.

'And Jason? Would he be on the telly as well?' I continued to press.

'Well, again, if Jason signs up and we're able to get agreement from all parties and we're given the go-ahead from the commissioner and the channel give us a slot and we're able to get enough material in the time allowed and the dozen and one other hurdles we'll have to clear to put together this show, then yes, hopefully Jason too,' CT confirmed.

'What, me and Jason on telly?' I could hardly believe it.

CT looked around the table for help and eventually Charley came to his rescue with the Janet and John version.

'Yes, you and Jason on the telly,' she explained. 'Would that be OK?'

'Because if it's not, I might ask you to sign something to say that you're happy to relinquish the rights to this idea in order for me to take it elsewhere. Obviously, you would be compensated in the event that the show went ahead and...' CT started to tell me, but I picked up on the word compensated straight away and asked him what that actually meant in terms of beer tokens. I mean, if he was happy to pay sixteen hundred for a pinboard, how much was he willing to shell out for a cracking idea like *Building Site* (working title)?

'Well, er... I can't really say until we've been allocated a budget and had the lawyers look at it in terms of...'

CT saw that he was losing his audience so he cut to the chase and suggested a working figure in the region of a thousand pounds.

'You're fucking joking!' I almost yelled in his face. 'A grand?'

'Well, obviously we could look into it and see if there was more available...' CT started, getting the wrong end of the stick.

'No no no, a grand's absolutely fine. Honestly, I'd be happy to settle for a grand, no problem. Just show me where to sign and give me a pen, quick,' I rushed him, my heart crashing at the thought of getting my hands on the easiest grand I was ever likely to earn. That was unless CT wanted some more ideas. In which case, all he had to do was take me and his chequebook down the pub and he could buy all the drunken nonsense that tumbled out of my gob he wanted.

'Well, we're getting a little ahead of ourselves here. All I wanted to know was that you're interested in principle,' CT told me.

'Right.' I nodded. 'Yeah, I see. So let me get this right, you want to know if I'm happy to be on the telly, and if not, you'll give me a grand?'

Hmm, I had to think about this one.

'Of course, you don't have to make up your mind right now...' he started, but I didn't give him a chance.

'CT, you drive a hard bargain but OK, then, let's do it,' I agreed, offering him my hand.

CT beamed and shook it enthusiastically as Charley, Clive and Russell all erupted in joyous celebration (like I was ever going to say no?). Only Simone remained unmoved, though this could've just been because most things paled into insignificance once you'd started knocking pinboards out for four figures.

'This is so exciting,' fizzed Charley, seeding my mind with a dozen doubts I'd beat myself over the head with in the weeks and months to come.

'Well, I was going to save this, but why don't we pop it open now? Champagne, anyone?' Russell announced, pulling a bottle of bubbly from the fridge.

'No thanks, but you can get me another Stella while you're there,' I told him.

I think I did about eight of them by the end of the evening and I decided to make a present of the remainder rather than ask Charley to hold open a carrier bag while I emptied CT's fridge again.

'Shall we walk?' Charley asked. 'It's probably only a twenty-minute walk home.'

'No, sod that, it's gone midnight and us celebrities don't

walk anywhere on our own legs at the best of times,' I told her, checking Simone's 'piece' for cab numbers.

Ten minutes later, I waved and kissed goodnight to CT, Russell, Clive and Simone as I saw fit and bundled Charley into a waiting minicab.

'Well, I think that went well,' I said, and, the odd cough and hiccup aside, I thought it had. Once we'd dispensed with the business of dinner and settled down to beer and baloney I'd had a genuinely nice time. Of course, I'm sure it helped that a lot of the baloney had been about how I was going to be the next big thing and how, come tomorrow, no one would even remember old whatsisface off *Car Pool*.

I'd actually had a good laugh.

'CT's nice, isn't he?' Charley said, in the back of the cab.

'Yeah, no, he's all right, I really rate him,' I agreed.

'What did you think of Russell?' Charley then asked.

'Russell? Yeah, he's a nice enough fella, I suppose,' I shrugged.

'You do realise he's CT's boyfriend, don't you?' Charley said, with an impish little grin dancing across her lips.

'Well, blimey, I'd guessed that,' I told her, stopping her smirk in its tracks. 'Two blokes who live together and cook each other lentils and have pink bog roll? How are they not going to be gay?' I wanted to know.

Charley stared at me, struck dumb by what I could only take as amazement.

'Well, we do have 'em in Catford as well, you know,' I pointed out.

15 Hugo and cry

If you were to ask any builder who they thought was the biggest blight on society, you'd probably be surprised by the answer. See, it's not anyone ethnic or Polish or gay or pen-pushing, as Charley and her friends seem to think we'd say – oh yes, for some reason they have us all somewhere to the right of Bernard Manning with tattoos for brains and fists for solutions, but they couldn't be more wrong. Half our site is either ethnic or black or gay – at least, all the roofers take it up the arse, according to the graffiti in the Portaloo. And Jason himself is, or at least was, half-caste until he got recategorised in the nineties so that now he's mixed race for another ten or twenty years or so until he starts to offend everyone again. But it doesn't matter to Jason, and it certainly doesn't matter to us. I mean, why should it? Live and let live, that's what we say. Just as long as people don't try to convert us to their religion, put us in a big pot and eat us or pinch our bottoms and smother us with kisses, seriously, who cares? Black people, Muslims, Hindus, homosexuals and even estate agents, they're all part and parcel of this big old wide world of ours and it's a narrow-minded fuckwit who can't accept that. No, builders are no more bigoted than any other profession. I mean, we still whistle at saucy old housewives and everything, but that's only because it is expected of us. And they love it. Oh no, on the whole, I'd say we are a surprisingly tolerant lot.

That said, there is one section of society that almost universally gets our goats up, and that we will unapologetically discriminate against and persecute to the ends of the earth.

Students.

For some reason... actually, no, scrub that, for dozens of reasons, we fucking hate students: lazy, spoilt, dopey, scruffy, long haired, constantly complaining, work-shy, cheque-writing, fucking dreary cunts. Ask any builder what they think of students and that's the sort of glowing tribute you can expect.

But weirdly, none of the above is what gets our goats up the most. What really does it is the fact that despite being lazy, spoilt, dopey, scruffy, long haired, constantly complaining, work-shy, cheque-writing, fucking dreary cunts, they all seem to think it's their divine right to tell the rest of us how to live. That theirs is the generation that has been chosen to show us the way. Most students are like lippy, backchatting little teenagers who think they know it all. But the thing with teenagers is that this confidence soon dissipates once they get handed a hod and told to load out a dozen muddy footings, or giving a broom and told to sweep up around the barber's feet, or a shirt and tie and told to add up a column of the chief accountant's numbers. Because work has the curious effect of slapping down your ego, while at the same time elevating your opinion of your elders, particularly if those same elders started out loading out footings, sweeping up hair or adding up numbers years before you came along. *There you go, son; been there, seen it, done it. Now it's your turn. Try to keep up – if you can.*

But students never go through this experience. Most little darlings go straight from bawling out their mums and dads for not buying Fairtrade bananas to bawling out the rest of us for not erecting statues of Germaine Greer on every street corner.

I could go on and do a few hours on this subject without pausing for breath but it's not that relevant. Suffice to say it was with mixed and conflicted emotions that I used to listen to Charley's university stories.

Not least of all because most of them featured that unbelievable arsewipe, Hugo.

Charley went to Bristol University some ten years earlier and met Hugo for her troubles. At first they'd just been friends, in the way that all good middle-class boys and girls always try to be when one of them doesn't fancy the other as much as they do. Anyway, they were both bright, both had issues with their parents and both wanted to save the whale, ban the bomb and free Nelson Mandela – despite the fact that he'd already been president for several years. Anyway, it was while working towards one or two of these ends that they found themselves in the library late one Friday night, passionate, enthused and yearning for revolution. Hugo had been spinning her a fine line in guff about the rights of the workers and the evils of an oppressive society for the best part of two months and Charley had all but choked on the hook. And this was when he made his move and gave her a big smoochy kiss on the lips, which only stopped when he tried to follow it up with a hand up the jumper.

Charley knocked him back and told him that she couldn't, that it was impossible, that she liked him and everything, but not like that. Besides, she already had a boyfriend at home, called Nigel, who she couldn't bring herself to cheat on.

Hugo told her she could do anything if she just put her mind to it. He *believed* in her.

One angry slap around the chops and a night of frantic tearful wanking later, Hugo apologised to Charley for crossing the line and promised her total sisterly respect from now on. All he wanted was her friendship – and possible her dirty bra and pants if she had any spares going. Some of these details, as you might have detected, have been added by Jason after a few sherbets so either run with our slant on the story or sieve out the facts as you find them.

Anyway, Charley forgave Hugo and apologised herself for overreacting and they became the best of friends for the next semester, studying together, doing homework together and giggling at the back of the lecture hall like a pair of budgerigars.

I find this a decidedly odd set of circumstances. There's something weirdly calculating and domineering about keeping someone close to you when you know they fancy you and would happily jump you in a heartbeat if you were to drop your guard. I think this is a uniquely female practice. Actually, I don't know. I'm sure there are some blokes out there who like to string along little fat birds for kicks, but by and large I think girls are probably better at it than blokes because they've got better self-restraint. I also think they are better at playing the indignation card, as it sounds more plausible coming from them, in that it's nigh on impossible to take them to task over their friendships with other blokes without leaving yourself open to all manner of accusations of small-mindedness, jealously and control freakdom. Yet you turn this one on its head and try nodding it your girlfriend's way when she wants to know why you've been seen all over Catford with that little scrubber from the chip shop and see how it sounds to the clatter of flying crockery.

I asked Charley what Nigel thought of her whole set-up with Hugo, and Charley assured me he was 'cool'.

Well, he shouldn't have been, for I know what happened next.

Charley and Hugo got heavily involved with the Student Union movement…

'Hold on, they have a union?' Jason choked on his pint.

'Yeah. It's one of the biggest in the country.'

'What, and like, they go on strike and everything?' he asked.

'I guess.'

'But, who'd care?'

It's something I've never been able to answer myself.

Still, Charley and Hugo got involved despite Jason's reservations, waving placards and doing whatever Student Union activists did. They complained to teachers, liaised with wet-nosed freshmen and generally swanned around Bristol with an air of self-appointed importance. And remember, this is Charley I'm talking about here, the women I adore, which should show you just how ingrained my prejudices against students are.

Anyway, at the start of their second year at university, the college decided to close the Student Union and sell off the building to try to recoup a few quid.

Now confusingly, the Student Union we're talking about here was not the action group that Charley and Hugo belonged to, but the subsidised bar on the campus grounds that all the rest of the students belonged to. This place was called the Union too, for reasons Jason can't explain, but it sold lager for £1.20 a pint at a time when the rest of the country were having to shell out £2.10 for it, so it was a very popular place.

Naturally, everyone was up in arms; the Student Union, the Student Union and other alternatively titled student folk. So, without delay the Student Union got its skates on and did what Student Unions do in times of crisis, they organised a sit-in – in the Student Union, no less. Probably not the hardest rallying call they've ever had to make.

Three hundred of them barricaded themselves in for three days and three nights, demanding a reversal of the decision and a seat on any subsequent review board, and amazingly, the university caved in. Incredible isn't it? That the board of governors quivered and climbed down because a load of scruffy herberts threatened not to leave the pub. I couldn't see me and my mates getting away with this. I think we'd have to make do with an SC60 through the letterbox and a fire hose through the catflap. But they got the decision. The Student Union was given a reprieve, the establishment assured everyone that it would remain open for another two years (by which time Charley and the other ringleaders would've left university and who gave a fuck after that?) and the Union folk were toasted as heroes.

Charley and Hugo obviously got a bit caught up in the moment and knocked poor old Nigel's picture off the bedside cabinet as they celebrated their historic victory by frantically banging each other long into the night.

Naturally, Charley felt devastated about her betrayal the next morning, but not so devastated that she didn't spend the rest of the month hopping in and out of beds and broom cupboards with her lover-in-arms, stopping only to drop Nigel a 'you're great, it's not you' SC60 of his own.

And that's how it happened. I guess that's how it always happens. Time and close proximity are like water for their erosive properties. Hugo's patient drip drip drip of respect and understanding slowly seeped behind Charley's resolve, so that all it took in the end was one almighty thunderstorm in the shape of a collective high for her defences to finally crumble.

I don't blame Charley for this and, oddly, I don't even blame Hugo. She was young and a long way from home. He was there, saw what he wanted and went after it. Each in their own way had their reasons. No, the person who I think was most at fault was Nigel. He'd waved Charley off at the station. He'd let her go. He'd thought he could hold on to her from a distance. He'd had the most to lose. And he had duly paid the price. It was his blame to shoulder.

Of course, he could've been banging half of Berkshire the moment Charley left and used her rolled up 'Dear John' note to snort a big fat line of gack off a big fat prostitute's arse to celebrate his new-found freedom. I don't know, it's possible, but for the sake of this particular story we'll assume he was all gutted about it.

So his relationship was history. But what could he do? Not a lot, because Nigel's time had come and gone. Just as Hugo's time would come and go too. Oh yes, he didn't last much beyond their mortar boards landing at their feet before he joined Charley's roll-call of exes. I don't know why precisely. Perhaps he just didn't stand up to long term scrutiny or perhaps she got distracted by some other doughnut (it wasn't me, by the way, I came along about eight years later), but whatever the reason Hugo bit the dust and slid down the 'see-ya' tubes to Dumpsville too.

So, what did *Hugo* do?

Did he drift off into her past and spend the rest of his days licking his wounds and praying for an Oscar or a lottery win to get Charley regretting her decision? Or did he up sticks and follow her to London, move in just around the corner from her, and start biding his time all over again?

Now this was very sticky ground for me to be speculating over, not least of all because I didn't want to lay myself open to accusations of small-mindedness, jealously and control freakdom, but it had to be said that Charley (and Hugo) had done it before, so it wasn't out of the realms of possibility that they could do it again.

It was unlikely. But then I'm sure that's what Nigel thought when he waved Charley off at Ascot station after a tender kiss and a lot of 'I'll write you soon' reassurances.

16 Hey, lads, guess who's going to be on the telly?

'Let me get this right; your mate's going to come down here with a camera crew and film us and then put us on the telly?' Big John said, his brow a tightly knotted mass of scepticism.

'All except the 'your mate' bit, yeah. That's the plan,' I confirmed, enjoying this particular Monday morning like I'd never enjoyed a Monday morning before.

'Smart, eh?' Jason reckoned, slinging the muck about with more than the usual flourish.

'Are you sure he's not just pulling your leg, Tel?' Big John asked.

'No, definitely. Well, pretty sure anyway. I don't think they're the type,' I said, though to be honest, at the back of my mind somewhere I had to admit it was possible. I mean, thinking about it, the whole evening could've feasibly just been one long middle-class joke on me, in fact. You can never completely rule these things out. It would've certainly explained the lentils.

'But why the hell would anyone want to film us laying bricks? Come to think of it, why the hell would anyone want to watch us laying bricks on the telly, like?' Big John couldn't work out, before going on to slap a couple down, presumably to see just how interesting it was.

'John, mate, they've got five hundred channels to fill these days, they're desperate for programmes,' Jason explained.

'Yeah, I know, but even so, *this*?' Big John still couldn't believe it, and he wasn't the only one. Gordon, the boss, was convinced that it was some sort of divine conspiracy to stop him skiving off down the pub in the afternoons for fear of copping a rolling pin over the head off the old lady when he got home.

'What are the odds?' he asked, when this particular consequence dawned on him. 'She's home in Bagshot, I'm at work in Wimbledon, but all she has to do if she wants to keep her beady eye on me is tune in to this week's episode of *Gordon's in the Boozer Again*?' he fumed. 'It's not right. It's not right at all. A working man should be entitled to a bit of privacy when he's at work.'

'Or not, as the case may be,' pointed out Robbie, right on cue, when he strolled by and made Gordon a gift of the hod of muck he'd brought with him.

'Don't worry about it, just don't sign up for it if you don't want to,' I reassured him. 'They can't use your pictures if you don't sign the forms, Gordon.'

'But I want to be on telly,' he sulked, giving us all a sneaky peek at the inner conflict raging within his head. 'Can't they just film me in the mornings and not film me in the afternoons?' he asked.

'Unless they all go down the pub with you, Gordon, I can't see there's much danger of them doing anything else, mate,' Jason reassured him, spinning his trowel around in his hand as if he was wagging his tail.

'And you'll all cover me? *Where's Gordon? Oh, I think he's down the compound*,' Gordon demonstrated, like we hadn't all been spinning that one to the site agent for the last year already.

Big John picked up rehearsals right where Gordon left off.

'*My, he has been working hard down there, hasn't he? Just*

look at him staggering back with his big red face,' he chuckled, winning laughs all around the band lift, save for one anxious subby.

'Bastards.'

I tell you, it's incredible the effect a little bit of exciting news can have on a man's performance. This particular Monday morning our walls flew up faster than that one they built across Berlin a few years back and soon we were on Dennis the brick hoddy's tail, moving from lift to lift before he had a chance to finish loading them out properly. Luckily, Dennis had also started tightening up his act in preparation for the bright lights and raced about like a whirling dervish all day long, throwing bricks this way and that, so that we never went short.

Naturally, as the day went on, the lads' collective conversation threw up more and more bizarre questions. Here's a summary of some of the best ones:

Would we have lines to read or would we just have to make up what we said as we went along?

Would we get paid for appearing in the programme?

Would we need Equity cards?

Would we have to wear make-up?

Would we subsequently qualify for other programmes such as Celebrity Come Dancing, Celebrity Master Chef *and* Celebrity Love Island?

'Actually, screw the dancing and *Master Chef*, let's just set sail for *Celebrity Love Island*. Any of those dirty actresses that Terry knows going?' Robbie said, sparking an altogether different conversation which must've had Ginger Spice, Natasha Kaplinsky and Kelly Holmes's ears melting off the sides of their heads.

'Charley's idea, was it?' Jason asked, giving me a look I could read like the front page of the *Radio Times*.

'As it happens, it wasn't. It was mine,' I told him, not even convincing myself with that one.

'What, you went up to one of her BBC mates, asked him if they were looking for anything to replace *EastEnders* with and reluctantly took one step forward?' Jason clarified, smoothing a bed of muck along the flank we were both working and buttering up the first in a succession of bricks.

You know, it's funny, but if you do something long enough, your actions become so effortlessly instinctive that they can often betray your thoughts better than a loose pair of eyebrows. Bricklaying's a bit like that. As I'm sure painting, harvesting, cutting hair or stripping down motors all are. Anything that requires your hands and a modicum of concentration really. And I ain't talking mind-reading here either, just body language. So when Jason cut and buttered his brick with a precision a diamond merchant would've been proud of, I immediately knew what he was getting at.

Of course, it helped that I'd had the same bees buzzing around my bonnet for the last couple of days too.

'What, so you reckon Charley's now just interested in me because of this whole telly programme development?' I said, voicing both our trowels' thoughts.

'Me? No, I don't,' Jason replied, with a shake of the hard hat. 'The question is, do you?'

Jesus, it was never ending, wasn't it? When was I going to get on an even keel with Charley and be able to relax without interrogating her every motivation? I just couldn't seem to let anything go, could I? What was the matter with me? Why couldn't I stop my brain from turning over? Maybe I was just too intelligent for my own good.

'No, I don't think that's it,' Jason said, spreading the next course of muck along the wall in a way that almost won him a punch in the gob.

OK, let's get real here. Charley hadn't gone out the night I'd met her with the intention of finding someone to brighten up all our evenings now that *Car Pool* Colin's star was on the wane. Our meeting had been nothing more than a complete and utter accident from the off and our continuing relationship had pretty much followed suit right up until this present minute. But had an idea occurred to Charley somewhere along that way that hadn't been there from the start? And was I only still in the picture because I was somehow tied in by this selfsame idea?

Again it was a possibility. But let's be honest, most things are, especially when you can't see inside someone else's head. I wondered if I should teach Charley bricklaying in order to get a peek into what she was thinking.

'She must be excited about it, though?' Jason suggested, his face a wall, his wall a face.

'Yes, she is excited about it,' I conceded. 'But who isn't? You're all excited about it too but that doesn't mean our friendship's all over the moment our ratings plummet.'

Jason smiled at that, but his smile didn't last long.

'Look, I ain't saying nothing. Honest I ain't. All I'm saying,' he said, not saying anything, 'is that I know you well enough to know that you're probably thinking all these thoughts yourself and that I really wouldn't worry about it if I was you.'

'No?'

'No. Because what will happen will happen,' he mused, like a fourth-division genius at the podium. 'And if she is only sticking around for the fame and fortune then that just gives you that much more time to wow her with the real you.'

'Or scare her off, as the case may be,' Robbie added, again right on cue as he went past with a hod of muck.

'Yeah, so just enjoy your Monday for once. Because tomorrow's Tuesday, and none of us can do anything about that.'

17 Sandra-ingham

They say that behind every great man there's a great woman, and this can be said of Jason (all except the 'great' part, that is). Sandra is his wife of God knows how many years. He met her yonks ago when we'd both just started out on the sites and this 'dirty little sixteen-year-old bird' who used to suck him off over the cemetery after four cans of cider bloomed into a wonderful woman without whom Jason would cease to function. Or at least, eat vegetables.

Oh, and don't think too badly of Jason for telling me what he and Sandra used to get up to in the cemetery when they first met because he told me at the time when we were both in our teens ourselves and you just do when you're that age. Besides, Sandra knows I know and even laughs about it herself, especially when I call her Woodpecker – and that isn't because of the cider she used to drink.

Anyway, Sandra's more or less been a fixture in Jason's life for as long as I've known him, which means she's also been a fixture in mine.

I regard her very much as the sister I never had. Something that narks the sister I do have off no end. But, you know, Jason's my best friend, so by extension Sandra's my best friend-in-law. That's how it works.

So naturally, when Charley came on the scene, Sandra took an immediate and active interest. Jason used to complain that Charley was taking over his life. All day long he'd get it in the ear'ole from me, only to go home and have to go through it all again with his eager spouse. Assorted bits of advice would then filter back to me throughout the week via Jason and I'd report results the following Monday, kick-starting the whole cycle again.

Well, I guess Sandra must've finally had enough of trying to run my love life from a distance because the moment she heard about CT's dinner party, an invitation was dispatched through Jason and me, requesting the pleasure of Charley's company the following Friday night. This was subsequently shifted to the following Saturday night on appeal when Jason pointed out that he was usually only fit to drop come the end of the week but the invitation was forwarded on nevertheless and Charley replied that she'd be delighted.

Of course, I'd told Charley all about Jason in the past and she'd always been keen to meet him, but Charley admitted to knowing very little about Sandra. I filled in the blanks where I could but before I got as far as what she used to do on days when business went to the crematorium, we were ringing Sandra's bell and greeting her in the flesh a mere wrench of the door later.

'Oh, it's so nice to finally meet you, I've heard all about you,' Sandra completely overdid it, almost curtsying when she took Charley's hand. 'Please, come in, come in.'

'Hello, Sand,' I said, kissing her on my way inside and shooting her a look that pleaded with her to go easy, but which she somehow managed to read as 'please giggle hysterically and ask me several times if you're embarrassing me'.

'Hello, Charley, it's very good to finally meet you,' Jason beamed likewise, stretching out his hand past his wife at the third attempt and shaking Charley's so enthusiastically anyone would've thought she'd just returned from the moon.

'Yes, you too,' Charley replied. 'Thank you for inviting me.'

'No, thanks for coming,' Jason said. 'Here, let me take your coat.'

'Oh yes, thank you. And here, this is for you,' Charley then said, handing Jason a bottle of red we'd picked up on the way round.

'Ah, thank you very much. Look at that, Sand'.'

'Oh, doesn't that look lovely,' Sandra gasped. 'Oh, thank *you*.'

'All right, enough of this,' I protested, before we all thanked each other into the nuthouse. 'Let's call a truce on the thank yous, shall we, until we see what dinner looks like.'

'Ooh, inne a mood?' Sandra reckoned. 'Don't know what you see in him. Right, then, love, you come with me through to the kitchen and we'll get you a nice little drinky.'

Sandra led Charley through to the kitchen while Jason hung back a step to give me a private nod of approval. Though it was during this nod that his eyes fell upon my empty hands and he realised the bottle of red he and Sandra had thanked us so comprehensively for was actually from both me *and* Charley.

'Didn't you bring any beers?' he asked, not liking the look of this one little bit.

'No, we brought wine,' I reminded him.

'Yeah, you brought *a bottle* of it. How far's that gonna get us?'

'Well, presumably you've got some in,' I said.

'I have, but what else have you been presuming? That you're going to sit around drinking it all night?'

'We are your guests. You did invite us,' I pointed out. 'Listen, this is just what people do when they go to dinner parties, apparently, they take a bottle of wine and that covers the admission, then the rest of the booze is laid on by you and you get it all back when you and Sandra come over to ours,' I told him. Honestly, what an oaf.

Admittedly I hadn't known any of this myself, not until CT's dinner party last week, when I'd committed the cardinal faux pas of turning up with a carrier bag full of wife beater, but I was learning from my mistakes. With the help of Charley, I was improving as a person.

Jason wanted to know why I couldn't have waited a week to have improved this side of my game.

'One bottle? That's, like, one fucking glass each, man, and then it's all gone. Couldn't you have at least got two?'

'Doesn't work like that, mate.'

'Oh, doesn't it? Somehow I didn't think it would,' Jason scowled. 'I've only got eight beers in myself.'

'Well, that's all right, I'll only have a couple,' I reassured him.

'But then I won't have eight,' he objected, pointing out the flaw in this plan.

'Oi, are you two joining us tonight or are you going to hang around by the front door all evening?' Sandra wanted to know.

'No, it's all right, we're just coming,' Jason called back, then told me he was going to work out a system where I owed him two pints in the pub for every can of lager I had of his tonight. I haggled him down to a pint and a half, so we shook on the deal, then went on through and joined the girls.

Well, I must say, other than the criminal lack of beer about the place, I did enjoy my evening at Jason and Sandra's. It's weird, but the odd curry, fry-up or Scotch egg aside, I don't think I'd ever sat down and eaten with one of my mates before. Well, you don't, do you? I mean, eating's just eating, isn't it? Having a bit of dinner when you get in from work or chucking a ham sandwich down your neck on the way out to soak up the beer is just something you have to do, like washing your armpits or occasionally changing your socks. It's just a functional thing. OK, me and Charley go out for dinner all the time, but that's different, because that's what you do with your bird because it's a romantic thing, but for blokes like me and Jason, eating's simply not a social activity. Yeah, we might occasionally drop our guard at chucking-out time and go and order dinner-for-four at the local Indian, but on the whole, when we arrange to meet up on a Friday night, there's not a lot of danger of us accidentally smacking lips because we've started sucking on opposite ends of the same bit of spaghetti.

I think it's different with Charley and her mates, though. They regard food differently. They're not sat around on a Friday night flinging back a load of olives and hummus in order to soak up the Chardonnay just so they can fit a few more glasses in before last orders without falling off their stools. They're savouring the experience of eating and making their highbrow, organic, Mediterranean grub the centrepiece of the evening. And I'm not just talking about the girls or Charley's gay mates here either. Even the straight blokes love kicking up a big stink about their food. I think it's a class thing. And I don't mean to sound like an inverted snob when I say this. There's no right or wrong about it. Only a difference of opinion. Something to do with the way we were all brought up, no doubt.

Now, I mention all of this for a reason, namely to explain the food and the dinner party that followed.

You see, Sandra was a builder's wife. She'd spent most of her adult life cooking to slake the ravenous appetite that walked in off the sites at the end of each day and consequently she'd had about as much experience of sun-blushed tomatoes as Charley had of marking out footings. So, when called upon to knock up a spread to impress, Sandra naturally went for quantity.

Sandra dished Charley out a slab of cottage pie that she should've paid stamp duty on by rights – crisp, golden, meaty, brown and steaming. And the grub didn't stop there. Chips, roasts, veg, gravy and doorsteps all filled the table between us until there was barely any room for conversation.

'Tuck in, go ahead and start, there's plenty more in the kitchen where that lot came from so don't be shy about helping yourselves,' Sandra reassured us all.

'It is just the four of us tonight, isn't it?' I had to double-check. 'I mean, we're not waiting on the rest of the lads by any chance, are we?'

Neither Jason nor Sandra looked up to answer. They'd already strapped on their feed-bags and were going for it big time; a special occasion and a table creaking under the weight of all their favourite foods stretched out before them.

'Oh, this is a lovely bit of grub. Well done, love,' Jason mumbled between forkfuls.

Sandra looked up just long enough to acknowledge her husband and string a load of grunts together that sounded something like 'yeah, that's all right, don't worry about it – eating' before getting her fork working again.

'Are you sure you don't want to wheel in the telly?' I asked, stopping them both in mid-shovel.

'What?' Jason asked, glancing my way and then Charley's.

All credit to Charley, if she was taken aback by Jason and Sandra's trough manners she didn't show it, even when Jason dispensed with the cutlery in favour of two doorsteps of bread and Sandra somehow dipped one of her tits into the gravy boat when reaching across the table for the spuds. She simply smiled pleasantly, chipped away at her cottage pie and cast me a quizzical look as if I'd noticed something no one else in the room had.

'I must say, I do love roast potatoes, but I can never get mine as golden as these,' Charley commented.

Sandra was thrilled to bits by such an admission and spent the next five minutes talking Charley through her own special system, which as far as I could make out seemed to involve nothing more than skinning them, boiling them and bunging them in the oven, but which she somehow made sound more complicated than repairing the Hubble telescope.

Charley promised to give it a go just as soon as she got home and Sandra couldn't have looked more chuffed had Charley asked her to cater at our wedding.

'So, how's everything going between you two, then?' Sandra asked next, for reasons best known to herself, before playfully singing: 'Do I hear wedding bells on the horizon?'

Even Jason put down his knife at that.

'Jesus, love, lay off the poor girl, why don't you?' he chided his wife. 'Please, take no notice, Charley, Sandra's hobby's marrying the rest of the world off.'

'Oh, I'm not saying anything, just a lovely girl like Charley deserves to have a nice husband come home to her,' Sandra kept digging.

'I know, but if you keep going on about it, she might come to the same conclusion and go off and start looking for one,' Jason said, giving me a wink and a nod to show me he was kidding. I was about to drag his face into the steaming-hot cottage pie by way of a retort when Charley caught us all off guard by confessing that she could never marry me because her parents would never approve of the match.

'Daddy always told me if I ever married beneath my station he'd cut me off without a penny and you can't get much farther beneath my station than Terry,' Charley pointed out. 'Still, a girl's got to have her fun, I suppose, so he'll do for the time being, but the moment I grow weary of him I'll upgrade him for a nice rich investment banker and just call on his services occasionally when I need my... what do you call the lead around the chimney again?' she asked me.

'Flashing,' I replied, cold to the core.

'Yes, that's it, when I need my lead flashing repointed,' she chuckled, before cutting one of Sandra's golden potatoes into four and lifting a quarter to her mouth.

It was only then that Charley became acutely aware of the

stunned silence hanging over the table and saw that she had a splendid uninterrupted view of each of our tonsils.

'Er… only joking,' she tentatively explained.

'Oh! Oh, yeah, we know. Ha ha ha!' Jason suddenly boomed, grabbing me by the shoulder and shaking me in agreement. 'I wouldn't let this common bastard near my dog, let alone my daughter if I had one either, so you tell your old man he's all right by me.'

Charley said she'd get straight on the phone.

I also played along and agreed that I wasn't fit to lick the dirt from such a well-to-do bit of crumpet's boots, though much of this was just a desperate attempt to talk over Sandra and stop her from asking Charley which bit she'd been joking about, me being a fucking pleb or her not wanting to marry me?

Mercifully, though, Sandra got with the team and spent the next ten minutes agreeing with Charley and Jason about what an oily undesirable I was until a few of their observations pitched up a bit too near to the truth for comfort and the whole conversation was ditched in favour of more potato talk.

I don't know what it was that knocked me for six about Charley's remarks. It had clearly been intended as a joke right from the start. She hadn't just accidentally blurted out her innermost thoughts and frantically tried to back-pedal with the old 'only joking' loophole when she saw her comments going down like Sandra in a cemetery after four cans of Diamond White. I can completely accept that.

And I can also completely accept that she may have felt a bit awkward about being backed into a corner over the question of *the rest of her life* and where exactly I fitted into it, and had tried to kid her way out of it. That was fairly obvious too.

No, I think what unsettled me most about Charley's joke was precisely what Charley had chosen to joke about. Namely, me, my lower-classness and our complete and utter lack of suitability. It was almost as if she'd peered into the darkest corner of my worst fears, seen that there was a dartboard hanging up there and hit the bull's-eye with her first dart.

It was a hell of a shot.

And I saw that Jason saw it too, as he gave me a right good eyebrow when Charley went to the loo, though neither he nor Sandra sought to wade any farther out into those particular waters.

Not at this time of night.

'Thanks very much for dinner. I had a really lovely time,' Charley told Jason and Sandra at the end of the evening, kissing them both on both cheeks and making Jason blush with surprise.

'You're most welcome,' Jason promised her. 'We're glad you could make it. It was so nice to finally meet you. Tel, I'll see you Monday, cock-a-doodle-doo, son. All right?'

'You too, mate. And thanks, Sand, that was handsome.'

'You're welcome.'

Etc.

We stepped out into the early hours of Sunday morning and struck out for my place. Before we'd got halfway down Jason and Sandra's garden path, though, Sandra decided to risk one last throw of the dice and called on after us, 'Oh, and Charley, don't mind us. He's all right really, I suppose,' she told her, meaning me, I'm guessing.

Charley looked back and smiled.

'I suppose.' She shrugged, before waving one last goodnight and turning back to loop her arm through mine.

And that was it. Not exactly a ringing endorsement but at least she wasn't calling me a dirty peasant and threatening to bin me for bankers any more.

Which, under the circumstances, was about as close to a compliment as I had any right to expect.

I wondered what her old man would say about that.

18 The Domino theory

When Charley was a little girl, she wanted to ride horses for a living. Showjumping, three-day eventing, equestrian stuff, you know, that sort of thing, not delivering milk. I guess this is quite a common ambition with young girls. They have a fascination and love for horses the way that young boys have a fascination and love for dog shit and scrambling over garage roofs. At least, that's what me and my mates were into when we were boys.

Anyway, most girls, though, can't afford to do anything about this inherent yearning. Horses are a lot of money. Stabling fees, vets' bills and carrots, they all add up. And up and up and up, more often than not. But a determined girl can always find a way. A girl who lived across the road from me used to shovel shit at the local stables after school just for a free half-hour at the end of every week, while Charley herself had to... well, actually, she didn't have to do anything as her old man was minted and she was the one and only apple of his eye.

Want a horse? No problem. What colour?

All she had to do was promise that she was serious about the whole thing, that it was no passing fad, and she could have what she liked. Charley duly promised.

Consequently, from the age of eight or nine she used to spend her every waking hour riding, grooming and cuddling a succession of smelly horses and all other times dreaming about them until around about the tender age of eleven she met Domino — her first love.

Naturally Domino was a horse as well, but it's OK to love a horse when you're eleven, so long as you don't expect it to be faithful when the paddock gate gets left open and Buttercup's swishing her tail about next door.

Now Domino wasn't just a biological motorbike to Charley. She really genuinely loved him and the pair of them forged a bond that was to last for most of her early teenage years. Build a time machine and go back to the eighties and you'd find Charley in jodhpurs no matter what time of the day or year you ran into her. She was totally dedicated to her horse, much to the relief of her old man, who'd forked out a few grand to get him for her. Not like me. Not like in our house. When we weren't flushing goldfish down the bog we were off up the pet shop buying some more. We should've probably tried remembering to feed the ones we had once in a while, but who could be arsed when they were only 90p a bag?

So Charley and Domino became best friends. They ate together, hung out together and grew up together. They also started competing in events and collected ribbons and cups from around the county. But it wasn't about the silverware for Charley (or presumably Domino), it was about being together.

Now, you could argue that Charley being an only child, her relationship with Domino took the place of a sibling relationship. That if she'd had brothers or sisters reading her diary every time she was out of the house, like my sister did, she probably wouldn't have felt the need to form such a close attachment to an animal. Possibly. Possibly not. Who knows. I guess it depends what you want to read into it. But these early years are so important in a person's development. They're when you learn how to form relationships. How to maintain them. And how to grow inside them. So this isn't just a story about a little girl who liked horses, this is a story about a girl and her best friend.

OK, so back to 1987 and everything had been going

swimmingly up until this point. Charley had found the love of her life, Domino had found someone to shovel his shit away from his feet and Charley's dad had found a way of making his daughter the happiest little girl in the world. Everyone was a winner.

Or perhaps not, as the case may be.

See, as Charley and Domino got older, the competitions she found herself taking part in got more serious. I'd like to say that Charley rose to the challenge and flourished like a true champion, but unfortunately she didn't. No matter how hard she tried, no matter how much practice she put in, she and Domino just couldn't get anywhere near the podium. There was always someone better than her. And more often than not, there were usually quite a few.

But this was OK, wasn't it? As it was more about being with Domino and taking part than about actually winning, wasn't it? Wasn't it? Of course, it's very easy to say things like this when you're doing well, but when the cups dry up and you suddenly find yourself simply making up the numbers, it's hard not to wonder where it's all gone wrong.

And who's not pulling his weight.

It's also hard not to get frustrated when the career and the future you'd always dreamed of are slipping away before your very eyes.

Two years of dragging her horse around the sticks saw the addition of just two 'thanks for coming' rosettes to her old man's optimistically roomy trophy cabinet, and before very long the competitions started coming and going without Charley and Domino.

I guess there's only so much polite applause one plucky competitor can take, so I can't really blame her for that, but another year of the silver drought saw the weekday visits to the stables peter off along with the cups. Where once Charley had run from school to groom, ride and water the love of her life as regularly as *Newsround*, she now began hanging out with a 'school friend' from next door. Domino got relegated to best-mate-to-visit-on-the-weekends-if-it-wasn't-pissing-it-down-too-much while school study-buddy and future fall-guy Nigel got to knock knees on the bed with Charley as they crammed for their finals. Nice work if you can get it, mate.

The wind continued to blow in this direction until one drizzly Saturday morning, Domino lost his footing while Charley was taking him for a rare trot around the fields and he dismounted Charley on to an exposed tree root, breaking her leg in a couple of places.

Naturally, Charley's dad was distraught – and not just about having spent all that money on baize and plinths – but at how close he'd come to seeing his precious daughter seriously injured. He feared her taking up the reins again and getting back on the horse, as the expression goes, but he needn't have worried because Charley had had enough. She packed in riding from her hospital bed, sold off all her gear and never sat on a horse again. Not even Domino.

Two years later she went to university, then about ten more after that another dumb animal started trotting around her paddock, hoping to get the odd handful of oats.

Anyway, the second animal heard all about the first from the horse's mouth and he came to the conclusion that, as far as horses went – hang on, I'm starting to confuse myself here. Let's drop all the synonyms and analogies for a minute and just lay our cards on the table.

In my opinion, Charley chucked in Domino a bit too lively for my liking. OK, so she wasn't winning her trials any more, and OK, so girls start to notice things other than horses as they blossom into womanhood, but still, it showed a remarkable ability on Charley's part to outgrow her own feelings.

One minute Domino was the love of her life. The next, he was just another fad of childhood put out with the jumble. The same could be said of Hugo at university. Worrying patterns were starting to emerge.

I always wondered what happened to Domino after Charley's old man sold him off. Did he go on to be part of another young girl's life on the equestrian circuit? Or did he go on to be part of a few hundred kebabs on the A10 bypass? I always wanted to ask but it was something of a sensitive subject for Charley so that I'd only really pieced together most of the above after collecting the facts from numerous conversations. She always got a bit choked up when she talked about Domino, and unlike Hugo, he didn't get down Signed For! much, so the conversations never lasted long, but I often wondered if that was because she missed her old four-legged friend or because she felt guilty about binning him so readily. Needless to say, I read more than my fair share into this whole sorry affair, enough to give Sigmund Freud a run for his money, but the lads reckoned I'd gone a bit off piste with this particular theory.

Horses are horses. And men are men, as Jason helpfully pointed out.

But people are people. And that's not just a rather good track by Depeche Mode. If you're fickle in your feelings about one thing then you're fickle in your feelings full stop. You can't change your personality. You might be able to lie to everyone including yourself for a bit, but time will always find you out.

That's what time does. It always exposes a person for who they are.

I thought about Charley and Domino more than I probably should have over the course of a few weeks before eventually putting that particular line of paranoia out to stud. Whatever else had happened to Domino, one thing was at least clear. He'd been loved by Charley once upon a time. And loved very dearly.

Even if it hadn't lasted.

19 Lights, camera, action

was surprised how quickly CT and the BBC got things going on the filming front. I had expected the whole thing to take years and years or simply turn out to be a load of old beer talk when all was said and done – like Lance Corporal War Hero from the Lamb. But sure enough, only seven weeks after it had first been mooted, CT and an assortment of cameramen, sound engineers and clipboard-tickers showed up in shiny new hard hats, brand-new Toe Tecs and designer donkey jackets to bring the whole site to an almighty great grinding halt.

I guess CT must've seen this sort of thing before because the first thing he did was call a meeting of everyone who'd agreed to take part in the documentary (which was everyone) to introduce his people and to urge us to ignore them from that moment onwards.

'You don't have to pretend we're not here, just try to forget why we're here,' CT told the assembled congregation. 'It'll be hard at first, but the more time that goes by, the more you'll get used to us until you'll hardly notice the cameras at all.'

Robbie put his hand up.

'Er, yes, Robbie?' CT asked, after consulting his clipboard.

'What if you're under the scaffolding and we see the scaffolding boys about to sling a loada tubes off the side? Do you want us to say something then?' he asked, winning laughs all round from the lads and one steely glare from Pete, the site agent.

'If you wouldn't mind, yes please,' CT replied with amusement,

scoring a few early points for taking the joke with good humour.
'But for the most part, we'll try to be as unobtrusive as possible.
We'll be shooting a lot of long-range footage and planting
microphones around the site so that we're not hovering over your
shoulders the whole time and hopefully after a few weeks we'll
become as familiar a *sight* on this *site* as Gordon here,' CT said,
prompting the whole compound to erupt with laughter once
again, this time Pete included.

CT looked baffled at having scored such a big laugh by simply
putting the words 'sight' and 'site' in the same sentence and asked
me if we'd not heard that one before.

'It's not that, mate, it's just... oh, you'll see,' I told him,
grinning from ear to ear and unable to look at Gordon, who was
chewing his top lip.

I'm not sure how many bricks we laid that first day. All I'll
say is, I was glad I was on a day rate rather than piecework. CT,
his cameramen, Barrie and Nat, sound engineers, Joel and Neil,
and production assistants, Jill and Elaine, aka Saucy Blonde and
Old Big Tits (well, fair's fair, we were a building site after all, not
New Labour's HQ) spent most of it checking the place over from
the show homes up by the road all the way around to the stakes
in the mud that represented the cul-de-sacs yet to be started,
and like an enormous spider watching its dinner, the site's eyes
followed them wherever they went.

Eric in the forklift was the first to start the showboating.
Riding his JCB around like a rusty yellow Domino and bouncing
it past the cameras at top speed as he dashed here, there and
nowhere in particular in an orgy of hat-tilting nonchalance.

Dennis was the next to tumble, running around the site as if
he had ants in his pants and forgoing ladders wherever possible to
jump stuntman-like off the scaffolding into the sand piles below
until Brian, the health and safety officer, gave him a bollocking
when he caught wind of it. Not that this fazed him, or anyone

else for that matter. The whole site seemed to lose the plot during those first few days of filming, with even the most normally miserable of bastards whistling, yodelling, juggling bricks and working at a rate that would've seen the estate finished and us all out of work two months earlier than scheduled had it continued.

Even Jason started wearing his hard hat back to front like he was some sort of bricky from da hood and only turned it around again when Brian started stapling posters up all around the site stating that protective clothing not worn as instructed was considered not worn at all and anyone found breaching health and safety regulations would be sent home, ending Jason's gangster-bricky phase.

Whether you believe me or not, the fact of the matter was that I was one of the few blokes not to go nuts when the cameras rolled up. And it wasn't because I was too cool for school or a consummate construction professional or anything like that, I just had other things on my mind. And you don't need to be able to bend spoons for a living to guess what.

All in all, it had been a little under six months since me and Charley had got together and our relationship had strayed on to a bit of a plateau. We were still seeing each other regularly and going for dinner, going for drinks and going to the pictures, but more and more it seemed to be in the company of her friends. CT and Russell, Clive and Simone, Adam and Lis, Ben and Nadia, Stephen and Louise, Greg and Katie. A never-ending production line of his and hers to share pancetta, Pinot and Polanski with. Don't get me wrong, most of them were nice enough, even to me. I just wondered what had happened to mine and Charley's time. Other than waking up next to her or sitting in a cab destined for Graham and Tanya's, Malcolm and Philippa's, Andrew and Sally's, or any number of other dinner parties, drinks and modern art exhibitions, I rarely got to see Charley on her own these days. We'd become a couple.

I know this was something I should've liked but oddly enough it wasn't. Because it seemed like the one thing couples were attracted to more than each other were other couples. And the one person they never seemed to talk to when they were out with other couples was the matching half of their own couple.

I lost count of the number of conversations I had about the TV show; when it would be on, how long the shoot would be, whether I'd be the star of it and whether or not I was free to come round and retile Clive's kitchen for nothing. I was not.

In fact, the one couple I never got to meet in all that time was her mum and dad, and the two weekends Charley disappeared back to Berkshire to attend family functions, my presence was noticeably not required. I guess parents and friends have different amusement levels when it comes to watching hairy-arsed brickies trying to butter bread rolls with fish knives.

Yes, it was still on my mind, that comment. You know, the one about me being beneath her station. That was still bugging me.

Why had she said it? Why had she chosen to make that joke? It must've been something that had crossed her mind in the past, otherwise how else could she have even come up with it? Everyone knows that all great jokes contain a seed of truth, which meant that this particular seed was planted somewhere in Charley's brain and that one day it would grow into a mighty oak of doubt and misgiving. Particularly when she was no longer winning ironic ribbons for being with me. And this is in spite of the fact that I know oaks don't grow from seeds, they grow from acorns, but an 'acorn of doubt' didn't sound right and a 'mighty tree' sounded like I didn't know the names of any big trees when I did. Just none that grew from seeds.

Anyway, all of this stuff must've taken a stroll around her mind at some point or another and if it had, then she had probably also got to wondering what our long-term chances were like, because you don't get yourself in a tizz worrying about parental approval and inheritances when you're simply sowing your wild oats, do you? Which meant that somewhere along the line Charley had also probably pictured us in fifty years' time, old and grey and holding hands, rocking backwards and forwards on our porch together and moaning about the price of robot oil, to see if she liked the image.

Cue thoughts of stations, Daddy and money.

Oh, what was the point? I knew how this was all going to end before it had even started so why was I even surprised? I mean, Christ, if this stuff had occurred to me, Tel the thicky trowel, then it had to have occurred to a clever girl like Charley. And her mates. And her parents – at least it would've had they known about me.

And that's probably what disheartened me the most. Because I could see it coming. I could see it coming from a mile off in fact. It was like going into a builder's merchants when you've forgotten your measurements, taking a chance and buying a couple of metre-wide sash-window frames, only to get them home and find you needed one-ten all along. I've done stuff like this before in my time. Most people have, I expect, and it's not the fact that your windows don't fit that gets you swearing when you get home, it's the fact that you sat in traffic for a hour and a half thinking to yourself, 'These windows are the wrong windows. I know they are. I fucking know it,' making the resultant 'See, I fucking *knew* it!' all the sweeter when you push them through your big gaps.

Not that Charley was getting me angry, you understand. That was probably just a bad analogy. I should stick to oak seeds in future. No, quite the opposite in fact. The whole situation was just making me sad because the more weeks that passed, the more it felt like I was turning on to the last straight of a ride that I didn't want to get off.

But I was going to have to. Because all good things come to

an end. And this was a very good thing. So the end was going to come with that much more of a bump.

I dwelt on this thought as I slowly chewed my egg sandwich in the passenger seat of Jason's van.

One day, Charley would finish with me. I knew this was going to happen. And it wasn't like knowing that one day I was going to die or that one day the taxman was going to catch up with me because this was something that was going to happen sooner rather than later and I was never going to be able to get rid of that apprehensive crease in my brow until I'd been through the worst of it, much like an amputation I kept putting off.

'Smile, then,' Jason told me, pouring us both a cup of tea from his two-litre flask.

'What?' I said, looking up from my sandwich.

'I said smile,' he repeated, handing me a cup and nodding towards the side window.

I looked around and almost spilt my tea when I saw my sullen puss reflected back in a big black camera lens.

'Shit.'

'Exactly,' Jason replied. 'Creep up on you, don't they?'

My reflection continued to stare back at me for another couple of seconds before moving off to stare at someone else.

'How long were they there?'

'About two minutes,' Jason guessed. 'Can't wait for that particular episode. I've always wanted to see myself eating Scotch eggs while reading the paper.'

'Who hasn't dreamt of that?'

'Think it'll make *Pick of the Day*?'

'I'm sure it'll be everyone's favourite bit,' I mulled.

We watched the camera team move from car to car, filming the lads and their lunch until the clock struck half past one and we went back to work. We'd started an oversite this morning and were just moving inside to take up the internal walls, but Gordon had other plans for me.

'Fancy doing a couple of chimneys, Tel? Roy's just lifted the scaffold on those gables we did yesterday.'

I looked around and saw that CT and Barrie had followed us inside and were settling in for a gripping afternoon of breeze blocks and banter, so I dropped my trowel into my bucket, grabbed my level and headed for the rooftops.

Grateful to leave the showmen to their show and return my head to the clouds.

20 The poshos are revolting

The following Saturday morning Charley phoned me up and asked me if I was doing anything that afternoon. Normally, I spent my afternoons in Catford doing my shopping, doing a bit of tidying around the flat and killing a few brain cells in front of the box before going up to Charley's for the evening, so something was afoot.

'Er, why's that?' I tentatively asked, wary of committing until I'd made sure that Clive wasn't laying a patio and wondering if I'd be able to give him 'a hand'. It wasn't that, though.

'It's just that a bunch of us are going on the World as One march and I just wondered if you wanted to come along too,' she told me.

'What's the World as One march?' I asked, suddenly in a patio-laying mood after all.

'You know, the anti-globalisation rally. It's been in all the papers all week,' she pointed out.

This may have been true, it may have been in the papers all week, but not everything that made it into the papers automatically made it into my brain. Party politics, Euro news, trade negotiations and celebrity sightings all went the same way as the previous evening's football reports when it came to my tea-break flick. In fact, few headlines got me turning the page faster than something like 'Tessa Jowell Climbs Down over Legislation', though I would've probably given 'Tessa Jowell Climbs Down over Ledge' a look if somebody underneath had snapped off a couple of sneaky pictures. That was around the sort of news I could just about handle at ten o'clock in the morning.

Anti-globalisation rallies were never going to get me forgetting about my sandwiches.

'No, sorry, I must've missed it. What is it?' I admitted.

'It's a rally against world poverty and the IMF,' she explained. 'It starts in Hyde Park and then goes all the way along Oxford Street and around Whitehall and finishes in Green Park. There are other rallies all over the world too, in America, across Europe, Australia, Japan and even China. Millions of us are marching on every continent to raise awareness,' she said, making me wonder why I needed to miss the Saturday afternoon matinee, then, when they sounded like they pretty much had things covered without me.

'Right, yeah, sounds... er, great,' I told Charley, in two minds over whether or not to ask her if there was going to be a beer tent or if this was a bring-your-own-booze sort of shindig. In the event, I decided to play it safe and simply ask how much tickets were.

'It's free, you lummox. There aren't any tickets. It's a rally,' Charley told me, a hint of amusement in her voice.

'Oh yeah, no, I know that. I mean, what about when they bring the buckets around? Do we just chuck in a couple of quid or something or are they going to want bank details, because I'm a bit skint at the moment what with the old...?'

'No, Terry, this is a political rally, not a fund-raiser. You won't be asked to contribute anything, just your voice,' she assured me.

'Oh. Oh, all right, then. Yeah, sure. I mean, if it's for a good cause,' I told her. 'Where shall I meet you, then?'

I've never been to a football match before but I've occasionally made the mistake of trying to drive through Selhurst on a Saturday afternoon when Palace were playing at home, so I've seen what crowds look like. Let me tell you this, though, those football crowds had nothing on the crowds that greeted me at Hyde Park – in terms of numbers or duffel coats.

I'd caught the train to London Bridge, then the Tube up to Bank and then along to Marble Arch, and the closer the train had got to my stop, the more the carriage had swelled. All along the Central Line the platforms had been mobbed, though at first I just put this down to it being Saturday afternoon and central London being what it was. But more and more people squeezed aboard our train until there was barely any room left for air. And that was when I suddenly remembered just how much I hated central London.

It probably took fifteen minutes to get from platform level at Marble Arch to the surface, though even once out of the station the whole place was still heaving. It was particularly packed around the entrance of the Tube itself, making me wish I'd chosen another spot to rendezvous with Charley and her mates. But luck shone on me when a nearby lamp-post became free and I suddenly had something to lean against...

... for the next forty-five minutes.

'Oh, hello. Hello [kiss kiss]. You haven't been waiting long, have you?' Charley said, all in an excited tizz with herself.

'Grumble grumble fucking grumble,' I replied, practically biting my tongue in two, though Charley wasn't really listening.

'Ooh, where's Clive and Simone? Are they not here yet?' she asked.

'I haven't seen them,' I replied. 'Look, just give them a call in a bit and arrange to meet them somewhere else, like across the road, or in the park, or in a pub. Anywhere. But let's just get away from here, can we, please?' I pleaded, my patience shaved down to punching point by a never-ending procession of worthies, Worzels and wankers who'd walked straight out of the Tube station and straight into me without so much as an 'excuse me, mate'.

'Hold on, just got to wait for CT and Hugo,' Charley told me, really topping off my day.

Not Hugo. Not that gooseberry.

'All right, geezer? Fucking mental, innit? *Wasstheword*?' Hugo gor-blimeyed when he bounded into view. I reluctantly shook his hand to say hello but pulled it free before he could go through his geezer pat-a-cake routine with me again. Hugo was the last person I wanted to see on this rally, but at least I was here to keep an eye on him and Charley.

Hmm, small-minded, jealous, control freakdom. Not good.

I shook this thought from my mind and passed my hand over to CT.

'Glad you could make it,' CT smiled, making do with a simple handshake. 'Surprised to see you here, to be frank.'

'Me? No, I love this stuff, I do,' I told him. 'What are we burning again today? Books or bras? I brought both with me this morning just to be on the safe side.'

After a token five minutes waiting for Clive and Simone, we chucked in the towel and upped stakes for Hyde Park across the road, and once through the gates we were able to fan out and reclaim a little personal space – a luxury I hadn't known since Holborn.

'Look at this, it's well naughty, innit,' Hugo reckoned, eyeing all the 'smash the system' placards through his new two-hundred-quid Police sunglasses before taking a shitload of photos on his iPhone and emailing them to himself at home. Unbelievable. Him and Charley. Unbelievable.

Unlike the crowds I got stuck behind at Palace, the individuals who made up this jumbled jamboree looked a right pick 'n' mix lot. Student types mingled with pullover-wearers, crusties rubbed shoulders with trendies, and anarchist punks queued patiently behind dyed-in-the-wool union rabble-rousers to sign petitions handed out by professional protesters. About the only people not here seemed to be people like me. But then again I guess it was Saturday afternoon, they were all at Palace or Spurs or QPR or West Ham, cheering on their teams and shouting names at the man in black rather than lobbying to have his debts cancelled.

We sidestepped our way farther and farther into the park, towards a big raised stage and the ever-thickening crowds, until we could go no farther. Smelly, dirty eco types and chubby little fat student birds hemmed us in on all sides so that it was like being back on the Tube all over again, despite the fact that we were stood in the middle of three hundred and fifty acres of open parkland.

'Do we have to be this close?' I asked. 'They have got microphones, you know. We'll hear them from back there too.'

'But I want to get a picture of Annie Lennox,' Hugo argued, keen to show his commitment to the cause. 'I heard she's going to speak.'

'Well, as long as she doesn't fucking sing,' I replied, scoring a turn of the head and an angry glare from some frumpy little tub of pent-up frustration in front of me.

Annie wasn't the only celebrity on show either. More than a dozen actors, pop stars and politicians pencilled themselves in to thump the poor and needy's drum for them this afternoon, and my mind couldn't help but drift back to the last big celebrity showcase that was supposed to have made a difference – Live 8. I didn't go to it or nothing, I just saw it on the telly, but I specifically remembered it because act after act came out onstage and gave themselves, the crowd and everyone who'd tuned in a big collective pat on the back for making history and changing the world. Hallelujah, and aren't we the bee's bollocks?

Yet here we were all over again. The same old faces, the same old placards, the same old poverty and the same old rallying cries. The only things that had changed were the T-shirts.

So what had happened?

I don't know. Smarter blokes than me could probably tell you, but I'll take an uneducated guess if you like and say that half, if not three-quarters, of all the people who turned out for these sorts of parties probably didn't really give a tuppenny fuck about world poverty. Not *really*. Of course everyone cares. Hugo cares. I care. My dad cares. The lads on the site care. How can you not when there are children starving in the world?

But there's a world of difference between caring and being seen to care.

A good proportion of the people at this rally, I reckoned, were more interested in having a cause to get in a strop about at parties and a nice little collection of wrist bands than actually changing the world. And I mean genuinely, seriously changing the world. All the students, the crusties, the trendies and the punks, the pullover-wearers, the rabble-rousers, the eating disorders and the activists; they looked on the surface like a wide and diverse cross-section of society, but to me they all looked like they'd probably grown up in the nicest houses in the leafiest suburbs and arrived here via three years of Student Union sit-ins.

Of course, this could just be me generalising and I'll be the first to hold up my hands and admit that I can't see into other people's souls, but this is how it seemed to me after six months on the Islington dinner party circuit. It was so often about image for so many of them.

I was there.
I led from the front.
I cheered the loudest.
I cared the most.
I manned the barricades.
And I got a picture of me with Annie Lennox.

It's a nice story to tell your mates and it shows you've got a social conscience if you've put in the hours weeping over the little people, but does it actually make the slightest bit of difference to anyone? I mean, *real*, *actual*, *serious* difference?

Of course it doesn't. How could it? Marching in a big circle around London, stopping the traffic and closing Oxford Street for the afternoon. How was that going to feed one starving orphan, African or otherwise? I couldn't figure it out, but like I say, I'm not really all that clued up about these things.

All I did know was that Charley, Hugo and CT – oh, and Clive and Simone, who'd just caught up with us – got paid about a quarter of a million pounds between them for flogging us ketchup, publicising celebrities, managing unit trusts, laminating pinboards and filming me eating my sandwiches, yet here they all were rallying against the unnecessary excesses of Western capitalism.

I'd heard Charley herself one night moan on and on and on about the Kyoto Treaty (that's the international treaty against carbon emissions and climate control, etc.), slamming America for not signing up to it and bashing Brown for not agreeing to stricter targets, yet when we got back to her place I found every light in her flat burning away and the heating on.

'Are you growing orchids or something?' I'd asked her at the time, to which Charley apologised and explained that she'd forgot. But this wasn't the only time Charley forgot about that planet she had a sticker of on her rucksack. Newspapers, bottles, jars and tins all regularly went in the bin rather than the recycling, the curtains usually stayed open at night while the heating was on, the taps stayed on while her teeth were being brushed and the telly, stereo and computer all ticked over quietly on stand-by whenever she wasn't around to use them. What's more, she had more shoes than some African countries and she never holidayed in Europe, let alone Britain, which meant costly plane rides and cubic tons of CO_2, according to Big John at work.

Don't get me wrong, I'm not exactly a saint myself. I only

close the curtains, turn off taps and lights, switch off the telly and head to Spain or Devon for my holidays simply because I can't afford to throw away good money after bad lighting and heating the street and seeing what the beaches in Bali look like compared to those on the Costa. If I'd had Charley's sort of money, maybe I wouldn't care if my heating bill was triple what it was or ever wear the same pair of socks twice or something, like millionaires are supposed not to. Maybe I'd live the comfortable, spendthrift life that financial security brings and look to other people on other continents for my worries. Then again, who knows? Too late to second guess how I might've turned out if I'd been born to money, so what difference did it make one way or the other?

She was who she was and I was who I was.

And we just had to make the best of it.

'Here, let's get a picture of you two together,' Hugo insisted, backing away a step and snapping off a shot of Charley and possibly me if there was enough room in the frame.

He pressed a few buttons and called the image up on screen, then giggled at it hysterically and told us it was wicked.

'Look at Terry's face!' He laughed, showing it all around and then to me, though I couldn't see what the problem was. It was just my face. The same one I'd had on all day. 'Here, now take a picture of me and Charley,' he ordered me, thrusting his iPhone into my hands and wrapping his arms around Charley's shoulders in a way that almost won him two hands wrapped around the throat. 'Make sure you get the stage and all the banners in.'

I reluctantly took a couple of pictures of Charley and Hugo pulling faces and raising their fists in militant defiance before handing him back his iPhone when the celebrity speeches started.

I can't remember everything of what was said that afternoon but here's a few highlights:

According to some barmaid off *EastEnders*, thirty thousand children died in Africa every day – something like one every three seconds – and this could be wiped out overnight with an aid and grants package in the region of £40 billion, half of which could be achieved by debt cancellation and a restructuring of something or other that I'd never heard of and didn't really understand.

Next up was a stand-up comedian who I'd only ever seen in crisp adverts who gave an impassioned plea on behalf of some poor little Ugandan girl who had AIDS, no money for medicine and no chance of seeing her fourteenth birthday.

Then some singer did her bit. Then half the cast off *The Bill* did theirs. Then a few more bods who hadn't had a hit in a while said a few words. Then someone I didn't know. Then some politician who looked like he needed the publicity. Then someone off *Big Brother* who looked like he needed a punch in the gob. Then someone else. And then someone else. And then someone else. Each having their say and each whipping up the crowd into more and more of a fervour until I could no longer hear what the people on stage were saying because the clamour for justice, vengeance and the president of the United States' gizzard had all but taken over.

Look, I'll say this right off the bat, that I've got nothing but sympathy for the world's starving. If they'd passed round a bucket, I would've put into it. If they'd handed me a petition I would've signed it. If they'd proposed putting a penny on all of our taxes to fly medicine out to them, I would've voted for it. I would've done any of these things and more (with the possible exception of buying Annie Lennox's new CD) but they weren't. In fact they weren't asking us to do anything, nothing at all except walk around London and shout slogans at all the Day-Glo coppers who'd been drafted in to chaperone us around the streets.

I simply didn't get it.

Style over substance, that's what it was. Style over substance.

'Down with the IMF! Down with the IMF!' Hugo was

shouting along, jumping up and down with the tubbies in front and filming himself on his iPhone.

'Where's this march going again?' I asked CT.

'Down Oxford Street and then Whitehall,' he replied.

'Think we'll be passing any pubs?' I wondered out loud, but before CT had a chance to answer, Charley spotted the crowds moving off.

'Hey, look, we're going,' she pointed out. 'Quick, everyone stick together.'

She linked her arm through mine and held on tight as the crowds around us started to jostle for a bit before finally moving. A few moments later we were marching through the park in step with a hundred thousand comrades, passing through the gates and straight out into a tunnel of coppers.

'Fucking look at 'em all! Fucking pigs!' some punchy scarecrow next to me screamed when he saw the lines of police on either side. 'Fuck the pigs! Fuck the pigs!' he began shouting, prompting one of the chubby little militants Hugo had been bouncing along with to start chanting the same.

'Pigs? Bit rich coming from her, isn't it?' I pointed out, but this was lost in the commotion as crusties all around us erupted into a chorus of 'Death to Bush'. Personally speaking, I couldn't see what this had to do with that poor little girl in Africa who'd had AIDS or how Bush, Brown, Blair, 'the pigs' or Daddy's death was ever going to help her or anyone else for that matter, but more and more people began joining in, waving their fists at the steely-faced coppers and flicking two fingers at the helicopters circling above.

To be fair, a lot of people in the crowd looked pretty upset at some of the more antagonistic elements they found themselves marching alongside and scuffles broke out all around us as a few of the braver do-gooders tried to take on the obvious troublemakers. By the time half a dozen punches had been thrown in half a dozen different directions the Old Bill nearby had no choice but to wade in, and before we knew it people were starting to get carted away.

'I think I can see how this one's going to pan out,' I shouted in Charley's ear, sidestepping some screeching Swampy who was going mental underneath a dirty great pile of determined-looking coppers and almost walking smack bang into someone who was having a game of overcoat tug-of-war with two more brave boys in blue.

'Bit boisterous, isn't it?' CT cracked, his face a mixture of concern and amusement.

A few of the more opinionated gasbags inevitably opened up at the Old Bill as they put their handcuffs to good use, screaming at them to 'let 'em go, you fucking pigs', only to find themselves face down on the tarmac two seconds later underneath a few 'fucking pigs' of their own.

'Come on, let's just keep walking,' I urged Charley, steering her away from one almighty hippy cull and between several others. 'Ooops. Sorry, mate. Mind your backs. Coming through.'

It's amazing just how quickly things descend into chaos. One moment I was part of a peaceful demo, taking to the streets to highlight the plight of those less fortunate than ourselves, the next I was part of a mob, hell-bent on trouble and a punch-up with the Old Bill. Halfway down Oxford Street – and I'm surprised we even made it that far – the whole march fell apart at the seams and all hell broke loose outside John Lewis.

'Kill the pigs! KILL THE PIGS!' came the cries again, as traffic cones, rubbish bins, newspaper stands and signposts flew past our ears in all directions.

I looked around and saw that we'd lost CT, Clive and Simone somewhere farther back, but Hugo was still with us – obviously, his head down and iPhone now well out of sight to save it being snatched out of his hand and used to knock some copper's hat off with.

'Fuck this shit!' he shouted, and for once I was in full agreement with the little tosser.

A lot of shops in the street had seen this coming and had had the foresight to board their shopfronts up in anticipation of the march. Those that hadn't came to regret it as unprotected doors and windows were put through in the name of the poor and needy, though I was still scratching my head to understand how this was helping anyone except poor and needy glaziers and coppers, who were all presumably on double time for this particular knees-up.

From out of nowhere, a loose elbow whacked Charley square in the face and she shrieked and fell back, clutching her mouth. I caught her before she hit the deck and shoved the fucking dickhead who'd swung it with all of my might, sending him head first into a knot of punchy crusties and as far away from us as possible.

'Hugo, help us here!' I shouted, pulling Charley to her feet and doing my best to shield her from all the pushing and shoving that was going on all around us. Hugo quickly came to Charley's aid and we sandwiched her between us and gave her the once-over to make sure she was OK. She had an enormous red mark on her face that would turn a lovely shade of blue given a couple of days, and her bottom lip was split down the middle and pumping blood all over her chin.

'We've got to get out of here,' Hugo shouted, and for the second time in as many minutes I found myself agreeing with him. Remarkable.

The protesters... or were they rioters by now? Well, let's stick with protesters for the time being. Anyway, these twats were now demolishing everything in sight and pulling up steel benches and street railings to use against the chipboard covers protecting Debenhams, Burtons, Next and a dozen or so other shops I'll be setting up standing orders with the day I'm rich enough to pull on brand-new socks every morning.

I couldn't understand why the Old Bill weren't steaming into them with all batons blazing, but Hugo pointed out that they'd pulled back and formed up into lines on each side of us.

'Oh, fantastic, just what we need.'

'I reckon we should turn back and go the way we came,' Hugo suggested, over the din of screams and the blare of sirens. This sounded reasonable to me, as the road up ahead was now jam packed up with protesters, while every side street and turning was barricaded with police horses and paddy wagons. About the only way left open to us was the way we'd just come. As things turned out, we'd been closer to the rear of the march than the front, so there was every chance we might be able to duck out of this mess before the Old Bill closed it off, hemming us in on all sides.

Unfortunately, before we got five yards, the left flank of our riot collapsed and protesters began sprinting in our direction, chased from behind by a roar of intimidation and a tidal wave of Day-Glo yellow. Instinctively, we turned with the crowd and legged it from the oncoming roar. Me, Charley and Hugo ran as one, ducking from side to side through the shifting maze of fleeing bodies and into whatever space we could find. I wasn't sure which way I was running, it's all pretty confusing when you're in the middle of a stampede. We just went with the crowd and after a few hundred yards found ourselves gummed up in the centre of an enormous cluster of bodies, bang smack in the middle of Oxford Circus.

I don't know how many of us there were in there, but there was barely a square foot of open tarmac anywhere to be seen. The place actually looked like it had been flooded – flooded with people. We lapped at the walls and the chipboard covers of the surrounding shops and flowed out across the Circus in a nice even dollop, so that only the tops of the street signs could be seen above the sea of jostling heads.

'Shit, you know what, I reckon we should've stayed where we were. Crouched on the floor and let the Old Bill run straight over us,' it suddenly occurred to me. 'Because I don't think we're making it to Green Park any time soon.'

Oxford Circus ran off in four main directions: Oxford Street to the east and west, and Regent's Street to the north and south. All four ways were now blocked by an enormous knot of luminous jackets and ten or so thousand protesters raged, snarled and hurled their remaining mobile phones at four banks of perspex shields as they struggled to either break free or win themselves a coconut.

Noticeably, we no longer counted the pullover-wearers or the real trendies among our ranks. Most of the people caught in this trap were crusties, punks, rabble-rousers and the professional troublemakers who'd probably had something like this in mind all along. As for the rest of the march, I couldn't tell you. Either they'd all done a runner once the trouble had started or made it to Green Park and were now listening to Annie Lennox congratulating them on a job well done – that was, if she wasn't in here with us lot, chucking bottles at the Old Bill and kicking McDonald's window in on behalf of the people of Tanzania.

'Leth get out oth here,' Charley lisped, holding her bottom lip to try to stem the flow of blood.

'Yeah, come on, let's go home,' Hugo agreed, and together we turned and tried to push our way back through the tangled mass of torsos blocking our way.

It was impossible trying to chop our way through as a threesome, so we unlinked arms and fought our way through as individuals. Hugo led the way, followed by Charley and then me. The closer we got to the police lines, though, the tighter the crowds became until, twenty feet from the front, we ground to a halt. The crowds had formed up to push back against the police, but the police were trained for this sort of thing and able to hold their lines.

'Kill the pigs! Kill the pigs!' the chant continued unabated, and I was rapidly losing my patience with the rest of Oxford Circus.

'Oi, you want to stick a sock in it so we can all get out of here?' I told one spotty little anarchist who was hanging on to a lamp-post and screaming blue bloody murder from the safety of the rear.

'Fuck off,' he spat back, outraged that anyone should try to oppress his free democratic right to incite murder. I half considered giving him a quick taster of Mr Left and Mr Right while Charley wasn't looking, but that would've been like taking a spark to a powder keg, so I settled for flicking him several of my fingers before continuing towards the front.

'It's too jammed, we can't get through,' Hugo called back, a dozen or so feet short of the swaying ranks at the front. We looked about and saw there were fewer people off to the sides, so we struck out in that direction, chopping, squeezing and pushing our way through the masses towards the boarded-up shop windows of Benetton's.

Once again, we got to within about twenty feet of the grey stone walls before grinding to a halt.

'Thith ith impothible,' Charley protested with frustration.

Over the chants of the crowd, I heard the cold metallic voice of authority appealing for calm through a squeaky loudhailer.

'You have been detained under Section One of the Public Order Act and we are permitted to hold you for as long as necessary to protect persons and property and...' the voice got as far as telling everyone before it was drowned out by the ever-popular 'Kill the pigs! Kill the pigs!'

The voice did have one coincidental effect on the crowd, however. As it had come from the other side of the Circus, the east side, some of our ranks broke away from the west and made their way across to confront it, leaving enough gaps for me, Charley and Hugo to squeeze through to the front.

When we got there, we found a line of grim-eyed policemen, three deep at least, behind a see-through barrier of perspex shields.

'Sorry about this, mate, but can we just get through there, please?' I asked the copper directly in front of me. The copper didn't answer. He just stared into oblivion and stood his ground, bracing himself against the swell. 'It's all right, mate, we ain't with these fucking idiots, we just got caught up in it, that's all,' I tried to explain, but the copper either didn't care or had been taken on during 'hire a deafo' week.

'Pleath let uth throogh,' Charley then tried, with about as much success as me, until I pointed out that she'd been injured in the trouble and needed looking at. This finally brought a flicker to the copper's face, so he told me to step back and swap places with Charley.

I did as he said, assuming he just wanted to give her the once-over, but the moment she stepped towards him, the shields parted and Charley was immediately sucked inside.

'Hold on,' I said, as the shields closed behind her and I watched in vain as she was passed back through the lines and disappeared from sight. 'Wait, we're with her, can we go too, mate?' I asked, pointing to Hugo and myself, but the copper was once again deaf to all requests and back to practising his poker face.

'Would that be all right?' Hugo double-checked.

When Hugo didn't get a response he looked at me and asked me what we were going to do. I didn't know; join in with 'Kill the pigs' was about all I could think of.

'Here, I'll give my dad a ring,' Hugo then said, pulling his iPhone out of his pocket and making me and the copper look at each other for the briefest of moments before he remembered his training and snapped back to neutral behind his clear perspex shield.

'What's he got, a tank or something?' I asked, but Hugo was already busily jabbering on to his old man.

He talked for about five minutes, explaining exactly where we were, what we were doing here, how none of it was our fault and how we were worried things were going to really kick off in a minute, before pocketing his phone and telling me and the copper to both hang tight.

'Seriously, Hugo, who is your dad?' I asked again.

Hugo didn't want to say in front of the police, who were now suddenly all ears, so he told me he was no one special and left it at that.

'Really? Mine neither,' I replied, picturing both of our dads coming down here in their vests and slippers to have a go at everyone and pull us from the crowd.

'Our bloody tea's on the table an' all, you little bastards,' they'd say, then clip us around the ears and drag us both home for our fish fingers.

Half an hour passed and I was just starting to believe that Hugo's dad really was nothing special when a call came up from the rear and the coppers in front of us shouted back to confirm their numbers.

A few seconds later an inspector poked his head over their shoulders and looked directly at us.

'Is one of you Hugo Baker?' the inspector asked, to my complete and utter amazement.

'Yes, that's me,' Hugo confirmed as quietly as he could.

'Have you got any ID on you?' the inspector then asked, so Hugo pulled his wallet out of his pocket and held his Oyster photocard against the clear perspex shield for the inspector to inspect. 'OK,' he agreed, giving the coppers either side of him a pat, before disappearing again.

'Fuck me, I don't believe it. Just who the hell is your...' I started to say, but I was cut short when my po-faced copper mate told me to step away from the shield and Hugo to step towards it.

'Just hold your fucking horses, John, I've seen this one already,'

I warned them both, grabbing Hugo and hanging on to him until I'd double-checked something with the copper. 'Are we both getting out of here or are you just letting him go?'

'No, it's both of us,' Hugo reassured me.

'Oh yeah? And how d'you know that?' I asked.

'Well, I did say, didn't I? I told my dad we were both in here so I'm sure he told them to get us both out,' Hugo reasoned.

'Yeah, that's right. And I'm sure on my birthday and bank holidays he kisses my picture goodnight at bedtime just before he kisses yours,' I agreed, my fingers still tightly wrapped around his arm. 'But let's just check first before we go rushing off anywhere, shall we?'

We looked at the copper behind the perspex shield and put the question to him again, and I have to say his answer didn't exactly inspire me.

'Let go of your mate's arm and step away from the shield if you please, sir. I won't tell you again.'

I see.

'No, wait,' Hugo said. 'He's with me. You're meant to let us both out.'

'Look, sir, you can either come out or you can stay where you are. It's all the same to me,' the copper replied, fully sympathetic with Daddy's little boy and his mate's plight.

Hugo looked at me and scratched his chin. That's right, it certainly was a tricky one and no mistake, but miracle of miracles, Hugo came up with the perfect solution.

'Terry, let me go through and speak to this inspector and I'll get him to let you out too.'

'And what if he says no?' I asked, on the off-chance the inspector didn't give two flying fiddlesticks about me.

'Well then, I'll just call my dad again and get him to put in a word for you too.'

'Why don't you just give him a call now?' I said, but I already knew it didn't make any odds. Hugo had been given a green light, so whatever else came of today, it was pointless us both hanging around here indefinitely. He knew it and I knew it. Personally, given the choice between being trapped somewhere alone or being trapped somewhere with Hugo, I would've happily taken alone every time, except in circumstances where I needed to use him as food...

And when Charley was already out there somewhere.

'Come on,' Hugo tried again, tapping my hand.

I chewed all possible considerations over as he nodded hopefully at me, before reluctantly releasing the fucker. Well, what else was there to do? Let Charley hear I'd held him back for no good reason? She'd see right through it.

You small-minded, jealous control freak. You didn't trust me? You thought I'd cheat on you? With Hugo? Like I did to Nigel? How could you think that?

No, it was an unhappy set of circumstances and no mistake. A no-win situation, I believe they call it. All I could do was act reasonably and hope it caught on. I let go of Hugo and ground my teeth.

'All right, but you talk to that inspector. Explain the situation to him and get him to let me out too,' I told him, and Hugo nodded enthusiastically like it was a done deal.

'No worries geezer,' he said, holding out a fist for me to knock knuckles with. I played along just this once, just to get out of here, but made a mental note to jump in front of a train if I ever found myself playing potatoes or comparing cocks with Hugo on a regular basis. 'Wicked, bruv, just you hang tight.'

Hugo turned and told the copper he was ready and I could see from the copper's face just how choked he was at having to let this particular one go.

A moment later, the shields parted like a super-fast supermarket doorway, and Hugo was sucked through. They closed right behind him again and Hugo disappeared from sight, leaving me in the firing line of a dozen pairs of suddenly suspicious eyes.

'Fucking copper's narc,' I heard someone say behind me, while others started to talk loudly behind my back about how they couldn't remember seeing me protesting at the pigs at any point during the last half an hour or so.

'Oh, for crying out loud,' I groaned, my mind awash with wishes, the most prominent of which was the one where I was wearing a comedy rucksack stuffed full of spring-loaded boxing gloves.

The coppers in front of me had precious little sympathy either. They now hated me as much as the twats behind did, lumping me in with Hugo as some spoilt little brat who was born with a silver spoon in his gob and a 'get out of jail free' card in his top pocket.

'Seriously, mate, I don't know him. He's just my girlfriend's... friend. The one with the bloody lip who you let through earlier. Remember?' I explained to the copper, but he didn't look like he cared much. Like he'd said, it was all the same to him. I just had to sit tight and wait until he was told by his superiors to let me out.

So that's what I did. I waited. I waited and waited and waited. And eventually the inspector gave the order and I was let out.

Six hours later.

Along with everyone else.

21 Done by the pigs

*I*went home when I finally got out. I'd had a text message a few hours earlier from Charley letting me know that they were all in the Workers' Social (where else?), but I just wanted to get away from London, get away from the crowds and get away from people. I felt like punching something – or someone – and that's not the sort of mood I could be around Charley in. I was starving hungry, miserably knackered, busting for a piss and so far from the end of my tether that I could actually see where the other end was tied.

Had I walked into the Workers' Social, seen them all happily tucked up and blissfully drunk and then got a welcoming cheer from that *cunt!!!!* Hugo, I think I would've fucking strangled the little bastard. Seriously. And it wouldn't have been for not wangling me out of that mess with him – if he'd even tried. Or for sniffing around my girlfriend, or for causing me no end of small-minded, jealous, control-freaking anguish. All that was immaterial. I was beyond motivation. I would've simply strangled him because strangling him would've made me feel better. My fists were outraged that three of their best mates, my back, my legs and my poor old aching plates, had been made to suffer so much for so little and they were in no mood to need reasons. Any loudmouthed Mockney cock-smoker in a flat cap and Police sunglasses who stood up to give me a gleeful cuddle would've happily done.

So I went home.

I went home to protect Hugo. I went home to protect Charley. But most of all, I went home to protect myself. I went home. I had a load of chips. And I murdered a bottle of Scotch.

It ruffled my hair all the next day that Charley had just pissed off to her swanky wanky pub without so much as a backwards glance. It didn't matter that there was nothing she could've done for me once the inspector had given me the thumbs-down. That was beside the point. The point was she'd just gone off and enjoyed herself with her mates while I'd been boxed in that misery. And not just me, as it turned out. Simone had got caught in the Oxford Circus box too and had stood for six hours along with me and ten thousand others waiting for the last few cries of 'kill the pigs' to finally flicker out while Clive worried himself legless in the Workers' Social over a Pad Thai and a couple of bottles of Chardonnay.

Again, it didn't matter to Simone that Clive couldn't have done anything about her situation, it simply didn't sit well that he'd abandoned her to fill his belly while she'd been marooned in the middle of all that mayhem. If you still can't understand why me and Simone were so pissed off, let me put it this way. Imagine you were sentenced to hang tomorrow morning. There you are in your cell, waiting for the priest's seven o'clock wake-up call, all last-ditch pleas for clemency turned down, with nothing but a couple of chess-playing screws to keep you company. Your family can't do anything to save you, and equally they're not allowed to be there to see you off, which must be as terrible for them as it is for you. Even knowing all of this, though, wouldn't it still knock you in the chops if you subsequently found out that they'd all bought some chicken drumsticks and gone across to next door's barbecue for the evening while you'd spent your last few hours on earth wearing out your slippers and listening to Mr Barrowclough ask which way the horses went again? Well, that's kind of the way me and Simone felt.

Charley phoned up at lunchtime to see if I wanted to come up and have a traditional Sunday dinner in Signed For! that afternoon, but I still didn't feel like seeing her, Hugo or any of the rest of them.

'You're not mad at me, are you?' she asked all indignantly, catching me by surprise and putting me on the spot.

'Oh no, no, of course not,' I blurted out automatically. I even went on to make up some bullshit excuse about how I'd hurt my foot in the crush and couldn't walk on it in order to allay any suspicions that I was in a mood, only to spend the rest of the afternoon kicking myself for not just telling her the truth. That I *was* mad. That going on the march had been her stupid idea. That chucking bins at policemen or smashing Burton's windows had nothing to do with the poor and needy in Africa. That not everyone had a rich daddy who could come to their rescue when they'd got themselves into trouble or buy them a house to save them from having to dip into their own fifty-grand-a-year salary. That Signed For! was a shit pub full of wankers. That Rocket Man Sauce sounded absolutely disgusting. And that I was fed up for the moment of being someone's fucking novelty boyfriend.

As you can see, there were a number of strands to my thoughts and I spent the day staring across the bar of the Lamb trying to knit them together into some sort of nonsense.

'Not with your rich bird today, then, Tel?' Tony the landlord nosed.

'No, not today,' I simply replied, giving him a scowl that stripped the smile clean off his face.

Old Stan in the corner just nodded at that, as if he'd been there forty years earlier and knew the difficulties of crossing the twain only too well, so I sent him over a half of stout to show him my appreciation and we drank to our own silent thoughts.

On Monday morning, CT made a point of looking me out and asking me how I was doing. I didn't feel like levelling with him either so I simply shrugged and asked him if he could do us a favour this particular morning.

'Sure, what is it?' he replied, in all seriousness.

'How many guesses you want?' I asked, pushing the boom out of my face, before turning my back on Barrie's camera and taking to the ladder with my tools on my shoulder.

Naturally, I'd told Jason and Robbie all about my weekend on the ride into work that morning and they'd both agreed I'd been hard done by.

'They're just wankers you get on these things, you get them everywhere,' Robbie had told us. 'The football used to be full of 'em a few years back. Hooligans and firms and them lot, all shouting their mouths off and slinging seats at each other. None of 'em was ever interested in watching the game, they just used to come for the ruck. Fucking Football Factory twats, most of 'em. I couldn't stand 'em.'

Which was all well and good, but it wasn't the 'kill the pigs' brigade I was annoyed at any more. They were just twats. Robbie was right. That was all they were and that was all they ever would be, certainly as far as I was concerned. I had no other expectations of them.

No, most of my bitterness had moved on from them and was now swooping in large ambiguous circles around Charley's shoulders. Not even Hugo's, because I'd suspected him all along and hadn't expected any better of him either – just Charley's.

I was annoyed at her.

I couldn't put my finger on exactly why, but equally I couldn't shake it off either. I was annoyed at her. Like the worm who'd finally turned, or the poodle who'd had one too many silly fucking haircuts, I just felt like having a bark, pissing all over the furniture and taking a big bite out of the postman's arse.

I was annoyed at her.

Halfway through the morning Gordon asked me to help him gauge up a footing we were due to move on to that afternoon. In layman's terms, gauging up a footing meant running lines off the site engineer's profiles to mark out where your corners should be and, most importantly, what height they should be built to. Footings are hardly ever poured flat so there's usually one corner that needs building up more than the others or a dip in the middle of a flank that needs building out so that all four corners and walls are perfectly level with each other by the time the house reaches the DPC (damp course prevention) level. It's just a question of adjusting the first few courses of brickwork or blockwork here or there to take into account and overcome any unevenness in the concrete.

Like most things in life, this unevenness has a name. It's called a 'pig'.

Your governor might say to a couple of his blokes who are about to build a footing flank, 'That wall has a two-to-one pig in it,' so that one of them will start at his end with two courses of bricks and slowly shave them away, while the other bloke will start at his end with one course of bricks and slowly build them up, so that by the time the wall meets in the middle, it's at the same height all along. Naturally this is all gauged out and you've got marks and lines to work to, but that's basically what's involved in layman's terms.

And it might not even be a dramatic as a two-to-one pig. It might just be a one-to-one-and-a-half pig or even less than that. It doesn't really matter. A pig's a pig and you can't build on a pig. If you try, you're asking for all sorts of trouble. It might not seem that noticeable way down below in your footings, but by the time you get to your second storey or above, your house is in serious danger of tumbling over on top of any estate agent who tries to knock a For Sale sign into its front garden.

A pig, even a slight pig, becomes more and more exaggerated with height. I mean, just look at the Leaning Tower of Pisa. If the subby on that job hadn't shown up with a busted theodolite I doubt we would've even heard of the town, yet here we are almost nine hundred years after the mayor first thought a bell tower might look nice in his front garden and he's *still* got the builders in. Something tells me my Italian cousins are on a day rate for that particular job.

But then, this is just what happens when you try to build on a pig.

Which all led me to thinking about the pigs in mine and Charley's relationship. There were so many that had been there right from the start, which we'd both tried to ignore. And they weren't little two-to-one pigs either. They were whopping great inequities that we had no chance of making up in the joints. And the longer we went on, the more the cracks began to show.

CT and his little camera crew came over to film us running lines between the datum posts and asked us what we were doing, so Gordon gave them a quick tutorial and pointed around the footing to show them where the various rooms and windows were going to be before they turned the camera on me.

'Sounds like a nice house, Terry. Would you like to live here?' CT asked, presumably to try and prompt some sort of response out of me before the day was over.

'This place?' I said, looking around the various mounds of mud and clay. 'I couldn't afford this place on my wages. In fact, come to think of it, I don't think I could afford this place as it is now, before we've even built the fucker, on my wages.'

I half expected them to put down the camera when confronted with such language, but they just carried on filming, happy to leave the site's bad language to whoever worked the bleeper in the cutting room. Blimey, he was going to earn his money on this programme before this day was out. Perhaps he could buy this fucking house.

'I sense you're in a bit of a prickly mood, Terry,' CT said.

'Oh, really, Captain Mind-Reader? And what gives you that idea?' I replied. 'Did you sense that in the pub on Saturday night while I was stood around twiddling my thumbs for six fucking hours?'

CT didn't say anything for about twenty seconds, presumably so that Tom Baker or Tom Hanks or whoever else they were going to get in to narrate this load of old nonsense could fill in the audience as to why I had the right steaming arsehole this morning.

'Do you hold Charley responsible for what happened on Saturday?' he then asked.

I looked at Gordon, who was winding in his measuring tape with one eyebrow raised my way. I thought for a moment then turned to CT again.

'You know what a pig is?'

CT thought for a moment then asked if this was a trick question.

'Do you mean the animal?' he asked cautiously.

'No. And I don't mean what your mates were shouting at the police on Saturday either. I'm talking about a pig in brickwork. Do you know what a pig in brickwork is?'

'No,' CT replied, so I pointed at the concrete between me and Gordon.

'This straight has a pig in it. About a two-and-a-half-to-one,' I told him, which was absolutely terrible, even by our shonky groundworkers' standards. They must've poured it about five minutes before last knockings to have left a pig that bad in it. 'A pig is an unevenness in your footing. Have you ever heard of the expression, "to get on an even footing"?'

CT had.

'Well, this is where that expression comes from,' I told him, indicating the ditch I was currently standing in. I have no idea if this is true, to be honest. I doubt it. I think it's probably more likely a sword-fighting expression from the olden days. Half the expressions we use these days seem to be, but CT wasn't to know this. Or if he was, he wasn't letting on, so I continued banging on about the importance of getting on even footings and the inherent dangers of building on pigs before leaving him to pick the bananas out of that bucket of pilchards, which is an expression all of my own, though sadly one that has yet to catch on with any great effect.

CT nodded, like this was all very interesting, which it clearly wasn't, even by BBC3 standards, so I upped the ante and talked him through the merits of brick foundations over concrete block foundations until I finally killed the camera.

'No, it's OK, it's just the tape,' Barrie told CT, dropping the camera off his shoulder and popping open the side.

CT said nothing while the tape was being changed. He just stood on the edge of the footing and stared down at me with a semi-amused smile on his face. Likewise, I clammed up during the switch, reluctant to spill a drop of this gold without having some professional eavesdropper catch it for posterity, and before a minute was out we were up and running again.

'Of course, things can get tricky once you start piledriving your footings...' I was in the middle of saying when CT cut right through my blarney and asked me if I was going to call Charley at all this week.

'What's that got to do with anything?' I insisted, a little irritably.

CT let the question hang in the air for a few seconds, either for maximum effect or because his mate in the sound van had accidentally turned over two pages of *1001 Dynamite Responses* and lost his place.

'I just wanted to know if you were planning on calling her, that's all,' he finally said.

'I thought we were talking about footings?' I said.

'I don't know what we're talking about, Terry, but it's certainly not footings,' he pointed out.

I responded with a snort and a shake of the head before getting back to the business of quietly marking out the corners off the profile lines. When CT saw he'd got all the footage he was going to get out of me, he tapped Barrie on the shoulder and Barrie lowered the camera.

'We'll shoot some stuff up on those roofs over there where the tilers are now, OK?' I heard him tell Barrie, sending him on ahead to get set up while he hung back and had one final word with me. 'Give her a call, Terry. Some time this week. I know she wants to talk to you,' he told me, before thanking Gordon and turning to catch up with his cameraman.

'What was all that about?' Gordon asked ten seconds later when CT was out of earshot.

I just shrugged and carried on marking out.

'*I* thought we were talking about footings,' Gordon then said, his face the picture of confusion.

'Yeah, so did I,' I lied, dipping the tip of my trowel into a dollop of smoothed-out green muck and writing the word 'PIG' as a heads-up to whoever was going to work on this particular corner.

22 Upcoming talks

The expression 'I know she wants to talk to you' kept getting snagged on sticking-out corners of my brain. Charley didn't want to *hear from* me. Or *see* me. Or *be with* me. She wanted to *talk to* me, which sounded ominously specific and came with its own wailing klaxons and cold, clammy hands. I pretended for a moment that I couldn't guess what she wanted to talk to me about and idly speculated as to the subject of said forthcoming conversation.

Perhaps she thought it was time we took the next step and started leaving socks and underpants around each other's houses. Unlikely.

Perhaps she thought it was time we spiced up things in the bedroom and asked some of her thoroughbred mates to come round and drop their keys into a bowl in the middle of the coffee table, because they're all into that sort of thing these thoroughbreds, you know. Even unlikelier.

Perhaps she wanted to agree with me that Saturday's march had been a load of bullshit and that ninety per cent of the people who took to the streets to be part of it did so just so they could say they'd been there, which is why the whole thing descended into some sort of Mardi Gras for angry brats. Possibly the unlikeliest.

No, Charley didn't want to talk to me about any of these things. That was pretty obvious, even to me. Charley wanted to talk to me about our future, or lack of one, to be precise.

'I've been thinking...' she would say as sadly as possible,

hoping that these few words would speak for themselves and save her having to spell out exactly what she'd been thinking (helped no doubt by a few quiet words from that guttersnipe Hugo).

If I didn't immediately leap in with a 'yeah, yeah, I know. It's OK, there's no need to say anything', she'd then have to dig a little deeper and see if any of the following lit up any light bulbs when she tried them out.

'I'm not sure we're in the same place…'

'It's not you, it's me…'

'I just think we're very different people…'

'You're going to make someone a really great boyfriend one day…'

'Things have just run their course…'

'We had some great times but all good things must come to an end…'

'Listen, dummy, do you need a diagram or what…'

I wondered if I could ride it out by playing all my stupid cards at once so that I missed everything Charley tried to tell me, though I wasn't sure I fancied us still being together to celebrate our diamond wedding anniversary if this was my long-term strategy.

And I wasn't about to argue my way out of the inevitable dumping either.

'Actually, Charley, we *are* right for each other. In fact, we're really well suited if you just gave me a chance, dropped that arsehole Hugo from your life and stopped trying to make me eat puy fucking lentils all the time…'

No, I'm long enough in the tooth to know that once your other half starts expressing doubts about their commitment to the cause, it's basically game over from that point onwards. You simply can't argue yourself back into someone's heart. Nigel had known this ten years earlier. And I knew it now. All you can do is take it like a man, keep your dignity and try as best you can to leave them with the awful nagging doubt that they may have done the wrong thing, so that when they come begging back to you three months later, you can tell them to fuck right off and emerge from the whole sorry mess feeling like the winner.

Not that I'd be feeling like any sort of winner any time soon after all I'd put up with.

You know, it's unbelievable, I'd really given this relationship my best shot. I really had. I'd travelled north to her neck of the woods. I'd drunk in her awful pubs. I'd eaten her awful foods. I'd watched her awful foreign movies. I'd made the effort with her aw… with her friends. And I'd gone on her fucking awful marches. I'd even resisted the temptation to smack Hugo in the gob, which really was above and beyond the call when you think about it, but at the end of the day, none of this had counted for Jack Johnson.

Because Charley wanted to 'talk to' me.

Thinking about it, my post-demo disappearance and subsequent phone call boycott were possibly the first and only time I'd ever openly expressed any irritation at anything Charley had done. Don't get me wrong, I hadn't spent the entire last few months walking around holding her hand and muttering 'fucking stupid cow' under my breath, but then by that same token I hadn't always voted with my conscience over every little decision either. Rather than say anything that might've sparked a bit of friction between us (like the now infamous eggs Benedict incident), most times I'd just ended up biting my tongue in order to keep the peace. And if this resulted in me eating the odd vegetable I didn't like or nodding enthusiastically to some opinion a big fat raspberry might've better suited, then so what? I was a big boy. It hadn't done me any harm and certainly hadn't done Charley any harm either, so why not duck all the silly little disagreements and just get on with the business of enjoying each other's company?

That was the way I saw things. I think it's the way most blokes see things, i.e. anything for a quiet life.

Women see things differently, though. For some reason – and I don't know why this is – most of the women I'd been out with felt the need to be agreed with as far as everything was concerned. Even the things that didn't affect them in any way, shape or form. In fact, especially the things that didn't affect them. Like I said, I have no idea why this is, but if life's taught me one thing, it's that there's no such phrase in the female vocabulary as 'OK, let's just agree to differ' except when they're confronted with conclusive and corroborated scientific evidence that proves beyond all reasonable doubt that they are talking out of their arses on a given point. This is the only time a woman will 'agree to differ' and possibly the reason most of the Foreign Office's diplomats aren't women.

'Excuse me, Mr Mbuko, but do you know you've got a plate in your mouth? You do? Well take it out, then, it's stupid. No, I don't care about your heritage, take it out now. There are people staring.'

This might seem a bit of a sexist thing to suggest, but then just because something's sexist it doesn't automatically mean it's *not* true, does it? Men and women *are* different. And women *do* do things that blokes don't (and vice versa, by the way). Just look at that palaver over the aforementioned eggs Benedict, for example. Why had it mattered to Charley what I had for breakfast that morning? Why had it bothered her so much that I'd ordered a can of Fanta as well as a cup of tea? Why had I had to try her horrible haddock Florentine? And why had I had to like all these things, with the exception of the Fanta?

Also, and on other occasions, why was some long, drawn-out, boring, moody Chinese movie where everyone was able to fly and hit treble top with three samurai swords blindfolded more intelligent than what I'd wanted to go and see at the pictures (the latest James Bond in case you're interested)?

Why was an enormous tree trunk suspended from the ceiling of the Tate Modern and wrapped in clingfilm *not* a pointless load of old horse shite? It had certainly looked it to me.

Why was the Congestion Zone charge a fantastic scheme that needed to be extended to every corner of the country, regardless of how little sense that made?

Why had I been wrong not to be outraged that the AIDS charity, the Terrence Higgins Trust, received a fraction of the donations that donkey sanctuaries up and down the country received? I mean, people can avoid getting AIDS, can't they, but donkeys can't avoid being donkeys.

Why had I been wrong to question the saintliness of the homeless? I had just been stating a fact that *Big Issue* sellers *do* look like the last people on earth who'd ever put their hand in their pocket to buy a copy of the *Big Issue* if things were the other way around.

And why had I been a Nazi for not thinking it absolutely scandalous that students had to pay back their student loans when they started earning a certain wage? A university degree seemed like the key to a nice healthy career and salary. Why shouldn't students be expected to foot a little of the bill themselves when they were going to be the ones who reaped the rewards? No one was forcing them into highly lucrative jobs in the City or the media at gunpoint. There were still plenty of ditches in this country that needed digging for people who didn't want to fork out for their own Student Union bar bills. No degrees required.

Why had I been wrong about all of the above and more? All of these things had come up at dinner parties or drinks parties over the course of the last six months and I'd clammed up or performed three-point turns every time Charley had developed a scowl. I'd compromised and compromised and compromised again in an effort to keep the peace with her and I'd done everything in my power not to annoy or upset her in any way in all that time because I was so utterly nuttily about my smart, beautiful and heart-wrenchingly adorable girlfriend.

But enough was e-*cunting*-nough!

I'd gone through shit and back on Saturday, I'd paid my dues in full and this time around I had the right to have the almighty hump.

I had that right.

And I deserved a heartfelt apology and a generous helping of love and understanding. I had that right. But I wasn't going to get an apology. And I wasn't going to get any understanding.

Instead, I was going to get *talked to*.

Un-*fucking*-believable.

How was that fair? How was that right?

It wasn't. There's your answer. It wasn't right and it wasn't fair. But it was tediously and predictably typical. A normal, ordinary working bloke tugs his forelock for six straight months and has no grounds to say boo to a Christmas goose because that's all normal, ordinary working blokes have the right to expect. Some privileged, spoilt, rich little public school girl has it all her own way for exactly the same six months and the first time buttercups don't make her chin glow yellow she digs out the binning brush and has a spring clean. Why was I even surprised?

You know the thing that I really hated, though? What I really hated was the fact that I didn't hate her. I didn't hate my Charley. I was on the verge of being ejected from her life because I'd become a bit problematic for a little ironic fling, but I didn't hate her. I was angry, bitter and as miserable as a sackful of puppies heading for the river. But I didn't hate her. I couldn't. I simply didn't have it in me.

However... that would almost certainly change if I allowed her to take one last walking holiday up and down my back without ever catching sight of my spine. Oh yes, a few months of stewing on one final humiliation to accompany my dumping would really set the agenda for the next few relationships to come. Of that I had little doubt. And I didn't want that. I didn't want to turn into a sour old bastard who was driven by spite, a carousel full of baggage and an insatiable appetite for seeing mascara running down women's faces. I'd always been such a nice bloke up until now. A bit thick and a bit of a worrier (no shit, Sherlock), but nice nonetheless. Ask anyone.

'What's Tel like?'

'Tel? He's all right. Nice bloke. Bit thick and a bit of a worrier, but nice nonetheless. Why d'you ask?'

But that would all change once I was damaged goods; haunting the corner of the Lamb, starting every sentence with 'you're better off without them' and poring over Dear Deirdre's pages for giggles. I didn't fancy that for a future one little bit.

But that was what was in store for me. I knew it as plainly as I knew I loved and was going to miss Charley. I knew it in my bones.

So what could I do to save myself from this fate? What could I do to emerge from this relationship with my dignity intact? After all, I'd always known that this day was going to come. Always. Our whole romance had been based on borrowed time, from the moment she'd said 'yes, it might be nice to go out' to the inevitable 'we need to talk', I'd always known we'd only had a certain number of dates. I hadn't known how many we'd had. One? Two? Thirteen? A hundred? I'd never been sure. All I'd known was that I'd recognise the signs when my time was nearly up. And time was very nearly up now. The stabling fees had been cancelled. The jodhpurs had been sold. And I was going the same way as the loyal but suddenly surplus Domino.

All I could do – my one and only shot at saving my sanity –

was to finish things on my own terms. That would go some way to redressing the disappointment.

I had to have the final say.

So there it was, my Hobson's choice. I finally saw what I had to do.

I had to take the initiative.

I had to dump Charley.

23 The planning department

espite CT's continued urging, I didn't phone Charley all week. I hadn't phoned her at the start of the week because I'd wanted her to know that I was in a big boo with her and I didn't phone her throughout the rest of the week because I didn't want to give her a chance to dump me before I could dump her. Timing was everything with a dumping.

Fortunately, other than her Sunday lunch invitation, she didn't try to call me.

I figured female pride wouldn't allow her to either, not after I'd rejected her half-hearted stab at reconciliation in which she tried to pass off a plate of overpriced roast beef as a wordless apology, and in fact I even banked on it keeping her at arm's length until I was ready to do the dirty. Fortunately, female pride is something you can stick your house, your life savings, both your kidneys and all your pets on if you want. There are few greater certainties in life short of the retaliation you can expect by slapping a Mafia don's daughter around on her wedding day while goading him that he hadn't got the balls to do anything about it or wandering around Tyneside in a 'Paedophile & Proud' T-shirt. Of course, it would be a different story if I was going out with another bloke. My phone would be ringing off the hook the moment the pubs chucked out with that deckchair blubbing his eyes out about how sorry he was, before booze got the better of him and the tariff suddenly turned into a drunken 0898 phone call.

There really was only one remaining problem.

I didn't want to dump her. I didn't want to do it.

I loved Charley and I wanted to spend my life making her happy, if only for the selfish reason that my happiness and hers were intertwined. I loved her. I absolutely adored her.

'Which is why you've got to do it,' I told my miserable reflection on Friday evening when I stepped out of the shower, almost poleaxing myself with remorse at the realisation.

I still hadn't heard from her, of course. I hadn't even got a text, which either confirmed everything I'd feared or told me she'd finally worn down her thumbs to nubs sending smiley faces to her mates.

So I had a shave, ironed a shirt and ran a comb through my hair, but these things did little to shevel my dishevelledness. My mobile finally found its voice just after seven but it was only Jason phoning to see if I was still in the mood for a drink. Now there was an understatement and a half. Yes, King Kong was a bit big for a gorilla, wasn't he?

I strolled up the road to the Lamb and found an empty bar stool right where I'd left one the previous evening.

'Evening, Tel,' Tony nodded when I took my seat. 'Lager?'

'Evening, Tony. And you, Stan. Yes please, mate.'

Tony poured two pints and set them both down on the bar towel in front of me.

'Cheers,' I said, picking up one and emptying the top three inches into my face.

Jason appeared less than two minutes later and embraced the waiting pint like a long-lost friend.

'Evening, Jason,' Tony nodded.

'Evening, Tony. Stan,' Jason replied when he resurfaced. 'Cheers.'

Yeah, we were a couple of Friday night fixtures all right. We didn't even have to ask for two pints these days, we just got a second automatically the moment we walked in to toast the start of the weekend, as Tony knew the other would never be far behind. You would've thought this might've caused a few problems whenever either of us were on our holidays and it probably would've if we didn't always go away on holiday together. Me, Jason, Sandra and whoever I was seeing at the time. We'd always go as a foursome. This year we'd be going away as a three.

Neither Jason nor Sandra knew this yet, though, so I decided to keep it that way for the time being. Finishing things with Charley was going to be hard enough without a load of uninformed and ill-thought-through advice to cloud my judgement. I knew what had to be done. And that was enough for now. There'd be plenty of time to pick the bananas out of this particular bucket of pilchards after I'd done the necessary.

'I had your mate CT bending my ear all afternoon today, you know,' Jason told me in between gulps. 'On camera and all. Can't that bloke do anything without pointing a camera at it? What's he like going to the pictures with, that's what I want to know.'

'Don't know. Why don't you ask him? I'm sure he'd go with you.'

'Yeah, I'm sure he would,' Jason smirked knowingly, prompting Tony (who was earwigging near by as ever) to ask if this CT was some sort of big movie fan, then. We decided to spare ourselves the inevitable gay teapot impressions that would've accompanied the truth and simply confirmed that this CT was indeed some sort of big movie fan.

'I like a good movie myself, I do,' Tony told us, sensing an in. '*Platoon*, that was a good one. And *Saving Private Ryan*, d'you see that one?'

I had. Jason hadn't.

'*A Bridge Too Far*, that was another good one,' Tony continued. '*The Great Escape. Full Metal Jacket. Hamburger Hill. The Dirty Dozen. Kelly's Heroes.* Er...'

'*Priscilla, Queen of the Desert*?' Jason suggested.

'Nah, don't think I saw that one,' Tony reckoned, scratching his head.

'Really?' Jason replied.

Tony was unfortunately called away to pour a few pints so we never got the chance to ask him which (if he *absolutely* had to choose) was his favourite Meryl Streep movie. Instead, we returned to the question of CT.

'So what exactly was he bending your ear about?' I asked. 'And you can cut out this "your mate" bit an' all, all right?'

'He was bending my ear about you.'

'Me?'

'Yeah, he wanted to know what you'd been saying about Charley.'

'He what?' I replied, stunned that CT should be trying to make a public spectacle out of my private feelings. 'Hang on a minute, on camera? He wanted to know what I'd been saying about Charley – on camera?'

'I swear to God, man. It's outrageous, I know.'

Outrageous wasn't the word. I could hardly believe it. It was one thing to stick your oar into someone else's puddle on the quiet side, but quite another to go around trying to tape the whole thing. That was taking stirring to an all-new level and it was bang out of order. Plain and simple. My only guess was that CT had been hoping to lull Jason into dishing the dirt on me under the guise that it had something to do with the programme, so that he could *then* show it to Charley so that she'd *then* have a reason to justify dumping me. Or something like that.

Jesus, my head hurt.

'And what did you tell him?' I asked.

'I told him to hop it and mind his own fucking business. What d'you think I was going to tell him?' Jason replied.

'That's not on,' I fumed, feeling even more wronged than usual. 'Going behind my back like that.'

'He's been doing it all month, mate,' Jason then told me.

'Has he?'

'Straight up. I never really put two and two together up until now but...' he started, until Tony cut in to ask Jason if he wanted to borrow a calculator.

'Here, Tony, do us a favour, will you?' I pleaded with him, before turning back to Jason. 'Go on.'

'Well, he'd always just ask us about you. You know: "How's Terry?" "How are you getting on?" "What's new with you and Charley?" That sort of thing. I thought he was just being friendly because he's mates with Charley and he knows you, so I always thought he was just making conversation, a bit of common ground and all that. But I'll tell you, man, this afternoon! He smelt all wrong.'

'In what way?' I pressed, noticing that even old Stan was all ears.

'Well, I don't know, he just did. Went beyond the usual "good morning" and "how's Terry?" malarkey. Especially with you having the arsehole all week. I just thought he smelt like a nosey cunt, so I told him to sling his hook and go and film some bricks somewhere else. Big John told him the same.'

'He was asking Big John about me an' all?'

'Tel, he's been asking everyone. For weeks. Like I say, I just figured it was 'cos he knew you. You know, like whenever I get invited to any weddings on Sandra's side, I don't know anyone usually so I just spend the whole night asking everyone how they know the bride until it's time to go home or I'm too drunk to care. It's just what you do when you don't know anyone else, innit? But no, I think there's more to it than that with your mate CT, like he's trying to stir it or something, and it really showed this week,' Jason said, downing the last of his pint and shouting two and a half more in for me, him and old Stan.

Any lingering doubts I might've had about me and Charley

were now well and truly shot. I couldn't believe I'd been so daft as to think things could've actually worked out between us, love will conquer all and that load of old kippers, but that twain really was some leap, wasn't it? And as if I needed any further proof, here was one of Charley's best mates going around behind my back, trying to get the nuts and bolts on the whole mess so that they'd all have something to giggle about at their next dinner party. That really put the henna tattoo on it.

'So what's his game, then?' Jason asked. 'What's he after? Haven't you and Charley kissed and made up yet?'

'No, we haven't.'

'Why not?'

'It ain't as simple as that.'

'Why ain't it? What's up?'

'Nothing.'

'Nothing?'

'No, nothing.'

Jason paused to consider this for a second.

'When are you seeing her next?'

'Who says I am?'

Jason raised an eyebrow, then nodded like he finally understood.

'Oh, sorry, mate. Given you the elbow, has she?' he puckered, ruefully.

'No she fucking hasn't! And what makes you think *she'd* be the one giving *me* the elbow if elbowing time came around anyway?' I demanded. 'She ain't exactly queen of the desert either, you know.'

'Uh-huh,' Jason uh-huhhed.

'You know, I'm fed up with everyone thinking I'm playing second fiddle to her. Some rich bird born with a silver spoon up her arse and I should be the one who's grateful for the zucchini gratings that fall from her table!' I brooded.

'What's zucchini?'

'It's like a courgette.'

Jason responded with a blank look.

'You know, a courgette? Like in cooking.'

'What?'

'Oh, look, it's like a cucumber only for cooking with.'

'You cook with cucumbers?'

'No, you cook with fucking zucchinis!' I snapped, rapidly losing my patience. 'You only cook with cucumbers if you don't know what a zucchini or a courgette is and you're just looking at the fucking pictures in your cookery book.'

'You've got cookery books? When d'you get those?'

'Oh, for fuck's sake!'

I rubbed my face and took a big wallop of my pint to signal my increasing frustration before getting back to my original line of martyrdom.

'I'm talking about Charley here.'

'What about her?'

'Well, I'm just saying, I'm the man, ain't I?'

'It's a tight one but I'd just about give you the decision, yeah,' Jason conceded.

'Well, I should be the one calling the shots, then, not the one who's running around after her all the time.'

'Is that what you want?' Jason asked.

'No,' I said. 'Of course not. But you know what I mean, don't you? It's just bollocks, this is. It's just bollocks.'

'Things going all right, then, are they?'

I didn't even deign that with an uppercut.

'Anyway, who says you're playing second fiddle to Charley? Is that what CT and the rest of her mates say, then?' Jason then asked.

'It ain't what they say, it's what they think,' I told him.

'Hang on a minute, you can read minds? You never told me about this. That's amazing. Here, do me. What am I thinking now?'

'I don't know, something about Saturday night, you and CT in the back row of the pictures with a couple of zucchinis, is all I'm getting,' I replied.

'Tel, look, mate, I don't know what's going on with you and Charley and it's none of my business, but if she ain't making you happy then you've got to ask yourself if it's worth it,' Jason advised from the safety of his long and happy marriage. 'I mean, you and Charley ain't exactly been making out like Romeo and Juliet for some while now, have you?'

'Well, neither have you or Sandra,' I pointed out.

'Phhp, of course not, we've been together almost fourteen years. We've earnt the right to drop all that bollocks, but I bet old Romeo wasn't sitting around after only six months cunting Juliet off to his mates because she kept trying to get him to eat cucumbers,' he said.

'Maybe not, but then they were all right back in the old days, weren't they, just riding around, picking flowers and living happily ever after. It's not like that these days, mate,' I objected.

'You ain't read *Romeo and Juliet*, have you?' Jason commented.

'I ain't *seen* it either. And neither's Tony, I'll bet, so what's your point?' I asked.

'Tel, I just think you got off on the wrong foot with this relationship and you've been off balance ever since,' Jason said. 'You know, most people meet, they shag, they go back for seconds and they end up thinking "hello, I quite like this person, perhaps I'll stick around for a little longer", but not you. You've been walking around like you've got the *Mona Lisa* under your arm from day one. How are you meant to relax and be yourself when you're constantly expecting a tap on the shoulder?'

'What's all this got to do with CT?' I asked, suddenly wondering where the start of this conversation had disappeared to.

'All I'm saying is you reap what you sow,' Jason explained. 'So perhaps they are all laughing at you behind your back. I don't know if they are. They might be. Then again they might not be, but if they are, it's because you've shown 'em the way. It ain't just dogs who can smell fear, you know,' which was Jason's final piece of advice before Tony successfully wrestled the conversation away from my personal inadequacies and on to his own with discussion about the complete works of Steven Seagal.

It ain't just dogs who can smell fear? Hmm.

Well, it ain't just dogs who have teeth either. I'd show 'em.

24 Getting my retaliation in first

I still didn't want to call Charley, as I was worried she'd bin me before I could get a word out edgeways, so I texted her instead, figuring six months of time served would hopefully protect me against any 'Hi T, lng time no :-0… Soz but thngs nt workn. Thnk we shud jst b :-) bye Cx' type replies.

I took the initiative for once and picked a place to meet. And it wasn't the Workers' Social either. I suggested we met at St Paul's. As in the cathedral.

I hadn't been struck down with religion or anything and I wasn't trying to make any symbolic points, I just wanted our meeting to be on my terms. And every time I'd suggested a place to Charley in the past, she'd always trumped me with somewhere *better*, which had generally put me on the back foot from the off.

'Fancy a drink in town this evening? I know a pub in Trafalgar Square that's never that busy.'

Better still, there's a great little bar just off Haymarket that serves cocktails in teapots and has bowls of goldfish on every table.

'Er, yeah, OK. Then afterwards, if we're hungry, maybe I can treat you to an Indian if you fancy it?'

We could do, but have you ever tried Iraqi?

Well, just let her try and come up with a flasher church than St Paul's Cathedral. I couldn't think of anywhere.

Also, and rather more importantly, I needed Charley to actually show up and I wasn't entirely sure she would if I simply suggested some neutral pub, restaurant or park bench somewhere after a week of radio silence. Charley might've smelt a rat and taken the opportunity to leave me stewing in my own pilchards as one final 'fuck you very much' before disappearing from my life completely. And I wanted to have my say. Face to face. I owed that much to myself.

So St Paul's Cathedral was my ace. Impressive, neutral and intriguing enough to entice her along.

I arrived a little before midday and walked around to the main entrance. One side of the building had scaffolding going up to the first roof, so I stopped for a moment and tried to picture what this place had looked like three-hundred-odd years ago when it had been rebuilt after the Great Fire. It probably wouldn't have looked too unlike some of the big building projects I'd worked on in the past. I'd done a few offices, a couple of supermarkets and even a prison out in Kent in the past, so I reckon I could've found my way around this site without too many problems. I reckon I could've probably even got a job if I'd showed up with my own tools and the boss had been hiring. Things hadn't changed that much in three hundred years. Technology, materials and designs had perhaps, but the actual work itself had always been done by blokes like me. It might've been Sir Christopher Wren's name on the big marble tablet on the wall inside but I didn't have a doubt in my boots that it was being kept company by a couple of hundred less obvious engravings that probably hadn't seen the light of day in three-hundred-odd years. And I was sure these names warmly greeted a dozen or so new arrivals every time a fresh set of scaffolding went up to steam-clean the masonry, repoint the lead or install the dean's new Sky+ dish.

I walked around and through a big set of revolving doors, bought two tickets for admission and left Charley's with the woman behind the desk, before heading for the Whispering Gallery.

Situated a hundred feet and two hundred and fifty-nine steps above the church floor, the Whispering Gallery is basically one big circular walkway with seats around the inside of the dome. It's so called because apparently if you whisper into the wall on one side of the gallery, the sound travels around the smooth stonework so that your mate can hear what you've just said right the way over on the other side. 'Blimey, the bishop's banging on a bit this morning, isn't he? Fancy a pint at lunchtime?' being one whisper I bet this wall had heard a fair few times in the last three hundred years.

Another whisper, according to the tour guide I passed on the stairs, was 'will you marry me?' Lots of people proposed to their other halves in the Whispering Gallery. Hats off, I guess it's quite a romantic thing to tickle your girlfriend's ear with.

I wondered how many had used the place to dump theirs.

Now, I wasn't going to be such an arsehole as to whisper it into the wall to her or string tin cans across the gallery or nothing. But likewise, I did quite like the sanctity of the place and felt it bullet proofed me against the sort of violent reaction that was as likely to be heard in the crypt downstairs as on the other side of the gallery.

Oh no you ain't! You ain't dumping me, because I'm dumping you first, you wanker!

That sort of thing.

Not that I expected her to flip out this way, but it was always a possibility. People do funny things when they've just been dumped.

I sent Charley a text to let her know where I'd be, then turned off my phone. And this wasn't just to avoid getting a last minute SMS dump either. St Paul's was a church. A house of God. Mobiles were strictly off limits. If visitors wanted to send messages from this place, it had to be done the old-fashioned way with their hands together and their knees bent.

I found a seat against a quiet wall of the Whispering Gallery and looked at my watch. It was now just after a quarter past twelve. I'd asked to meet her at half past and arrived early to get the lie of the land. I knew she'd be late. Probably a quarter of an hour, maybe even half, which normally would tear into my guts and fill my head with visions of being stood up, but I expected it now. I'd got used to it, so I was able to take a moment and prepare.

To be honest, I wasn't sure what I'd do if Charley didn't show up; rethink my whole strategy, probably, but the one thing I wouldn't do was enter into some sort of slanging match with her. I'd liked Charley too much to want to us go down that route. I knew some couples who sniped and bitched at each other for months after they'd split up. Years even. Sometimes for longer than they'd even dated in the first place. I guess it's just easier like that sometimes. We invest so much raw emotion into a relationship that some people have real problems letting go without seeing a return on their investment, whether it be hugs and kisses or sticks and stones. We all want to know that we mattered to the other person at one stage or another, even if it was just for a short while.

Equally none of us want to simply sink into the mists of time without laying down some sort of marker to be remembered by. And that goes for relationships as well as church walls, so some people hang around long after they should, slinging accusations at the former loves of their lives and ordering them fifty home-delivered pizzas a night.

But that wasn't for me. I was determined to do this right. Things hadn't worked out and that was too bad. Really. But I'd do the right thing and bow out with my dignity intact so that Charley would eventually come to realise that the uncouth, uneducated and unclipped bricky who she'd thought was beneath her was, in fact, the best fella she'd ever met.

For all the fucking good that would do me...

To my surprise, on the dot of half twelve, Charley stepped through the door and clocked me almost straight away on the far side of the Whispering Gallery. The very sight of her made my heart almost turn and run and for one headlight-staring moment I wondered if I had it in me to go through with it. Wouldn't it be simpler and easier just to let her do it to me, to save me from having to do it to her? Quite possibly, so I had to quickly remind myself why exactly I was getting my retaliation in first...

...if I could remember.

Oh yes, all that stuff.

Charley looked a little breathless herself and I was about to draw a few hasty last-minute conclusions to shore up my resolve when I remembered that she had just walked up two hundred and fifty-nine steps. She was allowed to look breathless. Just this once.

What didn't add up was just how confident she looked.

She looked happy, smiling and assured, like she didn't have a worry at her door, while I had spent the entire last week wringing my handkerchief out into a bucket over the state of our doomed relationship. It was funny, but it hadn't even occurred to me up until this final moment that Charley might show up with anything other than a matching expression to mine. Yet here she was, as happy as a florist's daughter on Christmas morning with a pocketful of pixie wishes.

That just about summed us both up in a nutshell as far as I was concerned and convinced me there really was no more of this relationship to run.

Come in, Tel the trowel, your time is up.

'Hiya [kiss kiss], I wasn't sure if you were joking when I got your text about meeting here,' Charley said, plonking herself down next to me.

'You found it OK?' I asked.

'Oh yeah, I've been here before,' she told me, which didn't surprise me in the slightest as Charley had generally been everywhere and done everything before. That said, I could walk into the Lamb in Catford tomorrow and have a pint of my favourite lager put on the bar without having to say a single word, so it wasn't like I didn't have anything to show for the last ten years either.

'Have you been up to the Golden Gallery yet?' Charley asked, but I just shook my head and told her I hadn't. 'Oh well, perhaps we can...'

'Charley,' I said, taking a deep breath and seizing the moment. 'We need to talk.'

Charley's eyes narrowed and her smile slipped a few degrees, but I didn't give her a chance to respond, too concerned was I that she'd pip me at the death with a lightning-quick 'I agree, we do, but let me just say what I've got to say first' strike of her own.

'I think you're great and I... I really, really like you, but... I... I just think... I... I think I'm going to have to call it a day. You know, between us,' I finally got out, my innards in knots over words I could scarcely believe I was speaking. 'Look, it's not you, it's me,' I added, figuring I might as well use that one up before she could.

Charley stared at me with uncertainty, then broke away from my guilty gaze to look into middle space, clearly flummoxed by what I'd just said.

'I just think we're very different people,' I continued in earnest. 'We're into different things. We're from different places. And we've got different parents. Er... we're just... you know, different. And honestly, I'm not saying that I don't like you, because I do, I just don't think... we're really [what was that expression? Er, that was it]... going anywhere,' I explained. 'You know what I mean?'

'No, I don't,' she suddenly snapped, obviously annoyed that I was the one doing the dumping. I guess she was probably more used to being the dumper than the dumpee.

'Look, it's not you...' I tried once again, but Charley just cut through my default setting with an angry hiss.

'Stop saying that,' she barked, before pressing, 'Is this about last week?'

'No,' I denied. 'Of course not. Er, well, yeah, sort of, I guess.'

'Look, it's not my fault that you...' she started to say, but I stopped her right there as I didn't want her thinking that this was a single-issue dumping. It was much more than that. Much, much more.

'No, no, OK, it's not about last week,' I corrected myself.

'But you just said...'

'Forget about that. Forget about what I just said. I didn't mean it. I was just... [saying the first thing that came into my head?]. Look, don't worry about last week. OK?'

'No, Terry, it's not OK. I don't know what's going on. What's going on?' Charley asked, which was a girlie classic and one my ex, Jo, used to use on me all the time. It's a simple technique that girls learn at an early age that turns the tables on us mug blokes. Basically, the way it works is this: there's a problem; you both know about it and you're both constantly reacting to it, but neither of you can say anything about it because the moment you do, the other one can then accuse you of being petty, oversensitive, stroppy or suspicious, so that all at once the argument becomes about that rather than about how much time they're spending down at Morrisons. It's a lost cause trying to talk out your concerns with women because at the end of the day, it's never their fault. It's always yours.

At least, it was always mine. And I can only go on experience.

'Charley, we're just not right together,' I simply said, causing Charley to turn away for a few seconds before rising to her feet.

I fought the overwhelming urge to grab her hand, drag her back down next to me and plead with her for forgiveness, but the dogs were in the traps and the rabbit was already running. This race would be run.

As it was, Charley didn't dash off anywhere, like I thought she would. She just stepped away from me a yard or two and leaned against the safety rail with her back to me. I watched her for a moment or two and took the opportunity to try and untangle the knot of reasons in my brain so that we both knew what we were talking about, but without resorting to all that 'then you did this, then you said that' bollocks, and I couldn't find the words.

Couldn't we *both* just acknowledge what we *both* knew? That our ironic little stroll on the other side of the tracks was over. No harm done. Very sorry and all that, but goodbye and the best of luck.

'You know, I'd love to know when you came to this conclusion because you've never said anything to me,' Charley then objected. 'And what do you mean, we're not right together anyway? What is it I'm doing that's not right?'

'Charley, please…' I tried, but Charley was determined to play the apportion game.

'No, I want to know,' she insisted. 'Tell me.'

'Charley, it's not you…' I almost said again, but managed to veer off at the last moment and repeat instead that we were very different people.

This didn't do for Charley, though. She wanted specifics, presumably to prove to me that I was the one in the wrong, not her. But seriously, what were the specifics?

She'd been born to rich parents whereas I'd been born to a couple that had met on a hop-picking holiday?

She'd gone to a posh school whereas I'd gone to a comp? Occasionally.

She mixed with actors and producers, doctors and lawyers whereas I mixed with a shovel?

She liked lentils and grown-up grub whereas I still liked the odd can of Fanta?

These weren't reasons for ending a relationship. They were actually pretty stupid in themselves if I'm honest here. I knew this, but that didn't matter because they weren't the real reasons we were splitting up. The real reason we were splitting up was... er... er...

For a moment there, I almost couldn't remember, but then it came back to me. It was all down to Charley. She was the one who was getting ready to dump me (possibly for Hugo or Domino? Not sure, I was confusing myself now), not the other way around. I just got in there first, which, when all was said and done, was the real reason she felt aggrieved. That yet another horse had thrown her off her back before she could shoo him away.

That I'd noted the differences between us and decided that they weren't for me, when really I should've been the one down on bended knees thanking her for even looking at me.

How dare I? How dare I finish with *her*?

This was the real reason my announcement had come as such a blow to her. I'd simply beaten her to the punch.

This was all this was and this was what I had to keep telling myself. Because if I lost sight of it even for a second, I'd be leaving myself open to one hell of a fall when the ball was back bouncing in her court.

Still, there was no reason to be horrible about it. I didn't want to be horrible and I didn't want to upset her, no matter what the reasons were, because I seriously did care about her. After all, it was the reason I was doing what I was doing.

'Charley, please, I don't want us to part on bad terms,' I said,

genuinely meaning every last syllable of it. 'Because I really did...
do like you. I've had so many good times with you – even just
being with you – but nothing lasts for ever. And it's just time to
call it a day,' I muttered, the lump in my throat making me barely
audible, even in the Whispering Gallery.

'I just wish you'd tell me why,' Charley insisted, but I'd said all
I could without the whole thing turning personal.

'I'm sorry,' was all I replied. 'Really. I'm really, really sorry.'

Which didn't say the half of it.

We stood in silence for a moment, neither knowing what to say
next and neither wanting to be the one who lost their composure,
and eventually Charley accepted the situation.

She collected her wits, nodded, then shook her head a couple
of times and told me she had to go.

'OK,' I unhappily agreed, almost accidentally telling her that
I'd give her a call in the week. But then I remembered I wouldn't.
Not this week. Not next week. Not any other week. This was the
last time I'd ever see Charley. And it was breaking my heart.

Just what the hell was I doing?

'Bye, then,' Charley frowned. We paused for a moment,
wondering whether or not to kiss, but dilly-dallied for so long
that the moment and kiss were lost for ever.

'Bye,' I replied, just as she turned and walked. 'Take care.'

I watched Charley head back around the Whispering Gallery
to the exit and got ready to wave when she looked back from the
doorway. But she didn't look back. She just darted on through
and disappeared from my life for the very last time. Utterly gut-
wrenched and exhausted, I slumped back into the wooden seat to
give her a fifteen-minute head start, feeling absolutely sick to the
stomach.

I'd just dumped Charley.

Oh my fuck!

I'd just dumped the woman of my dreams.

I couldn't help but wonder why.

No, it was no good thinking like that. What was done was done and done for a good reason. I knew that. And while I didn't exactly take comfort in the knowledge, I knew that I knew it. Which was about the best I could say about it.

And if you like, I'll tell you something else I knew. About this place, St Paul's. I knew that Sir Christopher Wren had designed it back in the 1600s after the old cathedral had been destroyed in the Great Fire of 1666. I knew that Nelson was buried in the crypt downstairs. As were Wellington, Florence Nightingale and Lawrence of Arabia. I knew that the great dome had been a symbol of Britain's defiance during the Blitz, that Prince Charles and Lady Diana had got married here in 1981 and that, after Big Ben, St Paul's was the most instantly recognisable landmark in London. It was certainly the most blatant, towering some three hundred and fifty feet above the Square Mile and being easily visible from Hampstead Heath to Crystal Palace.

I knew all of these things and more, but most importantly, I knew that every time I saw St Paul's Cathedral from now on, I'd think of Charley.

Just as I knew (or at least hoped) that Charley would think of me.

25 :-(?

I spent much of the next day checking my mobile to make sure that it hadn't rung in my pocket without me hearing it. It hadn't. Neither had it run out of battery power, forgotten how to receive a signal or clogged up with an avalanche of texts. It just hadn't rung or received anything. Anything. From anyone. Which, by definition, included Charley.

I couldn't decide whether I was surprised, disappointed, suicidal or monumentally relieved at this. Probably, if I'm honest here, disappointed, with just a dash of wrist-pondering for effect, because deep-deep-deep-deep down, at the back of my mind, in a corner of my brain I usually reserved for lottery-winning daydreams and flying-saucer fantasies, I'd half hoped she would call. I know it's nonsense. After all, I had just unceremoniously dumped her out of my life, so the chances of her calling were right up there with lottery wins and flying saucers, but still, I hadn't completely given up hope. Which was totally the wrong frame of mind to be in but, human nature being what it is, was all but inevitable. I mean, don't we all hope and pray for a happy ending when everything goes tits up? Don't we all pray for last-minute miracles? Whether we find ourselves up the financial Swannee without a penny to paddle with, in dire health straits, seven goals down to our arch-rivals or in midair following an ill-thought-through balcony short cut. Don't we all hope and pray for six beautifully bouncing balls, a revolutionary breakthrough in deathitis tablets, five minutes of utter insanity from the referee or a passing mattress lorry to save us from that terrible onrushing reality we're bracing ourselves to pancake across?

I know I did.

I hated it when shit things happened to me. And yesterday had been about as shit as I'd ever known. And contrary to all my expectations, it didn't soften the blow that at least I'd been the one who'd done the dumping because this just scribbled one enormous fucking question mark right over everything I'd done yesterday.

What if I'd been wrong?

What if I'd been wrong about everything?

Fuckkkkkkkkkkk...!

It didn't even bear thinking about, which was ironic really because up until yesterday, when I could've done something about it, this particular question hadn't even occurred to me, yet the next morning, when everything was too late and sunk beyond salvageable, I suddenly couldn't stop thinking it. Which did leave me wondering just whose side my brain was meant to be on anyway because the bastard seemed to have it in for me.

And all of this misery, all of this agony, all of this uncertainty could've been so easily wiped away with one call from Charley. Even a single text.

Hi T, how r u? :-(. U 3? Wnt 2 ><? Hv2 u Δ @ me& % wth £ if thts ;-/!!! Cxxx

I would've loved to have got one of Charley's bizarre hieroglyphic texts the following day, not least of all because I could've read absolutely anything I liked into it.

But she didn't text. She didn't call. And she didn't race around to bang on my door in the pouring rain until I swept her up into my arms and promised her I'd never bin her again.

Charley was gone.

And that was the way she was going to stay, no matter how she felt. If indeed she did feel otherwise. See, in my parents' day, perseverance was seen as a quality, faint heart never won fair maiden and that whole heap of false hope, but these days, if you showed the slightest bit of interest in someone who didn't respond exactly the same way, all your courageous heart ever won you was a restraining order and a caption in your local paper informing the rest of the community that you were a 'nuisance'.

And this wasn't just true for blokes. Any girl who's ever sent her ex-boyfriend a conciliatory card at Christmas to show there were no hard feelings has never been seen as anything other than a dangerous bunny-boiler ever since Glenn Close did her bit for broken-hearted women everywhere.

And who wanted that?

It was humiliating enough to be dumped by some stupid thicko tradesman who wasn't fit to kiss your Guccis, without everyone thinking you were desperate to win him back. After all, Charley could do ten times better than me. Maybe even twenty times if she really pushed the boat out. She knew it. Her friends all knew it. And I knew it too. She could've had anyone she wanted. Guys with money. Guys with good jobs. Guys with flashy cars, fancy Armani suits and their own skiing equipment – that they actually owned. No problem. A girl like Charley. That was how great she was.

Why would she even think about calling me again?

She wouldn't. It was as simple as that. Of course not.

And as if to prove it, she didn't.

Not once. Not even by accident while deleting my number from her phone.

In three days' time, I would finally come to accept this and move on with my life. I wouldn't move on very far, admittedly, only from desperation to devastation, but it would still be a step away from where I found myself Monday morning when Jason came calling for me.

'All right, squire. Fuck me, you look rough. Late night, was it, you old bastard?'

'I didn't get much sleep last night,' I explained.

'Oh yeah,' he winked, nudging me in the ribs from the safety of the driver's seat. 'Back in Charley's good books are you, then?'

I turned my bloodshot slits in his direction and caught the full force of his chirpy smirking worry-free delight and immediately realised today was going to be the worst day of my life.

And it was still only a quarter to seven. There was so much of it left.

'Here, pull over here so I can pick up a few beers, will you?' I told him when we passed a parade of shops. 'You want any?'

'Yeah, get us a …' he started, only stopping when he saw I was serious. 'Here, Tel, are you all right? What's the matter, mate?'

I swallowed a few times to try and summon up the words, but they had such a long way to crawl from the pit of my stomach that it took almost a full thirty seconds before I was able to spit them out.

'Me and Charley… we split up,' I choked, then let out a blub of misery before I was able to slam down the hatch again.

'Oh no, Tel, you haven't, have you?' Jason responded, shaking his head with deep regret. 'I'm so sorry, mate. Get rid of you, did she?'

'No she didn't, actually, you big cunt, I got rid of her!' I snapped back, prompting Jason to furrow his brow and ask a question I'd been asking my pillow all night long.

'Really? What d'you do that for?'

'I don't know,' I replied, my head almost fit to burst. 'You told me to.'

'Uh? You what?'

'On Friday. You said I should bin her if I wasn't happy with her,' I said.

Jason looked suitably confused and told me he never said any such thing.

'All I said was, if she wasn't making you happy, you had to ask yourself if it was worth the effort, or something like that. I never meant for you to bin her. I just meant for you to have a think about what you wanted.'

'Oh right, tell me that now,' I exaggerated.

'Don't give me this,' Jason countered. 'You've never done anything I've told you to do in your life, so don't come the old "I was only following orders" bit with me. You did what you did because you decided to do it. Now you're all gutted and looking for someone to grumble at so you're grumbling at me, but if you've given Charley her marching orders then it was for more than something I said in the pub on Friday night that I can just about remember. At least, I fucking hope so for your sake, mush,' he told me, turning us south on to the Sydenham Road.

Of course, he was right. My relationship with Charley had come a cropper on the rocks and I was trying to blame the seagulls when I'd been the one at the wheel. Actually, that wasn't true. Charley had been the one at the wheel, I'd been the one stoking the boiler down below. But then stoking the boiler was just as important as turning the wheel, as you couldn't steer if you didn't have a stoked boiler, so if the boiler stoker down below downed his shovel, then it amounted to much the same thing as turning on to the rocks.

Oh, what was I talking about? I knew even less about boats than I did about women, so what was with the seafaring analogies? I wasn't sure. I think I was just a bit bored with my usual bricklaying analogies, but the seafaring ones hadn't worked out as well as I'd hoped so I decided to switch back for the time being until I grounded myself in something else.

'You're right,' I finally admitted to Jason. 'Sorry, mate. It wasn't nothing to do with you.'

'That's all right, I know how it is,' he accepted, before asking me how I went about calling it a day with Charley, then.

I told him all about it. My lunchtime date, St Paul's Cathedral, the Whispering Gallery and her reaction, omitting only the real reason I'd picked somewhere so memorable to do the dirty.

'Well, it's a shame, I know, but if it wasn't to be, it wasn't to be, mate,' was Jason's opinion, as he pulled up at Thornton Heath roundabout next to a yawning Robbie.

'*Mawning*, chaps, have a good weekend, did we?' Robbie enquired when he drew back the side door and climbed in with his hod.

'Tel split up with Charley,' Jason quickly gossiped, clearly unable to wait until I was out of earshot to spread the breaking news.

'Nah, you ain't! Shit, that's bad news, man. What reason she give?' he asked, more or less answering his own question, in roundabout terms.

'No reason, Robbie. No reason at all,' I told him, too finished off to even put him straight.

I wondered how many of Charley's mates would make the same assumption when the news broke up in Islington. Pretty much all of them, I guessed, which meant that stupid old predictable Tel had managed to somehow catch a lot of clever people off guard with his weekend's work.

It was absolutely no consolation.

You know what, when you split up with someone, it's awkward enough bumping into one of their mates after the event as it is. All that 'yes, I'm having the time of my life what with all the great times and enormous successes I've been having just lately that I hardly even think about old whatsername any more' old bullshit you have to go through until they're far enough out of earshot that you can start crying again. And that's usually only for five minutes. Try having the bastards following you around at work all day long and pointing a camera at you whenever you open your gob. See how you like that. It takes 'putting on a front' to a whole new level.

CT was waiting for me from the off. As was Barrie and Joel with camera and boom. They normally didn't arrive until after ten o'clock but today they were here at half seven. What a coincidence.

'They're starting early, ain't they?' Robbie said, climbing out of the van with the mixer handle to start knocking up.

'You don't think that CT's here to film you, do you?' Jason asked, staring at the film crew through the van's dusty windscreen.

'That's exactly what I think,' I replied glumly, when I saw Barrie shoulder the camera at our arrival.

'What, because of you and old Charley?' Robbie couldn't believe it. 'No! That's bang out of order. You want to knock his fucking lens in if he points it at you.'

'No, don't do that. Don't give 'em the satisfaction,' Jason advised. 'They're looking for a reason to paint you as the villain, mate, make you look like a wanker for dumping Charley. Don't give it to 'em. That's the best way to give it to 'em.' Jason then turned to Robbie. 'You neither, Rob. Sunday best, boys. Pass the word.'

'Hang on a minute, you dumped Charley?' Robbie double-checked.

'Yes, I dumped Charley. Is that so unbelievable?' I replied.

Robbie didn't respond, he simply shot Jason a pair of raised eyebrows, slid out of the van and went to give Dennis a knock.

'Chin up, mate, chin up,' Jason said.

'What the fuck's he even doing here this early?' I wanted to know, incensed that I had CT to deal with on top of everything else.

'He's just nosing around, just like last week. Rise above it and don't give him anything you'll regret six months down the line. Be bigger than him.'

At this moment, Gordon came over and leaned in.

'Here, what's this Robbie's saying about matey boy trying to stitch you up?' he asked.

'Tel's split up with Charley,' Jason replied for me, positively first with the news today.

'Have ya?'

'Yes, and I dumped *her*, all right,' I pre-empted him.

'Oh. Oh right. Well, that's the main thing, I guess. So what's with Gladys? He out to start trouble, then, is he?' Gordon replied.

'No, you know him,' my official spokesman continued. 'He's just looking to make us look like arseholes, only this ain't the time, so I say we don't give the bastard nothing.'

Gordon thought about this and nodded in agreement.

'You all right today, Tel? You want to go home?' he asked.

'Nah, don't do that,' Jason interrupted. 'Worse thing he could do.'

'Yeah, I'll be OK. Get me head down and lay some bricks. That's what I need,' I told him.

'All right,' Gordon agreed. 'There's a couple of table lifts and chimneys loaded out if you want to get away from the lads. As long as you promise not to chuck yourself off the side,' he laughed, then stopped when he saw that I wasn't.

'Don't worry, Gord, I ain't going to do myself in. I dumped her, remember?' I told him.

'That's true,' Gordon agreed.

So once again I found myself thirty feet above the deck, staring out across a cloudy grey sky, well away from the hurly-burly of Monday morning.

CT hadn't approached when I'd climbed out of the van and neither had he followed me up here. Instead, he was filming the lads who were starting an oversite on the far side of the estate. I wasn't sure how much he was going to get out of them this morning seeing as Jason had them closing ranks on him like a well-drilled detachment of teenage girls. I hoped they wouldn't make their needle too obvious, as I'd tried to leave Charley on the best possible terms so that she'd think fondly of me whenever she glimpsed St Paul's, not hock one out and curse my name over the lads' treatment of her friend. Not that there was anything I could do about it if they decided to go that way. Blokes being what they are generally as a rule can't be talked out of blanking, threatening, smacking, burgling, firebombing or, most disastrous of all, having a quiet word with, a third party once they get it into their heads that they're doing their mate a favour. I just had to keep my fingers crossed and try to set an example.

Not today, though.

Not so soon afterwards.

I simply couldn't face it.

That's why I quite liked finishing off chimneys.

A lot of brickwork, such as when you're just running in a big long featureless wall, can be pretty straightforward. There's still a skill to it, don't get me wrong, but if you're a time-served trowel, you can easily switch on to autopilot and either lose yourself in your thoughts, have a natter with your mates or listen to the radio. The corners are already built, you're simply laying to the line, so there's not much to distract yourself with. But chimneys are different. There's a little bit more to them. You have to keep an eye on your measurements and your levels as you're taking them up. They have to be sturdy enough to independently withstand thirty or forty lashing British winters. The flues inside have to be set with heat resistant muck and sit flush. And they usually have to be finished off with a little ornate flourish of brickwork, usually involving a couple of different types of brick, more often than not flettons and either engineering bricks or Staffordshire blues.

So a table lift and chimney represented a good morning's work and enough of a challenge to focus my mind away from the events of the weekend.

At least, until I came to the smooth muck flaunching around the chimney pot.

It wasn't until lunchtime that CT finally came over. Remarkably, he wasn't accompanied by either his cameramen or his sound operators.

'Hey, Terry, how are you?' he asked, hanging on to the van's roof as he looked through the open window at me.

I thought better of telling him that I was 'absolutely fucking fantastic' and settled instead for downplaying it with an 'OK'.

'I heard about what happened with you and Charley at the weekend and I just wanted to say that I'm really sorry,' he explained, also looking across at Jason and the mess him and his cheese Sandrich were making all over the driver's seat to share his sincerity around.

'Yeah,' I thought to nod, then added, 'Thanks.'

'I just want you to know that whatever's happened between Charley and you, as unfortunate as it is, I hope it doesn't affect us,' he went on, presumably trying to salvage his shooting schedule in the face of the lads' change of attitude towards him and his crew.

'Yeah, you say that now,' Jason butted in on my behalf before I had a chance to answer, 'but how do we know how you're putting this programme together or what the voiceover's going to say until we see it? You could be making old Tel out to be a right cunt for all we know and we wouldn't know jack shit about it until it came on the telly for everyone to see and then what if we didn't like it? Tough shit all round.'

CT looked gobsmacked at the very suggestion and asked us if that's what we thought of him.

Once again, before I could get in between the two of them, Jason was speaking up on behalf of the silent thoughts I'd hoped to keep silent.

'Oh, come off it, Top Cat, you TV people are all the same. Everyone's best mate when you want to get your pictures, then right stitch-up merchants once you've got what you need,' Jason said through a mouthful of Hovis and Red Leicester. 'I've seen those documentaries on the telly with old Paul Daniels and Noel Edmonds and Robbie Williams and you always make them look like right wankers,' he pointed out.

Me and CT glanced at each other and the names on Jason's list and for the briefest of moments were of one mind, before CT assured us we had nothing to worry about on that score.

'I'm not here to do a hatchet job on anyone,' he promised us both. 'That's not even the style of documentary we're making. It's a seven o'clock family spot. We're just looking to make a fun and factual day-in-the-life show. We're not out to make anyone look bad.' CT then turned and spoke to me directly. 'You don't think I'm trying to portray you badly, do you, Terry?'

I didn't know what to think. Not any more. Events were out of my hands and in the laps of everyone else. If CT was going to stitch me up, then he was going to stitch me up. If the lads were going to get arsey with him, then they were going to get arsey with him. And if Charley was going to hate me, then she was going to hate me. There was nothing I could do about any of it any more, not least of all because I simply didn't have the energy to. I'd finally chucked in the towel.

'CT, I just want to come to work, get my head down and

lay some bricks. And that's all I want to do,' I almost pleaded with him.

CT weighed this up for a moment, then let out a long sigh.

'OK,' he accepted. 'You have to do what's right for you. I know it can't be easy having us here so, look, we won't get under your feet or make things difficult for you. We'll just let you get on with your job if you like,' he assured me.

As it turned out, he was as good as his word.

26 Laying bricks

Six months ticked by. Christmas came and went. And brick by brick, the estate slowly neared completion.

In all that time I didn't hear from Charley once, though she never wandered farther than a frown's throw from my face. I gave up trying to make sense out of our time together, the conclusions I'd leapt to and the decisions I'd taken, and made do with tormenting myself with dates, places and times.

A week earlier, it had been six months exactly since my last glimpse of Charley. It had been in St Paul's in the Whispering Gallery. She'd slipped through the doors to the stairs without looking back. She'd been wearing her blue suede jacket, her black cotton trousers and her knee-high heeled boots underneath; her hair had been untied, she'd worn a pale pink lip gloss and, most memorably of all, just the tiniest dab of Allure that I could still smell whenever I closed my eyes. I couldn't remember what I'd been wearing that day. I was pretty sure it wasn't my donkey jacket, hard hat and half a bottle of Brut, even though that was what my prankster memory was desperately trying to convince me I'd gone in, but it didn't really matter. All that mattered was that single point in time, because that was the last time I'd seen Charley.

And as if to complete the symmetry, in just under two weeks' time it would be a year to the day since I'd first met her. What she'd been wearing or smelling like that evening, I had no idea. I could only speak for the next morning when I'd first encountered her wearing nothing but a smile and a generous stench of champagne, but I circled that particular Saturday night in my mind all the same. Just so I could mark it with a few sad thoughts when it came around.

Despite these mental etchings, I'd managed to work alongside CT for much of the winter without Charley cropping up in the conversation. In fact, she'd been rather conspicuous by her absence and there had been times when it had been almost torturous not asking him how she was, if she was happy, how her Rocket Sauce campaign was getting along and if she'd moved on and was seeing anyone new. Anyone I might know, like a cunty four-eyed ex who'd been hanging around like a bad smell for years? Incredibly, I managed not to ask him any of these questions somehow, though by New Year's my tongue felt like an old bit of boot leather.

Still, it had actually turned out quite good to work with CT, to know that he was seeing Charley on a regular basis and that stories of me were possibly filtering back to her, so I stayed on my best behaviour, put my best foot forward and entertained myself with silly scenes in my head in which CT told a rapt Charley every detail of my working week over couscous and baby otter's cheese.

'...and he had grapes in his sandwich box the other day. He even offered me one. He's eating a lot more fruit these days and cutting down on the crisps and sausage rolls and has even switched to wholemeal bread. He says it's better for his bowels.'

'Wow, that's great. That's really good that he's looking after himself. I was worried he might go to pieces after we split up, but he's obviously made of stronger stuff and really getting on with his life, isn't he?'

'He certainly is.'

Then Simone and Lis, who'd be at the same dinner party (Hugo's dead or in prison for downloading kiddy porn at this point – hey, it's my fantasy!), would lay a comforting hand on each of Charley's shoulders and admit that they'd been wrong about me all along.

'He was actually a great bloke, wasn't he?'

'And a great catch too.'

'Why did we all think he wasn't as good as us?'

'I don't know, because he was.'

'Yes, he was.'

'I feel really bad about it now.'

'Me too.'

'Do you think there's still time?'

'To get him back, you mean?'

'Yeah, to get him back.'

'If that's what you want in your heart of hearts, poppet, then you have to go for it.'

'Really?'

'Really. You can't go on crying yourself to sleep in that big old empty bed of yours every night and living a life of celibacy.'

'I know, but what if he's not interested?'

'He will be. If he really is as great as he sounds – and from what CT tells us, he certainly seems like it, what with the fruit and wholemeal bread and bowels and everything – then he'll take you back in a shot. He'd be a fool not to.'

'Then goddammit, I'm going to do it.'

'Good for you.'

'That's fantastic.'

'We're all right behind you.'

'It's the right thing to do.'

'Absolutely. Also, we were wrong about these lentil things. They're actually really horrible, aren't they?'

'Well, I didn't want to say anything before but...'

Then, just before Christmas, CT and his crew packed away their equipment, thanked us for making them feel most welcome and said their goodbyes. They'd got all the footage they needed, so that all there was left to do was knock the programme into some sort of shape in a nice warm cutting room somewhere in the BBC. Well, I couldn't blame them for that; January on the site's not the funkiest time of year.

CT would still swing by from time to time, just to double-check a few facts for the voiceover or to get some linking footage. They had Dirty Den off *EastEnders* doing the commentary on the programme, which was pretty smart, though all the lads were gutted that we wouldn't actually get to meet him in person, not least of all because we knew we'd spend the next five years having our ear'oles bent by blokes in pubs all wanting to know what Dirty Den off *EastEnders* was like.

'Actually really posh. And really short,' were a couple of the lesser career-finishing rumours we'd start for chuckles.

I always made a point of saying hello to CT whenever he was in. I'd have a bit of a chat with him, help him with anything he needed help with and share my flask with him if he fancied a cuppa. I even showed him how to lay bricks one quiet Friday afternoon and there are probably still two or three hundred bricks on the estate that were laid by him, Barrie, Neil and Elaine when they put down their cameras, booms and clipboards and became brickies for a day. But by and large it was a pretty uneventful six months. All I really did for most of it was lay bricks, go home, have my dinner and have a few pints at the weekend. Usually with Jason. And usually in the Lamb.

Jason reckoned I needed to get myself back out there. 'Get back on the horse, chat up a few birds, have a few laughs and get some shags under your belt,' he advised, which, well-intentioned nonsense though it was, was still nonsense, even by Jason's standards. I was in no fit shape to be chatting up or shagging anyone, especially some of the Michelin women who got in the Lamb on a Friday night and whose arrival would elicit a flurry of elbows to the ribs. No, what I really needed was time. Time to forget. Time to move forward. Time to heal.

So time's what I got.

Unfortunately, the thing about time is that it takes time. Days, weeks and months can drift by with no discernible effect. All you really notice is time itself. The dates in the calendar and anniversaries that come along. It's a hard thing to tell if you're missing the person you're trying to get over less and less with each passing day because, as a rule, you're not. You care about them just as much as you did when you last saw them, only you're not able to express any of this emotion as you don't ever see them, so it stays where it is, hanging over your head like a big cloud and pissing in your beer whenever it's Miller Time for everyone else.

And the regrets?

Jesus, don't get me started. That fucking eggs Benedict incident haunted me for weeks on end after we first split up. I would lie awake at night cringing over memories of me turning my nose up at what is essentially eggs on toast, kicking up an enormous hoohah and making myself look like a right Prince Charles. I mean, what was I thinking?

And as for going straight home in a big boo after the demo instead of meeting them in the Workers' Social, how could I have thrown away a night with Charley so easily? It almost made me want to weep.

But you know the thing I regretted the most? Or at least, the thing I regretted most often. It was that final kiss we never had in the Whispering Gallery when we came to say our goodbyes. It killed me that I hadn't just bundled her up into my arms, held her tightly and pressed my lips to hers one last time. Why hadn't I done that, for God's sake? Why had I dithered while Rome had burned? There had been nothing more to say, nothing more to do; a kiss, a cuddle and an embrace? It would've been the most natural thing in the world to do. God, how many nights had I lain awake beating myself up over that lost kiss? Almost feeling it. Almost tasting it. I would've given anything to have had the chance for that one last kiss again. Anything. But the kiss was gone. I'd bottled it. Just as I'd bottled everything. What was wrong with me?

You know, thinking back on it, I'd almost bottled our whole relationship that first morning after the night before, playing it cool on the doorstep like Mr D'Arcy with the horn for his lordship's wife instead of simply asking Charley out, so I guess it was fitting that I'd bottled something at the last too. How d'you like that for symmetry?

Only that first time I'd received a reprieve in the shape of a second chance when I'd walked off with her mobile phone. I'm generally better the second time around. I rarely make the same mistakes twice and I know I wouldn't if I got another chance with Charley. Because I've seen what life's like without her and I have to say it's not a patch on what it's like with her.

There was only one problem.

There was no reprieve.

There was no second chance.

What was done was done.

The bricks were laid. The muck had dried. And Charley was on the other side of the wall.

She was gone.

27 At the keyhole

Well, the day finally arrived and a very exciting day it promised to be too. No, this had nothing to do with Charley, though I managed to shoehorn thoughts of her in there anyway. I'm talking about the day our programme came on the telly.

CT had given us a call a couple of months earlier to let us know that the show had been scheduled and the good news didn't stop there. For reasons I found difficult to follow and a bit tedious trying to, our programme had been switched from BBC3 to BBC1, which meant that a few people might even get to see it now, including Robbie, who's telly still didn't even get Channel Five.

Personally speaking, I was quite surprised we had to wait until it actually came on the telly as I thought CT and his bosses might've invited us into their offices for a sneaky preview, though I guess they decided against that on the grounds that they didn't want cement dust walked all through the BBC.

Still, it was exciting nevertheless, and there wasn't a bloke on the site who didn't buy a copy of the *Radio Times* the moment it came out to see what it said about us.

And here it is, here's what their big write-up said about our show:

7.00. NEW Building Site *Docu-soap following the fortunes of a gang of brickies.* 9947 Txt.

*   *   *

Now I'll admit right off the bat that I hadn't expected us to be on the front cover or nothing but by that same token I had thought our write-up might've given a bit more away than the unknown soldier's epitaph. It also annoyed all the hoddies, chippies, spreads, roofers, plumbers, sparkies, groundworkers, painters, scaffolders, sales staff, surveyors and everyone else who'd contributed to the programme over the last six months something rotten as it made the classic assumption that the only people who mattered on any given building site were the brickies. I guess it's a bit like when Americans appear on *Parkinson* and refer to our country as a whole as England, prompting Jocks, Taffs, Micks and weird little islanders up and down the length and breadth of the United Kingdom to put their boots through the telly.

Still, I was one of the brickies, and an English one at that, so what did I care?

One of the lads suggested we all got together to watch it when it came on and this suggestion was enthusiastically received for about thirty seconds until Jason pointed out that as hardly any of us lived near each other, nine out of ten of us would have to drive and therefore be unable to drink, spelling a death knell to that particular idea.

In the end, me, Jason and Robbie agreed to get together to watch it up at the Lamb when it came on, so that's where we found ourselves at seven o'clock the following Wednesday evening, with the pints lined up on the bar behind us, watching the end of the regional news with increasing palpitations.

Hardly anyone else was in the pub this early, and those that were – old Stan, Paul, Peggy, Tony the landlord, of course, and a few others – knew the occasion and marked it with a cheer when the programme started.

I'm sure I don't even need to tell you that my thoughts flickered to Charley in those first few seconds.

I wondered if she'd be watching. And I wondered what she would think when she saw me. Or indeed, if she'd see me, seeing as I'd kicked up such a strop six months earlier that CT had more or less promised to stop pointing the camera my way. This was something I kind of regretted now, but what could I do about it? Moan my guts out about not being on the telly when I'd already moaned my guts out about not wanting to be on the telly? And perhaps while I was at it I could tell Jason he was my best friend, Robbie he was my second-best friend, old Stan he was my third-best friend, and then sit on the steps crying my eyes out until everyone had agreed to make me their best friend. If I wanted to be childish about this sort of thing.

These thoughts were thankfully banished with a roar when Robbie came on screen throwing sand and water into a mixer only to suffer an almighty great splashback for his troubles. Dirty Den introduced us to Robbie and told us how old he was, how long he'd been a hoddy and a bit about his daily duties and I fought the urge to turn to him and ask him for his autograph.

Robbie's slapstick moment was followed by a procession of familiar faces from all corners of the site, including a shot of Jason nodding at the camera nonchalantly as he walked past, his tools slung over his shoulder and his face chiselled into that haunted thousand-yard stare that only the most battle-hardened of brickies wore on their way back from the front line.

'Twat,' Robbie observed for both of us, and Jason looked dour and admitted there was a lot more Vietnam-vetting from him to come.

'I thought it looked cool,' he muttered, the colour drained from his face.

Gordon distracted us further, taking the camera on a quick tour of an oversite the lads were working on before snatching up his trowel and slashing into the muck and bricks with such a vigour that it pretty much guaranteed that particular section of wall would've had to have been rebuilt the moment the cameras were off him.

As for me, I was nowhere to be seen, and I was just starting to think that I'd snubbed my fifteen minutes of fame as well as the love of my life when the camera pointed to the horizon and zoomed in on me working on one of the countless chimneys I'd built over the last twelve months. I recognised the house straight away and remembered roughly when I'd been up there, but I wasn't allowed to dwell on these thoughts for too long as Jason was talking about me directly to the camera.

'*Had a bit of a rough weekend on the love front did old Tel, so we like to bundle him off away from us on a Monday morning and let the poor kitten get on with it,*' Rambo laughed, prompting half a dozen similar remarks from the lads, a couple of which came dangerously close to mentioning Charley by name.

I turned to Jason in disbelief and he was suddenly even more ashen faced than before.

'What was all that about?' I demanded.

'I don't know. I can't remember. I may have said a couple of things about you, but I didn't think they'd put them in the programme,' Jason simultaneously confessed next to me and laughed like a drain about on-screen.

'*Never let a woman get the better of you because that's what happens,*' on-screen Jason reckoned. '*I've always said I'd rather live my life on my own terms and alone rather than dance to someone else's tune.*'

'When did you ever say that?' I challenged him.

'On the telly. Just then. When you were working on that chimney,' he told me, before adding: 'Sandra's going to kill me. Can I stay at yours tonight?'

'No you fucking can't.'

Dirty Den then cut in to take us across the site and for five minutes we followed Dan the chippy around a joist lift while he looked for a pencil that was actually perched behind his ear. Then we went off and watched the plumbers putting rads into a half-finished home, then the site agent knocked on the door and came in for a cameo, before once again we headed off to a different location to watch a couple of spreads flinging plaster up and down the walls like a pair of H-Block lifers with a tune on their lips. All in all, it was a bit like being at work, only I actually got to hear what the wankers said about me behind my back.

'I'm sorry, mate, honestly, I know I said some things I shouldn't have but you know how it is; we were just taking the mick. Didn't mean nothing by it,' Jason apologised again, quickly waving Tony over to top up my pint, but I told him not to sweat on it, it was fine. After all, no one had been a better mate to me over the last year than Jason, and part and parcel of being mates with someone is the joy of ripping the piss out of them in times of need.

It really is 'just what you do'.

With the best intentions in the world, no one can offer an unlimited supply of tea and sympathy without cracking a few gags along the way for their troubles, otherwise we'd all go mad or grow tits. So no, I wasn't angry or annoyed at the lads for putting the boot in behind my back, as I'm sure I've probably done the same to others in my time.

It was just weird seeing something that I'd so clearly never been meant to see. It was the ultimate 'listening at keyholes' experience and a little unsettling, to be honest.

Before we knew it, half an hour was up and the on-screen lads were packing away their tools for the evening and making for their motors behind a scroll of rolling credits. They even included a little scene of me waving goodnight to the roofers and climbing down from my chimney as Dirty Den told us to tune in next week for more 'high drama from the boys from the building site'.

And then it was over. As quickly as it had come, it was gone.

'That was wicked, wasn't it?' Robbie reckoned, as Tony, Paul and Peggy came over to slap us all on the back and agree. Only old Stan sat his ground, perhaps a little intimidated to be in the company of three such enormous celebrities.

Almost immediately our phones started popping with beeps as everyone we knew sent us texts or tried to call us to say they'd been watching and as much fun as it was for about an hour, eventually we had to turn them off just to get a little peace.

Ha, famous at last and already sick of it.

Still, we toasted ourselves long into the night, which was pretty stupid considering it was a work night, and inevitably pulled a trio of gorgeous kebabs on the stagger home.

When I got in, I turned my mobile back on to see who else had left a message and it beeped away like R2D2 making a dirty phone call. After thirty or so seconds, R2 blew himself out and I checked the enormous list of text and voicemail messages for a specific name. But it wasn't there.

I had enough messages on my phone for it to qualify as heavy reading but the one text I'd spent the last couple of months kidding myself into believing I would receive never came.

Perhaps not everyone had been watching after all.

Naturally, the entire site showed up for work the next day with an almighty hangover. I'm not sure how much actual work got done that day but I reckon if we'd all pooled our efforts, we wouldn't have housed a divorced ant.

Tommy seemed to have taken his new-found celebrity status most to heart and spent the best part of the day asking us if his face really looked as fat as it did on the telly.

'The camera adds ten pounds, don't you know?' Big John told him.

'Yeah, and those sausage-and-egg sandwiches you've been

living off all year have probably contributed a couple of ounces too, you fat fuck,' Jason suggested.

As you'd expect, most of the day's chit-chat was taken up with the obvious and we jabbered on about almost nothing else until the conversation finally burned itself out the following morning. CT chose that particular afternoon to drop by to see how the show had been received, briefly reigniting the whole tedious topic again, but that flying visit aside most of us were done with the conversation until the following Wednesday.

Naturally, we all tuned in again, but this time around there wasn't the same level of excitement or anticipation that had heralded in the first episode. Don't get me wrong, it was still exciting and there was still a buzz about the place that day, but it didn't quite feel like the life-changing, seismic event that the previous week's episode had. We were still here. We were still working. And we were still able to walk up to the corner shop for a Scotch egg without being mobbed by crazed and adoring teeny fans.

Nothing had changed for us.

And Charley still hadn't rung.

It was all very disappointing.

But things didn't stay disappointing for very long.

No, as the weeks went by, the disappointment soon gave way to disbelief as more and more episodes were screened. Week after week, we tuned into a show I began thinking should've actually been called *Stick It to Tel* rather than *Building Site* as this seemed to be the recurring theme. Again and again we'd cut away from some token scene of roofers roofing or plasterers plastering to eavesdrop on one of my mates nattering around the mixer about my chances of finding a diplomatic solution to my relationship. Sometimes the lads were aware of the cameras, sometimes they weren't, but mine and Charley's problems inched their way towards centre stage a little more each week.

It was like CT was growing in confidence the more shows he got under his belt. There had been just the merest mention of us that first week and he'd got away with it, so come the second, there we were again, only this time in more detail. And then the third. And then the fourth. And so on. All spread out for teatime viewers to pick over and digest.

Talk about reopening old wounds. It was more than a little jaw-dropping.

All our rows were there too, like a collection of porcelain squabbles; the wanky bars, the dinner parties, the posh food and her dodgy time-keeping, the fact that Charley earned more in a year than I would in three (and that's before subtracting all the unpaid rainy days I'd lose) and our niggling little disagreements over newspapers, celebrities and the need to clip kids around the ear on a regular basis. They all made unwelcome appearances. Even the classic old theory about posh birds and rough bits of trade made it in there thanks to a moment of profound insight from Robbie, which pretty much ticked my entire card.

All there, and all snaking their way through the series like pockets of rising damp.

I tell you, when CT set out to do a job on someone, he really did a job. I had to give him that much if nothing else.

Naturally, whenever my name was mentioned by either Dirty Den or the lads, the camera would find me in the distance and zoom in on me, either finishing off one of my chimneys, trudging around a footing or forlornly picking my nose in the van.

By Christ, I cut a sorry figure and no mistake.

In fact, the only mistake I'd made was to give CT the benefit of the doubt that his loyalties to Charley wouldn't cloud his judgement and lead him to portray me as some sort of enormous lovesick mug – which I guess I had been at times, but still, that was no excuse for letting the rest of the country in on the joke.

What an arsehole.

And by that, I mean CT.

By episode five, pretty much half the programme was now taken up with the lads' gossip about me and Charley and our petty trials and tribulations. It had simply ballooned out of all sense of proportion.

Gone was any anger I'd initially felt at CT; in its place instead was honest-to-goodness incomprehension. Forget how my late-lamented love life wasn't anybody else's business, I simply couldn't figure out how CT had thought it would be of interest to the viewers. I mean, blimey, there was some pretty tedious shit flying about on this building site of ours, I'll tell you.

One week there was a little subplot where Charley hadn't phoned me. *Boo hoo*.

Then there was the incident where she hadn't wanted me to meet her parents. *Whahh!*

Then there was that hilarious spat where I'd gone to a party with some of her mates one weekend and Charley had once again spent the whole night talking to Hugo instead of me. *Lord take me now!*

All brought to the attention of the Great British licence-fee-paying public courtesy of *the fucking lads*.

I mean, 'Christ Almighty. Big deal. So what?' was basically what my neighbours heard me shouting at the telly every Wednesday at seven.

I didn't want to have to relive this puerile drivel week in week out and surely I wasn't alone in this. I would flinch each time my name was mentioned and grit my teeth whenever I saw a tiny me looking away into the middle distance with starry eyes. It got to the point where I longed to see that wet blanket either pull himself together or take a long walk off a short length of scaffolding.

I mean, what had happened to Dan the chippy's pencil? Hadn't he found it yet or what? Why weren't the BBC dedicating a prime-time half-hour slot to that drama? It was on a similar par with my hullabaloo.

I really, really, *really* couldn't credit how CT had thought he could get away with it either. And by that I don't mean he had anything to fear from me or the lads because he didn't. We might not greet him with big sloppy kisses if he ever dared show his face on our site again but no one was of a mind to turn his lights out. Not even me, who it could be argued had every right after being stitched up like some middle-class kipper's mum.

No, I was talking about his bosses at the Beeb.

Surely they weren't going to take kindly to him using *their* show for his own private muckraking. I mean, how could they? All that money, all that manpower and all that screen time and all they'd got for this substantial outlay was six episodes of some sullen bricky walking around with his thumb up his arse. Nice. It was possibly the equivalent of Gordon asking me to set out a footing on a three-bed semi, only for him to come along half an hour later and see that I'd decided to spell out 'TEL IS THE GREATEST' with all the bricks instead. That would be a sacking offence at the very least with possibly a referral to the site psychiatrist – if such a person existed. But they didn't. I wondered if they did at the BBC. I hoped so for CT's sake because he was going to need all the wordy sick notes he could lay his hands on if he wanted to keep his job after *Building Site*.

I even half thought about suing. Actually, I never really thought about it. Jason suggested it one night while we were on the lash, which was about the only time it made any sense. Come the next morning, two ibuprofen and a double egg-and-sausage sandwich later, I knew I didn't have a leg to stand on (much like the previous evening). I'd signed a waiver agreeing to be filmed, I'd had nothing more than my pride hurt and at the end of the day I'd said and done all of these things.

Or at least, Jason and the lads had.

Maybe I should sue them?

At the end of the day, I was just embarrassed by the whole affair and wanted nothing more than for it all to go away. Even if there had been grounds and I'd had a spare few grand burning a hole in my bank account for the lawyers, the prospect of slinging 'you said this' and 'you said that' backwards and forwards across an open courtroom for two weeks didn't exactly get me whistling.

All I'd ever wanted was to be able keep my dignity, keep my pride and end things with Charley amicably. It had been the whole reason I'd bought two tickets to St Paul's and deleted her number from my phone the very next day, because I hadn't wanted to expose Charley to my soft underbelly.

Me moping around like a wounded kitten.

Me looking like a sap.

Me looking hurt.

But most of all, I hadn't wanted Charley to feel bad about dumping me... hang on, I dumped her, didn't I? For some reason, I always remembered it the other way around. Anyway, I didn't want her feeling bad whichever way the cards had fallen, which I guess was my real concern. I was big enough and hairy enough to take all of this nonsense on the chin. But I was genuinely worried about Charley, though admittedly for selfish reasons.

I didn't want to give her any excuse to hate me.

Or to remember me poorly.

Or curse our time together.

Or feel embarrassed that we'd been close at one time.

And what tumbled out of our screens for six weeks gave her every reason and then some to feel all of the above, culminating in Jason's observation in the final show that my collywobbles were born long before I met Charley.

'See, the way Tel sees it,' Jason told Big John as the camera eavesdropped, 'is if Jo could walk out on him for some supermarket manager without so much as a cheerio, then what chance did he have of hanging on to a bird like Charley?'

Which was funny because I couldn't remember saying anything of the sort to Jason, which probably meant that this pet theory was all his own work – though that didn't necessarily mean there was no truth to it.

I don't know, but I didn't really have time to think about it because I was suddenly far too busy reeling from CT's final parting shot.

When exactly he'd filmed it, I couldn't tell you, but he'd saved the best for last and played it out masterfully.

It was one final humiliation for poor old Terry to chew on.

Jason had just finished speculating as to the reasons for my and Charley's break-up when the shot changed and suddenly we were looking down over the site from above. I guess CT must've rented a helicopter and buzzed the place at the weekend because I don't remember him flying overhead any time during the week, but that was really neither here nor there. All that mattered was that from above we could suddenly see what I'd only intended God, the birds and passing rocketmen to see – my chimney-top declarations.

Oh… bollocks…

In complete honesty, I didn't realise I'd done so many, but there they were in all their glory, around the tops of every chimney flue and as blatant as the horrified expression on my face.

Terry ♡ Charley, 2008
I love Charley, Terry 08
Terry + Charley, xxx
x Charley x 3/5/08
T&C 4ever
T+C=♡ 2008
Charley Charley Charley Terry Aug 08

```
With all my heart T2Cxx
Be mine T+Cx
```

And most pointedly of all:

```
I miss Charley, T
```

These messages were repeated again and again and again, in every flaunching, on every chimney, on every house and on every street of our little estate. Scored in soft muck and hardened for posterity. Messages that should never have been seen. Messages that should never have been read. And messages that should never have *been*.

Much like Charley and myself, I guess.

28 Hitting the roofs

Jason knocked on my door around half nine that night.

'I've been trying to phone you for the last two hours,' he said, when I finally opened up.

'I unplugged it,' I told him, my eyes bloodshot with beer, tears and shame.

'What d'you do that for?' he asked in all seriousness.

'Well, I didn't suppose anyone would want to speak to me this evening, so I was trying to save the battery obviously, you twat. What d'you think I unplugged it for?'

Jason pondered this for a moment and agreed it had been a stupid question.

'So,' he speculated, following me into the flat, 'watch anything on the telly tonight?'

I slumped on the sofa and chewed on my lip. This was where it started. I'd successfully managed to dodge the consequences of my actions for two measly hours, but now Jason was here to crank open the floodgates.

I guess this is what inevitably happens when you do something stupid. On such occasions all you ever really want is for the source of your embarrassment to go away, be forgotten or at least be swept under the carpet and never spoken of again, but before you can get to that point, you have to run the gauntlet of smart-arse quips or overly concerned arms around the shoulder (the smart-arse quips being infinitely more preferable).

'Get it over with,' I told Jason, before ripping open another can of lager.

'Tel, mate, I ain't here to have a go at you, but what were you thinking?' he asked, curiously sounding like he was having a go at me.

'What do you mean, what was I thinking? You read my housing estate, didn't you? You know what I was thinking,' I replied, then conceded, 'or rather, wasn't.'

'But Jesus, Terry, we all know you're cut up about Charley and everything but you could get the sack for what you did,' Jason then said, which knocked me along the sofa by a good six inches as this upshot hadn't even occurred to me.

'You don't think I might, do you?' I suddenly fretted.

'I don't know, mate, you might do. I mean, you defaced God knows how many houses and left the company open to as many compensation claims. At the very least they might have you up on all the roofs repointing every flaunching in your own time or have your wages docked to pay for the job. And that's if you're lucky.'

Oh, bollocks.

I tell you, when it rained it fucking poured, didn't it? And to think, only thirty seconds earlier I'd been worried that everyone was going to laugh at me, but now all I could see was a horizon of angry faces all demanding my head because I'd vandalised their properties. The calls would start at the top of course with the chairman of the company, and they'd tumble downwards through the shareholders, regional manager, site agent and finally Gordon, before knocking me on to the dole with a thump.

All I could do was hope that the blame would stop with me. I'd feel dreadful if I'd landed Gordon in it or cost him any money or future contracts. That would be more than I could bear. Christ, how was this all going so disastrously pear shaped?

'I'd better give Gordon a ring,' I concluded, and endured a five-

minute tongue-lashing from said subby before he finally calmed
down enough to tell me to keep my chin up.

'Look, no real harm done, lad, not when you think about it.
Nothing structural or nothing, so we'll just go see Pete in the
morning and offer to put it all straight, OK?' Gordon proposed,
before telling me to stop apologising. 'See you in the morning,
boy.'

It was only after I'd hung up that I noticed no mention was
made of money and I asked Jason if he thought I should offer to
cover the costs when I saw him.

'Stop trying to pre-empt everything, mate. Just see what
they've got to say and go with that. I mean, it's not like their
share price ain't done all right these last six weeks, so don't go
making any offers they might take you up on,' Jason insisted,
then chuckled, 'even if you have just knocked them out of the
FTSE 100, you big, dumb, love-struck idiot.'

The next morning came around surprisingly quick, despite the
fact that I hardly slept a wink. The alarm went off at half-six and
I got out of bed to the sounds of my own pitiful whimpering.

I know this is probably stating the obvious here but there's
something about facing the music that holds a particular
foreboding for us stupid people. It's not like going to the dentist's
or having your lungs swapped out in a transplant operation,
it's an altogether different kind of dread, because there's zero
accompanying sympathy.

I did it. And now it was time for me to face up to it.

What's the matter, don't like it? Good, that's the point. Facing
the music's all about not liking it. In fact, the more I didn't like it,
the better. That was music-facing in a nutshell. That was being
sorry and being made to feel sorry. That was what today was all
about.

I knew all of this as I washed my face and I knew all of this as I brushed my teeth. I would've known all of this as I made my sandwiches too but I didn't make any sandwiches, not this particular day. I didn't deserve sandwiches. All I deserved was a flask, but even then I stewed the tea slightly to stop myself from enjoying it too much.

That was all I deserved.

Jason was already parked up and waiting for me when I emerged. I braced myself for the first dig of the day but Jason just told me not to worry about it. What was done was done. The worst they could do was sack (and possibly sue the arse off) me but that was it, and in thirty or forty years' time we'd look back on this day and laugh.

'Can't wait,' I glumly replied, as Jason twisted the key in the ignition and drove me towards my fate.

I didn't say much during the van ride over, Jason did enough jabbering for the both of us. Then when Robbie climbed in at Thornton Heath roundabout, the conversation clock reset and the whole thing started all over again.

I realised this was how it was going to be for the next few weeks: the same questions, the same digs and the same bewildered looks, and I wondered if it was at all possible to rent a big marquee, fill it with everyone I knew, everyone I'd ever known and everyone I was ever likely to know, and invite them to ask me 'what the fuck' for an hour or two to get my humiliation dealt with in one fell swoop. It would be logistically difficult to arrange and probably pretty pricey, but it might be worth it all the same. Especially if Jason set up a stall selling rotten tomatoes and old cabbages. We might even make a bit of the money back. Enough to pay for a few chimneys in fact. Worth a thought.

Unfortunately it would have to wait, because like my night's sleep, the van ride was over all too quickly and suddenly we were here.

We were at work.

We rounded the corner and pulled on to the estate, but all at once Jason suddenly hit the brakes.

'What the shit...?' he spluttered, staring straight ahead towards where we normally parked.

'What is it?' Robbie asked in the back, climbing forward to peer over our shoulders. 'Who are all them lot?'

'Christ knows. Jesus, you don't think they're here for us, do you?' Jason fretted.

Fifty yards ahead, where normally only beaten-up old Escorts and sleeping hoddies lingered, a swell of bodies turned to greet us. I don't know how many people were there, maybe two or three dozen. Definitely too many for us to mow down, so I suggested we stuck the van into reverse and got out of there as fast as our tyres could carry us.

'Before they drag us from the van and murder us,' I added. 'Come on, I've seen these films. I know what happens next.'

A ripple of excitement bristled over the crowd and suddenly the front row made a break towards us.

I yelped with fear and Jason knocked a few hundred quid off the value of the van as he tried wrestling us into reverse before suddenly we were careening backwards at top lick. Robbie was already ripping through our tool buckets in the back looking for weapons in case we had to make a last stand as the mob outside were now howling up a storm.

'Go go go!' I urged Jason, but inexplicably he slammed on the brakes. 'What the fuck are you doing?' I demanded, but a horn blast and a rear window full of concrete lorry answered that question for me.

I turned back just in time to see the first few ranks of our pursuers wrap themselves around the front of the van and start demanding me by name.

'Terry!'

'Terry!'

'Terry!'

'Terry, did she call?'

'Terry, do you still love her?'

'Terry, what message do you have for our readers?'

The three of us stared at the melee in dismay and disbelief as more and more faces poured in from every angle to fill the windscreen.

'Terry, when did you first start writing your messages?'

'Terry, where else have you been writing them?'

'Terry, did she call?'

Eventually Jason succumbed to his need to continually point out the obvious.

'I think they're here for you, mate.'

29 Lofty reactions

I've never been the centre of attention before, which is fine by me, by the way. Don't get me wrong, this ain't a 'no one ever loved me' bid for sympathy. It's just a fact. I'm more of a background sort of person. It's where I'm most comfortable. I like to have my opinion heard as much as the next bloke. And I like to have friends. But I'm not one of these people who feels the need to hog every conversation or jump up on stage at the drop of a karaoke microphone. I'm just a normal fella, I reckon. Perhaps even normaller than most, if that makes sense or is an actual word. I'm certainly shyer. I don't know.

All I do know is that it freaked me out no end having every eye within a hundred yards of me boring into my skull. It made me feel very weird indeed, like I was naked or something.

And if this wasn't bad enough, you try having sixteen simultaneous conversations first thing in the morning and see how that starts off your day. They weren't aggressive or nothing, the reporters. They weren't like in the movies, all shouting, screaming and knocking my teeth out with tape recorders. They were all perfectly polite and patient. There was just sixteen of them and they all seemed to want to ask five different questions at once so that I couldn't keep track of whether I was telling them I hadn't heard from Charley, was looking to get back with her or ever sat outside her flat in my van at midnight crying.

'No, I mean yes. What? No, it's not my van. Er...'

Lurking towards the back of the crowd were Gordon, Dennis,

Big John and Nobby, all of which had already held their own press conferences and were now reaching in to pluck me from the limelight.

Naturally, the cameramen and journalists tried to keep pace with us but we successfully lost them at the gates when Brian, the health and safety officer, pointed out that they needed Toe Tecs and hard hats in order to be admitted beyond this point. Incredibly, one enterprising young hack had foreseen this and dressed for the occasion, so Brian pointed out that they also needed to be builders and actually work here to get in, which somewhat pissed all over his brand-new shiny Toe Tecs.

'Blimey, are all them journalists?' I asked the lads, looking back at all the jostling faces at the gates.

'No, not all of them. Some are just fans here to get a look at you, would you believe. Looks like you might get mobbed going up the shops for that Scotch egg after all,' Big John chuckled.

'Shit, and I didn't bring any sandwiches either,' I suddenly realised.

Instead of going to work, Gordon led me straight to the site office for a sit-down with Pete, the site agent. I'd expected only hostility and humiliation when I got to work but what I actually found was generosity, humour and understanding. Though it took me a while to realise this.

Pete's secretary, Grace, smiled at me full beam when I stepped into the office and told me that her mum had even cried at the end of the programme.

'I'm sorry, tell her I'll repoint her chimney first, I promise I will,' I replied, to universal amusement.

Pete looked up from his phone call and told whoever he was talking to that I'd just arrived and that he'd call them back, before hanging up.

'Morning, Terry. And how are you today?' he asked in a

weirdly over-familiar way that got my fur standing up on end before we'd even started.

'I'm really sorry, Pete. Honest I am. It was a really stupid thing to do and I promise I never thought anyone would ever see any of them, I swear,' I told him.

'Well, what d'you do them for, then?' came the question I'd been dreading and the one I still can't answer today.

'I don't know. I was just... being stupid, I guess. I've never done anything like that before and, to be honest, I never realised I'd done so many. I seriously wasn't thinking but I promise I'll put 'em all right out of my own pocket,' I volunteered, ignoring Jason's latest advice. Well, why break the habit of a lifetime?

'No you will not,' Pete told me in no uncertain terms. 'Do you have any idea just how many phone calls we've had this morning regarding your handiwork?'

'That's why I said I'd repair it all,' I implored, desperate to head off the sort of legal action that would see me moving into an address that boasted cardboard furniture and trains running backwards and forwards across the roof. 'Please,' I implored.

'Terry, these ain't complaints,' Pete then said. 'These are people who want to buy.'

'What?' I replied, my pleas suddenly smacking face first into one of my own brick walls.

'These are people who want to buy the houses. The phone's been ringing off the hook in the sales office. We've got five appointments to see every house and we've even got interest in the houses that ain't even going to be houses for another six months yet. The place has gone potty,' he explained.

'But why?' I asked. 'Didn't they see the programme last night?'

Pete stared at me like I'd just asked him where babies came from.

'No, Terry, they didn't. This is all one massive coincidence,' he replied with deadpan sarcasm. Well, fair enough, but come on, I'm not exactly an Oxford don at the best of times and this morning I was feeling particularly fuzzy headed.

'So, people saw the programme last night, saw what I'd done and still wanted to buy the houses?' I talked through, for the benefit of myself and the Portakabin walls.

'Not still wanted to buy, but wanted to buy *because* of what you'd done. They're asking for specific houses by the specific chimneys, the most popular of which seem to be the two houses with Terry ♡ Charley, 2008 on them. You should've done more of them, they're shifting like fucking hot cakes, they are,' Pete pointed out.

'I don't get it.' I shrugged.

'No, you really don't, do you, you silly bastard?' Pete shook his head. 'Go on then, go and do some work. I've got Reuters to get back to.'

I thanked Pete (for what I wasn't quite sure) and was just leaving the office when he called after me:

'Oh, just one other thing, don't deface any more houses unless we tell you to, eh, there's a good chap.'

The lads and a lot of questions were waiting for me and Gordon outside and we chatterboxed like a Thursday morning post office queue until Pete appeared at the doorway and pointed out that he hadn't been joking about us doing some work.

'Come on then, chaps, hi ho, hi ho,' Gordon sang, leading the lads off to a band lift across the way while me, Jason and Robbie headed for the van. See, unfortunately, when all this madness had kicked off, we'd had to abandon the van where we'd been surrounded and all our tools were still inside.

'Does either of you fancy getting mine for me?' I suggested, pulling up twenty yards short of a fresh barrage of demands and camera clicks.

'All right, I'll get them for you this one time, but don't you go thinking that, now you're a big celeb, you don't have to carry your own tools,' Jason warned me, before being swallowed by the mob.

'Terry! Terry! Terry!' called the crowd, when they clocked me again.

I didn't fancy getting sucked back into it all over again and thought about moving away and waiting for Jason and Robbie by the bottom of the ladder, but I'd wandered too close to the journalists and was now within shouting range again. I could've just ignored them, of course, but I didn't want to appear rude, like fame had gone to my head or something, and before I knew it I was answering a whole load of new questions, mainly about what Gordon and Pete had just talked to me about.

'Did they tell you to stop writing your love messages?'

'Will you still be building all the chimneys?'

'Was there any talk of disciplinary action?'

'Did the company know about them from the start?'

And so on.

Again I didn't know which questions to answer first and tried to explain that it had all been one big, stupid mistake, and that I should've never done what I'd done, but I couldn't tell if they were listening.

'Please, I don't want any of this. Seriously, you'll just stir it up for me,' I pleaded, setting three dozen pencils frantically scribbling.

'But has Charley called, Terry?' the mob continued to demand.

'No,' I reluctantly admitted, hoping this would quell their questions.

'But you're hoping she will, right?' the hard-hatted journalist asked, trying to pin me down.

'I don't know,' I parried.

'You don't know if you'd like her to call or you don't know if she will call?' he pressed.

'No,' I replied, before quickly changing this to 'yes' when it occurred to me that I wasn't entirely sure what I was saying 'no' to.

'So when she does call, where will you take her? What's your ideal make-up date?' the conversation moved on, even though I couldn't remember confirming whether I wanted Charley to call or not.

'No, wait, I didn't say that. I think you've got it wrong,' I insisted, but no one turned their pencils around to rub anything out. Quite the opposite in fact. 'Please,' I pleaded, 'this is all getting mixed up.'

But suddenly I knew none of it mattered. They'd just go off and write what they wanted to write and there was precious little I could do about it. They'd fit their stories together like crazy-paving slabs and twist the facts and half-truths to fit any story they wanted to sell until I looked like some bunny-boiling bricky from the back of beyond. And when everyone was done having a right good laugh at my expense, and Charley was hoarse from cursing my name, I'd be left to stew in my own stupidity for the rest of my days.

There's an expression that I believe's particularly apt for times like these – *when you're in a hole, stop digging.*

I thanked everyone for their interest and was about to walk away when Jason and Robbie emerged from the crowd with my tools and something more besides.

They had Charley.

Charley was with them.

There was Charley.

The sight of her proved such a shock to the system that my brain simply froze up and for a good ten seconds I stood there gawping at her with my gob swinging open like a mixer winding down at tea break.

There was Charley!

I hadn't seen her in eight months. I hadn't even seen a picture of her in all that time, because I'd never been able to pluck up the courage to ask her for one in case she'd thought I was being uncool, so all I'd had to go on these last few lonely months was a dog-eared, rose-tinted memory of her.

But suddenly, she was there.

She turned her green eyes to mine and blinked. I would've blinked back, but I was suddenly far too busy drinking in the sight of her: the way she looked, the way she moved, the way she shook her head and frowned at me in disbelief. It was like I hadn't seen her in a thousand years, yet she'd never been away.

'Coming through. Mind your backs, chaps,' Jason was saying, as he and Robbie led her through the scrimmage.

Luckily, no one else seemed to notice Charley. Not the journalists, the fans of the show or any of the dozen or so other nosy parkers who'd taken the morning off to swing by and catch a glimpse of Britain's biggest doughnut. I guess no one else knew what she looked like, so the lads were able to walk her through the crowd and right up to the gates before she was finally stopped by Brian.

Intrusive questions continued to be hurled at me, but I could no longer hear them, Charley had taken possession of all of my senses and it took me the longest possible time before I was even able to breathe.

A few of the assembled press finally started to twig that something was afoot and looked about their ranks for the source of my astonishment. I guess we might've still got away with it had Brian simply let Charley through, but he was being a stickler for H&S rules this morning and in no mood to make exceptions.

With nothing else for it, Robbie made the supreme sacrifice and handed over his hard hat and Toe Tecs, and it was only when he started tying Charley's laces that the press finally clocked her for who she was.

'Come on, quick,' Jason urged her, dropping the hard hat over her blonde locks and bundling her through the site gates.

She barely had time to find her stride before the camera flashes started exploding behind her and for the briefest of moments she was lit up like an angel – though this could've just been me putting her on a pedestal again. I never learn, I don't.

'Come on,' Charley shouted, grabbing me by the hand as she and Jason raced past.

Jason realised he was probably surplus to requirements after about fifty yards or so and dropped out of the race, but me and Charley sprinted on until we reached the site's brick drop and it was here, shielded by a few thousand flettons and a couple of hundred spiders, that she pushed me against the stacks and told me what a wanker I was.

'I'm sorry…' I started to say, but Charley cut right across me.

'Shut up!' she snapped. 'Just shut up! Don't say anything for two minutes and just listen to me for once, will you.'

I went out on a limb and mumbled 'OK', but figured it was probably best to leave it at that. I guessed Charley was in more of a talking mood than a listening mood this morning.

'You're a wanker, Terry. A total bloody wanker,' she told me, like this was news to me. 'I don't know what to make of you, I really don't. My head's all over the place. I mean, what the fuck, Terry? What the fuck?'

I sensed this was a rhetorical question so I didn't try to answer it.

Finally, Charley calmed down long enough to collect her thoughts.

'Do you have any idea how much you hurt me?' she asked,

screwing up her face and wiping her nose on the back of her sleeve. 'You hurt me like you can't believe, Terry. You really really hurt me. And for what?'

'I didn't mean to...' I tried, but she just slapped me down again.

'No, Terry, just button it. I've spent the last six weeks listening to your side of the story, so now you're going to listen to mine,' Charley told me in no uncertain terms, threatening me with a pre-sharpened wagging finger. I saw that there was nothing more for it but to assume the being-told-off position and let Charley vent her chest. Hang on, that wasn't the expression, was it? I tried to remember what the expression was but stopped when I found myself looking at her tits in an effort to jog my memory.

'Terry, I liked you. I liked you ever such a lot, in fact. And I thought you liked me, too,' she told me, in that 'disappointed' way women seemed to perfect when they met me.

'I did,' I told her.

'For *me*, I mean, Terry. Not for my money, not for my lifestyle, not for my friends, or my job or my expensive dimmer switches. I thought you liked me <u>for me</u>,' she underlined.

'I did,' I repeated, with a mope.

Charley's scowl melted a little.

'I know you did. And I never doubted it. Not even for a second. So why did you think I thought otherwise?'

I opened my mouth in an effort to explain but realised I couldn't. I mean, how do you explain paranoia to the person you've been paranoid about without suggesting that all along you secretly suspected they were a fucking arsehole?

'Er...'

'And do you really think I only went out with you was because you were *a bit of rough*? I mean, how insulting is that?' Charley asked me and the onlooking spiders.

'What? No, I never said that...' I tried once more, but Charley pointed out that I'd never said anything.

'Not to me anyway. You saved all your talking for the boys on the bloody site.'

'No, what I said was...'

'And what's all this shit about Domino?'

'What?'

'You heard. My horse, Domino. You think I got rid of Domino because I just got bored of him?'

'No, I never...'

'No?'

'No,' I professed.

'Then why did Jason say that on the programme last night?' Charley demanded.

'I don't know. I don't know why he said any of it,' I tried to explain. 'Oh God, everything's just got exaggerated and blown out of all proportion. I don't even know if I'm coming or going any more.'

'So why do you think I got rid of Domino?' Charley demanded.

'I don't know,' I squirmed.

'No, come on, tell me,' she pressed.

I twisted in the wind a little longer before realising she wasn't going to be satisfied with my default 'don't know' answer. 'I guess... I guess you probably just grew out of him or something. I mean, people do when they're that age. It's just what people do,' I tried to sympathise with her.

Charley fixed me in her sights and pursed her lips.

'Domino broke his leg when we fell, the same as I did,' she said. 'Only you can't mend a horse's leg like you can mend a person's, so the vet had to put him down.' Charley now looked away, off into the middle distance and into her past. 'And it broke my heart when he did. That's why I never rode again. Not Domino. Not any other horse. I couldn't ever bring myself to again.'

'Oh!' I grimaced.

'Yes, oh!' she confirmed, taking me down a dozen more pegs and finally completing my humiliation. 'I was no bloody good at it anyway. I realised that even before the accident, which is why I was concentrating on my exams, but to suggest that I got rid of him because...'

'Charley, please, I'm so sorry, honestly, I didn't know,' I tried, but I was suddenly having trouble forgiving myself for this one.

'You didn't know anything,' Charley pointed out. 'About anything. And you never said anything. Why didn't you talk to me, Terry?'

I stared at her incredulous green eyes and finally crumbled.

'I don't know,' I confessed. 'I... I guess I was just afraid of losing you.'

Charley cocked her head.

'You must have a really low opinion of me,' she said, shaking her head.

'No,' I told her, now broken to the point of misery. 'I think you're wonderful. I always have.' I dropped my eyes from her scowl to my boots and told her how it really was. 'It's me I have the low opinion of.'

Charley turned back and looked me square in the eye. She didn't say anything for the longest possible time. Neither of us did. And I was just starting to think we were locked in a staring competition when she finally blinked.

'I'm not your old ex, Terry. The one who ran off with the shelf-stacker.'

'Supermarket manager,' I corrected her. Well, come on, I had *some* self-esteem left, didn't I?

'Supermarket manager,' she acknowledged. 'And you're not my horse, as truly bizarre as that sounds.'

I signalled that I understood with a stamp of the hoof.

'So I want you to listen to me, and listen carefully, because I'm only going to say this once,' Charley said in a manner that made what followed even more surprising. 'You are one of the kindest, warmest and most generous men I've ever met. I couldn't believe how lucky I was to be going out with you. And I loved being with you. I absolutely loved it.'

Charley took a step closer to me and dropped her eyes from mine.

'You know what, I've never had that much luck with men in the past,' she said, which was frankly a ridiculous notion, something akin to Mr T telling me he'd never found a necklace he liked, but Charley looked for all the world sincere. 'I've had boyfriends and I've dated a few guys in my time.'

'Like Hugo?'

This caught her attention and she narrowed her eyes suspiciously.

'Yes, like Hugo,' she confirmed. 'I only dated him for as long as I did because we were at university together. And that's what everyone did at uni.'

'Date Hugo?'

'No, go out with the first bloke who came along, no matter how much of a prat he turned out to be,' she said, before a thought occurred to her. 'In fact, I should get commitment points for sticking with him for as long as I did. Talk about a lost cause. What was I thinking?'

'But you still see him, don't you?'

'As a friend, Terry. As a friend. Are you threatened by that or something?'

'No,' I lied. 'But all the lads just thought it was a bit odd him still hanging around after all these years.'

Charley almost laughed. Almost. 'Well, you tell the fucking lads from me that he lives around the corner. Of course I'm going to still see him occasionally.'

'But why does he live around the corner? Why did he move to

Islington after you did?' I braved… er, on behalf of the lads, who I thought might be curious.

'Because he's a trendy little middle-class boy who works in the media. Where else is he going to live, Terry? Catford?'

Which was a fair point.

'I guess,' I conceded.

'Yes, you do, don't you?' Charley suddenly seized upon.

'What?' I asked, momentarily confused. 'What d'you mean?'

'I mean you guess. You don't ask, you don't find out, you just guess. Well, guess what else, Terry; before I met you, I'd never been in a relationship that I thought had a future. That I thought was going anywhere. That I even wanted to go anywhere,' she said, pursing her lips to deliver the killer blow. 'Until I met *you*.'

Boy, if it was her intention to poleaxe me, she certainly knew where to land her kicks.

'I honestly had no idea you were getting ready to dump me. None at all. And you can't have any idea how miserable you made me when you did. I couldn't understand it. I couldn't understand it at all and hated myself for months afterwards trying to work out what I'd done to deserve it.'

'You didn't do anything,' I quickly tried to reassure her.

'I know that *now*, you dickhead. I've been watching this programme on telly all about my fucking love life, remember? But back then, I just thought you didn't like me any more. Or that you'd had enough. Or that you didn't want to commit. Or that you'd met someone else. Or… or… I don't know.'

This all really caught me four-square and true.

'How was I to know you were having some big crisis of confidence about the scary uptight bitch you were going out with? Jesus, Terry, why couldn't you talk to me? Why did you always have to guess?'

'I don't know,' I simply repeated, and almost left it at that.

But then miracles can occasionally happen, even to thicky brickies, and it finally dawned on me that I wasn't talking to her *again*. And that this was exactly how I'd fucked up everything in the first place and how I was almost hosing away my thoroughly undeserved second chance now by not throwing my cards across the table and straining every sinew against an avalanche of honesty.

'Charley, please...' I said, grabbing her by the arms, turning her to face me and taking a deep breath. 'I... *like* you.'

Well, it was a start.

Charley frowned.

'No, wait, I mean...' I then took a *really* deep breath. 'I *love* you.'

Charley failed to respond with a similar declaration, which was somewhat unnerving, and I suddenly realised I was going to have to go for this all guns blazing and lay myself bare without the slightest hint of encouragement.

'Charley, I'm so so sorry,' I apologised, figuring it was a good place to start. 'I didn't mean to hurt you, I really didn't, and I didn't think I was. I just thought...'

'What?' Charley pressed.

'I just thought I was saving myself a lot of misery by jumping before I was pushed,' I finally admitted, chucking in my carefully crafted front and handing Charley the advantage I'd so cravenly clung to for the last eight months. I half expected her to leap on these words and dance a merry jig all over them, until all I could see was her laughing face when I closed my eyes at night. But then I guess that had been the problem all along, hadn't it, because Charley did no such thing. She just thought for a moment then asked me the obvious question.

'And did it?'

I sighed, with almost-amusement.

'No, not really,' I admitted.

'As long as it was worth it, then,' Charley replied, then another thought occurred to her. 'Also, what was that shit about St Paul's Cathedral? Why did you pick that place to dump me? Was that some sort of dig about my dad working in the City?'

'What? No, honestly. I didn't mean anything by it. I just...' My mind raced ahead thirty seconds and saw my future self being called a malicious cunt in light of a full and frank explanation, so I decided to save that chestnut for a sunnier day and plumped for a somewhat simpler version. 'I just thought it was somewhere quiet we could talk. Not a bar, or a pub, or a restaurant. You know?'

'Nice. You couldn't have just dumped me by text like normal blokes do? I can't seem to go into town these days without having to go past that place and it's like a constant shitty reminder of a really shitty day,' Charley told me.

'Er, yeah, sorry about that,' I cringed, knocking back the full explanation even farther from sunny-day admission to deathbed confession. 'In fact, I'm sorry about everything. I can't believe I messed everything up so badly and I'd do anything to be able to turn back the clock. Anything.'

'Anything except pick up the phone, obviously,' Charley pointed out.

'Well, yeah, of course. Up until five minutes ago I still thought I was the one who was getting dumped by you,' I said, thinking about that for a moment before realising I was suddenly confusing myself.

Charley let out a long sigh and leaned against the bricks. 'Jesus, Terry, I know psychologists who don't do half the head-churning you do.'

I agreed and offered up the only explanation I could.

'It's a manual job, bricklaying. It gives me a lot of time to think. Sorry,' I shrugged.

Charley thought about this, then told me she'd buy me a radio.

'Really? What colour?'

This almost jogged a smirk out of her. But not quite. I wasn't sure we were quite there yet.

Charley pushed herself off the bricks again and looked around.

'Terry, do you want to go and get some breakfast with me? I think we've got a few things to discuss.'

'OK. I'd like that,' I said. 'Come on, there's a gap in the fence by the toilets. We should probably slip out that way if we want to avoid all the reporters.'

'Wow, glamorous. Is this the sort of celebrity lifestyle I can expect from now on with you?' Charley smirked, following me up a muddy path as I led her to a bank of lopsided Portaloos around the back of the compound.

'Maybe. If you want to give me a second chance,' I said. 'If you think I deserve one.'

'Do you think you deserve one?' Charley asked.

'Jesus, Charley, I never thought I deserved the first one,' I told her. 'But if you give me a another, I swear I won't make the same mistakes I made the first time around. Honest I won't. I'll never hold out on you again.'

Obviously, it wasn't just Charley I was swearing this to, but myself. I'd behaved like a right groundworker for most of our relationship, from the very start in fact, and that was simply no way to behave. From now on, I was going to be straight down the middle with her, about everything, and let the chips fall where they may. I'd seen how badly things could get when I tried to do the thinking for both of us and I couldn't go down that road again. There was just no future in it.

Which was suddenly what we were talking about — a future. We had a (possible) future together. How had that happened? After everything that had gone before and soured our pot, Charley was here, wading through a water-filled forklift track with me and discussing our future. Unbelievable. Mind you, not as unbelievable as a girl like Charley taking an interest in a bloke like me in the first place. I mean, how unlikely was that? But there you go.

'Why don't we talk about this over breakfast?' Charley suggested, stepping from side to side to avoid the slippery mud ruts.

'OK,' I agreed, but then stopped dead when a related thought hit me straight between the eyes.

'What's up?' Charley asked, when she saw that I'd stopped.

'I don't like eggs Benedict,' I told her.

'What?' she blinked.

'I just thought I'd say right off the bat that I don't like eggs Benedict. I don't want eggs Benedict for breakfast. So I'll probably just have a bacon sandwich or something instead, OK, because that eggs Benedict thing isn't for me, OK? Just letting you know where I stand,' I told her, bracing myself for her reaction.

Charley let a smile spread across her face and slipped her hand into mine.

'That's a start, Terry. That's a good start.'

30 One year later...

'Did I ever tell you what happened to my dad?' old Stan asked me over half a stout in the Lamb the following spring.

I told him he hadn't and pulled up a stool.

'Well, when he was a young man, younger than you are today, he had a bit of an accident,' he said.

I nodded cautiously and wondered where this was going. Thoughts of old Stan telling me that this same thing had just happened to him and could I follow him into the toilet flickered through my brain.

'He used to be a painter for the council, see, back in the early twenties. Outdoor work, it was mostly; park gates, lamp-posts, park benches, that sort of thing,' old Stan said. 'Well, anyway, one day he was up this ladder doing some guttering or something, not quite sure, anyway, it's not important, when the rung he's standing on breaks right from under him and he falls on to these railings. Gets speared, he does, right through the belly and the legs and the arms and everything. Gawd, dreadful it was,' he elaborated, with a sad shake of the head.

'Jesus!' I exclaimed. 'Did he die?'

'What? No, but he was really badly injured. Anyway, he... here, hang on a minute; early twenties? How old d'you think I am, you cheeky git?'

'Eh? Oh yeah, of course. Sorry about that. Just my maths,' I apologised.

'I should think so an' all,' old Stan bristled. 'Anyway, where was I? Oh yeah, that was it. So me dad's all laid up in hospital and at death's door for weeks, see. Had the last rites and got measured up for his wooden overcoat and everything, he did, before he finally pulled through. But even then he was in a terrible state. Legs gone, back gone, could hardly sit to lean, let alone get up and walk about, so what sort of future did he have?'

'A bleak one?' I ventured.

'You're not wrong, son. See, it weren't like it is these days. There weren't no wages being handed out to people who couldn't work back then. If you went to the wall in the twenties, you went to the wall,' old Stan told me, and Tony the landlord, who'd wandered over to join Stan's stagger back down Memory Lane.

'Didn't he get no compensation or nothing, then, your old man?' Tony asked.

'I was just coming to that,' old Stan insisted, irked at having his big story rushed. 'See, a bloke from the union come down and told me dad that they'd take up his case with the management, see he was paid his due and looked after, right. I mean, it was the council's fault after all, weren't it, what with the ladder breaking and everything, so he told him to sit tight and concentrate on getting himself better. But above all else, whatever else he did, he weren't to sign nothing, not without someone from the union being present,' he told us, with a knowing nod.

I think I saw where this story was going after old Stan's twist in the tale practically set off the sprinklers.

'Sign it all away for a couple of magic beans, did he?' I guessed.

'Well, no. I mean, he thought he was doing the right thing at the time, because his governor from the council come down and told him that they'd love to see him all right, but that they simply didn't have the wherewithal to pay him a big lump of compensation. Told him that if they was held to ransom by the union, then they'd have to lay off half a dozen blokes just to find the money. Well, all them blokes were me dad's mates and he didn't want to see 'em out of work on his account, so him and the governor struck a deal; if me dad waived his right to compensation, he'd have a job for life with the council.'

'Was that it?' Tony asked. 'Nice deal,' he guffawed.

'But you're judging it by today's standards, Tony, and it's not the same. Back then, a job for life was like winning the pools. It meant security, which was unheard of for working men back then, let alone men like me dad who'd been injured and who couldn't actually work. I mean, you have to remember that the country was full of blokes who'd been injured in the Great War and who couldn't work and there was precious little support for them, so what chance did a painter who'd fallen off his ladder have? None whatsoever,' he shrugged. 'So he signed and gratefully accepted his job for life,' old Stan told us, though it was clear from his tone that there was more to his story than this.

'Go on, then, what happened to him?' I asked, taking my cue to do so from old Stan's knowing nod.

'Well, five weeks later they give him the push. He hadn't even finished convalescing in the hospital when me grandmother came and see him and brought him the letter. Some old flannel about legal responsibilities, limitations and liabilities. It was just a load of double-talk, though, to justify themselves going back on the deal. Me dad said it was the first and only time he'd ever heard me grandmother swear and it was then that he realised what they'd done to him. But what could he do? He couldn't go back to the union because they'd told him not to sign nothing and he couldn't go to the law courts because his job had been promised on the strength of a handshake. He was sunk.'

'He could've gone to the papers,' Tony suggested.

'What, in a country full of hard-luck stories? This was only seven years after the Somme, remember? Where was the news? No, that was it, he'd had his chips,' old Stan said sadly.

'Stan, is there a moral to this story, because the only one I can make out so far is don't trust Catford Council and I knew that already, so I'm assuming there must be more to it than this,' I double-checked.

'Well, yeah, there is, because it was in the hospital, during all this, that me dad met me mum. Of course, she wasn't me mum at the time, she was just another nurse treating him, but they grew close over the course of his convalescence and they just sort of fell in love.'

'A nurse, eh? He's a sly one, your old man, eh,' Tony clucked, much to old Stan's bemusement.

'Well, yes, quite. Anyway, back then girls didn't have careers like they have today, not like your Charley, they had families, so their security depended on them finding themselves a good husband to provide for 'em.'

'OK, I see what you're getting at. And your lame old man was a pretty shaky bet,' I said, filling in the blanks for myself.

'That he was. And me mum was an attractive girl in her day. She could've had her pick of the suitors if she'd wanted to – doctors, solicitors, bankers, anyone, but over all them she chose me dad.'

'Funny, my old dear spent the best part of thirty years saying exactly the same thing about my old man,' Tony told us, 'usually while slinging plates about.'

'Ton', d'you mind?' I told him, sensing Stan's story was running out of legs as it was, without Tony bowling jokes in front of it all the time. 'Sorry, Stan, go on.'

'Well, that's it really. They got married when me dad got out of the hospital and lived with me grandmother for a couple of years until me dad got back on his feet. In every sense of the word. It was a rough old time for 'em at the start, but they made the best of it because they had each other. And that's how it is for some folks. It's all about what's in here,' old Stan said, pointing to his heart, 'not what's in here.'

He moved his finger down a few inches and for one stupid moment I wondered if he was trying to find his pancreas, before I realised the bulge in his jacket was his wallet.

'You got a good 'un there, young Terry. Treat her right,' he winked, lifting his glass.

'Yeah, and she's got a few quid in the bank,' Ton whistled in agreement. 'Nice.'

Old Stan looked at me, rolled his eyes and finished off the last of his stout.

'Want another one, Stan?' I offered, when he set his glass back down.

'No, son, let me get you one. You shouldn't be buying anyone drinks today. Not today,' he insisted.

Old Stan told Tony to do the honours, reached into his jacket and pulled a shiny new twenty out of his pancreas.

'Blimey, Stan, you printing it or something?' Tony asked him.

'Well, no one ever lets me buy one, do they?' he explained.

'So, Stan, what happened to your mum and dad? Did he ever get back to the painting?' I asked.

'No, he couldn't. He was never the same again after his accident, so he taught himself to cut hair. Set himself up as a barber and eventually opened up a little shop in Lewisham, him and me mum. He did the fellas, she did the women. Shop ain't there no more, of course, but they made a good living out of it,' old Stan said, before a little twinkle entered his eye. 'And get this, some years later, his old Catford Council governor came in the shop for a haircut. You know, the one who'd done the dirty on him all those years earlier. Well, he recognised me dad in the mirror after a few minutes and apologised for what he'd done. Said he'd had no choice. Some new councillor had come in off the back of a local election and gone through the books with a fine-tooth comb and a hatchet. It hadn't been his fault. That sort of thing.'

'So what did your old man do?' I asked.

'Nothing; just give him a short back and sides. But me mum cut his ear off when me dad was cleaning his comb out in the sink,' old Stan chuckled. 'Should've seen the mess it made.'

'Gordon Bennett! Didn't she get done, then, your mum, by the Old Bill, like?' Tony asked, as he plonked our new drinks down on the bar.

'Nah, everyone knew me dad, and what had happened to him, even the local coppers, so they just put it down to an accident at work – an industrial injury. Well, these things happen all the time, don't they?' Old Stan smiled, before sinking into a fresh half of stout.

'Oi, you ain't got time for that. Come on, we're going to be late,' a voice behind me nagged.

I turned and caught sight of CT standing at the door, frantically tapping his watch.

'It's all right, we've still got forty-five minutes. And Charley's bound to be late anyway. It would be an absolute miracle if she weren't,' I replied. 'Besides, we can't go without Jason, but God knows what he's doing because he went to the bog twenty minutes ago and no one's seen him since.'

'Maybe he fell in,' Tony smirked.

'Maybe he's cleaning it. Somebody oughta,' old Stan suggested.

Jason emerged a few minutes later, straightening his tie and dabbing his mouth with a paper towel. 'Sorry about that, chaps, just a few butterflies,' he explained.

'What were you doing, catching 'em for the zoo?' I asked.

'Well, it's all right for you, you're not the one having to do the big funny speech, which thanks to him is now going to be in front of a load of TV cameras,' Jason said, aiming an accusing finger at CT. 'I'm bloody bricking myself, I am.'

'Relax, it'll be fine.' I smiled. 'These things have a habit of working out.'

'Well, they won't be if we're late,' CT insisted. 'So come on, the car's waiting.'

'Oh, all right,' I relented. 'Come on, then, let's get going. Cheers, Stan. Tony. See you in a couple of weeks' time.'

'Yep, see you, son,' old Stan replied, tipping his glass in my direction. 'All the best.'

'Good luck, chaps,' Tony added, his thumbs to the ceiling.

Luck?

I didn't need any more luck. I'd already had all the luck in the world and nothing could, or would, ever change that from this day forth. I'd done my utmost to throw it all away, but when luck's in your corner, you're impervious to all idiocy. Even your own, believe it or not.

Oh yes, luck was something I had in abundance and no mistake. I had it when I woke up in the morning. I had it when I came home at night. I had it over dinner in the evenings. And I even had it on quiet nights in when I curled up on the sofa to watch Rocket Man Sauce adverts.

Luck?

I didn't need any more of the stuff. I'd already had all the luck any thicky bricky could ever hope to find.

In Catford, Canonbury or beyond.